I plowed headfirst into the elevator —and smack dab into . . . *him*!

I've never fainted in my life, but sure as hell tried to right then.

Still coherent, I heard the doors close behind me and turned to see no other soul had gotten in. *Damn!* I pushed myself away from his granite chest and stood tall. Well, as tall as my five-six could get next to what had to be his six-three. I shut my eyes and asked Saint Theresa to have the elevator get down in warp speed.

The damn thing stopped!

My eyes flew open. There he stood . . . with his hand on the emergency stop button.

Guess Saint Theresa was busy.

A Dose of Murder

LORI AVOCATO

This is a work of fiction. Names, characters, places, and incidents are products of the author's imagination or are used fictitiously and are not to be construed as real. Any resemblance to actual events, locales, organizations, or persons, living or dead, is entirely coincidental.

AVON BOOKS
An Imprint of HarperCollins*Publishers*
10 East 53rd Street
New York, New York 10022-5299

ISBN: 0-06-073165-6
www.avonmystery.com

First Avon Books paperback printing: October 2004

Printed in the U.S.A.

10 9 8 7 6 5 4 3 2 1

This book is dedicated to my dad, Stanley Gansecki, whom I miss very much.

Acknowledgments

To Sal, Mario, and Greg, for all their support throughout the years, and for staying out of my office when asked to.

For my mom, Helen Gansecki, my sister, Margaret Braddon, cousins Alice Meattey, Liz Nawrocki and Barbara Nawrocki (all descendents of the *real* Pauline Sokol and supportive family members).

To Stanley Gansecki, my dad, who is watching from heaven.

And Pauline Sokol, my babci (grandma) who, too, has passed through the Pearly Gates.

To the late Eileen Hehl, fellow writer, who encouraged me to use my nursing background in my work.

To Jay Poyner and Erica Orloff, fabulous agents who believed in this series from the query letter to the final draft.

To Erin Richnow, editor, whose suggestions only improved this work and who "gets" my sense of humor.

To Kimberly Peterson Zaniewski, my best cheerleader and writer friend.

And to Barbara L. Hodgins, a real-life investigator, who helped with my research of a field I knew little to nothing about. So, any errors are solely my fault.

To all CTRWA, NEC/RWA, NJRW, LIRWA and Rom-Vets members who rooted for me throughout my career. Thanks.

And to anyone else that I forgot. Thanks and sorry.

A Dose of Murder

One

"Open wide." If I had to repeat that order to this kid one more time, I'd stick my head into the autoclave and roast my brain until it popped like a kernel of corn. Of course, first I'd have to remove all the instruments that are sterilized in the darn thing. That's how my day was going. That's how this damn career was going.

No, that's how my *life* was going.

I glared at the closemouthed kid sitting in front of me in the pediatrician's office I'd offered to work in for a week—and groaned.

What the hell was I thinking?

I had a permanent job at the Hospital of Saint Greg's. I didn't need this. Why did I insist on doing favors for others all the time?

Stinky Lapuc, the little boy sitting in front of me with his mouth clamped shut tighter than a clam facing a pot of boiling water, glared at me from his perch on the examining table. I called him "Stinky" because the dear must have eaten beans prior to his visit at the office. His real name on the chart was John. Boring. I liked "Stinky" better. It had character. He had gas.

I waved the throat swab in front of his beady, watery eyes.

"Open wide, my dear," I repeated in my best Cinderella's Fairy Godmother voice. "Open wide and let Nurse Pauline Sokol take a peek at those handsome tonsils you have." If not, kiddo, this swab gets poked into your tummy until you open. Okay, I'd never poke a five-year-old, but the way I felt right now, I enjoyed a moment of thinking I was capable of child poking.

Today while my feet hurt worse than Stinky's possible strep throat, I stood there and looked at the swab in my hand. Before I stuck it into his bacteria-laced throat, I wished, for a second, that it was a magic wand and I could whisk myself away to Club Med.

Because, although I don't have a mercenary bone in my body, I also didn't have any money in my savings account, and a magic wand was the only way I'd get there. Admittedly, I'm a shopoholic, but hey, I'm single—not something I'm proud of by the way, and don't get my mother started on that—and could shop till I dropped. But not today. Today even shopping didn't pique my interest. Hell, I was tired of taking odd jobs on my vacations. I was tired of my regular job as a unit director in Labor and Delivery who hired and fired staff. I didn't have the stomach for the firing. Frankly, I'd been considering the fact that I was . . . *burned out*.

Nursing had been my life, yet now . . . I needed a change. But I couldn't afford to just quit with no future plans.

Stinky looked as if he needed to cough or yawn or something, so I aimed my swab. "Open wide, sugar-doll."

His mother, Mrs. Lapuc and cousin to Andrea Lapuc, who went to high school with me and stole my boyfriend Stephen, gave me an odd look. "You think you could get him to open?" I asked in my most professional voice, although that poking thing wouldn't leave my thoughts.

She took the boy by his collar. "Do what she says or no dessert tonight."

Amazed that the old threat was still used by parents today (My mother had used it as her dinner mantra until I was about thirty. No, wait, she still uses it on me), I stood at the ready.

Stinky hesitated. Then, as if watching a drawbridge go up in slow motion when you're the last car in line and you have to pee, I took the swab from the holder, held it at the ready, and saw his little lips part. It wasn't enough yet, so I gave a pleading look to his mom.

"Dessert."

That did the trick.

Or so I thought, until he bit down on the swab, leaving half of it in my hand. "Don't swallow!" I reached toward his lips. "Open."

He looked at me, then the remainder of the swab shot out with the force of his tongue clearly behind it. I looked down. The swab was stuck to my left breast. "Excuse me." I walked out of the room, screamed inside my head and promptly went to get another one.

"Don't do that this time," I said, giving another pleading look at his mother when I came back in.

"He doesn't feel good, you know."

And I hated my career.

"That's why he's behaving like this," she said, then grabbed his arm. "Open!"

He did, and the swab hit its mark before he clamped shut like Jaws again, and I had my—hopefully—last patient taken care of. I gave the mother instructions about the test and turned to go.

Mrs. Lapuc bundled Stinky up although the office had to be a hundred degrees. Outside was snow covered and maybe in the thirties, but this wasn't Alaska. It was Connecticut, for crying out loud.

Babies cried. Toddlers ran rampant. Older kids, I'm guessing by the colorful language, yelled words to the nurses that even I didn't use in the privacy of my home when alone, and the odor of diapers, full and ripe, mixed with medicine that no kid in their right mind would take unless under threat of mother.

The soreness in my feet spread to the tips of my shoulder-length blonde (natural, I swear!) hair, which was wrapped, nurse-style, upon my head. When I got to the nurses' station and had given the swab to Maryann, the full-time nurse who'd know better what to do with it, I collapsed into a chair. Thank goodness it wheeled itself into the counter with the weight of my fall and not out into the hallway where I could have bowled over one of the little patients.

I leaned back with my hands behind my head and momentarily shut my eyes. Then I heard a rustle from behind and didn't care if an attack of some sort was imminent, as long as a group of out-of-control kids didn't wheel me into a closet, since I am, admittedly, claustrophobic. I didn't budge.

"The Lapuc kid's swab is negative," Maryann said.

Relieved it was her and not that wild group or some crazed pediatric patient with a scalpel behind me, I managed to shake my head. "Good."

"Want me to tell his mom? You look beat."

To my surprise, one eye opened. The left one. It had always been my strongest and the deepest gray, which came from my Viking ancestors who'd invaded Poland years back. I didn't know I had it in me to open either eye. "That'd be great." With my one-eye vision, I watched her shuffling papers, signing things, writing notes. God, I was tired. "How do you do it? How do you manage to stay awake all day and not commit hara-kiri at the end of your shift?"

She laughed. I wished I had the energy to join her. It seemed as if it would be fun to laugh. I think I remember laughing in 1992.

"You get used to it," she said as she turned and walked down the hallway.

Used to it? I sat bolt upright. That was like saying to drink Scotch you'd have to "acquire" the horrible, throat-burning taste. I didn't want to acquire a taste for Scotch or get *used* to this never-ending state of exhaustion I'd been in the last twelve years.

I looked into the highly buffed side of the autoclave. There I was. Thirty-four years old. Bags threatening to materialize under my eyes and a possible wrinkle forming on each side. Crow's-feet. I might have crow's-feet! Okay, maybe they were from leaning my hand against my face, but I was starting to look . . . older. Still, I told myself, I wasn't bad-looking. In fact, in my youthful, self-absorbed teens, I actually won Ms. Hope Valley, twice. Blonde Polack beats voluptuous brunette Wop. That's what I'd put in my diary.

Now I was burned out from nursing, had no husband—actually no love interest at present, and I refused to count Dr. Vance G. Taylor even though we'd been on and off again for the last five years. In high school he wore pocket protectors and was called "Vancy." Today, well, I'd give him this. The guy was a living doll who still wore pocket protectors. Looked like a younger version of George Hamilton. Year-round tan included. Not even ethnic. True WASP, Vance was. And well off to boot. An orthopedic surgeon.

But there just wasn't any spark between us. At least not on my end. My mother, bless her heart, couldn't understand that one. *Take a number*, I thought.

Maryann came around the corner. I'd seen her reflection in the autoclave as she came from behind. "You ready to call it quits for the day?" she asked.

I looked at her in the silver metal. "No, I'm ready to call it quits . . . *for good*."

"You have no job?" my mother asked as if I'd grown two blue heads and just arrived from Venus. She looked about as shocked as she did when my oldest sister, Mary, had said she was leaving the convent and getting married. That news came after Mary had gotten her bachelor's degree compliments of the Sisters of Saint Francis—and before she left. Talk about Catholic-induced guilt. Mom had won the prize that year. Now she might be in contention again, thanks to me.

"I'll get something else." I let my legs dangle off the stool while I rested my head in my palms on the turquoise Formica counter.

My parents had lived in this house for forty-three years,

and never upgraded the decor. Each time I came back for a visit, I half expected Donna Reed to come waltzing in with Lucy on one arm and the Beav on the other.

The aroma of kielbasa and sauerkraut hung in the air, and tonight mother was cooking meatloaf. Since both parents were purebred Poles, the house had absorbed the aroma somewhere around 1970, and not even my mother's Renuzit air freshener (fresh mountain pine) fetish could get it out of the air.

In truth, it'd grown to be a comforting scent. Smelled like a fake Christmas tree.

Right now I needed comfort. I inhaled deeply. Ah.

"Of course you'll get something else, Pauline. There's a critical nursing shortage in this country. With the baby boomers retiring, it's getting worse." She sliced a potato and plopped it into a pan of water.

At first I only stared. Mom sounded like a commentator on the five-o'clock news. Who knew the woman who left high school in her sophomore year to marry my father before he went to fight in the Korean War could come up with such a timely statement as that?

My father came into the room with my uncle Walt Macie. Walt never married, and had lived with us all of my life. He actually was a Maciejko, but somewhere along the line he and his brother, Stash, Americanized the name to "Macie."

At the age of eighty now, Uncle Walt spent his days at the Elk's Club, Bozuchowski's bar (better known as the local hangout) and Boz's, or played cards at the senior citizens center. Many a day my mother had to smooth the ruffled feathers of some widow whom Uncle Walt had connived into playing for cash.

Usually he only played for home-cooked meals or his favorite homemade chocolate chip cookies. I knew they weren't good for his adult-onset diabetes, but I never scolded him since they made him happy, and I often told my mother to let him enjoy.

I wish I could be as happy as Uncle Walt and his cookies—diabetes or not. Hey, he was eighty years old, for crying out loud!

Despite my stupor, I managed a smile. "Hi, Daddy. Uncle Walt." My head refused to leave my palms, so my words came out slurred.

Uncle Walt walked to my mother and took a slice of raw potato. He popped it into his mouth. "Pauline been drinking, Stella?"

Mother looked at me. "I only wish."

I groaned.

I should've politely left and gone back to the condo I shared with Miles, one of the nurses at Saint Greg's. "I'm not drunk. Wouldn't waste the calories on liquor." *Or the money*, I thought, and hoped Miles would spot me the next month's rent. He would, I knew, but I hated to take advantage of my friend.

Daddy came closer. "What's the matter, my little *pączki*?" A *pączki* (sounds like "paunchki") is a Polish donut. A huge one. Fat and filled with prune filling. My father always called me his *pączki*. When I was young, I paid no attention. At my age, though, I wanted to run out of the room screaming. Thank goodness I didn't fit the bill of a round, stuffed donut.

Still, he meant well. My father was the hardworking silent type who retired after forty years in a factory making tiny parts for airplane engines, and I loved him. Even when he referred to me as a donut.

I sighed. "I'm burned out, Daddy. I can't go back to nursing . . . for a while. I need a rest."

My mother clucked her tongue and set the pot of potatoes on the stove. "Rest, *shmest*."

Uncle Walt lifted his Steelers cap off his head and rubbed his naked scalp. He and I were the only two Steelers fans in the house. Not that I lived here, God forbid. But the rest of the family—hell, just about the rest of the state—were Patriots fans, since this was New England. He looked at me. "Good for you. Take a rest. Come play cards with me."

"Er . . . as tempting as that sounds, I need to work. Only not in nursing."

Mom wiped her hands on the towel hanging over the white enamel goose's head next to the sink. She'd crocheted turquoise around it to match the Formica. I'm pretty sure she did that way back in 1969, before I was born. "Not in nursing?" She made the sign of the cross. "You've studied nursing in all those schools, Pauline Sokol. Good pay, too. Now what are you going to do? What job can you get to support yourself? Of course"—she turned and hung the towel over the goose—"you could move back here . . ."

The next thing I knew, I was opening the door to my condo and running in as if fleeing a stalker. I had no recollection of leaving my parents' split-level or driving my Venetian red metallic Volvo back here and praying it didn't break down.

But here I was.

Miles had been napping on the couch and woke in a startled state. I must have been in such a hurry that I made too much noise. "Hey, sorry if I woke you."

He rubbed his eyes as I collapsed into the comfortable white leather chair across from him. Spanky, our little joint-custody shih tzu-poodle mix weighing in at five pounds, eight ounces, jumped at my legs. I lifted him up and gave his tummy a tickle.

"You look like shit," Miles said, sitting up.

"I'm guessing you're not talking to Spanky." I leaned back and groaned. "I hate my life. I hate my career. I hate the thought of moving into a split-level that smells like sauerkraut."

"Jesus." He stood up, rubbed his eyes and without another word walked out of the room.

Before I could nuzzle Spanky's little body, Miles appeared with two bottles of Budweiser. He'd even popped the tops. I took mine from his outstretched hand and after a long, slow, welcoming sip, I said, "I quit my job today."

"The one at the pediatrician's that you're filling in for?"

I shook my head no.

He glared at me. "First you scare the shit out of me in my dead sleep. Then you guzzle that brew as if it were calorie free, you, Ms. Health-nut, and now you drop a bomb like that on me. What the hell gives?"

"It's true. I have to leave nursing . . . for a while. Miles, I've been a nurse for the greater part of my adult life. A registered nurse with a master's degree, no less. Shows you how many years I've put into this profession. Twelve. I even talked my supervisor at Saint Greg's into not making me give a two-week notice since I was on vacation anyway. I just couldn't go back. Thank goodness I was able to coerce Liz Pendleton to fill in for *me* at the pediatrician's office until Kathleen gets her sunburned butt back."

Miles could only stare. Probably because I kept talking and he couldn't get a word in edgewise.

"Things have changed, Miles. When I graduated from Saint Francis Hospital School of Nursing, got a degree from Southern, then a masters from Yale, I thought I'd be a nurse for life."

"I always thought—"

"Yeah. And even when those degrees hung freshly in their frames, I took jobs that no one else wanted. Still do. Extra jobs that exhaust me. Today I sunk to nearly poking a throat swab into the tummy of a kid—"

He shook his head. "You'd never do that."

"I know. Maybe that's my problem. Maybe I'm not daring enough. My life needs a jolt of some sort. Got any ideas?" I stared at him to make sure he wouldn't hold back.

Miles had connections all over town. That's what made him such a perfect roommate. How else could I have ever afforded leather furniture, a kick-ass gigantic television, which, I might add, made my Steelers appear as if they were running in the living room, or this condo near the lake? Miles pulled strings like a marionette artist and knew someone who knew someone for whatever anyone needed.

He was my closest platonic male friend. Of course his being gay had something to do with that. On more than one occasion I'd told him I'd marry him if he'd convert. I'd meant to Catholicism, he, of course, thought along the sexual lines.

For that I went back and forth with Dr. Taylor. Lately, though, it'd been a long time since *that* subject had come up. I made a mental note to have him invite me to dinner. It'd been some time since I'd seen him, and Miles had mentioned that he'd heard Vance had a new job. Yes, it was time to call him.

I needed *that* right now.

Miles sat back on the couch and wrapped himself in the mauve-and-black afghan one of his old boyfriends, Leonard, had knitted for him. I never liked the guy, but he'd been a whiz with knitting needles. Good thing he didn't break Miles's heart, or I'd have dealt with Leonard.

"Okay," he said, "no need to explain. Been there, done that."

"That's right. You traveled around the Caribbean on your sabbatical a few years back."

He lifted his bottle toward me. "Bon voyage."

I took a sip. "Don't I wish."

His eyes softened. "Damn. You really can't afford to get away."

It wasn't a question. Miles was a smart guy and one hell of an OR nurse. He was my closest friend, and the only one who knew I'd lost my shirt and most of my savings by stupidly co-signing a loan for a fellow nurse, Jeanine Garjullo, who I thought was a friend. We'd actually been roommates in a cottage on Long Island Sound for the first few years I'd worked at St. Greg's.

My "friend" took off with the new Lexus she bought with the loan last year and left me with the bills. One payment every month for so many years I'd lost count but I knew I'd be older than Uncle Walt when the final amount was due. That's when Miles let me move in so I wouldn't have to go home to my parents. I could see the headlines in the *Hope Valley Sentinel*. Thirty-four-year-old middle child, the only single one, moves home with parents.

Made me cringe.

"Bingo. I need a non-nursing job that makes me enough money to live on."

Miles leaned his head back, tapped a finger on his tooth. He always thought better like that. "Perfect."

I jumped up—forgetting poor Spanky, who ended up on all fours much like a cat since he was about that size—and yelled, "What? *What* is perfect?"

Miles smiled. "I have a relative in the insurance business. Owns his own place. Insurance agency. He'll hire you. Wear a nice suit tomorrow for an interview. Skirt. Not pants. Good thing you're such a looker. I'll make the call."

He was up and poking the pager to locate our portable phone, which had a mind of its own and always snuck off so we couldn't find it. The beeping came from the kitchen. I watched Miles walk through the swinging doors and contemplated which of my two suits I should wear to an insurance company interview: the black one that I used for funerals, or the red one I'd had since the late eighties, when "power red" had me thinking—mistakenly I might add—that I could get my staff to listen better if I wore it.

I'll go with the black, I thought, as I heard Miles mumbling, then saying, "Tuesday morning. Nine it is," because for some odd reason, I felt as if I *were* going to a funeral.

I looked at my watch. Three after nine. I uncrossed and recrossed my legs and looked at my watch again. Three after nine. Still. Waiting in an insurance office for a job was frustrating, to say the least. It didn't help that I hadn't been on a job interview since before the invention of the wheel. I'd forgotten how I hated this kind of stuff.

Pauline Sokol was never one for change.

If I were, I'd be backpacking it around Europe. Lack of money or not. Or at the very least, I would have moved out of the oh-so-very-ethnic town I was born in, grew up in, and, not adjusting well to change, would meet my maker in, no doubt.

A shuffling sound from the other side of a door to the waiting room took my interest. There hadn't been a receptionist at the desk when I came in, so I politely sat in the waiting area, silently chanting, *I can do this. I can do this.* This became my mantra, although I really didn't know what "this" was. Miles had given me no specifics except that I should be here at nine in my suit and meet his cousin Fabio Scarpello of the Scarpello and Tonelli Insurance Agency.

Miles had told me there was no Tonelli, but Fabio thought it would bring in more business to have two names on the sign above the door.

I looked across the room that mirrored my mother's taste in fifties furniture and wondered about Fabio. Maybe this wasn't such a good idea. That thought hovered in my mind as my legs stuck to the fire-engine red Naugahyde couch. The floor was black-and-white checked linoleum and I wondered if the same people installed it as had my mother's turquoise-and-white checked flooring.

Before I got too deep in thought, I smelled something. A cigar—a cheap one. I looked up. To say Fabio was handsome would be a mistatement. He had deep brown eyes like Miles, but Fabio's had sunk into their sockets, probably from years of reading insurance forms. His nose wasn't big, but it hooked over, very beaklike. Miles was adopted into the Scarpello family, and, looking at the ethnic Fabio, I said a silent prayer of thanks in honor of my roomy.

"So, you're going to work in . . . investigating." He wasn't asking a question per se—more ogling me in wonderment.

I stood, held out my hand and blinked. I have no idea why someone thinks blinking can help clear up a misunderstood word, but I knew Fabio had meant *insurance*, even though it had come out as "investigating." Odd. The man was odd. "I'm Miles's roommate, Pauline Sokol."

Fabio's grip felt wet, although I'm sure his hands were dry. Perhaps oily was more like it. He had the nerve to wipe his fingers on his baby-poop brown (I was still having flashbacks of the pediatrician's office) polyester suit after shaking mine. Single-breasted polyester jacket with plaid pants, no less. Despite a shudder, I knew I was doing the right thing.

"So," I said, "will I be doing filing or answering the phone or—" Something mindless, please, sir.

He scrunched his eyebrows at me. "Investigating. Need a hearing aid, doll?"

"I . . . no." I thought better than to argue with my new boss. Miles had agreed to spot me the rent, but I couldn't ask him to pay the monthly payment on Jeanine's loan. In other words, oily Fabio Scarpello or not, I needed this job.

"With your medical background, you'll be perfect, doll."

"You really did say investigating. As in snooping on people?" If he called me "doll" again, I'd borrow a filled diaper from one of my nephews and leave it in Fabio's office overnight.

"Snooping is exactly what it is." He flicked the ashes from his cigar into a nearby ficus plant. I only hoped that if it was silk it was flame retardant. He grinned. "Yep, snooping."

At the moment Fabio looked more intelligent than I felt. Oh God. What a thought.

"You'll get a video camera, some equipment. You buy them. If you need, I'll float you a loan. . . ."

Loan! Oh . . . my . . . God! I heard the word, saw his mouth keep moving, but all my brain could detect was the L word. Like I would ever sign my name on a piece of paper that had the L word on it ever again. No way! I had decided soon after Jeanine rode off into the sunset in her shiny, black Lexus that I'd never be able to buy a house for the rest of my life. Because no way could I force myself into applying for a loan.

Now Fabio was talking loan. I wanted to scream, but at least was able to control that action, since screaming during a job interview had to be a no-no.

"Got it?"

I looked at him. He was waiting for an answer, but I'd drifted off into "Nightmare on Loan Street" and hadn't heard a thing. I gave him my best smile and mentally scrambled for a lie. "I'm so sorry, sir. I didn't get what you said." He glared at me. I knew he was thinking I couldn't do the job, so I added, "Recent ear infection and all."

"Oh. Hope it gets better."

And I hope God doesn't punish me with a real one. "How kind."

"Anyway. Get me evidence of fraud from the cocksuckers who claim injuries, collect, cost me *mucho* and then go on about their merry way." He now spoke so loudly my ears hurt, and I think I felt an infection coming on.

I stared at him. The words snuck out of my numb lips. "I'm going to be an insurance-fraud investigator."

He clucked his tongue like my mother always did. "Only for the medical cases. I've got a beauty of a one too. Don't pay any attention to the bullshit about murder."

I slapped myself in the head. "Duh. Medical cases. Of course. I knew that."

Fake slap or not; truthfully, I didn't know what the hell I was getting myself into.

Wait a minute! *Murder?*

Two

I crossed and uncrossed my legs about a million times. Damn. I should have gone with the power red suit. That skirt was longer. This black one crept up my legs, and Fabio's slimy stare followed it every inch. Yuck. Conversation. I needed to say something to get his attention. My skin was starting to *feel* his staring, and I suddenly had the urge for a shower.

I'd get Miles for this.

No, I told myself, he knew exactly what he was doing. Miles knew his cousin and how the man's mind worked—one step up from the gutter. The job was mine on looks alone, and Miles knew that. Not that I considered myself such a looker, but I'd heard rumors since "developing" around age twenty. I suppose Miles knew I'd have a hell of a time changing careers in my early thirties with no other education other than in nursing, and that sending me to Fabio was the best thing to do.

The guy was a genius. Miles, that is.

The only thing I'd get him on was the suggestion to wear a suit. If I had pants on, Fabio wouldn't have such a view. I crossed my legs at the ankles like ladies are supposed to do.

Maciejko women—my mother's family—were known for

their legs. My grandmother on Mom's side, who we fondly called *Babci* since it meant grandmother, had a set on her that looked as if she ran the New York marathon annually. Look out New York City Rockettes! Hardworking Poles could look damn fine if they didn't overdo the shots and beers and kielbasa.

Fabio shuffled his foot. Got my attention.

"So, when would you like me to come back?" Now that I was going to be gainfully employed, I should go out and celebrate. Charge something on my credit card, with the "light at the end of the tunnel" theory that I'd be getting a paycheck soon to cover the bill.

He slid his gaze from my legs, lingered far too long for good taste on my chest and finally made it to my head. Something about Fabio I noticed right off the bat though: He didn't look me in the eyes. He had an annoying habit of looking over my head.

I actually turned to see if there was something behind me, but saw only tan-and-brown woven wallpaper peeling at the top near the corner wall. I turned around.

"Come back?" he said, and turned toward the door he'd slunk in from. "I need someone *today*, doll. Dick Stacey quit out of the fucking blue. If that ain't enough, Mike Morton is home with the gout. Gets it every few months because he won't lay off the sauce. That leaves you to pick up the slack, doll." With that, he walked out the door.

Feeling a bit like Alice chasing the rabbit through Wonderland, I couldn't decide whether to follow or stay safely in the waiting room. This "doll" sat there dumbstruck.

Suddenly, like the Cheshire Cat, a head appeared behind the Plexiglas window of the reception desk. It belonged to a woman wearing a skintight white suit with black polka dots on the collar as well as the ribbon in her bright (and I don't use that term lightly) yellow hair, and on her gloves. Gloves? Hadn't seen them on anyone since 1979, except in the winter. These weren't wool though; they were a stark white with tiny black dots on the ruffles.

She looked at me and shoved the window door to one side. "Hi, *chéri*. What can Adele do for you?"

Motionless for a few seconds, I could only stare. *Adele could be a prostitute*, was my first thought. What? *Stop that, Pauline.* How snobbish of me to think that because her cleavage could hold an entire pencil box full at one time, and that her use of the endearment could be misinterpreted, she could be a streetwalker. Despite the overdone blue eye shadow, the fire-engine red lipstick and the cheeks that looked like, well, red polka dots, she would be rather attractive if she toned it down.

Shaking my confused, stupid thoughts out of my head, I smiled. "I . . . I'm going to be working here."

She leaned over to get a closer look. That cleavage kept me staring at the wall behind her. Similar to what Fabio had done to me, but I wasn't showing cleavage today, and I figured, he'd stare anyway, at any woman.

"Work here?" she asked.

"Why, yes." I managed to get back to some state of normalcy. Adele's outward appearance had confused me at first, but some kind of motherly warmth emanated from her. She had the best smile I'd ever seen, with teeth whiter than her suit. "Mr. Scarpello—"

"Fabio, *chéri*. 'Mr. Scarpello' was used for his father, may his soul rest in peace. Using it for"—she motioned with her head toward the back door—"*him* is tantamount to disrespect for the dead." She held out her hand. "I'm Adele Girard."

I liked the way she rolled her Rs. "Nice to meet you." I shook her hand. "I'm Pauline—"

She waved toward the door. "Come back here and get comfortable."

As I walked to the door where Adele stood leaning against the dark brown paneled wall, Fabio stuck his head out of what I assumed was his office. The royal blue carpet smelled of mildew and had more spots on it than Adele's collar had polka dots.

"Miles sent her here. Have her fill out the paperwork for

taxes and shit like that, then send her to me," he said, and then pulled his head back into his office like a giant ostrich hiding in the sand.

I figured Fabio might have good reason to hide.

She waved a "don't pay attention to him" hand at me. "Come in here."

Adele proved to be as warm as her smile. She got me coffee and a donut that resembled a *pączki*. I took the coffee and passed on the donut and learned that Fabio had taken over the business when his father passed away two years ago. Everyone missed him, she'd said.

And by her tone and the actual things she said, no one was too fond of Fabio. Duh.

"But . . . Adele will give him credit for not running the place into the ground," she said in her adorable Canadian accent, which she'd told me she couldn't shake, having spoken French since birth. "He's a shit most of the time, but so filled with greed, *chéri*, that he actually has this place making money. One thing his father wasn't too good at. No, Mr. Scarpello wasn't a greedy man. God rest his soul to all eternity." She made the sign of the cross on her head.

I felt compelled to join her.

After mounds of paperwork had my John Hancock on them, I took the donut Adele had again offered, knowing what I needed was a good sugar high. Now I had to go see Fabio and find out what the hell I'd actually be doing.

"What?" My voice came out so high pitched I might need to change to soprano from alto in the church choir. Naw. It was only a logical gut reaction to Fabio's words. "I have to do *what*?"

His forehead wrinkled like the prunes my uncle Walt ate on a daily basis, claiming regularity is how he lived so long, and said, "Shit. Don't you listen . . . Oh, that's right. Ear infection."

I was ready to say "What infection?" but remembered my earlier lie. I wasn't good at lying. Catholic-school-induced conscience and all. How good could I be at spying? And all by myself, as Fabio had just explained. Lord, what was I doing?

Fabio shoved a folder across the desk. Of course it had to make several detours on the way since his desk was covered in files, dirty napkins, filled ashtrays, old donuts on paper plates and who knew what else—I sure didn't want to find out.

"You read through the information in the file. Your first one stiffed Workers' Comp. Fake back injury. I need you to prove the fucker is faking it. You get yourself some detective equipment, like I said before. Video, camera, those kinds of things. No need for a gun yet—"

My throat constricted so I squeezed out, "Gun?!"

He shook his head. "Miles is going to owe me big time, doll, if you keep this up. No gun, I said."

"But you also said 'yet.' "

"Yeah, right. Some suspects don't want their little money-making schemes found out. They get a little testy about it." He shrugged. "Sometimes you need protection."

I took a long sip of now-cold coffee. When it settled enough that I was certain it wouldn't spew out of my mouth, I managed to say, "Testy? I'm guessing someone who is crooked enough to commit fraud, wouldn't *ever* want to be found out."

Fabio winked. "Atta girl, doll. You're catching on. Brains *and* boobs. Miles said you were smart."

How smart could I be if I was sitting here talking about spying on criminals?

"Any questions?" He took a partially smoked cigar from an ashtray overflowing with butts of cigarettes and dead cigars and started to relight it.

I hesitated. Had to, in order to clear my confusion, astonishment and impending fear. A short pause. There. Now I might be able to come up with some questions. "Actually, Fabio, I do have several—"

"Go have Adele introduce you to Goldie. Nick's out on a job. Goldie's a vet. Goldie'll show you the ropes." He spun around toward the window, set his feet on the counter and leaned back.

I guessed a nap was in order but didn't stay around to find out. I left my coffee cup on his desk, thinking it wouldn't be noticed in the debris and knowing if I tried to carry it, my trembling hands would spill coffee all over my suit. No sense wasting money that I didn't have on a cleaning bill.

Adele had her head bent forward with earphones tucked beneath the polka-dotted bow in her hair. She typed on a keyboard, obviously transcribing notes. And with gloves on, no less. I hated to interrupt but needed some motherly comforting—and had a feeling Stella Maciejko Sokol wouldn't volunteer when she heard about all this.

The gun part wouldn't leave my thoughts.

I tapped at the door, but Adele didn't turn around. So I went inside and gently tapped on her shoulder. Her head flew up, the wire of the headset caught on her flailing hands and a giant potted fern took the brunt of her actions and ended up on the floor.

"I'm so sorry!" I scrambled to help pick up the pot. Luckily it was plastic made to look like pottery and didn't break.

Adele looked at me, took a deep breath and sighed loudly. "Adele doesn't do well with sneaking up on her. Not since eighty-eight, when I was convicted."

I couldn't help myself, yet I'd never been the nosy type. "You were convicted?"

She straightened her hair while looking in the shiny part of the electric coffeepot next to her desk and reapplied her cherry red lipstick. "Embezzling. Learned my lesson. Thank the good Lord Mr. Scarpello found it in his heart to hire me after I got out."

Got out? Geez. She was adorable but an ex-con. Pauline Sokol never did well with change and this is exactly why. I figured it wasn't prudent to ask for any more details, since she wasn't offering.

Then she said, "My old lady was sick. The big C. Ate her

up to nothing. And, to boot, no medical insurance. I needed that money. The jury was right to convict me. Don't matter the need, you can't steal." She held up her gloved hands. "Burned in the joint."

I could only nod. Adele sat silent for a minute. I figured she was thinking of her mom, so I said, "Fabio said I should have you introduce me to Goldie. When you're ready."

"Oh . . . sure. Sure thing." She leaned near and touched my arm. "Don't be afraid now, *chéri*. Goldie *can* help you. Don't pay attention to the outside."

Outside? Outside of what? Oh . . . my . . . God. And here I thought the "gun" thing was frightening.

The hallway behind Adele's office narrowed toward the end. Stale cigar smoke coated the walls, causing the burnt scent to overpower the musty odor that permeated the reception area. Two doors, one on each side, were at the end. One open. One closed. I guessed that one was Goldie's.

Through the open one I noticed a young man and a woman at desks, typing on keyboards, talking on phones. Adele said that was the extent of the office staff and she'd introduce me later. "No one there can help you, *chéri*," she said as she hesitated outside the closed door.

"Maybe we should call first?" I stepped back, not even admitting how stupid that sounded.

Adele looked at me. "Hmm. I never thought of that. We have an office intercom, but it don't work, and Fabio is too cheap to get it fixed." Again she touched my arm. "Don't you let meeting Goldie get to you. Adele is right here. Just remember that Goldie is . . . well, Goldie."

Instead of it getting creepier that she spoke of herself in third person, I convinced myself that it was motherly. I told myself not to be afraid with Adele standing next to me.

After a quick knock with her still-gloved hand—Adele's other hand gripped my own—a muffled sound came from inside.

"Is someone in there with Goldie? Because if they are, we could come back," I said.

Adele tightened her hold on my hand. "*Chéri*, that is Goldie," she whispered to me.

"But it sounds like—" A man? A woman? One with a baritone voice? No, what the hell did it sound like?

The door swung open.

I pulled back behind Adele. She stepped to the side and let me face Goldie . . . alone.

A hand with long fingers that piano players would kill for reached out to me. I cringed, then reluctantly reached out.

"Hey, suga, you must be the new mole."

Adele stepped back toward me. "*Chéri*, this is Goldie Perlman. Ex-Army intelligence."

I glared at what had to be six feet of well-endowed woman in front of me. Goldie had on silver skintight slacks, looked like the stretch kind. Her feet, maybe size eleven, well, maybe twelve, sported gold spike heels with pearl-covered bows on them. Ack. My feet hurt looking at them. Not good for running, I'd imagine. Then again, with her size, she probably didn't have to run from anyone.

I looked past the pants to her shirt. A tiger's face nearly jumped out at me until I realized it was three-dimensional artwork, or at least looked like it. So real, yet sparkly too. Lots of gold and bronze colors. Actually very pretty, but not my taste. The two golden tiger's eyes glared at me.

I moved to the side, out of tiger view.

She smiled, revealing a set of damn fine white teeth with a slight overbite. But they sparkled like the shirt and pants. Her makeup, muted earthy tones, was done to perfection, as far as I could tell. Of course I'm no expert, since all I ever use is Maybelline pink blush and matching lipstick. Miles always nagged at me to buy more expensive stuff or at least to let his friend Carl, who worked at Macy's department store, do a makeover.

Goldie didn't need a makeover.

She was beautiful. I tucked the idea of asking her for help

with my makeup into the back of my mind. I shook her hand and winced at the grip. Wow. She must work out more than I did.

Geez. She really didn't look like my idea of an investigator. More a movie star.

Adele smiled at Goldie. "How's it hanging, *chéri*?"

Goldie chuckled. "Long, honey child. Long."

They howled.

I started to join in, then froze. Hanging? Long? *Long!*

I looked up at Goldie. *Really* looked at her, past the beautiful skin, the perfect nose that any Pole like myself would kill for, those darn teeth and—I swallowed so loudly that Adele and Goldie glared at me.

Goldie was a *he*.

Now I realized his wrists were too thick to be a woman's. Should have been a dead giveaway, but I had been mesmerized and didn't notice. Okay, that didn't bode well for my investigative skills.

Adele must have seen my mouth gape open. She reached out with a gloved finger, very nonchalantly I might add, and ever-so-gently pushed my lower jaw closed. "Miles introduced Goldie to Fabio. Goldie is from New Orleans."

As if that would explain why a six-foot-tall, maybe Cajun, man would be dressed up in an outfit snazzier than any I owned for New Year's Eve and still look as if he could win the Miss America title after waking up with wrinkles in his cheeks and his auburn hair spiking out all over. He was *that* good-looking. Shit. Maybe I could fix him up with Doc Taylor to get him off my back.

I realized why I was here and decided I'd hang on to the doc a bit longer. I really needed *that*, soon.

Miles's friend. Now it made sense.

I'd been so overwhelmed by the job, Adele and Goldie that I hadn't put two and two together. Miles might have mentioned Goldie a time or two, but . . . I had no idea he looked like this.

Feeling as if I really had stepped through the looking glass, I smiled at Goldie. "Pauline Sokol. Nice to meet you."

Adele slapped herself in the head. "Where are my manners? Sorry. Oh, Pauline is the new investigator Fabio might have mentioned to you—" She turned toward me. "Goldie calls all of you moles."

Goldie laughed. "Come on, suga, we need to talk." He pulled me into his office, and Adele clattered down the hallway.

With Southern manners any mama would be proud of, Goldie showed me into his office and offered me a drink. As I looked at the moss-covered tree growing in the corner, the zebra-striped couch next to the glass coffee table resting on elephant legs and Goldie's desk made of chrome and more glass, I mumbled, "Scotch, neat."

"A girl after my own heart." He turned to open a mahogany cabinet near the window then pulled out the hidden bar.

"I mean . . . coffee." Scotch? Where'd that come from? This was getting worse. I couldn't help but stare. Even his voice didn't give him away. I'd seen Ru Paul on television a few times, and Goldie could give him a run for his money, although Ru was gorgeous too.

He looked back. "I'll take the Scotch. You get the Joe."

As I sat and sipped the coffee latté he'd whipped up, I decided I liked Goldie. Although the most flamboyant friend of Miles, I automatically considered Goldie a friend of mine, too. He told me how he'd been in the Army, worked intelligence as Adele had said and went back home to New Orleans, where he wanted to open his own private investigating firm but never did.

After nonstop work and burning out (been there, done that), he met Miles at a Mardi Gras parade. Amid the ruckus and the gaudy plastic doubloons thrown from the floats, Miles convinced him to move north and work for his uncle, Mr. Scarpello.

Goldie said he never looked back.

"Now, Fabio gives you the file and you're pretty much on your own. You get yourself some good equipment, suga. Not that cheap stuff that breaks down before you know it and you're paying twice as much cuz you have to buy more. A good video camera is a must."

"Thank goodness I have one already."

He polished off his Scotch, wiped a long finger across his bottom lip. "Let me guess. One of those older models that is about two feet long with a dick of a microphone sticking out on the end long enough to poke someone in the eye?"

"Why . . . yes." That wasn't a good thing? Not the dick in the eye thing, but the long microphone?

"Suga . . ." He walked to the wall unit and turned on the television. While I watched Emeril pour some batter into a Bundt cake pan, Goldie snapped off the tiger's left eye from his chest.

"What are you . . ."

He opened the eye, which still stared at me, and took a cord from the back of the television and connected it. With the aplomb of a Boston Pops conductor, he waved his hand toward the TV.

A few seconds of snow, followed by a blue screen, and then . . .

"Oh shit!"

I materialized on the screen, standing in the hallway and obviously trying to hide behind Adele. Whoever said television added ten pounds was correct. I decided I would run an extra lap that night. "How'd you do that?"

He shook his finger at me. "See how you'd be too obvious with your dick camera?"

"Completely." I did, but those ten extra pounds wouldn't leave my thoughts.

"We've got a lot of work to do, suga. The right equipment is a must in this business. Come on."

After hours of Goldie's Fraud Investigation 101, I really did need that Scotch. I settled for a Coors while Goldie poured himself another Scotch.

"I had no idea there was so much to the job. I might be in way over my head."

Goldie leaned back in his black leather chair with leopard armrests and said, "I have no doubt that you are, suga. But what the hell." He lifted his glass in a toast. "Life is short. Go for it."

I looked around the room that obviously Goldie had furnished himself and said, "I'll do just that."

But, truthfully, inside I screamed, "Help! I'm about to drown!"

I poked my toe out from the bubbles. One thing about Miles: He knew how to live. I always teased him that he was born with an interior-decorating gene.

Our tub was sunken into the floor of the bathroom, all salmon-colored marble. Gold water spigots shaped like dolphins sat at one end, and at the other were the controls for the stereo system, phone and the jets that were now massaging my sore muscles.

I'd done that extra lap and two more.

No man was going to look better than Pauline Sokol!

Alongside the tub was the tan folder, on suspect Ms. Tina Macaluso, that Fabio had given me. My first case! What a rush! What was I doing?

I'd read it over and over, until my bathwater cooled. Still I remained submerged in thought. Goldie had made this investigation stuff sound so easy—and obviously it *had* been, for *him*. Then again, he was ex-Army Intel.

He probably did great with the investigating—it certainly didn't look as if money was a problem for him. And he'd said Fabio gave decent bonuses for good work. Adele had said Goldie's conviction rate of frauds was in the hundreds and the monies recovered in the millions.

Damn.

I could do this. I could get my first case solved. Goldie's "Go for it" had said as much.

Tina Macaluso was a dead woman.

Three

Okay, Tina Macaluso wasn't really a dead woman, but she'd soon be tucked neatly away in jail if I had anything to do with it, and I might get a Christmas bonus this year. Then again, I think in Goldie's Fraud Investigation 101, he'd said the DA didn't incarcerate most of the time. The money just had to be paid back.

According to her file, Tina had conned the Global Carriers Insurance Company out of $33,892.77. Wow.

And I planned to help them get every penny back. Sure, I'd like to see her butt in jail, but I'd settle with her getting caught and having to pay the money back. It rankled me that others got money so easily. From an insurance company, no less, and me without any coverage until after my probation. That alone made me feel driven to succeed with this case.

Although being the honest person that I was, I had to admit that I had no idea how to do it. Still, I wasn't going to let on to Fabio about my shortcomings. Goldie had offered to help, and I'd damn well take his offer.

With my toe, I lifted the knob that opened the drain and as the water ran out, I stood, toweled myself off and stuck on my robe. I padded to my room and looked out the window.

Snowflakes skittered across the lawn. Although not a major storm, the roads would be slick. Still, I had work to do.

It was odd making my own hours. The urge to sit and watch the *Jerry Springer Show* with the morbid curiosity that draws one to rubberneck during a car accident had to be tamed by the stark reality of my bank account. Once dressed, I grabbed my purse. Time was of the essence, Fabio had said, and besides, he only paid "per job." No salary. Ack.

Also, being a newbie on probation, I wouldn't get anything until the first assignment was completed. If I did a good job in a timely manner, I could get some interim pay from then on. It'd be only part of the payment for the full job, so I'd have something to live on until I made the big bucks.

More cases—more money.

Right now, I had nada.

I stuffed an old pair of binoculars that I'd used for bird-watching back in my nature-loving days of the eighties, a 35 mm camera with film from my cousin's wedding two years ago still inside (please don't get my mother started on that), and two chocolate power bars into my bag and looked at the video camera on the counter. A prehistoric elephant was smaller. Still, I couldn't buy anything new yet. Goldie needed all his stuff for a job he was working on, and couldn't stop since he was nearly finished. So, no loaners.

Okay, I'd wing it.

Adele was a whiz at getting personal info on the claimants, I'd found out through Goldie. She'd given me Tina's address and where she worked. Damn if Tina wasn't a nurse too. Small world. Goldie had said he'd start me out first thing on Monday with "on-the-job training" by working on this case with me. But that was days away, and that money thing wouldn't leave my thoughts.

Hey, what could it hurt to start on my own?

I let Spanky out and back in, gave him a hug and made sure he had enough water before going out the door.

Out in the parking lot, I climbed into my Volvo and drove

out rather exhilarated. There was something mysterious, almost orgasmic about heading off to spy on someone—legally. My fingers danced across the steering wheel while the tires crunched along in the snow, and Frank Sinatra crooned on my favorite AM station. Wow. Who would have thought a non-nursing job could cause such excitement.

What a natural rush!

I reached over to my purse, dug out my cell phone and punched in Doc Taylor's number. Got his voice mail. Shoot. "I'm free for dinner Saturday. Call me." No need to mention *that* was the real reason I'd called.

Snow had my windshield wipers going nonstop. Damn. It wasn't going to be the best of days for surveillance. Surveillance. Pauline Sokol on surveillance. My laughter mixed with Frank's singing as I turned onto Maple Avenue.

Hope Valley wasn't a metropolis, to say the least. But it was a decent-size town and had a decent-size hospital. A very ethnic New England town. Immigrants from Italy, Poland, Russia, Germany and several other countries had settled here. I can only assume they heard the name and thought it would bring them good luck and lots of hope. They remained in their little ethnic groups: Even the Catholic church in each neighborhood was attended by predominantly one nationality. Needless to say, the Sokol family belonged to the Polish one, Saint Stanislaus Church.

My great-grandfather must have had the same idea when he arrived in the United States at the ripe old age of eighteen on the S.S. *Ethiopia* from Glasgow, Scotland, landing on Ellis Island. Not that he was Scottish. That was only his point of departure from Europe. He and his soon-to-be wife, Amelia, came from what they referred to as White Russia in Poland. Thus my very ethnic clan ended up in Hope Valley.

Hope Valley had some manufacturing left from the 1900s, a mall and—of great interest to me now—one of the biggest insurance companies in the country. Global Carriers was several blocks over and certainly the biggest outside the

Hartford area. I turned down Pine Street, heading to the residential area Adele had told me about.

Tina Macaluso lived in a trendy New England subdivision near the Connecticut River. Houses in her neighborhood, circa 1700s, gave me the feeling that I'd driven back in time. The wooden structures were mostly saltbox style. No split-levels with aluminum siding like my folks' house. Nope. This neighborhood had ordinances that said residents had to comply with rules like no electric door openers, no chain-link fences and nothing that made them look as if they were in the twenty-first century.

I pulled up alongside a slate blue house and looked at the number. One hundred seventy-one. Macaluso's. Perfect.

I looked at my watch. I'd been there three minutes.

Now what?

Ack. I should have waited until Monday to come with Goldie, since I had no inkling as to what to do next. I popped a Celine Dion cassette into the tape deck, leaned back and waited. Normally I was a country buff, but hey, who didn't enjoy a little Celine once in a while?

A neighbor drove by in a silver Jaguar. Obviously this was the ritzier part of Hope Valley. She slowed alongside me and looked through the haze of snow. I smiled, leaned back. She moved on. Good. I sure didn't need any interference on a job. I had enough to figure out on my own.

After forty-three minutes and the two power bars, my feet hurt. Cold does that to little toes. I'd turned up the heater, but the outside temperature dropped in proportion to my increasing the controls. The only excitement so far was when the light in the upstairs room of Tina's house came on for a minute and then went off. Somehow I thought that wasn't going to do me any good.

I decided to "will" Tina to come out the door and do something stupid. Something that a person getting paid by Workers' Compensation shouldn't be doing with a "back injury."

I shut my eyes to have that "will" thing work better.

An engine purred in my left ear. My eyes flew open. I

turned to look out the window to my side, but could only see a blur of black through the frosted pane. I wiped off a circle and peeked out.

Shit!

I pulled back, then looked out again.

A black SUV of some sort was pulled up right next to me! Real close. That wasn't the part that had me pull back. Oh no. It was the occupant.

He sat staring at me. Not just any *he*. More a younger version of George Clooney—and hey, he'd been voted the star folks would want to come knocking at their door by a whopping 41.2 percent—so this younger version was no slouch. The guy, who was actually scowling down at me now, since his SUV towered over my Volvo, had the same look as George, only his hair was jet black without the sprinkles of gray.

From what I could see at this angle, and yes I did unabashedly peer up as high as I could, he wore a black ski jacket, black leather gloves and aviator sunglasses—also tinted black. I could picture him swooshing down some trail at Mount Snow. Maybe I should be more scared than excited, watching him stare at me like that.

And here I had thought *surveillance* was an orgasmic experience.

The window on his SUV slid open.

I opened mine. "Afternoon."

"Need something?" The tone wasn't friendly, more like a what-the-hell-are-you-doing-here kind of tone. But that voice! Scratchy in a sensual sort of way with a wee bit of a laid-back tone thrown in. Had my insides a-quivering.

Did I need something from him! Be still my heart.

I had to once again face the fact that I wasn't a good liar. That was something I'd have to brush up on with Goldie. So, I looked at him. "Nope. Thanks anyway." Then I shut my window and wouldn't allow myself to look back. He must live near Tina. God, I hoped he wasn't her husband. Then again, Tina was married to a doctor, and this guy looked too streetwise to be a doctor.

I convinced myself that he didn't even know Tina. Besides, I could spot a doctor a million miles away—and this guy was no doctor. What was I thinking? He had me all confused. I'd learned from Adele that Tina's husband was an orthopedic doc—go figure—and that she worked in his office.

After a few minutes I heard the crunching of snow and figured that he had driven off. I turned to see him pull up in front of the tan house next to Tina's. I switched my windshield wipers on full tilt. Through the now-clear windshield, I could make him out, using his cell phone. Damn. Now what? What was he doing here, ruining my surveillance? Why hadn't he just pulled into his driveway? This secluded neighborhood wasn't the kind of place one just tooled around in, so he must have had a reason for being there.

His damn car was a Suburban—long enough for a family of four to live in. Well, who cared? I had to be professional and concentrate on the job. Earn some money. That's what I'd do.

A next-door neighbor came out, looked from the black Suburban to my Volvo and walked to her mailbox. When she opened it and took out a handful of mail, I wondered if I should ask her if she'd ever seen Tina lifting something heavy—or who the heck Mr. Instant Orgasm was. But wait a minute. That didn't seem like a good idea. It could tip Tina off that the insurance company was on to her, and maybe have some half-crazed wife running out to slash my tires if Suburban over there belonged to her.

I couldn't afford new tires so I forced my hormonal imaginings to Dr. Taylor. Tried to picture him in my thoughts—naked. I waited a few minutes. Nothing. Somehow it didn't do the trick.

Although my car was now toasty warm from the heater, I realized that asphyxiation could come into play if I sat with the motor running too long. Also, not much of a mechanical wizard, I figured the tape player was sucking my battery's juices dry. So, I shut everything off.

Just then the front door of Tina's house opened. A heavy-set woman in a neon yellow parka, black leggings, and a furry yellow hat came out—with a shovel in her hands! I lunged across to the passenger side and pulled the binoculars from the bag. With my gloved hand, I wiped the frost from the window and wondered how "staker outers" kept their breath from fogging up the glass.

Then I shuffled around in the manila folder to find her picture. It wasn't a very good one where you could see her face, but she did look like a plus-size kinda gal. Had to be her.

A scraping called my attention back to Tina. The "injury" that had kept her from working the ortho clinic must have felt peachy today, because she was getting that walkway cleaner than my mother's dishes. Obviously a snowblower wasn't usable in this neighborhood, since the sidewalks were all crushed stone.

I leaned a bit closer. Tina looked familiar, but the damn hat kept falling forward and blocking her face. I zoomed in my vision by squinting. Wait a minute! Antonina Scarlucci! I'd gone to nursing school with her back in the late eighties. Talk about a small world. Of course, several of us had remained in Hope Valley after graduation. But to spy on someone I knew? Damn. I hated that, but then again, she was a criminal, in my book. I vaguely remember her cheating on a biology final, come to think of it.

That's right. I'd heard she'd married Donnie Macaluso, who was a doc. And, something to give me pause, Tina's family was rumored to have ties to the old Mafia. Gulp.

But I had a job to do.

Excitement had me fumbling between the front and back seats, where my gigantic video camera had fallen. I hoped it still worked. And, I hoped Tina couldn't see me or the dick of a microphone. I pressed the ON switch, hefted it up on my shoulder, and started to mentally spend the money I'd get for this case when I hit RECORD.

Tina shoveled away.

Occasionally I had to re-clean my window. But I was getting her on tape, so it didn't matter. The Workers' Comp claim would soon be dismissed. I'd have to get more evidence—something closer to prove it was Tina—because of the damn hat, but hey, this was a start.

Truthfully, she looked like a giant bumblebee. Much like the old *Saturday Night Live* clips of John Belushi. The giant bee shoveled until she reached the street sidewalk.

This investigating stuff was a piece of cake.

A tiny black battery flickered in the corner of my view.

Ack. I hadn't had time to charge the battery. Okay. Professionals don't panic. I zoomed in to get a clearer shot. She held the shovel in one hand, flipped her hat back with the other (Oh yes, there is a God!) and bent to shovel snow the plow had piled in front of her driveway. It had to be heavy! This was going to be—

Fuzz

Click.

Black.

Black?

The video camera went black. Dead battery.

I leaned back, blinked my eyes since the strain of looking through the camera hurt, and cursed. Just like the proverbial sailor.

Professionals don't panic, I reminded myself again.

I dropped the camera onto my lap with a *thump* and expelled a whoosh of air from my mouth at the weight. I grabbed my bag and hauled out the 35 mm. Two shots left. Good thing I'd never had the film developed. Had to be because I was so sick and tired of *attending* wedding after wedding. With a quick prayer that two-year-old film doesn't go bad, I looked in the viewfinder. Foggy window. After a quick wipe of the glass, I leaned the camera near.

Tina resumed her shoveling.

My finger was poised on the shutter.

Behind her I noticed a light blinking. A blue light. I looked through the camera to see a cop car pull around the corner and slow near the SUV. Good. Maybe he'd get arrested for being a Peeping Tom. Despite my wacko thought that I wouldn't mind someone who looked like him peeking at me, I watched a few minutes.

The cop looked too friendly with him. Uh-oh. They were laughing! Then they both looked at me!

Oh no! Who *was* that guy? My finger slipped. *Snap*. Damn. A wasted shot.

I probably shouldn't hang around. Besides, hunger pangs reminded me it was after six. When all else fails, I think of food, and getting the hell away from here. Okay, when I sense the police are about to question me, I think of food. Tina'd have to wait.

My parents would be sitting down to eat right now. Mom always served at six, twelve and six. No matter the day of the week. When we were kids, she made us get up at 6 A.M. for breakfast. As teens we'd sleepily shove something down, then sneak back to bed until around noon, when she'd wake us for lunch.

I hurriedly flung the stupid camera into the backseat and vaulted across to the driver's side. Thank goodness I was only blocks away from my folks' house, or I'd get there in time for only dessert.

The cop got back into his car, turned into a nearby driveway and started to back out—in my direction.

I started the engine, dusted the snow from the front window with the wipers at warp speed and watched Tina lift a statue with one hand. Ack! I shouted, "You damn camera! You just cost me big! A waste of time." Boy, someone her size was strong.

As I drove past the SUV, I couldn't help but slow, smile and scoot away. Wow! That wasn't like me at all—but the look on the mystery man's face was all worth it.

Deliciously pissed.

In my rearview mirror I could see Tina, still shoveling, and cursed at my behemoth of a video camera.

I needed to talk to my folks—about my new job.

About buying equipment.

Making a mental sign of the cross so as not to take my

hands from the steering wheel, I asked Saint Theresa for her help—yet again.

I added another prayer that she wouldn't get tired of me praying to her about all my causes and threw in that if she wanted to have the mystery man follow me and . . .

Never mind. Saints shouldn't get involved in things like that.

I spun out of the circa 1700s neighborhood before the cop could follow me.

"Why would you need a new video camera?" my father asked through a mouthful of potato pancake. "Didn't I give you my old one?"

I scooped a dollop of sour cream onto my pancake and added another of applesauce. It had to be Friday night. Mom always cooked meatless Polish meals on Friday. I hadn't realized today was Friday. Seems days ran together since I'd become an independent investigator—although I'd just started. But I didn't miss the daily nursing grind. "Yes, Daddy, you did. But I need something smaller."

Uncle Walt scraped a forkful of potato pancake across his dish. Mother raised an eyebrow at him, but he ignored her. "Smaller is better these days. Ask all the chicks at the senior citizens center."

My parents rolled their eyes. I lost my appetite, thinking they were going down *that* road with Uncle Walt. After I set my fork down, I made a mental note to call Doc Taylor again. He really, really needed to take me out to dinner soon.

My mother put the rest of the pancakes on my father's dish without even asking. Of course, after forty-three years of marriage, they had some kind of matrimonial mental telepathy between them. He started to eat them all.

"I still don't understand about this new job. I'm thrilled you found something, although you could have taken a break and stayed here with us instead of living with that homosexual man," she said.

"We aren't 'living together,' and Miles is my best friend."

She'd always called him that, but treated him as one of her sons soon after she'd found out his parents had died in a sky-diving accident.

"Oh, nothing against him, darling, he is a doll. It's just that family should be taking care of you when you have no money, although I told you numerous times you needed to start a vacation club savings account—"

"I have a job now. I told you that I'm going to help out at Miles's uncle's insurance agency."

"I know, darling—" She started to stack the dirty dishes in front of her. "But when you said you'd be working there, I thought filing, answering phones. Not going out and spying on people. What is this world coming to?"

I wasn't going to share that I'd felt the same way about the job originally. Hell, I'd never be caught dead admitting that I thought like my mother. After a quick shudder, I said, "They need to be spied on, Mom. Some people cheat the insurance companies out of millions."

Daddy looked up. His eyes widened. If he weren't such a pious man, I'd think he'd want to hear how they did that. Instead he said, "They should buy lottery tickets. They could win big and win honestly."

After retiring, and playing the lotto 364 days of the year, he still hadn't won "big" on the daily numbers. He didn't buy a ticket on Good Friday, out of respect.

"Anyway, I need a very small video camera, a digital camera and a few more things. So—" The plea stuck in my throat. How I hated to ask my parents for money. It would be the third, fourth, and fifth degree until I described every detail of my new job. I'd *owe* them. Ack.

I looked up to see Uncle Walt waving at me while my parents ate. "What—"

He waved frantically, then laid a finger over his closed lips. Okay, I get it. He didn't want me to go on about asking for money. I'd humor him until dessert. Tonight had to be bread pudding. Not my favorite, though. My mother makes better desserts than Bellinski's Pastry Shop, but Friday night wasn't the time to come looking for good sweets.

Uncle Walt got up. "I need help . . . in my room."

My father started to get up. Uncle Walt pushed a hand on his shoulder. "Pauline has smaller fingers."

I looked at my hand and wondered if Uncle Walt was hitting the Vodka too much. But I stood and followed him.

Mother clattered the dishes as she must have gotten up to set them by the sink. She refused a dishwasher every Christmas from us kids. Said she could do a better job than any machine and didn't want to waste the cabinet space, although she had two empty drawers and one cabinet under the sink where she only kept a bucket in case of leaks. I've never known the sink to leak.

Uncle Walt waved me into his room. The old maple furniture always smelled freshly lemon polished. The drapes were a deep brown, matching the carpet. Beige doilies that my mother had crocheted sat under the lamp on his dresser. He walked near, turned to look at the door and again held his finger to his lips.

I smiled to myself and remained quiet.

He pushed in the small piece of molding above the top drawer. I was about to tell him that he might break it by doing that, but before I could, a little button appeared. He pushed it, releasing some mechanism that made the thing pop out like a drawer. On closer inspection, it *was* a drawer.

"Wow," I whispered.

Uncle Walt turned around. I would have given every penny I had to get a snapshot of the pleased expression on his face. His watery blue eyes sparkled. The thin, cracked lips beneath the wrinkles of his face curled up on each end. Uncle Walt, the crafty senior. "How much you need, Pauline?"

He reached in and pulled out a wad, and I mean a wad, of money.

"Shit. Where did you get all that?"

Walt's gaze flew to the door. "Shush. Don't worry. It's all legal. Years of hard work."

And poker games with highly pensioned widows, no doubt. "You should put that in the bank—"

"Bank shmank. How much?"

"I can't let you—"

"Humor an old man. I've never been able to do much for you kids, Pauline. Especially you, since you don't have any kids yourself. I get to buy for the little ones, but you . . . you're still single."

Thank you very much for the reminder.

"You're the only reason your mother lets me eat an occasional cookie or piece of cake."

I smiled, told him how much I needed and made him take my written IOU. I said I'd pay him back. He said he wouldn't take the money. We agreed I'd give it to Saint Stanislaus Church once I'd earned it back.

I left my parents' house with my stash, hurried back to my apartment and called Goldie at home to tell him about the money.

"Shit. Nice uncle. Wish I had one of those." I could hear the sadness in his voice and found out he'd grown up shifted from one foster home to another. Didn't know any uncles, let alone parents. He sucked in a breath and told me where to order my spy equipment.

When I hung up, I booted up Miles's computer and searched the Web for detective equipment. Amazing what someone could buy online with a credit card. After spending all the money from Uncle Walt, I was set.

As soon as the UPS man arrived in a few days, I'd be out the door on the tail of Tina Macaluso once again.

Back injury—yeah, right.

Another Saturday night sitting home alone eating a delivered pizza with mushrooms, eggplant and sausage was beginning to look better and better as I shoved on my black patent-leather heels.

Spanky sat on the bed, watching. Smiling. I'm sure he smiled when I slid the shoe over my foot. Men.

The shoes went perfect with the slinky black dress Miles had insisted I buy on our last shopping trip to Lord and Taylor before I quit my job. Seemed like years ago.

Even though the shoes made my "Maciejko" legs look damn good, I couldn't bring myself to get excited. Seemed a waste of good sex-appeal equipment to be waiting for Doc Taylor to arrive.

Because, I had to admit, my thoughts were for the occupant of a black Suburban with a tiny silver cross hanging from the rearview mirror. Oh, yes, I noticed the small things.

As if my life wasn't complicated enough.

Now I lusted after a stranger. Albeit a gorgeous one.

Four

"You look . . . sexy tonight," Doc Taylor said when I opened the door and he walked in. I think a tiny bit of spittle seeped out of his lips.

It wasn't that Vance wasn't appealing. He, too, was sexy as hell in a professional sort of way. Not professional like a gigolo, but more a doctor or lawyer sort of way. The good-looking kind you'd see on the soaps. Vance could win an Emmy on appearance alone.

What the hell was wrong with me?

I should be jumping his bones right now. If I broke one, it wouldn't matter. He was an orthopedic surgeon and, I'm sure, could fix himself right up.

I reached up and kissed his cheek. He looked taken aback, as if it should have landed on his lips. "It's been a long time—"

He grabbed me in a bear hug.

"Hey, watch those precious hands of yours," I said.

He released his grip as if I might break one of his highly insured fingers. Vance's sense of humor—actually lack of—never failed to astonish me.

"I'm kidding, hon."

He laughed. Forced it.

"It *has* been too long. My secretary called you many times. Doesn't Miles's machine work?"

I wanted to ask if she was going to take me out, but looking at his face, I knew there was no other way to work things. She made all his calls for him, social *and* business.

Vance had grown up in a family of doctors, living in a ritzy neighborhood in Greenwich. I'd met him during his residency at Saint Greg's. His family never laughed at my jokes either. For that matter, I'm sure they didn't root for me to become Mrs. Doctor Vance G. Taylor.

Still, Vance had this notion in his head that we were in love. At least he said he was. I cared about him deeply and would nurse him back to health if, God forbid, he should become ill. Yet, I couldn't see myself as Mrs. Doctor Vance G. Taylor any more than his parents wanted me to be.

"I guess Miles's machine is on the blink," I out and out lied. Next, I made a mental confession followed by good reasons why I had to lie. If God didn't buy it, I'd be sunk. I knew Vance's secretary had called several weeks ago, but until lately, I hadn't felt the urge for . . . that. So, I ignored the calls. "Good thing I called you."

He leaned near, nuzzled my neck.

For a few seconds, hormones readied to dance throughout my body—but they fizzled out as usual. "I'm starved. Where we heading?" I knew better than to try to make plans for us. Vance did all the "man" stuff, and, right now I didn't have the desire or the strength to argue. A few years back I tried, but to no avail. He played by a different set of rules. Ones written in some good ol' boys' yacht club in the days before feminism. So, who was I to argue?

"Thought we'd head over to Harbor Bay. I'm in the mood for surf and turf."

Vance was always in the mood for surf and turf, and his version was Maine lobster (at outrageous market prices) and prime rib. Harbor Bay was a damn pricey restaurant with the best seafood in Hope Valley, located on the bank of the Connecticut River.

"Sounds like a plan." When he lifted my black coat off the chair to help me put it on, I asked myself if I really should be going. I mean, it might seem as though I was using Vance. In some respects I guess I was, but I'd never once lied to him about my feelings. I never used the L word with him, although he'd told me that he loved me plenty.

When I'd try to break up, he'd refuse. I came to the conclusion that Vance used me as much as I used him, and neither of us was hurting each other. He really wanted someone for an occasional date and bedding.

I needed him for the occasional date and . . . *that* too.

I followed him outside to his waiting Mercedes. Vance drove a silver one with a license plate that had MD on it. Sometimes I worried that someone would follow us for free medical help when we headed out.

Freshly fallen snow crunched under our feet and my damn toes nearly froze in the stupid sexy heels I'd worn. Vance looked at my feet.

"You should have on boots."

"Yeah, right." Once in the car I made him put the heat on full blast and told myself he was right. What possessed me to dress this way for Vance?

A little voice in my head, the voice of my Catholic-school-induced conscience, said it was because I'd been infatuated with Mr. Suburban and was trying to ignore that fact by seducing Vance.

Oh what a tangled web we . . .

At the restaurant Vance gave the keys to one valet while another opened my door. Vance and I hurried inside, where he promptly ordered a 1973 Dom Perignon (which cost more than I made at my ex-nursing job in a month) for him and a Coors for me. I didn't do Perignon.

"What have you been up to, Vance?" I asked, once the

nearby fire had crackled me toasty warm. The Coors didn't hurt either.

He took a long slow sip of his drink, swished it around in his mouth, swallowed and said, "Working as usual. How about you?"

It dawned on me that Vance wasn't privy to my career change, so I told him the bare facts of burning out on nursing, stopping short as to my current career. Just didn't seem right to tell him, so I said Miles found me a job with his uncle. Period.

"My God, Pauline, you sure you know what you are doing? Giving up a career in nursing to do who knows what."

My second lie of the night rolled off my tongue. "Of course I know what I'm doing, hon. Don't worry." I didn't know "what" either.

The waiter handed us menus. Vance ordered for both of us—something else I gave up trying to change years ago. The guy had fabulous taste and other than that blackened mahi-mahi back in 1999, I loved anything he ordered.

We chatted and dined until the cognac for him arrived followed by the crème brûlée for me. No wasted calories on liquor for Pauline Sokol, with an admitted sweet tooth. I did keep it under control most times and got my chocolate fix from those power bars. Tonight, though, I needed sugar.

He took a sip of his drink, paused and, I would imagine by the pleased look on his face, savored the taste. "Did I tell you I took the job near Saint Greg's?"

A spoonful of the smooth, sweet custard-like dessert poised in midair, I said, "Miles *did* mention you were looking for a change."

"Two physicians in one practice aren't enough."

Money wasn't an issue for a Taylor, so I assumed he meant with only one partner, he was on call too often. I had to smile at that one. A doctor who didn't want to work scads of hours a day. "Whereabouts are you, then?"

He held his snifter up to the light, swirled, leaned nearer

and then sipped. "Over on Dearborn Road. Very convenient to the hospital."

Dearborn. Dearborn. Sounded familiar. Actually I knew the street was perpendicular to Ashley, where the hospital was, but why was that street so familiar? I took another bite to think it out.

"Hope Valley Orthopedic Group," he said in a matter-of-fact tone.

I looked up, spoon clenched in my mouth. "Wope Walley Orfopedic—"

"Take the spoon out, Pauline. I can't understand you."

I yanked out the spoon and flipped a droplet of crème brûlée across the table to land on Vance's expensive silver silk tie. "Jesus, Pauline! What the hell?"

Yikes! Vance was a neat freak, and wearing expensive pudding didn't sit well for him. I grabbed a napkin and started to wipe. He took my hand away and motioned for the waiter, who scurried over as if Vance were on fire. "Seltzer water. And hurry."

"I'll have it cleaned. You're working at the Hope Valley Orthopedic clinic?" My voice sounded horrified.

Vance raised an eyebrow. "I am an orthopedic surgeon. There are five of us in the practice. . . ."

I knew he was talking since his lips kept moving, but all I could hear was my mind screaming, "He's working with Tina Macaluso and her husband!"

Five

"Oh . . . my . . . God. You look beautiful!"

I had to grab onto the doorjamb of Goldie's office Monday morning when I got a look at him. Shock did that to me. I'm not a vain person: Other than that year as a sixteen-year-old cheerleader, when I thought I was the cat's meow, I really didn't give my looks a second thought.

I wasn't ugly—that I admitted. And my figure was a slim size four. *That* I attributed to my obsession with aerobics and jogging, which came around age twenty-two, when I dated a health-nut doctor my first year on the surgical ward at Saint Greg's. He turned out to be a royal jerk. I turned out to become obsessed with exercise and to this day can't stop. Nor would I want to.

Up until the last few years—okay, since turning twenty-eight a few years back—I had dated regularly and played the field more than my beloved and all-time favorite Steelers running back, Jerome Bettis. But lately, dates were far and few between. My mother tried to add her two cents with reasons like "More girls were born in 1970 than boys" or "Hope Valley had a plethora of girls because of the good food." Never could figure out that one. Still, it must have made her feel good, since neither of us could figure out why my "dating well" had dried up.

Again, Vance didn't count—'cause I wouldn't let him.

So I shouldn't feel jealous, I thought, looking at Goldie. But damn it all, he *was* gorgeous, and he made me feel like a frumpy over-the-hill housewife whose husband cheated on her and whose kids ran roughshod over her. "You look fab. You look . . . damn it all, gorgeous with a capital G. And not for Goldie either."

"Morning, suga." He smiled.

I couldn't help but stare. Whitest teeth I've ever seen. The words, "Hey, Goldie," somehow came out with my jaw dropped down to my chest.

His hair today was blonde, frosted heavily. I ran my fingers through mine and decided I needed to make an appointment with Farrar, a fabulous hairdresser Miles had turned me on to at the Do Drop In salon. But truthfully, I told myself, Farrar, wizard that he was, could never make mine look as good as Goldie's.

Ack.

Today Goldie's tiger shirt had been replaced by a zebraprint one with matching leggings. Fine legs. I constricted my calves several times in hopes that my "Maciejko" legs would shape up like his. Golden bracelets clanged on both wrists. I couldn't help but stare.

"Doesn't that noise make it difficult to do surveillance?" As soon as the words came out, and Goldie's forehead wrinkled, I felt stupid. "I mean—"

He laughed. "I know what you mean, suga." He jingled the jewelry a few times. "Actually, I'm less conspicuous with all this on."

I could only stare longer.

He looked me in the eye, which broke my concentration, and we both howled. "It does seem odd, but true." He motioned for me to come in. "Few pay much attention to me after the initial staring. Then I just blend in."

Maybe on Fire Island. I walked in, sat on the zebra sofa. Goldie offered me coffee, which I accepted. As he bustled about, pouring, milking, sugaring and stirring, I could only continue my observation. Had to be good for my future cases. I mean, I could watch him all day in wonderment, so of course I could follow a case, no problem.

Goldie turned and handed me a mug of steaming liquid. The pungent scent tickled my nose.

"Smells wonderful."

"N'Awlins's best. Chicory café au lait. Secret is the hot milk." He'd gotten himself a cup in a matching mug with purple, yellow and green Mardi Gras masks on it.

I could only wonder if Goldie missed his home state. Instead of dredging up possible painful memories, I told him all about my "date" with Vance and that he'd taken on a new job. Goldie asked about Miles, and I sensed he still missed him. I tucked that tidbit into the back of my brain. Then I mentioned my "visit" to Tina Macaluso's house.

He gave me a high five. "You go, girl. But, suga, you gotta have better equipment. For the surveillance." He looked at me and smiled. "You got the right stuff for your date though."

First I laughed about that date stuff, then I sighed. "I know. I was hoping to borrow yours until mine gets delivered."

He got up and opened the college-type refrigerator that was camouflaged in black to match the countertop. "About that, suga. Can't today. My case is running longer than I'd expected. Fuckers."

My heart sank as I took one of the cannoli off the tray he held out toward me. But, liking Goldie as I did, I smiled and lied, "No problem." Lying was starting to get disturbingly easy for me since changing professions.

Goldie licked ricotta cheese from his finger. Today his nails, longer than my pinky finger, were a brilliant black with tiny stripes across them. Damn it. Matching zebra nails. Only Goldie. With one finger in his mouth, he mumbled, "I'm hooking you up with Nick."

I swallowed the last of my cannoli and eyed a second one

until this little voice in my head said Goldie must wear a size *one*. "Nick?"

"Um. Nick Caruso. Freelances for Fabio. Been doing it for years. Actually taught me all I know. You'll like Nick. Fabio has a list of freelancers he uses. Most you'll never meet. Calls them in when he needs extra help or one of us full-timers is tied up on a case." He took another cannoli.

I cursed estrogen. How come he could eat two cannoli and probably *lose* weight, and if I took another one, it'd be added to my hips by nightfall?

Goldie got up. "Come with me, and I'll introduce you to Marilyn and Tommy while we wait for Nick. They're office staff. Work the sales end. Nothing to do with investigating."

I walked taller knowing I was an "investigator."

Marilyn Bleaker was a rather frumpy woman with glasses that perched on the bridge of her nose. Tommy Nelson, balding and near fifty, I assumed, appeared rather shy. After a cordial introduction, greeting and goodbye, I followed Goldie back to his office. He said Tommy had a wife and five children. I said a silent novena for all of them and declined a second cup of Goldie's miracle coffee.

We chatted until a knock sounded. Goldie yelled to enter.

Good thing I'd finished my coffee. If I'd had a mouthful when Nick came in, I'd have spewed it all over the faux fur couch.

Nick Caruso wasn't exactly as handsome as Goldie was gorgeous, but Nick was, in my opinion, attractive. Of course this was from a woman who hadn't exactly been zooming around the dating circuit lately. Okay, ever.

I looked at him and smiled. Where Goldie's hair, today, was blonde, Nick's was gray. Prematurely gray by the look of him. Couldn't have been past forty. His voice came out a deep, mellow tone, and I told myself I'd have to call Doc Taylor yet again. And yes, I realized how sad that was.

Nick shook my hand. "Nice to meet you."

"Yes . . . I mean, you too." *Get a grip, Pauline. It's not as if you've never seen a nice-looking guy. Vance is no tuna.*

Nick wore a pin-striped navy suit and looked ever the successful businessman. The outfit really added to his appearance. I couldn't help but think he was on his way to some office, and I asked Saint Theresa to make sure he was straight. How pathetic was that? "Am I keeping you from something?" I said.

He gave me an odd look.

Goldie's eyebrow rose, but not as fast at the heat up my cheeks.

"I mean, you look as if you are going to work."

"He is, suga. With you." Goldie laughed. "Nick likes to get dressed up like a manly man."

"Fuck you, Perlman." They laughed.

There wasn't any tension between them, I noted.

"Great. Shall we get started?" I said, with not an inkling of what to do.

"Oh, Nicky, I didn't know you were here."

I swung around to see Adele leaning against the door frame for support. I thought she'd suffer the vapors, the way she was staring at Nick. Guess she found the "businessman type" attractive.

"What a way to start a Monday morning," she purred. *Purred* was a perfect word to describe the way she spoke to him. Very feline.

I looked around. Not a hint of crimson on his cheeks. Either the guy was used to compliments like that or he was a fabulous actor. He merely offered a smile.

I turned back. Adele blushed brighter red than the snug-fitting suit she wore. Today the ribbon in her hair was navy and white. Her shoes navy. Despite being Canadian, Adele's attire was more American than the US flag. She motioned for me to come to her. "Can I see you a minute, *chéri*?"

"Sure." I turned to Goldie and Nick. "I'll be right back."

"We'll be here," Nick said.

I think Adele moaned. Or maybe it was I who did.

Out in the hallway she leaned near. "Nick Caruso. Isn't he nice-looking?"

"He is, in a businessman sort of way." I wondered why she called me out.

"Single. Forty-one. Ex-Air-Force fighter pilot. Flew commercial for a while. Too tame for him. Was married several years back, but didn't work out. What's new nowadays?"

I looked at her. She expected an answer, but I was stuck on the "single" part. "Oh . . . yeah."

She gave me a curious look. "Unfortunately he plays the field."

"Afraid of commitment?"

"No, *chéri*. Nick Caruso is not afraid of anything. He's the second most masculine, sure-of-himself man I know."

He was attractive in that entrepreneur sort of way, but there weren't any real sparks from my end. Sure the hormones acted up some, but he looked a bit too much like Vance. Albeit a bit more human—more real. Then it dawned on me what Adele had just said.

"Shoot, Adele! Who the hell is the *first*?"

She laughed, turned and said over her shoulder, "Nick's nemesis."

"Nemesis?" Couldn't wait to hear about this guy.

But all Adele said was "Jagger."

I turned back to go into Goldie's office, wondering what a "Jagger" was. I thought of asking about Jagger, but figured I shouldn't bring him up in front of Nick since Adele had implied the two didn't get along. Goldie, however, I would interrogate later.

Goldie gathered up his equipment after giving me a technical tour along with Nick's two cents. We walked out of the office. I followed them to the parking lot, watched Goldie stuff the equipment into the backseat of his banana yellow Camaro. Had to be from back in the sixties, but highly polished, and I knew by its condition that Goldie took care of it like a baby. Not what I'd expect for a surveillance vehicle, but then again, I was driving a Volvo.

"Let's head to Dunkin Donuts for a coffee," Nick said.

I turned toward him. "Sure." That was all I managed, not

knowing if I should get into my car or follow him.

"Take your car, Pauline. I have some business to do around one."

That answered that question, I thought, as I slipped into my car and watched Nick get into a black-with-black-interior '98 993 Porsche. I knew this because Uncle Walt was a car buff, and I used to read his magazines when I lived at home or used my parents' john.

And here I thought all investigators used generic white vans. Showed how much I knew about surveillance—or anything in this business.

On the bright side, Nick and Goldie had to be making a bundle to drive those kinds of cars. The Porsche, used, sold for around sixty grand.

Knowing that made my day.

I followed Nick's Porsche along Maple to Oak to Olive Street and onto Main. He pulled into the parking lot of Dunkin Donuts and parked next to a patrol cruiser. I figured he thought his car would be safer next to a cop's.

I yanked my rearview mirror toward me and checked my makeup, hair and teeth. Good. No cannoli particles stuck between them. I only wished I'd worn something better than faded jeans and my Steelers parka. Here I was, contemplating my next outfit for tomorrow when it was only ten. Today when dressing, I'd thought I had to look as good as Goldie but soon gave up, and now I was thinking I'd have to look good so as not to embarrass myself in front of Nick or any other men I might meet in this new adventure.

What a great job this was turning out to be.

Nick had thrown a navy overcoat on, since December in Connecticut was nippy. No more snow today. The sun sparkled on the covered ground, making me glad Christmas was only three weeks away.

Once inside, Nick ordered for both of us, but he asked me what I wanted first. Of course, he drank his coffee black, and he smiled at the extra cream and three sugars I used.

"You should try it virgin," he said.

My mind got stuck on the "virgin" part. Sex was an issue I'd been trying to push to the back of my mind since I first saw him. And here he had to say the word *virgin*. Now it flooded my brain. I looked at him holding his coffee and realized he meant *black*. Drink it black. "Uck."

"You get to savor the taste, not mask it with all that cream and sugar." He put his hand on my lower back to guide me to a table in the back.

Be still my heart.

Right now I could down a gallon of black coffee and not taste a thing. He held my chair and then sat across the table. "Maybe sometime I'll try it. But I've been hooked on all the cream and sugar since I was a kid. My brothers and sisters and I used to sneak coffee at my grandmother's. She got milk delivered to her house in glass bottles, no less. You were supposed to shake the bottle to mix the cream—"

"From the top."

I looked at him. "Yeah."

He laughed. "I used to do that with my sister too."

"Small world." The stupid cliché snuck out after my nervous rambling. "So, we stole the cream off the top and used it to make coffee the color of sand. Now, I'm so used to it—"

"Be daring. You'll need to be, with this job."

His tone had deepened. Grown serious. My heart sped up a bit, and it wasn't from the caffeine. I looked at him, waiting for an explanation.

"Goldie tells me you're a nurse." He took a long slow sip of his coffee.

So much for an explanation. "Yes. I got burned out and needed a change."

He chuckled. A deep sound that vibrated from his chest. Nice. "This job will be a change for sure. But sometimes you might need to use your background."

"Use it?" I thought he meant knowing if someone was faking an injury.

"Sure. Go undercover. There are plenty of nursing registries that handle filling-in staff. Doctor's offices are sometimes under suspicion. You could get in there—"

"I thought I was only going to spy on people at their houses!" My words came out in a horrified tone.

Nick reached over, touched my hand. At least I think he did, since it instantly numbed. "In the future. Okay. This Macaluso case should be a good starter for you to get your feet wet. Very simple."

He went through more surveillance stuff, and when we got to the equipment part, I told him mine was on order and due any day because I'd paid for rush delivery. No sense in embarrassing myself with a confession about my ancient, gigantic video camera or the fact that I still had pictures from my cousin's wedding in my camera, and she now had two kids.

Goldie I could laugh with like one of the girls. Nick . . . Well, I refused to embarrass myself in front of him. Even if I'd told myself he wasn't my type.

"Got the file on Tina?"

"Yes." I foraged around in my bag, which had gotten bigger and heavier with the camera in it. The old video was stowed in my trunk, right where it belonged. I handed him the folder.

He thumbed through it and mumbled something like "Christ."

I figured he wasn't praying. "Something wrong?"

"Macaluso's husband is a partner in an orthopedic group."

"I know. I went to school with Tina."

He looked up. Took a sip of coffee, which emptied his cup. "Good. Let's take a little trip."

"To her house?"

"The office."

I stood when he did and followed him to the door. "Word on the street is, that practice is under suspicion."

"Medical malpractice?"

"Medical insurance fraud."

Six

One had to be astute to be a nurse. After all, people's lives depended on a nurse noticing a change in their condition then calling the doctor. So, I prided myself on being astute.

Nick Caruso knew something.

Something about my case. About Tina Macaluso and her husband's practice.

I followed Nick to an office building on the corner of Dearborn and Fenway. We pulled into the parking lot. Doc Taylor's car was in a reserved space. I really didn't want to run into him. Still, maybe I should tell Nick that I knew someone who worked there. What I wouldn't tell him is that I slept with that someone—on occasion.

We got out and walked to the door. The building was much bigger than I'd expected. Red brick. About ten stories. Here I thought Vance would be working in a small building with only that one practice. By the sign in the lobby listing all the occupants, I realized it was a regular professional building and that the ortho group was only a small part.

Nick looked at the list. "Come on. Let's get a cup of coffee."

I thought I'd float back out to my car if I had another cup.

Surely the man wasn't thirsty. And, besides, I ruminated, I'd have to pee if I drank any more. I didn't relish the idea of telling Nick I had to go to the little girls' room. That was another thing that annoyed me about men and women. Men are like camels. Women are like leaky faucets.

"You really want another cup of coffee?"

He looked at me as if I were nuts. "Part of the job. Good diversion." With that we got onto the elevator and he pushed the ninth-floor button.

The door opened to a cafeteria that took up most of this level. Only a few employees were having an early lunch and several patients or clients of the legal groups in this building—I guessed since they had coats with them—were eating as well. Nick walked over to a table opposite a group of what appeared to be nurses, both male and female.

Odd that he'd chosen that table, since the rest of the room was nearly empty. I sat anyway. "I'll pass on that coffee."

"Get something to eat, then. Anything." He motioned toward the lunch line. "Look as if you belong."

Duh. We couldn't just sit here not eating or drinking. "I'll get a salad. Can I get you something?"

"Coffee, black."

I got up and walked to the line, certain Nick wasn't watching me. He'd had an eye on the group of workers since we'd gotten there. No doubt he was eavesdropping.

I took a tray, slid it along the metal bars of the line and picked out a small green salad. The chef salads looked good, but since I really wasn't hungry, I didn't need those calories. I'd be facing a few extra miles tonight if I ate when not hungry. I got Nick's coffee and a water for myself. I could take my time eating the salad and sipping on the water for several hours if need be and not have to worry about added pounds.

The guy in front of me at the cashier turned around.

"Sokol? Hey, Pauline Sokol!"

I looked up. "Eddy? Hi, Eddy." Eddy Roden and I went to nursing school together along with Tina. I'd heard Eddy had shifted from job to job throughout the years. I knew he'd gotten fired from Saint Greg's for calling in sick one too many times. He'd gotten thin, had grown one of those foolish clumps of hair below his lower lip, needed a tooth cleaning, and wore navy scrubs. Guess he'd gotten a job in this building.

"You working here, Pauline?" He paid the cashier and stood there with his tray while I paid for mine.

Ack. I hadn't been ready with a lie. "I . . . er . . . no."

"What brings you here?"

"A . . . a friend works here."

"Whereabouts?"

Let it go, you jerk. I looked to see Nick watching me. He gave me a look that said to find out what I could. I reminded myself that I was on a case and if anyone who worked in this building knew something, I needed to question them. Now, I needed to turn the questions in Eddy's direction and not mine.

"Ortho group—"

"No shit! That's where I work."

My tray slipped. The cup of water flew off, splashing onto Eddy's white sneakers.

"Christ, Pauline! You're still klutzy, I see." He set his tray on a nearby counter.

I grabbed a handful of napkins and shoved them at him. Klutzy? What nerve! Okay, I was a bit clumsy at times. I was working on it, though. "Sorry, Eddy." As he wiped his shoes off, I asked, "How long have you been here?"

"Couple months. Sucks."

Hmm. "Doesn't Tina Macaluso work here? Didn't we go to school—"

"Fat, lazy-ass Tina's old man is one of my bosses. Cocksucker."

A smile crossed my face. A disgruntled employee. First ones to sing. Maybe he could inadvertently help with my case. I couldn't wait to tell Nick.

"So, what you doing for a living now?"

"I . . . left nursing for a rest. . . ."

He glared at me.

Damn. That trying-to-lie thing was back. "I'm working at a friend's uncle's place. Sorry about the shoes, Eddy," I hurriedly added, before he could continue on about my job. "I'll let you go, so your food doesn't get cold."

"I've got a chef salad, Pauline."

"Oh, yeah. Well, enjoy!" With that I turned and hurried to get myself another glass of water.

Back at the table I sat, slid Nick's coffee toward him and opened the plastic wrap that covered my salad.

"Who's the guy?" Nick asked.

I was ready to say he wasn't my type, as if Nick were jealous. Then it dawned on me that I was working. It was still difficult to wrap my brain around the fact that I had flexible hours, traveled around town and could eat a salad at eleven twenty in the morning if I wanted to. Or, in today's case, as part of my surveillance.

I leaned closer to Nick. "Eddy Roden. I went to nursing school with him and Tina. Get this, Nick"—I looked around the room as if it were bugged—"Eddy works for Tina's husband." I took a sip of water.

"No shit."

I nearly choked on my water. Swallowing quickly, I said, "You knew that?"

"Knew she worked here. Thought we'd see if she was around and find out . . . whatever." He shrugged. "You have to do your homework in this business, Pauline."

My heart thudded inside my chest. Nick looked at me. I think he heard it. "I thought I was only going to get some video or pictures of Tina—"

"What better place than her husband's office—where she also works? What'd the kid say?"

I wasn't going to mention that Eddy was my age, and Nick hadn't referred to *me* as a kid. Okay, maybe I really didn't want him thinking in juvenile terms with me. *Woman* was more like it. After all, I was a professional investigator—or at least I wanted Nick to believe that. I told him about my conversation with Eddy and how we'd gone to school together. Then my conscience kicked in. "I know someone else who works for that practice." I took another little sip.

Nick looked at me, took a sip of coffee all the while staring over his cup. "Doc Taylor?"

I nearly choked. "How the hell . . ."

He grinned.

My nerves crackled.

"I said I did my homework. Doc Taylor is new to the practice and about your age. I put two and two together—"

"And concluded I'm sleeping with him?" Oh . . . my . . . God.

The corner of Nick's lip curled at the same time my internal temperature spiked to one hundred four. A few more degrees and I'd be peacefully dead so as not to have to face the embarrassment of what I'd just blurted out.

"Actually, I put together that you might have worked with him at Saint Greg's or something along nursing lines. Sex wasn't my first thought."

That meant sex was one of his later thoughts.

I shoved a mouthful of salad between my lips, nodded for no good reason and turned to look away.

Speaking of sex . . .

My mouth dropped open (this was becoming a bad habit). I forced myself to swallow, and couldn't take my eyes off the doorway.

Before the thought that Mr. Suburban had just waltzed in could materialize, I heard Nick mumble, "Shit."

I turned my gaze to him.

He was glaring at Mr. Suburban and cursing under his breath.

When my mental faculties returned, I asked, "You know him?"

"Jagger."

"Oh my God!"

"Shush!"

I hadn't meant for that to come out so loudly, or out loud at all. But Jagger? Adele's Jagger? *Of course, Pauline*, I told myself. How many *Jaggers* could there be in this world? And didn't the guy have a last name? Or was that his last, and he needed a first?

What did it matter?

He'd had time to get himself a Coke and bag of Wise potato chips while I had my mental meltdown. I looked back to Nick, who was watching every move Jagger made. "What's a Jagger?"

Nick chuckled. "Good way to put it."

It was the only way I was capable of asking right at the moment. Jagger had on his black parka, sunglasses he'd shoved on top of his head to cover the dark hair, and I could swear he had a tan since the last time I saw him. Oh God! Had he seen me at Tina's close enough to recognize me now?

Something told me that Jagger was also astute when it came to women. Not being vain, I wondered if I'd made enough of an impression on him that he'd recognize me.

Please, God.

I looked back at Nick. Now, Nick was nice-looking, but Jagger was . . . damn it all, an instant orgasm. Had to do with him being good-looking in a more rustic, outdoorsy, *dangerous* kind of way. Where Nick dressed as if he'd stepped out of a Fortune 500 club (and reminded me too much of Vance, "stability" and Pauline Sokol's old life), Jagger looked as if he'd stepped out of a forest with a giant buck in tow—still alive.

Vance was boredom and solidity.

Nick was class.

Jagger was sex. Walking sex.

I wiped a droplet of drool from my chin and smiled at Nick as best I could. He'd been staring at me as if he could read my mind. What a thought. I felt flushed. "So . . . how . . . you know him?"

"Jagger and I go back to the military. Gulf War. We flew

sorties in February of ninety-one"—he looked off into the distance as if he could see something I couldn't—"Desert Storm. Air bombardment. Four hundred killed in an air-raid shelter in Baghdad. I took a desk job in Intelligence after that. Jagger separated soon after and became a PI. Seems investigative work fits ex-military pretty well. Never talked much after he left the service, and I don't know if he still works for himself."

I could only stare. Wow. They'd both left what they must have loved because of the accidental loss of civilian lives. War casualties but no less hard to take. But why the rivalry?

And what the heck was Jagger doing here?

I finished my salad and sipped on my water to give Nick time to compose himself. Not that he looked all that flustered, but I hated dredging up a past that for him must not have been too pleasant. I envied that he'd done so much in his life while I'd lived in Hope Valley since birth, except when I'd attended college in Hartford.

He finished his coffee and looked across the room. I turned to follow his gaze.

Jagger was sitting with Eddy Roden.

This was getting confusing. "What does this Jagger do?"

Nick looked back to me. "You would have been better off to go with the 'What's a Jagger' question," he commented.

"Why would he be here to see Eddy? You don't suppose they are friends?"

"Jagger only has enemies."

Yikes! "But they're talking as if they didn't just meet." I could see Eddy grinning, leaning near as if telling Jagger some private joke. Eddy was sleazy. I remembered him as being nerdier in nursing school. He got up and walked toward the door.

"Go tell your buddy goodbye."

"What?" At first I thought he was talking about Jagger. Then I realized he wanted me to talk to Eddy for the case. I took my empty tray in my hand and forced myself to stand after making sure Jagger was still in his seat.

Our eyes met. Damn!

Talk about looking through someone. No, talk about mentally stripping someone. Okay, that was me trying real hard to strip Jagger. His eyes were boring into me. I turned away and still looking at him, tripped on something—and smacked right into Vance.

"Pauline? What are *you* doing here?"

Seven

"What am I doing here? What *am* I doing here?" Over Vance's shoulder I could see Nick staring at me. When I turned away, I caught Jagger's glare.

"What am I doing here?"

Vance looked annoyed. I've seen that look many times, so it didn't take any special skills to read his body language. "Yes, Pauline. You're acting weird. What are you doing here?"

"I . . . came to see *you*, silly." Good one!

Vance looked suspicious. "You came to have lunch with me?"

I looked down at my tray. There sat my empty salad dish and empty water cup. "I wanted to surprise you." I'm a master of that emotion today. "Yeah. I . . . see? I have a dish ready to get a salad and cup of water too. I could only guess at the time when you'd get to have lunch, so, here I am." I swung around to see if Eddy had left.

Whew. He had. All I needed was him coming over to ask why I was eating a second lunch. Despite Vance being the flustered one now, he followed me to the lunch line, where I got a second salad—low-cal dressing this time—and another cup of water. I looked back at the table to see Nick was gone.

Well, he did say he had some business to attend to.

So much for my surveillance lesson today.

Across the room I saw Jagger get up and walk toward the tray return. Good. All I'd have to do was chitchat with the Doc, then get in my car and head over to Tina's. Headstrong Polack that I am, I decided I could do a bit on my own again. I refused to think about what a bust my first trip to Tina's had been.

After my second glass of water met up with all the coffee, I did, in fact, have to excuse myself from the table. Vance was used to that, and I wasn't the least bit embarrassed with him. After you've slept with someone, you don't worry about potty breaks. He was about done anyway. "It was nice having lunch with you. I have to get back to work. See you."

As I grabbed my tray, he added, "Maybe we can do dinner again this weekend."

I sucked in a breath and thought of Jagger and Nick. "Yes, I'll need *that*. . . . Dinner, that is." I scurried toward the door. The cafeteria was bustling with employees and patients now. When I pushed the elevator button, the doors opened immediately. I didn't stop to look behind in case Vance had followed me. Instead, I plowed headfirst into the elevator—and smack-dab into—Jagger.

I've never fainted in my life, but sure as hell tried to right then.

Still coherent, I heard the doors close behind me and turned to see that no other soul had gotten in. Damn. *You are a professional, Pauline*, I scolded myself. So, I pushed myself away from his granite chest and stood tall. Well, as tall as my five six could get, next to what had to be his six three. Suddenly my urge to pee dried up. "Sorry."

He nodded.

Good. Maybe we could get to the ground floor in silence. I yanked at my hair to help hide my face in case he might recognize me. Then I shut my eyes for a second and asked Saint Theresa to have the elevator get down in warp speed.

The damn thing stopped!

My eyes flew open. I knew that not enough time had elapsed to get to the ground floor. There stood Jagger—with his hand on the emergency stop button.

Guess Saint Theresa was busy.

Okay, I know all prayers are not answered and there's always a good reason. If *this* guy was going to attack me in the elevator—that may be good reason enough.

"What were you doing outside Macaluso's house?"

Not even a "Hi, I'm Jagger." I leaned back and decided he was too mysterious to want to have sex with—in person, that is. Being practical, I decided I'd stick with fantasizing about him. "I . . . What were *you* doing there?" When in doubt repeat a question or at least confuse the hell out of your attacker. Truthfully, I didn't consider Jagger an attacker. Not physically, at least. Not since Adele and Nick knew him. I'll bet Goldie did too. Besides, as mysterious as he appeared, he didn't seem like a wacko or a threat.

"I asked first."

I was tempted to say, "So what?" but decided not to get into an argument. The guy looked as if he was packing. Not that I knew much about that, but I knew a bulge like that in his jacket wasn't from a wallet. Maybe I was a natural at this job. The observation part anyway—thanks to my nursing skills. I tried to ignore my heart racing and my fingers tap dancing against my sides.

He stood, waiting.

I couldn't say I was on a case. There had to be some rule that an investigator had to remain anonymous, so I said, "I went to school with Tina." Besides, he must know Eddy, and if I said what I was doing, he could tell Eddy, and Eddy could tell Tina. Then I'd be out of my payment. I thought about that as I continued to examine his appearance.

He had to work out to have pecs like that. Even with a jacket on, I could tell the guy was built. There was some magnetism kicking in. One exercise fanatic to another.

Jagger looked at me. His left eyebrow rose. His teeth gritted, and I think he growled. "What the hell does that have to do with you sitting outside her house watching her shovel?"

"Good question." A bead of sweat trickled down my cheek. Suddenly I realized it wasn't because of my infatuation with this guy. The elevator wasn't moving. In my sexual fantasy about Jagger I'd momentarily forgotten my phobia—claustrophobia. My pulse sped even more. My gut tightened, sending much-needed blood to my vital organs to keep me alive during an anxiety attack. But feeling the elevator at a standstill with the door shut, I felt as if those vital organs would explode.

That thought about fainting was getting all too real.

There was no air in here. Well, no fresh air. A ringing started in my left ear, and then collided in the center of my brain. I tried to take a deep breath. No luck.

"You all right?"

My hands started to tremble more. The sweat now poured down my cheeks. I felt cold, then flushed. Then cold again. My heart had to be hitting the inside of my chest, at the speed it was going.

"Hey. I asked if you were . . ."

Suddenly his arms were around me. The elevator darkened, spun, and then winked out.

"We're on the ground floor."

The voice floated on a current of air. A deep, sexier-than-hell voice. I felt a hand brush the hair from my clammy forehead. *It felt nice*, I thought, as I tried to open my eyes.

A man stood above me. Not just any man.

Jagger.

The elevator door was open. I looked from him to the lobby and realized I was on the carpeted floor of the elevator.

"Here." He took my shoulders and lifted me to a sitting position. "Take a few deep breaths."

I nodded and did. A musky aftershave hit my nostrils. I turned to look into his eyes. Where I'd seen specs in Nick's, there were none noticeable in the darkness of Jagger's.

"Let's get you up and out into the fresh air. You're not pregnant, are you?"

I looked at him as if he were nuts, and started to say "I've only slept with Doctor Taylor about twice a year and he uses the most expensive condoms," but decided it was none of Jagger's business and merely shook my head. A crowd had gathered around the elevator.

"Diabetic?"

"What?" He hoisted me up, held my arm and walked me toward the door.

"Diabetic. Are you a diabetic? Have epilepsy? Some other illness?"

"What *is* this? Some verbal physical exam?" My cheeks flushed when he looked at me. His hand rubbed low on my back.

"I'm only trying to figure out what happened back there."

Oh God. I'd either have to lie about having a physical disease in which case God might see fit to actually giving me one or tell the truth. Pauline Sokol, good Catholic girl. "*You* caused it."

Jagger let out a deep howl of a laugh. By now he'd opened the door and a cool blast of air hit us. Felt wonderful, yet I shivered since my hair was damp.

"I believe that's the first time a woman has fainted over me—that I know of."

I pushed away. "This woman fainted because *you* locked her in a closed . . . elevator—"

"Christ." He looked genuinely sorry, mixed with a little pissed. At himself, I was guessing. "You passed out because I stopped the elevator?"

"Everyone has a phobia. I'll bet even you do." Not in a million years did I believe that.

He leaned near in a naughty-boy sort of way and grinned. "When you discover what it is, let me know."

I pushed past him. "I have to go."

He grabbed my arm. "Not so fast."

Oh, no. He was going to pursue the questioning he'd

started on the elevator. My heart thudded at the thought of the closed, stopped elevator.

"I'm not letting you drive after passing out."

Hmm. Compassion.

And no further questions.

"I'm fine," I insisted, shivering outside in the parking lot.

Jagger cursed under his breath. "Look, lady. By the way, what's your name?"

Wow. I knew his name, but he didn't know mine. Still, with the tone he used, he didn't seem truly interested.

"Pauline. Pauline Sokol."

He held out a hand. "Jagger."

"I kn—" Shit! He couldn't know that I knew his name. Then he'd ask too many questions. Then I'd seem interested in him. Then he'd know someone had told me about him.

He raised an eyebrow at me.

I forgot he used to be a PI. The guy had to be perceptive. More than likely, he already knew my name.

"You what?"

"Nothing. Nice to meet you, Mister Jagger." I held out my hand.

He shook it, then, "Just Jagger."

I pulled my hand back. "Fine. I *am* fine too, and very capable of driving myself home." I had no intention of going home though. I'd go see if Tina was home, shoveling or doing something else I could catch her at.

"Look, Pauline. It's my fault you conked out. I'm responsible for getting you home. What if you pass out driving?"

I didn't want to remind him that the cause was claustrophobia. Too damn embarrassing. Shoot. Didn't seem I had much choice. Truthfully, I wasn't feeling myself yet. Wooziness had a habit of hanging on once one passes out, it seemed. This was news to me, since I'd never passed out before. "I'll call a cab. You must be busy. Don't you have to get back to work?" Good one. Maybe I could find out more about the enigmatic Jagger.

"Don't worry. Get in." He motioned toward the black Suburban.

Go for it, Pauline.

I waited a few seconds to see if he'd open the door. He was already in his seat. So, I opened the door, got in and discreetly looked around. "You live in here?"

The SUV was filled with stuff. Boxes in the backseats, stuff on the floor. Papers, bags, T-shirts. Man. Despite the amount of stuff, it did seem orderly. Not as if he threw stuff around randomly.

He turned toward me. There was no humor in his eyes. "I work out of here."

"Wow. I work out of my car too." Pauline! Why did I have to say that? My honesty often got me into trouble.

He turned on the engine and backed out of the space. When he took a left out of the parking lot, he slowed, looking in his rearview mirror. "Shit," he mumbled.

"Something wrong?"

"You in any hurry?"

Was he asking me out? "I . . . I'm flexible."

"Good." He did a U-turn on the street adjacent to the parking lot and sped up. "Put on your seat belt."

I looked down. I'd forgotten to put it on, and with the way he was weaving in and out of traffic, I sure needed it. It wasn't like me to ride without my seat belt. Maybe that passing-out thing had affected my brain. At this speed, my body was pushed back in the seat with my head pressed against the headrest. It felt like being on a ride in an amusement park where gravity keeps you in your seat as they spin you around. "*You* in some hurry?" I croaked out.

He ignored me and swung down Maple Avenue.

Suddenly I realized he was following someone. A green Toyota Corolla in front of us. Jagger slowed. The car took a right onto Oak Street.

Yep. We were following it. I squinted to see the driver. "Who is that?"

Jagger handled the Suburban like a pro. We weaved in and

out until the Corolla turned into a Stop and Buy parking lot. Jagger slowed and turned in too. He pulled to the side of the lot and stopped.

I leaned forward, thankful to be able to move of my own accord. The Corolla had pulled up near a black Lexus. Nice company—but still a painful reminder of the next car payment I owed. I figured Jagger wasn't going to tell me what the heck we were doing there. I only hoped it didn't involve shooting. There was that bulge. . . .

Before I could ask any more questions that I assumed he wouldn't answer, I watched the door of the Corolla open.

Out stepped Eddy Roden!

"Eddy?" snuck out of my mouth.

Jagger turned, stared, then looked back at Eddy.

What the heck was going on?

Eddy walked up to the Lexus. The door opened. I sat motionless and silent, which I'm sure Jagger appreciated. I held my breath in my throat, waiting.

A red leather boot stepped out followed by a black-panted leg. The rest of the woman, covered in a black mink jacket, followed her leg. Even at this distance I could tell it was real mink and not faux fur. Goldie would look fabulous in that jacket—only it would have to be several sizes smaller.

The woman leaned forward to talk to Eddy and her matching mink hat tilted to one side.

"Oh . . . my . . . God."

I looked at Jagger. His eyes met mine.

"Tina," we said in unison.

Then my eyes widened. Jagger's eyes pierced into me, obviously in question.

"How do you know her?" I asked, heading off his interrogation, which I felt certain would follow. Even though I'd said I went to school with her and Eddy, that was a long time ago. And, truth be told, I wouldn't recognize her if she barreled over me on the street. If it weren't for my seeing her the first day of my surveillance, she could have been any large woman in Hope Valley, for all I knew.

Jagger turned back, once again ignoring my question. Eddy gave Tina a manila envelope. She handed him a small white one. I turned to Jagger, who now had on his sunglasses, which he occasionally adjusted. Odd, since puffy gray clouds had the sun hidden. My gray eyes are sensitive to light, but even I wouldn't need sunglasses right now.

I contemplated that a second.

Eddy and Tina got back into their respective cars and drove off. Jagger took off his glasses and put then into the holder above his visor. He cranked up the engine and drove to the end of the parking lot. He looked at me as if nothing had happened. "Where to?"

Did I really want Jagger to know where I lived? Then again, he was an ex-PI, so he could find out if he wanted to. Damn, between him and Nick, I felt a bit as if my privacy had been invaded.

Something told me both *already* knew where I lived.

Eight

Jagger, in fact, did know how to find my home without directions from me, and as he pulled up in front, I dashed out of the black Suburban before he could say anything. He wouldn't answer any of my questions, so I figured I'd get inside and have Miles take me to get my car.

When I shut the car door, I heard Jagger say something. It sounded like either *you feel better* or *you look wetter*. Either way, I didn't want to hang around inside *his* car.

Too many male pheromones in that Suburban.

I ran up to our door and dug into my purse for my keys. After searching around for several minutes, I leaned on the doorbell. When I looked over my shoulder, I saw Jagger watching, a half smile on his face.

I inhaled and nearly dropped my purse.

The pheromones were seeping out of the Suburban.

Suddenly a sleepy Miles opened the door. "What the fuck, Pauline?"

I pushed past him, ran to the window. The Suburban's brake lights sparkled as Jagger slowed, then pulled out of the parking lot.

Thank God he left.

I sank into the white beanbag chair. Spanky ran up and

jumped into my lap. I hugged him and looked up at a confused Miles. "Couldn't find my keys."

"Stop carrying everything you own in that satchel. Your car break down?"

"I only wish. Nothing that simple though." I looked at him. "Oops. Forget you got called in last night to work. I didn't mean to wake you."

"No problem-o." He flopped on the couch, his navy silk robe revealing hairy slender legs. Goldie had it all over Miles in the legs department. Maybe that's why he was the transvestite.

I told Miles about my day and had to repeat several times that he should close his mouth. It wasn't all that shocking, and I repeatedly apologized for waking him since he was working nights.

He looked at me. "Maybe that's not the right job for you. I should call my friend Hammy. He owns a furniture store—"

I rubbed Spanky's ear. "I could never work with inanimate objects. I'm a people person."

"But there's weird stuff going on. I thought you'd just follow someone, take their picture and *boom*. Get paid."

I jumped when he said *boom*. Good thing I'd left off the part about realizing that Jagger was packing.

"I don't want this guy coming back and doing . . . something."

"Miles, dear"—I sighed heavily—"if you saw this guy you wouldn't mind him doing something to *you*."

Miles shook his head.

"Okay. I'll call but I already know Jagger is well-known." I got up and looked under the pillows for the phone. "Will you take me to get my car?"

He looked at the brass clock on the salmon-colored marble mantel. "Shit. I have a date for a late lunch in twenty minutes. Tony in Physical Therapy. Just a friend, in my book."

Miles hadn't been out in a long time. I couldn't ask him to miss his date.

"No problem. Maybe Goldie can take me."

I noticed Miles's eyes perk up at the mention of his old friend.

He jumped up and headed toward the stairs. "Let me know if he's coming here." With that he was gone.

I leaned against the wall. Miles was acting strangely. Was he still interested in Goldie? I wouldn't blame him if he was, but didn't want him hurt if it was all one-sided. He was like a brother to me.

My real brothers would cringe at that thought, but Miles was a living doll.

I headed into the kitchen and pressed the phone's PAGE button. From upstairs I heard Miles shout, "In my room."

"Throw it down." I walked to the stairs. He stood there in his silken tiger boxer shorts. *Damn, what a waste of a good male*, was my first thought. Then I reminded myself that Miles was Miles and his choice of partners was part of his makeup, and I wouldn't want him any other way. He threw down the phone.

I held the receiver and realized that I didn't know Goldie's cell phone number. He'd said he was out on a case so calling the office to find him would more than likely be a waste. Then again, Adele so far proved to be a whiz at finding addresses and other tasty info on suspects so she might have his cell number. I didn't want to ask Miles, since I really didn't know the extent of his connection with Goldie.

I punched in the office number and heard Adele's "Scarpello and Tonelli Insurance Company."

"Adele, it's me."

A pause. "Me who?"

A bit deflated, I told myself I hadn't been working there long enough, and in fact this was the first time I'd spoken to her on the phone. "Pauline." If she said, "Pauline who?" I might break down into tears, with the kind of day I'd had so far.

"Hey, *chéri*. What's up? You finished with your case?"

"Should I be?" I asked frantically. Did Fabio have a time limit and not pay after a certain amount of time had passed?

She giggled. "Takes as long as it takes. What do you need? Address? Workplace?"

"I have all that on Tina. What I need is"—*info on one Jagger.* But that's not why I called. "Do you have Goldie's cell phone number?"

"Sure. But he's in his office. Want a patch through?"

Yes. No. Yes. But first, who is *this Jagger?*

"Thanks." I couldn't ask her about Jagger. Something inside said I really didn't *want* to know and more than likely wouldn't ever see him again. No way would he come to where I lived. So, let sleeping dogs lie, as my mother would say.

"Tell me every detail you know about Jagger." I grabbed Goldie's arm and pulled him into my condo. "Every detail."

Goldie looked at me and smiled. "So, you met *him*."

It wasn't a question, but came out as if Jagger were some genius sage. He knew Jagger all right.

Spanky ran in from the hallway and jumped at Goldie with all of his five pounds. Goldie snatched him up, rubbed his tummy and set him down. I picked Spanky up so he wouldn't jump at Goldie's calves anymore. He could put a run in Goldie's hose. They were silvery with sparkles in them and matched his skirt and jacket. On his right lapel was a porcelain woman's face with purple feathery plumes sticking out of the top like a hat. Dangly purple orbs hung from Goldie's ears. He'd pulled his hair back in a sophisticated bun.

Damn it, but he looked good.

"You gonna offer Goldie a coffee or something?" He looked around.

Miles. He must be looking for Miles.

"Sorry. Where are my manners?" I set Spanky down and motioned toward the kitchen. "Come in, please. My roomy is out."

Goldie followed me through the swinging doors and

stopped. He'd been here before, I could tell. Slowly he walked to the bay window and paused, looked out at the English garden Miles prided himself on where it lay, snow covered, in the tiny patch of land we were alloted with our condo. After a moment he came to the counter, sat on one of the wicker stools and leaned an elbow on the white granite counter. "Miles does have a flair for decorating."

I wanted to laugh, thinking it was some gay joke, but then I looked at Goldie and didn't, thank goodness. There was a sadness in his green eyes that made me want to walk over and hug him. Instead, I took a bag of coffee out of the fridge and scooped some grinds into the filter of the Mr. Coffee. "Miles is not seeing anyone regularly." I filled the machine with water and turned around.

Goldie tapped a nail, now shiny silver, on his tooth. "No shit?"

"No shit. He's at a late lunch with a coworker but will be home later."

Goldie smiled.

What teeth.

"Okay," I said, reaching for two mugs. Miles insisted we use the bone china for daily use. When he wasn't home, I used paper and plastic, but Goldie was company, so I set out the good stuff. "Hungry?"

"I could eat."

I opened the pantry and walked in. I'm a neat freak from the word go, but I have nothing over Miles. The spices sat in alphabetical order, the cereals were color coded and the canned goods were stacked alphabetically by content. I took a package of Oreos from the shelf under the heading "Snacks for Pauline." Miles didn't indulge in junk food but graciously catalogued mine. I was a health nut but lived under the assumption that one might need things like junk food, pantyhose or Maalox every so often.

I came out and set a few cookies on a dish. The coffee had stopped perking so I poured us each a cup. "Ever drink it black?"

"Hell, no. I love sweet things."

"Nick said to try it black sometimes to get the true flavor."

Goldie laughed. "I can only guess what else Nick said. He make you hot, suga?"

Despite the heat searing up my cheeks, I said, "Not as sizzling as Jagger did."

Goldie howled and pounded on the counter. Spanky ran out of the room. "Okay, let me guess. You did see Jagger today. Spill, and I'll tell you what I know."

Through three cups of coffee, six Oreos (Goldie had seven), and after splitting a ham and cheese on a croissant, I told him about my day.

"Lord, suga. You have been indoctrinated."

"Indoctrinated? You mean my days could go like that again? He locked me in an elevator for crying out loud!"

"Jagger's a pip. One hell of a guy though. He'd never hurt you."

"Now that's a relief." I didn't want Goldie to know I'd invite Jagger in, without fear, if he came a-knocking at my door, any old time.

Goldie licked his finger. "No, it isn't. You were so taken by the hot-damn Jagger, you weren't even coherent enough to be scared."

"Damn you." I smiled.

"Jagger's an enigma. Don't lose any sleep over him. I like you too much for you to fall for someone so far out of your reach."

I huffed. "Thanks a lot."

Goldie touched my arm. His nails glided across my skin. "Suga, I don't mean it like that. You're a hell of a looker yourself and have legs to die for."

"Really?"

"You know it. I only mean, Jagger isn't your type. He's like a current of air. Sweeps in, sweeps out. I wouldn't want you hurt. Hell, I'm not sure if he's anyone's type."

Touched, I patted his hand. "Thank you." He removed his hand to take a sip of coffee. I did the same.

"Okay, you want the skinny on Jagger. Sure you don't want it on Nick instead? Nick plays the field. But that's better than Jagger."

"You saying he's involved with someone?"

"I'm saying I have no idea about his love life, and I'm guessing neither does anyone else. The guy comes and goes, sans attachments. He has a past with Nick—"

"Nick already told me about their being in the military together." I stood and gathered up the dishes. Goldie got up to help. I'd never felt so close to someone so quickly. Well, Miles and I were like siblings, but Goldie was more a "girlfriend," and I'd known Miles for years.

"I've never been convinced by the reason either of them gave as why they got out of the service. Great fighter pilots. Both of them."

"Those casualties in Baghdad."

"Bullshit. Nick and Jagger wouldn't get out because of that. They'd suck it up and trudge on. Nope. I never bought that. There's more to it than meets the eye." He took off his jacket to reveal a white silk long-sleeve blouse with a ruffled front.

"I'm sorry. Were you going somewhere?"

He laughed. "After we get your car, I'll make the rounds."

"You need a guy." I sighed.

"We both do, suga." We laughed.

"Call Miles," I said without thinking.

Goldie paused, then rinsed out the mugs while I washed off the counter. I think he smiled though.

"Anyway," he continued, "Jagger headed out to California. Married some chick he met out there, but it only lasted a few years."

I felt my muscles relax. They'd clenched when Goldie first mentioned that Jagger had married.

"Children?"

"None that I ever heard about. Anyway"—he looked at his watch—"let's head out to get your car. I'll fill you in on the way."

"Fine." We let Spanky out and back in, locked up and got into Goldie's Camaro. The interior was bright pink. Pepto-Bismol pink. So Goldie. A pair of spongy black dice hung from the rearview mirror. I felt as if I'd stepped back into the past.

Goldie started the engine and we drove out of the parking lot. "Okay. Where was I?"

I could barely hear him over the muffler. "No kids that you knew of." I didn't want Jagger to have kids. How selfish of me. Still, that was my honest gut feeling. I wanted him totally unattached. As if I could attach him. *Yeah, Pauline. Right.*

I was amazed that someone like him had interested me. I assumed it was because he was so very different from all the men I'd ever met. Men of my past. They could all fit around my mother's dinner table at once. She'd love that.

"Worked for a PI firm out there. As I understand it, he was trained by some ex-Navy Seal turned LAPD who had retired. Jagger worked high-profile cases including murder but always gravitated toward insurance fraud."

"Why's that?" We turned down Maple. Goldie had taken the long way. What a doll.

He shrugged as he downshifted. "Several speculative rumors about that. The closest one I tend to believe is his old man owned an insurance company."

"And?"

"That's all anyone ever heard. So, Jagger works his way up to senior investigator then, after extensive training and *beaucoup* hours of work, in California he applies for a Private Investigation Agency license—then he moves to Connecticut."

"Did he get his license?"

"Don't know. But he moved, so that's a moot point. Soon he's working cases right under our noses. Adele says Jagger was around before Fabio hired her. She thinks he works for the state fraud unit."

"Really?" Hmm. A fraud investigator too. That might make sense.

"Me? I think he's FBI." We turned into the lot.

My heart leaped up to my throat. "FBI?" I croaked.

Goldie laughed. "What, you got something to hide?"

"I . . . no, silly. It's just that I never met anyone who was an FBI agent."

Goldie got out and opened my door. "Maybe you have—and just didn't *know* it."

I watched Goldie peel out of the parking lot as I fiddled around in my purse for my keys. Should have had them out before we got here, but I was so mesmerized by the stuff about Jagger, I could only sit and listen. "Yeah, right," I muttered, fingering the keys at the bottom of my purse. They slipped away and I peered inside. "Jagger, FBI," I said to myself.

"What are you looking for, Pauline Sokol?"

"My keys." What? Who the heck? I yanked my face out of my purse. Yikes!

Tina Macaluso stood in front of me!

"Oh, hey. Antonina. Long time no see. What have you been up to?" Other than bilking the insurance company out of thousands. I fiddled more and pulled out the keys. Then I stupidly held them up for Tina to see.

"It's Tina now. Not much, other than work. How about you?"

Work? Work? She'd been on Workers' Comp for weeks. "Oh, I worked at Saint Greg's for years."

She leaned near, pushed my hand down. "I see you found your keys."

"Oh, yeah." *Get a grip, Pauline. You're a professional.*

"You said 'worked.' What are you doing now?"

Had she seen me watching her? Oh Lord! Did she recognize my car? Hopefully not. "I . . . got a . . . well, I thought I'd do some odd jobs." Like follow you around and get your rather large butt on video.

"Oh, hey, I have something for you."

Ack! Maybe she saw Jagger and I watching her and Eddy.

I almost expected her to whip out a gun and accuse me of stalking her. Where was the line between stalking and surveillance anyway? "Something—"

"I've been out of work for several weeks now."

"Oh." *Fancy that.*

"Pulled my back out on the job." She faked a wince.

How'd I know it was fake? Hey, I'd seen her shovel as if the snow were made of Styrofoam. "You don't say. How'd you manage to . . . do that?"

"I work in orthopedics and tried to lift a heavy patient."

"From the floor?" The wind had picked up, and I was freezing my slender butt off. Tina had more insulation and that not-faux-fur jacket on. I stifled a shiver and waited for her lame explanation.

"No, silly. He was on the table."

"Don't you have strong males around for that kind of stuff?" Be still my feminist heart. Okay, I had to ask to prod her for further info.

"I can handle most things. Just happened to pull out my back this time." She pushed her hat back farther on her head. "It's as cold as Alaska today, Pauline. I can't stay out here much longer—"

"You able to drive?" And shovel?

"I—" She let out a deep, pathetic sigh.

And here I thought the wind was strong.

"I have to manage. Anyway . . ." She reached into her purse.

I flinched and ducked.

"You take drugs, Pauline?" She pulled out a little gold cardholder, opened it and handed her business card to me.

"Only Sine-Off during the spring." I was acting weird, but I thought she was going to pop me. Then I scolded myself that Tina was a Workers' Comp case and not involved in some Mafia fraud ring despite the old rumors back in nursing school about her family.

She shook her head. "I married Donnie Macaluso. Remember him from high school?"

"Donnie? Oh, yeah. Wasn't he a year behind us?"

"That's my Donnie. Only now he's a prominent orthopedic surgeon and part owner of his practice."

She waved her card toward me. "Take my card and call my husband's office manager, Linda Stark. She needs someone to fill in for me while I'm out."

I squinted at her. "How long you planning to be out?"

She rubbed at her spine. "Actually, I have to rush home and rest now. Lord only knows the pain I'm suffering."

You mean the devil, you fake. I took the card and tucked it into my purse. "Thanks. I just may do that."

I watched her get into her black Lexus and drive out. Then I hopped into my Volvo and followed her ass.

What pain? Ha! I'd show her pain when she had to pay back every cent to the insurance company. Fabio said that'd be her punishment. I was hoping for jail time, but, oh well.

Tina turned onto Maple and headed north on Oak. She made a few more turns that had me confused. Her neighborhood was south of here toward the river. She wasn't going that way and yet she'd said she "had to rush home."

The late afternoon sun sunk behind the mountains on the western edge of Hope Valley. Tina headed toward them to the "little Italy" section of the town. My parents lived in the Polish section, which was to the north of here. Speaking of my folks, I wondered what my mother was having for dinner tonight. I could use a good meal and reminded myself it was Monday. Meatloaf Monday. Always meatloaf.

My stomach growled. I'd only eaten those two salads, half a croissant and the six Oreos all day. For a second I contemplated turning onto Colony Street and going to eat with them. Tomorrow would be pot roast Tuesday, followed by Wednesday fish. Scrod. Always scrod. Then there was Thursday's roast pork and, of course, Friday's potato pancakes. Saturday I avoided like the plague,'cause kielbasa and sauerkraut didn't fit into my health-conscious diet. Neither did six Oreos, but I hadn't been myself lately.

When Tina turned into Hope Spring Valley estates, I

thought about Sunday being ham day and how my mother never lacked for what she would serve for dinner. All she had to do was look at the calendar to see what day of the week it was.

Yikes! The houses—no, mansions—in this subdivision didn't look like anything I'd ever seen in Hope Valley. It bordered on West Hartford, which was a town with plenty of money. This was a new neighborhood with only two streets complete. With the size of the brick houses, though, only about five fit on one side of the street. Trees, naked by the winter, bordered between properties.

Tina pulled into the last long driveway on the right. As she traveled its length the garage door opened. She had an opener for this house. That must mean she owned it.

Ack!

I know her husband was a doctor, but so was Vance. He came from money, but on his own I knew he couldn't afford two houses. No, make that a house and a mansion.

Damn.

Maybe Tina had bilked the insurance company out of money before.

Hell, it had to have been a bundle. I pulled around to the other street, which had mansions under construction. I could see Tina's house clearly through the leafless branches of the trees in her backyard. I pulled over and tried to make my Volvo invisible behind some construction equipment.

I opened my purse, dug around for my old 35 mm and hoped there were still some shots left, since I hadn't thought to get new film yet. I figured all this investigative stuff would come to me in good time. I looked at the camera. Good. One more shot left. I'd take a picture of her house. Why? I wasn't sure, but it seemed like a good idea and maybe pertinent to my case.

I grabbed my gloves from my pocket and tucked my hair under a black wool cap that I found on the floor. I'd used it sledding last weekend with Miles. It was his, but it would keep my ears warm.

A chill had set into my bones while I talked to Tina, and even the heater in my car hadn't successfully warmed me inside. Once bundled up, I opened the door, stuck the camera in my pocket and locked my purse in the trunk. No sense lugging it around. There sat the old video monster.

Damn it. I should have charged the batteries, but I thought I'd be working with Goldie's stuff today. I cursed at the camera and slammed the trunk shut. Oops. I looked around. Not a soul in sight. Good.

I pulled my hat lower and trudged across the snow-covered empty lots between two mansions under construction. I thought I saw someone in the front of the second house, but a wind must have caused the black tarp covering some construction equipment to move.

That same wind howled between the trees and right down into my bones. Damn, it was cold. On top of everything else, my eyes started to water. Oh well, a shot of Tina's house and I'd be outta here. Home in a nice hot bath.

"Bubbles and all," I murmured.

At the border of Tina's yard, I froze. Not from the wind either. Her back door started to open! And me there with only naked trees for cover. I dove behind a pile of snow some kids must have shoveled to resemble an igloo.

Frozen to my inner core now, I rifled around in my pocket for the camera. Tina walked through the yard toward a woodpile, where she not so gingerly grabbed several logs.

Where was my new equipment when I needed it?

I tried to aim the camera but couldn't move with the gloves on and covered in snow. With my teeth, I pulled one off, then the other, and told myself it wasn't really that cold. Just as I looked through the viewfinder, Tina's large form became shrouded in black.

What the heck?

I moved the camera up and down. Still black. Then the black moved. I readied to shoot the picture when the black became a flesh color.

A face.

A face glared at me through my camera.

I couldn't put the damn thing down, so I pressed the shutter, heard the *click* in the still winter air. And realized I'd just taken a picture of Jagger.

Nine

For what seemed like hours, I stared at Jagger through the lens of my stupid camera. Maybe I was hoping he'd disappear. Maybe I was hoping he'd help me up, brush me off and let me go without a word.

Maybe I was hoping it really wasn't Jagger.

No one had eyes that deep brown. Eyes that let you in only to lock you out at the same time. And eyes that could see into your very soul as if *you* were invisible.

Suddenly I felt myself being lifted up. I took the camera away from my eye—or maybe it fell away—as Jagger lifted me like a rag doll. A light one.

The guy had strength in those arms. They weren't only for show—or my enjoyment.

"Come on."

Without another word, he turned me around, away from Tina's house and led me through the woods. At the end of the lot, we crossed the backyard of the house under construction, and with his hand still pulling me along, walked to a white trailer.

"You work here?" I queried, although I have no idea where I got the strength (or balls) to ask that.

He only walked faster and gave me an occasional look. At the door, he opened it and waited.

"I'm guessing you want me to go in." I thought of his gun.

He swept his arm toward the stairs.

"How do I know you're not going to hurt me?" Attack. Have your way with me—if there really is a God.

"You don't. Get in."

"You must think I'm stupid—"

A silver Jaguar pulled around the corner. In what seemed like an instantaneous decision, Jagger shoved me up the stairs and inside. Truthfully, I think he actually lifted me. The office was sparse. Not what I'd expect in a construction site.

Then again, it was three weeks before Christmas, Connecticut, and the ground was covered in about eleven inches of snow. Not exactly the height of the building season.

We were all alone.

Be still my heart.

I looked to see him sit on the only chair next to the only desk, which held one phone, pencil and Dunkin Donuts coffee cup.

I glared at the phone.

"Not connected."

Damn. The guy didn't miss a trick. *Of course not, Pauline! He's FBI!*

Maybe he was. Maybe he wasn't. But he was definitely on top of everything that went on around him.

If he was FBI, I told myself, I needed to cooperate. I wasn't up on the law, but I thought I saw a movie about a witness not cooperating and his teeth were pulled out one by one. Wait. That was the Mafia, not the FBI who did it. Still, didn't Mary Richards on the *Mary Tyler Moore* show have to go to jail for not revealing her sources? Okay, she was a news reporter. I was a plain citizen.

Who'd been stalking Tina Macaluso.

Maybe Jagger was still a PI and she'd hired him to follow

me. Maybe she lured me here with that "fill in for her job" routine.

I yanked Miles's hat off, shook off the snow and looked at Jagger. "What?"

He grinned.

I turned toward the window and caught my reflection. Methuselah had nothing on my hairdo. Wildly I tamped it down. He sat staring. I contemplated telling him how rude it was that he didn't offer me a seat but thought better of the idea. Instead, I pulled myself up to my full height, shook my parka a few times and looked right back at him. Not too hard to do.

"Am I under arrest?"

"What'd you do?"

"I . . . what do you mean, what did I do?"

He lifted his feet, parked them on the desk. I hadn't noticed before, but he wore black cowboy boots. The bottoms were fairly worn. He looked the type. I wouldn't have expected wingtips.

He smiled again.

That alone unnerved me. I forgot the question. With him looking, all I could do was stand there, wrapping my Steelers parka tightly around me—and feeling naked.

Jagger was a master at the old staring game I used to play with my siblings. It had to be hours—okay, minutes that I stood there with neither of us saying a word. Finally my stomach growled.

He grinned.

"Yes, I *am* hungry. And I have a dinner appointment."

"Date?"

"Okay . . . date."

"Then let's make this quick." He pulled his feet off the desk.

I got ready to defend my honor, for as much as he was a hottie, I wasn't ready for *that*. The thought struck me that it was odd how something in my imagination seemed like such a good idea—a wonderfully orgasmic idea—yet when push came to shove in the world of reality, I wasn't ready to make love to Jagger.

"What are you going to do to me?"

"*To* you?" He looked genuinely confused.

"Why did you pull me in here? What were you doing out at Tina's?"

"How did you know she lived there?"

"I—" I'm on a case. Could I really tell him that? I could if I knew who he was. "I don't have to tell you that. If you don't have an arrest warrant for me, then I'm outta here."

I turned toward the door. That was all my feet would do. Damn them. I couldn't get out. I felt him staring at my back, almost gluing me to the spot.

"I still do not know why you think I should arrest you—"

I swung back around. "Ah ha!"

"Ah ha, what?"

"So you *can* arrest me."

"Look, Pauline. I could arrest you just as you could arrest me as a citizen or by calling 911 if you found me doing something illegal. . . ."

Shit. He confused me. "Isn't shoving me into this trailer illegal?"

He raised his hands. "Am I stopping you from leaving?"

No, my feet were. "What do you really want? I have to get to my parents'—"

His grin had me nearly in Nirvana. "I thought you had a *date*?"

"I never said . . . Okay, I don't. I have dinner plans at my parents', and my mother will be worried if I'm late." I pretended to look at my watch. "Oh, shoot. They're probably saying grace right now. Without me. My father takes medication for his blood pressure and my elderly uncle lives there—"

"All interesting, but I'm confused."

Who wouldn't be? "My point is they will all worry." I looked at my watch, really did, this time. Four thirty. Yikes.

Who eats at four thirty? "We always eat early on meatloaf night."

"Meatloaf night?"

"My mother makes meatloaf on Mondays. She makes a meal for every day of the week like clockwork, and makes enough to feed all of Hope Valley. I really have to go. I'm starved."

"I could eat. Let's go."

I walked to the door and stopped. *Let's?*

Okay. I really believed he was FBI and I had to do what he said. There was that gun thing. I mean the guy scared the stuffing out of me. He was everywhere I was. There had to be a good reason, and it had to involve Tina too. I would just bet. Maybe I could use him to further my case. That is, without him knowing it. Still, if he was FBI? Oh well, I'd still try to use him.

But to find myself sitting at my parents' table across from Jagger—my meatloaf sat on my tongue like a dried-up piece of cork.

Mom would die if she heard that analogy.

"So, Mister Jagger," my mother said as she served him another slice of meatloaf without asking.

He smiled. "Just Jagger."

She spooned a heaping portion of mashed potatoes onto his dish.

"Thanks, Missus Sokol. I'm getting full, though it is all delicious." He took a token—I was guessing—spoonful and ate it. His lips, full and moist, worked miracles when he chewed.

And not only on the food.

My mother remained silent, watching as I joined her.

I could only stare.

He had my mother mute. My mother! She set the ladle down and returned his smile, totally forgetting her question and obviously not caring. Me, I was dying to get his name thing cleared up, but felt certain it wouldn't be tonight.

Daddy and Uncle Walt ate and stared. I know Daddy was

observing Jagger for his intentions—but those were something else I felt certain wouldn't be revealed tonight.

If ever.

As if there were any intentions!

Uncle Walt kept asking about the black Suburban. Did it get good gas mileage? Did it do well in the snow? The ice? And on and on until Jagger promised him a ride around the block after dinner.

My mother insisted not until after dessert. If she'd known we were having company, she would have made something special, she told him. As it was, she said, she'd only thrown a homemade chocolate cake in the oven and added her secret two tablespoons of cream cheese to the frosting—which she revealed to Jagger.

And here I had never known it for years, and never would have found out if I hadn't walked in on her baking for my twenty-ninth birthday.

My mouth watered at the mention of chocolate. That had to be the salve I needed to pacify me after this pip of a day I'd had.

And Jagger sitting across from me.

I *needed* chocolate.

"When's dessert?" I asked without thinking.

My father looked at me. "Give us a chance to finish our meal, *pączki*." He took a huge bite of mashed potato, added a piece of meatloaf to it and topped it off with a side order of peas and carrots. Daddy always loaded his fork with a three-course meal.

Jagger looked up. He was going to ask what a *pączki* was, and I didn't want my father telling him that he called me a donut. So, I had to act fast. "Where are you from, Jagger?"

He looked at me. The question threw off the steadfast whatever he was. Good job, Pauline.

"Hartford. What's a *pączki*?" He aimed the question at my father.

I sunk down into my seat.

Even the fact that he admitted he was from Hartford

didn't help. My face was already hotter than my mother's meatloaf (and she was a stickler for serving food piping hot).

Daddy went on about how he's called me the little Polish donut name since I was born, weighing in at a whopping ten pounds, five ounces. How pink and round I had been, he added. Thank you very much, Daddy.

I looked past my mother to the brocade avocado green drapes that have hung in the dining room forever and contemplated if the drawstring was strong enough to make a noose out of.

Before I finished planning my demise, I heard a deep chuckle, and glanced up to see Jagger looking my way.

So, I straightened up in my seat, ignored my lobster complexion and said, "Hartford. Small world. So you've lived in Connecticut all your life?"

He took a sip of the Coors that my father insisted needed to follow the whiskey shot the Polish always offered their company. I'd be looped and on the floor if I'd had the two Jagger so graciously accepted and drank. Didn't look as if they'd fazed him.

"No."

I waited. Mother excused herself to clean up. Daddy sipped at his Coors and Uncle Walt kinda nodded off. Dessert would get him kicking again. And I sat there still waiting for more of an answer than a simple no.

None came.

Daddy broke the ice with, "Hartford. Did you hear that, Stella? Jagger is from Hartford. Not too far away."

From the kitchen Mom called, "Do you still have family there, dear?"

Dear?

"None left, I'm afraid."

Mother stuck her head out of the door. "Oh my. That means you don't have family to spend Christmas with."

I could hear her talking—knew what was coming. But her voice slowed in motion like that deep sound you hear in a scary movie.

"Spend Christmas with us. We celebrate twice. Christmas Eve we call Wagilia. Then you have to come back for Christmas Day. No one should be by themselves on Christmas. . . ."

Unless they're Jagger! I sat frozen to my seat. Maybe he'd decline. *Pauline, you nut case!* Of course he'll decline. Release your fists before your nails poke holes in your skin. He'll decline.

"Sounds wonderful. Thanks," Jagger said.

"Pauline, help your mother," Daddy said.

Help my mother do what? I could think of a few things right now, but I got up like a robot and started to clear the dishes. When I reached for Jagger's dish, his hand grasped mine.

Lord, I hoped my father didn't notice the little hitch in my breath.

And that—please, Saint Theresa—Jagger didn't hear either.

"I'll get it," he said, then pushed back his chair, stood and helped me clear the table.

One wouldn't think an FBI agent would do dishes.

My mother bustled about the kitchen getting the good china out of the hutch. When I'd arrived earlier, unannounced and with Jagger in tow, she had insisted we eat in the dining room.

On a Monday!

Even my parents had been affected by my new job and . . . Jagger.

"Get some ice cream out, Pauline," Mom said as she lifted the metal cover off the ancient cake tin she'd had since my birth. "Chocolate."

Hmm. Maybe Jagger had Mom needing chocolate too.

I did what I was told and got out the Hood chocolate ice cream, the scooper I knew she'd tell me to get next, and five clean forks.

"Get the ice-cream scooper and five clean forks too, Pauline." She never looked back but trudged ahead, cake in hand.

I looked at Jagger. He smiled.

Maybe he'd had a Polish mother too.

Then again, he didn't look Polish. More Mediterranean, although his name offered little clue. When I got to the doorway between the kitchen and dining room, he leaned near.

"We're not finished."

My knees buckled. I stumbled into his chest and poked a fork into his arm.

"Ouch!"

My mother stood behind him glaring at me. "What are you doing, Pauline?" She grabbed the silverware as if the forks were lethal weapons and ordered, "Get a clean fork. I'm so sorry, Mister Jagger."

He smiled. "No problem."

Dessert was fabulous as usual. Other than that bread pudding on Fridays, my mother could open her own bakery. Of course when you spend your life cooking for others, you're bound to get pretty damn good at it.

After Jagger and I cleaned up, he looked at Uncle Walt, who was fast asleep with a smudge of chocolate on his upper lip.

Jagger looked at my father. "Please tell him I owe him a ride, sir."

Daddy nodded. "You two kids hurry off before Mother has you playing Scrabble."

Again I had no memory of leaving my parents' house, yet here I sat in Jagger's Suburban. I did, however, remember that the last word I'd heard was *Scrabble*. The heater blasted warm air on my legs, and we were sitting in the parking lot of the Super Stop and Buy a few blocks from my parents' house.

At least he couldn't have his way with me in such a public area.

Damn.

I turned to him as he adjusted the radio to WMMZ, my favorite country station. Wow! We had something in common.

Trisha Yearwood came on, singing, "I Don't Paint Myself into Corners" from her *Inside Out* album.

I watched Jagger tap his finger to the beat and thought of how I'd painted myself into a whopper of a corner with this job.

He looked at me. "I'm only going to ask you one more time. What are you doing following Tina around?"

Yikes! The guy didn't let moss grow under his cowboy boots. "Who said I'm following her?"

"Me."

"Oh." I fiddled with the zipper of my jacket. "You have to take me back to my car, you know."

"Yeah."

Oh, great. Mono-word Jagger. I looked out the window and watched Mrs. Zuckowski wheeling her basket full of groceries toward her blue Caravan. Mrs. Zuckowski lived two doors down from my folks. Maybe I could scream that I was being held captive and for her to call 911. Then what?

Jagger would only find me another day.

Might as well get it over with. Besides, I told myself, maybe I really could use him to finish my case. "I work for Scarpello and Tonelli Insurance Company."

He didn't flinch. As a matter of fact, he could have been carved out of granite for all the body language I could read.

I knew I was about to ramble nervously and other than jump out of the Suburban, I couldn't help myself. "I work for Fabio as an investigator. You know, follow people around that are breaking the law. Well, at least they are bilking the insurance company. You know, fraud. I'm talking fraud here, which of course is against the law.

"Thousands of dollars they steal. These people that is. Actually, sometimes in the millions. They steal in the millions. I actually read about a case that was in the billions. Imagine that." I could only guess what Jagger was imagining right now. "So, I . . . well, I was a nurse for many years and burned out. You know, the responsibility . . . kids puking on your shoes . . . throat swabs on your breasts . . . working weekends . . . working with staff. Mostly female. Catty females. Rather have all gay males, but that's another story. I'll never take a job where I have to hire and fire staff again. It's not in my nature to fire—"

"Tina?"

Mono Jagger strikes again. Well, I was getting off track a bit. Okay, I admit my faults. "Tina is out on a Workers' Compensation claim for an injured back."

"And Fabio in his infinite fucking wisdom hired you, a nurse, to crack that case."

I knew an insult when I heard one. And that had to be one. "Yes. Yeah. So what?"

"What kind of experience do you have in surveillance other than sitting smack-dab in front of her house or—oh wait, that's right. You have the smarts to hide in a snowbank."

Now I was pissed. "I'm going to get her."

He shook his head, cranked the motor and shoved it into drive. As we pulled out of the parking lot, he said, "Stay the hell out of my way."

We rode in silence until I saw my precious Volvo covered in frost and sitting so lonely on the construction site. Jagger pulled up alongside, shoved the Suburban into park and waited. I opened my door and stepped out.

"I'm not making any promises. Besides, you didn't say what you were doing, or whom you work for. So, how can I stay out of your way if I don't know what your way is?" With that I turned and walked to my car with my heart pounding double-time and a prayer on my lips that he wouldn't follow me.

His tires screeched.

"Thanks, Saint T," I mouthed, dug around in my purse for my keys and shivered.

It wasn't from the cold, either.

Ten

When the shock of Jagger coming to my family's Christmas started to wear off, I decided I'd better get into my car and head home before I froze to death out here in the woods by Tina's mansion.

Then again, that didn't sound like such a bad idea.

A light came on in her backyard. I watched for a while, but equipmentless, I could only stare. Truthfully she could have come out and yanked one of the naked trees up with her bare hands and I could have cared less.

I just didn't have any investigating left in me right then.

"I need a bubble bath," I said to my Volvo. No reply. Surprising, with the day I'd had.

I got in, started the car, cranked up the heat and, even though the engine was still freezing, told myself the air blowing in my face was warm. At the edge of the subdivision I slowed, stopped and looked into my rearview mirror. There was Tina, hiking through the snow with a huge package in her arms. Damn. I'll bet it was heavy.

As I looked both ways for traffic before pulling out, I noticed a black Suburban sitting at the corner two streets down. That was out of my way, but I turned down the street, slowed when I passed and flipped Jagger the bird.

Not like me, but it felt so damn good!

Once back at the condo, I hurried inside, called for Miles and got no reply, let Spanky out and back in, then headed to my room. I left my damp jacket on the bed and grabbed my pajamas and robe.

Major bubble-bath day.

In the bathroom, I rifled through the scented bubble bath beads and picked out rose. Roses are sent to you when Saint Theresa hears your prayers. I figured I could use whatever help I could get tonight even though she is supposed to send them to you as a surprise.

Once the water was perfect, I slipped in, blowing bubbles about the room. The heat relaxed my muscles. I hadn't realized how tense I had been. Had to have something to do with starting out with Nick and ending up with Jagger. I shuddered.

Being coerced—make that ordered—to take him to my parents' tonight for dinner was nothing compared to what I'd face on Christmas Eve and Day when the entire Sokol clan arrived. I shut my eyes and refused to think about it.

And other than my birthday, Christmas was my favorite holiday. Shoot.

I wondered if Miles's late lunch had turned into an all nighter. Gee, I hoped not. I really was rooting for Goldie.

Well, whatever happened, happened. I wasn't about to push them together and possibly hurt either one. Miles I loved, and I could see Goldie becoming a dear friend. It dawned on me that thanks to Miles I had met Goldie. Right. If I didn't work for Fabio, I would never have met Goldie. How sad that thought was.

Or met Jagger. How shocking that thought was.

Speaking of working for Fabio, I had to accomplish something tomorrow. Anything related to the case.

I had to, or else I'd be unemployed right soon.

Then again, there was that nursing job at Tina's office. Maybe I should take it for a few days and see what happens. Then again, *nursing*.

I didn't have the stomach to go back yet, even if an office job might be a piece of cake. Surely orthopedic patients didn't spit throat swabs. Okay, I'd think about it tomorrow. Tonight I'd soak until soggy and forget the day.

"You in there?" Miles called.

"Oh, hey. I'll be out soon." Damn. I looked at my fingers. Not even wrinkled yet. And tonight I needed wrinkled.

"No problem. Just wanted to know where you were and that you hadn't fallen asleep in the tub again."

I blew bubbles toward the door. "That was six months ago, and I'd taken NyQuil 'cause I was sick. Give me a break, Miles."

"Hey, that sounds like your tea tone."

I smiled despite how I felt. Miles called it my "tea tone" when I needed a cup of hot, steamy decaffeinated tea because of stress or whatever upset me. It was one notch down from my "Coors tone." "What's the biggest mug we have?"

"Hold it right there."

I heard him running down the stairs, leaned back and shut my eyes.

Knock. Knock.

"Tea time. Cover yourself up."

I made sure the bubbles were shoulder-high although it wouldn't impress Miles to see my 36Cs. "Enter."

He opened the door, walked over and handed me my mug. Then he looked at himself in the mirror, groaned and hurried out, shutting the door behind.

"You look wonderful," I shouted, then took a sip of tea. "Ouch." Miles insisted on boiling the water, although I preferred my tea heated in the microwave.

"Horrible bags under my eyes. Impending crow's-feet. Forget that. Tell me about the need for tea. Couldn't be worse than this morning for you," he hollered through the door.

I talked about my day until the water cooled. In between sentences, Miles let out a few squeaky gasps followed by a muttered, "Christmas?" I had to smile as I stood and toweled off. When I had on my Steelers pj's and robe wrapped tightly for warmth—although Miles kept the condo heated like August in Miami—I took my mug and opened the door.

I needed the heat right now. Comforting. Similar to being in the womb of my 98.6 degree mom. Speaking of which, I could use a sniff of pine Renuzit.

He was sitting across from the doorway against the opposite wall, tea mug in hand. He looked up. "I'm calling Hammy at the furniture store. Investigating is not the career for you."

I held out my hand, which he used to pull himself up. "No you are not. You're calling Goldie."

His hand tensed. "What?"

"He misses you, Miles. I don't know what went down between you two—"

"Besides me?" He laughed, but it was a nervous laugh and it was not like Miles to use gay jokes.

"I'm serious. You should have seen him when he came to give me a ride. I promised myself I wouldn't interfere, but the way he looked . . . Please call him once. Then I'm out of it."

He nodded and let it go.

I followed him down to the kitchen, where he fixed two more mugs of tea. I'd be up all night peeing, but the Sleepytime hit the spot. I really needed tea tonight and was on the verge of asking for the caffeinated variety.

Miles sat at the counter and motioned for me to sit too. "I met Goldie at Mardi Gras one year."

I sat and kept my mouth shut—for a change.

"He was adorable. . . ." Miles looked off toward the garden. Earlier he must have turned on the walkway lights that led around the tiny brick path.

I could only imagine that he was thinking of their first meeting.

"Goldie was dressed as a lion. But he looked like Marilyn Monroe in drag, dressed as a lion. Adorable," he repeated. "We spent the rest of my vacation down there together. Three glorious weeks. When I had to come back to work here, Goldie came too. He'd planned to be a PI, but it didn't work out."

I took a sip of tea and decided to let it cool more. I could use a few Oreos with it, but didn't want to interrupt Miles by getting up.

"We moved in to that apartment I had on Dearborn near Saint Greg's before I bought this place. Goldie worked nights as a bartender, days in a Dunkin Donuts, where he met this undercover narc. They hit it off, but Goldie and I were tight.

"Least I thought we were. The cop taught Goldie all he knew about being a PI. Goldie was going to try to get a job as one so I sent him over to Fabio. He hired him, and he's been there ever since." He stopped to finish his tea. Then he stood, took the mug to the sink, rinsed it and stuck it into the dishwasher.

I remained silent and a bit confused. Who was the cop, and what happened between Miles and Goldie?

Miles turned around. "Turned out the cop was a jerk. He tried to get between us—and actually did. But not 'cause he cared for Goldie. The jerk used him 'cause he had just been dumped.

"Once he'd gained Goldie's confidence through all that he taught him, Goldie was mesmerized. He left me for the jerk, then *he* left Goldie when his ex came back. Goldie's and my relationship hadn't really cemented enough yet. That's why he left me. Goldie had a problem with trust and commitment.

"He didn't have great self-esteem at the time either. That's partly why he dresses the way he does. He's a good-looking guy, you know. So,'cause of the cop, we both ended up hurt. You know me, Pauline. I don't do forgiveness well 'cause of my mama. So, I refused to take Goldie back. He was embarrassed that he left, and we haven't seen each other in three years."

"Are you ready to now?"

He looked back at me. "Yes. I've never met anyone like Goldie."

I smiled. "Neither have I."

* * *

The next day, Adele let me into Goldie's office and I helped myself to a cup of chicory coffee. She said she did that every morning, and he expected it. When she hurried out to answer her phone, I sat on the faux fur couch and took a sip. Perfect. The coffee was delicious and was a good omen for my day—at least that's what I told myself.

"Hellooooo, suga!"

I looked up to see Goldie waltzing in. And waltz he did, in red spike heels, black chino pants and a skintight red-and-black-striped long-sleeve shirt. Slung over his arm was a raccoon coat. I couldn't tell, but it sure looked real to me.

"You walk in the snow with those on?" I looked down at my climbing boots that fit snugly around my leggings. I wore black ones today with an oversized black-and-white tweed sweater. I thought I'd better start paying attention to my wardrobe in case I had a day like yesterday.

He laughed. "I believe I walked *over* the snow today."

I smiled. "What's got you in such a good mood?"

He came near and yanked me up from the couch and planted a kiss on my forehead. "You really don't know?"

"Finished your case?"

He waved a hand. "They'll be paying back sixty Gs, but that's not it." He let me go and looked me in the eyes. "You really don't know?"

"No, Gold, but you're killing me with suspense."

"My Miles called."

I let out a whoop. He grabbed me and danced around. Adele rushed in with her arms flailing.

"What? What's the excitement about? Don't let Adele miss out on a thing!"

"Got my man back, Adele."

"Miles?" She hooted and kissed him on the cheek. Good thing she wore such high navy heels in order to reach.

Fabio stood in the doorway. "When all the excitement is over, I'd like to see some fucking work get done around here."

I felt the urge to defend my friends. "Goldie finished his case."

Fabio ran his fingers along his chin. "Fabulous, Ms. Sokol. And what about yours?"

Ack.

"I'm helping her wrap it up today, Boss," Goldie said.

Fabio held out a manila folder. "No, you're not. Here's your next one." He turned toward me. "Probation means you do your goddamndest, lady, if you want to be made permanent." With that he turned and walked out.

In unison, Goldie and Adele said, "Cocksucker extraordinaire."

Something told me they'd used that term for Fabio before.

We both mumbled some ripe curses after Fabio left.

"We probably should do some work before Fabio comes back in," I said to Goldie after we sat silently for what seemed like an hour, then I filled him in on the rest of yesterday. He had the same reaction as Miles, and gasped when I told him that Tina had two houses.

Adele had followed Fabio, and I heard her chiding him all the way down the hallway. I only hoped he didn't fire her. She was a gem, a friend, and I'd miss her terribly. That was if I kept my job.

Goldie stirred. "You're right, we'd better get to work." He opened the file Fabio had given him. "Shit. I won't be able to help you today, suga. This one's going to be a bitch. I'll be up at night following this jerk around. Night watchman. Sheeeet."

I stood up and pulled my sweater down. "Thanks for the coffee. Good luck with Miles, too."

He winked at me. "Want me to see what Nick is up to?"

"No! I mean, no thanks. I have to start out on my own sooner or later."

"What about Jagger?"

"Thanks for *that* reminder."

He smirked at me. "Now don't go getting your panties all in a knot over that guy, suga. I told you about him."

"Yes, but is he FBI? I mean I wouldn't have cooperated with him if I thought he wasn't."

Goldie tapped a black nail against his tooth. "I can't rightly say, suga, but that's still my best guess. Either way he won't physically hurt you, as I said, but he is one hell of a mysterious guy. I'd be tempted to lock lips with him myself—"

"You think he's gay!" I've never heard my voice sound so horrified, even when Doc Taylor suggested we get married about a hundred years ago.

Goldie laughed. "You didn't let me finish. I was going to say, if he swung my way. He doesn't. I can tell these things."

I wondered if someone who looked like Marilyn Monroe could really tell about another man. Then again, this was Goldie, and he'd proven to be quite knowledgeable about everything else. "You think I should have told him who I am? What I do for a living?"

"I think he already knew, suga. That's Jagger."

"What? You're kidding me!" But I knew he wasn't. It did seem as if Jagger wasn't surprised when I told him. Damn. I liked him not knowing since I didn't know about him.

"Maybe a good idea to take that temporary job Tina mentioned. You could see her at the office if she goes there." He shoved the file folder closed.

"I don't know. It might help, yet I'd hate to take a nursing job. Seems counterproductive to my sanity."

Goldie laughed. "But Fabio hired you for your background. You of all people should be able to tell if someone is faking."

"She's faking, all right. If I had a decent video camera last night, one that worked in the dark, I could prove it." I walked to the door, not really certain where I was going but knowing I'd better do something fast. "You think Fabio will fire me if I don't finish this case soon?"

Goldie hurried over, took me into his arms and held me.

"Shit," I mumbled to his chest.

* * *

This day had started out wonderfully with the chicory coffee, but it was taking a downward spiral to hell, I thought as I drove out of the parking lot—in no particular direction. I could head over to Tina's, but which house? They were on opposite ends of town and it wasn't as if I could run back and forth between the two to try and catch her.

I turned left onto Hillside Avenue and got stuck at the light. The road ahead was backed up to the intersection and there were no side streets to take.

Okay, this was getting to be a not so good day.

Chime. Chime.

Great. My cell phone. Who would be calling me here? I grabbed my purse and dug around until I found it. I pushed the green button and held it to my ear. "Hello."

"Package here for you." It was Miles's sleepy voice.

"Really?"

"No. I got up early on my day off to fool you."

"Speaking of having a late night, I heard about your phone call. Well, not any details."

"I wasn't speaking of any late night, but yeah. Goldie and I talked for hours."

"I'm glad. Now tell me more about the package."

"Geez. Such concern for my love life." He laughed. "It's sitting right here on the counter."

My hand started to shake and my heart did a three sixty in my chest. "Is it from Parker and Smith Inc.?"

"That'd be the one."

"Oh Miles! That's my equipment."

I heard him shuffling around and guessed he was getting himself some coffee. "Great. Now you can do the job like the consummate professional that you are."

"I'm not really that professional—yet. I will be though. Give me a few cases under my belt, and I'll be giving Goldie a run for his money."

"You go, girl. I'm off to the tub. Lavender bubbles to celebrate—"

"The arrival of my equipment?"

"My late-night phone call."

"You go, guy." We laughed. "I'm stuck in traffic, but will be there as soon as this bottleneck clears." I hung up and shoved the phone into my purse. Damn. Traffic stretched out for miles in front of me. Maybe I could back up into some driveway and get going in the other direction. I looked into my rearview mirror.

About five cars behind me was a black Suburban.

"Damn it!" My good day had had an upswing, and now it was cascading downward again. The guy must have better things to do than follow me around.

I didn't do anything illegal!

I decided to ignore him and motioned for the car behind me to move back a bit. The driver, a woman in a red Dodge Caravan, obligingly eased back a few inches. It was enough for me to back into the driveway of a white colonial. I eased through the space in the line and turned left, away from the congestion.

As I got near the Suburban, I floored it without a glance.

I wasn't sure, but I thought I might have seen a woman at the steering wheel out of the corner of my eye. If it was, she'd given me a hell of a look. I'd have to check out Jagger's license plate next time I saw the Suburban.

I was beginning to develop paranoia toward black Suburbans.

I drove into my parking lot, parked and flew out of the car. I was up the front stoop and into the kitchen in record time. Miles was sitting on the window seat, sipping coffee and reading *GQ*. No wonder the guy always looked smashing in the clothes he chose.

"Where is it?"

"On the counter like I said." He got up and hurried over. "Open it. Quick. I can't wait to see."

"You?" I grabbed a knife from the drawer and, despite Miles's groan of protest, sliced open the package and took out my new video camera.

"A beeper? What the hell?" He leaned near. "What? You think Tina Macaluso is going to beep you when she's committing fraud?"

"No, silly. It's a camera!"

"Holy shit. No kidding."

We looked at it thoroughly and decided it looked like a genuine beeper. Inside the package was my new digital camera too. "I can't wait. I'm off to Tina's now."

Miles laughed. "You go, girl, again! Good luck," he shouted as I patted Spanky a quick one and ran out.

This time I decided to go to Tina's colonial by the river. If she wasn't there . . . Wait, I had a brilliant idea. I ran back inside and yelled to Miles, "I'm a genius! Just wanted to let you know that."

He watched me grab the phone book from the kitchen drawer. "What's up now?"

"Well, I don't know where Tina is, so instead of wasting my time, I'm going to call her!"

"Brilliant, Columbo. You think she's going to do something stupid after you've called?"

"Yes. No. No. No. No." Exhausted, I sat down and took a cleansing breath. "You're right and I'm not that stupid. You're going to call her."

"Me?"

"Just call and hang up when you hear a female voice. Simple as pumpkin pie." Pumpkin was my favorite.

"Don't you think she has caller ID and will read the name?"

"Ack. Why didn't I think . . . Okay, no problem. Use your cell phone since it's unlisted."

"Brilliant, my dear." He dialed the number of the house by the river. We waited for a few seconds, then Miles's hand started to shake and he shoved his finger down on the disconnect. "She's there."

"Yes!" I hugged him and danced him around. "Oops! Watch out for my camera!" I patted the "beeper" in my pocket.

"You know how to use that thing yet?"

"No, but I'll read up on it waiting outside her house. See you later!"

With that I was out the door yet again, and found myself down the street from Tina's without remembering the drive over. I worried for a few seconds about these memory losses, but told myself it was only because my excitement had me driving so fast and thinking of nothing else.

The memory losses I suffered when running out of my parents' house, I decided, were nothing to worry about either. They were a coping mechanism for my sanity and a speedy escape from potential Sokol hell.

I'd pulled over to the curb three houses down. There was a giant RV in the drive, and it provided wonderful cover for me to hide behind. Tina might remember my car, but I wasn't sure if she knew the Volvo I was standing next to in the parking lot yesterday was mine or the red Chevy Blazer next to me. Still, I didn't want to take a chance.

"Okay, Ms. Investigator, now you are really going to crack this case." I wasn't sure if that was the correct term for investigating someone faking an injury, but it would glamorize the boring hours I might have to spend here waiting for Tina to do something. Now was a perfect time to read the instructions on my beeper/camera.

I opened the box it came in and took out the paper. Something caught my eye.

Tina's door opened.

"Shoot!" I dropped the instruction sheet. It floated to the floorboard beneath my feet. When I started to reach for it, she walked to her car, got in and drove out of the drive. I cranked my engine, waited a decent amount of time—not so long that I'd lose her—and followed.

"Tailing Tina Macaluso," I said out loud in a similar voice the cops use on TV.

She headed down Maple to Olive and out onto Main. It wasn't the route to her husband's office. Great. I hoped I didn't have to follow her around all day before she did something I could get on my new camera.

And I hoped I'd have a few minutes to read how to use it.

She pulled into the Spring Mountain Weed and Feed store. I turned into the parking lot of the adjacent real-estate business and turned off my engine when she got out and went inside. What on earth would she need there—in the winter?

I tried to look at the camera directions at the same time I watched out for her. What little I had time to read seemed simple, so I attached the beeper to the belt of my jeans, grabbed my purse and got out. I'd have to go into the store and see if she was doing anything worth filming. When I got to the doorway, I noticed a poster of winter birds. Purple finches. Although their feathers were more red than purple.

Birdseed!

Maybe Tina was buying a fifty-pound bag of seed. It was common for folks around here to feed the birds in the wintertime. Perfect! I walked cautiously into the store. No Tina near the cash register. Good. I was ready with a lie if she saw me. But she wasn't in aisle one or two. A young teen with bad acne sat on the floor, stamping cans of paint with the pricing gun.

"Excuse me," I said in a low voice.

"What?"

I jumped at his loud tone, then thought of the poster in the front doorway. "Where is the birdseed?"

"I can't hear you, lady." He gave me an odd look.

No wonder. I was acting odd. A bit louder I said, "Laryngitis. Where is the birdseed?"

"Aisle five." I think he rolled his eyes at me, but I'd headed off too fast to be sure or to give him a lecture on manners. I waited between the ends of aisles five and four by the shovels. A man came close. He looked as if he was going to ask me if I needed help so I gave him a nasty look. He turned down aisle four, and I decided I may never be able to set foot in this store again.

Tina's voice floated down the aisle. "So, you think they like more sunflower seeds?"

A young man's voice said yes.

I eased past the shovels to see Tina's back to me. Good. I opened my jacket enough to reveal my "beeper." Then I pressed the RECORD button. The man turned and walked toward me. Ack! I closed my jacket, swung sideways and pretended to look at household cleaners. He went past me. I looked around.

Tina was reading the posted ingredients on the shelves of birdseed. Good. I opened my coat again, held it away from the beeper/camera and waited. She read for what seemed like hours. I had no idea how long the video would work, but I had to wait.

Then—thank you, Saint Theresa—Tina bent over without even a groan, and lifted a hefty sack of seed from the bottom shelf!

My back hurt watching her. She lifted it over the side of the cart and set it inside. When she started to move, I swung around and scurried toward aisle six. From the end of that aisle, I watched her go through checkout and wheel the cart out of the store. I followed, ignoring the strange looks of the clerks, who probably thought I was shoplifting a hammer or something.

I stood behind a giant blue spruce and opened my jacket again. I got her lifting the bag of seeds from the cart into the trunk. From here I could tell it was a forty-pound bag. Wonderful!

She got in and drove off.

I should follow her but couldn't wait to get to the office and show Adele and Goldie that I'd made a major dent in my case.

My excitement couldn't be contained. I ran into Nick on the way into the office and babbled about my case. He laughed and graciously said he'd love to see the tape. Adele was genuinely excited and unfortunately, Fabio was standing in the hallway and heard my news.

"Okay, doll, let's see what you got," he said over my head.

Adele took me by the arm. "Goldie has the only VCR

here. You got the connection wire to hook your camera to the TV?"

I proudly held it up. Yes.

Pauline Sokol was on her way!

Goldie jumped up from his desk with excitement when Adele gushed on about me. "Everyone sit," he ordered, and took the camera and connection wire. "Allow me, Ms. Sokol."

"Gladly."

We all settled around his office. Adele sat next to me on the arm of the leopard-print chair.

My heart was doing a jig. It felt so good. Fabio might be able to use this tape alone and get his money back—and I'd get mine.

The room hushed when the TV went from snow to blue screen. Then, the picture cleared to the taping of Tina Macaluso committing fraud.

I could only stare in dumbfounded silence when Tina's knees came into view, followed by her large ass. I heard Goldie gasp. Nick gave me a comforting smile. Adele touched my arm and sighed and Fabio growled, "What the fuck? How we going to use this tape?"

True.

The entire video was of Tina—waist down—no face ever in view, since I'd worn the camera on my belt the whole time.

I covered my eyes with my hands and willed myself to die in Goldie's flamboyant office until I heard a faint chuckle. Hurt that one of my coworkers would laugh at me, I peeked between my pointer finger and the next one only to see that they sat stoically glaring at me.

I turned around to see who the chuckler was. Standing in the doorway for what I'd have to believe was the entire viewing stood Jagger.

Eleven

I stood with my head resting against Goldie's red-and-black-striped top—sobbing—in the ladies' room. It didn't even faze me that Goldie came rushing in like one of us females. Adele kept wiping my face with a damp paper towel and crooning, "It'll all be okay, *chéri*."

But it wouldn't.

I'd been humiliated in front of everyone—and Jagger.

I sobbed louder.

"I'm . . . usually . . . not . . . a crier . . . except"—I blew my nose on the toilet tissue Adele gave me, then took a long controlling breath—"at funerals and weddings. I cry at weddings, but that's 'cause I'm always a bridesmaid."

Goldie hugged me tighter. "You'll be a bride someday, suga."

"I don't want to be a bride anymore." Oh my God! I'd never even admitted that to anyone, let alone myself. Getting married and having kids took a backseat to career since the big change. "I want to be the best medical fraud insurance investigator that I can beeeeeeeee." It started again, the sobbing.

Goldie held me tighter yet again, and Adele had just about used up all the paper towels not to mention the fact that my hair was now damp from them. She meant well and moistened hair was the least of my problems.

Goldie went on about the small community of investigators around here and what a close-knit group they actually were. Well, he'd added, except for Jagger. I'm not sure why he rambled on about that other than my behavior had him out of whack too. "You'll learn how to use your camera and get Tina real soon," he tried to assure me.

But he didn't sound too convincing.

"I'm a failure at this job. I should have taken the time to read the instructions. I mean—" I pushed away from Goldie and forced a smile at both of them. "Thanks." After another whopper of a breath in and out, I said, "She lifted a forty-pound bag of birdseed with extra sunflower seeds in it, twice. Twice, and all I got was her knees and ass. You couldn't even tell whose ass it was, although she has a distinctly large one." My gaze caught Goldie's then Adele's.

We broke out in hysterics.

"Sheeeet," Goldie said, wiping his eyes. "Now you've got me tearing up with that one."

"It was rather funny. I mean, not getting any of her face to prove who it was."

Adele took the last paper towel and wiped her eyes. "Adele would give her right nipple to see the look on Fabio's face again. Shock. Delicious anger. Fabio fury. Wonderful. I think I peed in my pants!"

We laughed louder.

Goldie let go and took my hand. "Glad you can laugh about it, suga. That's the only way to get through life."

Wise transvestite.

I know he'd been through some of life's tough lessons, but Goldie was a trooper. My Polish stock were no slouches either. I would get my girl, and my paycheck, in due time.

"We better get out of here before Fabio cans all our asses," Adele said.

I nodded and followed Goldie to the door. He turned to me after Adele had walked past. "Jagger is like cocaine, suga.

He'll make you feel on top of the world—then fuck you up at the end. But, you can trust him with your life."

I stood digesting that info.

Goldie stuck his head out the door and looked both ways. "Come on."

I could only guess that he was checking to see if Jagger was out there and to help me save face—or what little face I had left to save.

After two cups of chicory coffee with double amounts of sugar in them (since Goldie said sweets would help and he was all out of chocolate—rats!), I sat on the leopard chair and finished reading the camera directions.

"I see the problem now."

He'd been writing in a file and stapling surveillance photos to a manila folder. "You sure, suga?"

"Stand up." I got up at the same time and hooked the camera onto my belt. "Walk toward me."

He not only walked, he pranced, he mamboed, he cha-cha'd, and finally flung himself on the zebra couch and sang two choruses of "I Feel Pretty."

Despite the laughing, I followed him along with my beeper still attached. Then we hooked it up to the VCR and watched Goldie's antics. "You should be in show biz," I said. Truthfully, the picture swayed about as much as Goldie but at least showed his face.

He leaned back, his hand on his forehead. "I'm getting seasick, suga. You've got to practice steadying yourself."

I curled my lip at him, got up, grabbed my purse and walked to the TV. While I disconnected the camera, I said, "Thanks for all your help. You're a doll."

"I am, aren't I?" He got up and chuckled. "Miles is taking me out to Madeline's for dinner."

Madeline's was a very exclusive, expensive French restaurant on the Connecticut River in Hope Valley.

We high-fived each other. "Yes! Have fun. Think of me eating a can of soup with Spanky tonight."

"Go to your mama's house."

I thought a minute. Tuesday. Pot roast. My mouth started to water because my mother made the creamiest brown mushroom gravy with her beef. Then, I thought of Jagger sitting across from me in Mom's dining room.

I'd more than likely never be able to eat at my parents' house again.

Great future. No house because no loans, and no more of Mom's home cooked meals.

"No. I'm going home. I need it."

Goldie blew me a kiss. "Tomorrow."

"You have a wonderful time," I called down the hallway after him.

But before I could turn toward the exit myself, a deep voice answered, "I already did."

I swung around to come face to face with a smirking Jagger. *You're a big girl, Pauline, and a professional. Don't collapse into a pile of nothing like the wet Wicked Witch in Oz.*

"Jagger." I nodded and started to walk past him. "Glad you had a good time."

He grabbed my arm. "You need to steady that camera on your belt and . . ."

I heard him talking but couldn't believe he was giving me very clear instructions on how to use my new camera. The guy was exactly right, from what I'd read in the pamphlet. I looked at him when his lips stopped. "Where were you this morning when I could have used that info?"

"Places."

Oh, boy. "Do you ever answer a question with something other than a mono word?"

He shrugged. "Sometimes."

"Well, at least that's two syllables."

"Your hair looks like shit."

"Latest fashion craze." I cringed inside.

"Let's get a coffee."

"I . . . Are you asking me out?" I nonchalantly tried to fix my hair. "Like a date?"

"No. I told you I wasn't done questioning you yet."

Was my face appealing in bright scarlet? I wondered that as he looked at me.

I watched Jagger over my coffee cup while we sat at the table farthest in the back at Dunkin Donuts on Elm Street. He ate a Boston cream donut as if it were the last morsel on earth. Something about him said he enjoyed the hell out of food and was comfortable in his body.

Who wouldn't be?

Okay, I thought, I have to keep this professional. I'd declined a donut since all I could think of was my ten-pound birth weight and that Jagger knew my father's nickname for me. But watching Jagger eat had me craving Boston cream. Truthfully, I craved whatever he was eating. Made food so sexy I felt like Meg Ryan in that restaurant scene with Billy Crystal in *When Harry Met Sally.*

"Tina lifted a forty-pound bag of birdseed. That's what was supposed to be on my tape."

I could tell he had a difficult time stifling his laughter at my expense, but I'd give him credit for self-control. He did, however, take an exceptionally long time wiping a smudge of cream from his lip and licking off his finger all the while looking me in the eyes.

I swallowed—hard.

And nearly coughed up all my coffee. So then I took a deep breath to calm myself. Pheromones had to be wafting across the table. I knew I had inhaled some even if they were scent-free. I held my cup near my nose and took a deep breath of the pungent liquid to use as a Jagger-pheromone shield.

"Getting her lifting forty pounds would have been useful against her claim," he finally said. He finished his coffee and sat looking at me.

"I don't know what else I can tell you. I'm going to go over to her house again and see if I can get any more video to use."

"You mean *some* video to use." He smiled.

I smiled back. "Right." Coming from such "strong as

bull" Polish stock, I held my head up and refused to be humiliated anymore than I already had been this morning.

"You have to practice using that camera and . . . I'll help you find Tina if you take that part-time job in Doctor Macaluso's office."

I glared at him. No sense asking how he knew. Small community of investigators indeed. I could only hope that he couldn't read my mind. For a few seconds I thought about Jagger's "suggestion." Vance worked there. Did I really want to work with him in the same office? I didn't want to lead him on: After yesterday's lunch, he'd already planned on us having dinner together this weekend.

I looked at Jagger. Sex with Vance was never going to be the same.

"I don't know. I doubt I'll get much vidco on Tina there." The payment Jeanine had stuck me with was due in a few weeks. Damn it. The money was sorely needed.

"You won't get any."

"Then why the hell should I take a nursing job *there*?"

"I want you to."

"Linda Stark, please." I held my cell phone in one hand, Tina's business card with the office manager's number on it in the other and watched Jagger across the table watching me.

What the hell was I doing?

I had a good premonition meter—always relied on it for my nursing—and this time the meter was telling me I could trust Jagger even if I didn't know who the hell he was. Even Goldie had said as much. So, I was letting Jagger talk me into taking the job for a few days.

"Yes?" a female voice came on the line.

"Ms. Stark, I'm a friend of Tina Macaluso," I lied and again flushed. Lying did that to me, but I plodded on despite my complexion, making a mental note to always wear something that doesn't clash with crimson when I'm with Jagger. "She suggested I fill in for her while she's out. Poor thing with that injury and all. We went to nursing school together."

Jagger had a toothpick—from where I don't know—and sat fiddling with it in his mouth oh-so-very casually.

Linda had me coming in to work the next day!

"Desperate," she'd said they had been, and the local nursing agencies sent most of the staff to hospitals or home care. Doctor's offices were last on their list. I hung up and sat back. "You have no idea how much I hate doing this."

"Yes, I do."

It was then that I truly realized Jagger knew more about me than I probably knew about myself.

I was going with FBI.

"Keep that thing on your belt until you need it. That way you can get it in seconds," Jagger said as I held my beeper/camera in my gloved hand. "Don't drop it."

"Gee, I thought I'd take videos of feet."

He ignored me and drove us right out to Tina's mansion, as if he knew exactly where she'd be. Didn't surprise me. Did amaze me. Did make me jealous. Did give me aspirations to learn from him.

We parked and found myself hurrying along a snow-covered empty lot to keep up with Jagger's long strides. The back of Tina's house was off to the left. Jagger led me to the bank of snow I'd dove behind last night. He kept looking at her house and doing things at the same time. Things like kicking the pile back into its original igloo shape.

Me, I would have been capable of only one thing at a time, but before I knew it, he had us huddled in the half igloo and had made a window of sorts to spy out of.

For some reason I didn't think Jagger would call it spying.

His shoulder pressed against mine. It was all I could do not to sigh. Even through the bulky down of my Steelers jacket, I *felt* him.

"Is it warm in here?" Oh shit! I couldn't believe that snuck out of my mouth.

Without a thought he said, "Snow is a good insulator."

"Yeah. Right. Insulator." Ack. I lifted the collar of my

jacket over my nose as if it was cold, but truthfully, it was my second Jagger/pheromone shield of the day.

"She's coming out," he said quietly. "Get your camera ready."

I fumbled around in the midst of my bulk and pulled out the beeper. "Here."

He looked at me. "This is your case."

"Oh, right."

He moved over slightly so I could get to the hole of a window. There she was, all right. "She's carrying something big. Looks heavy. I'll bet it's that forty-pound bag of birdseed!"

"Film away."

This time my excitement wasn't hormonally induced, although *that* never left my mind. I held up the camera. Just as I thought I was getting her carrying and lifting and spilling birdseed on the ground, I heard a dog bark.

It got much louder.

Jagger looked at me. "Ignore it and it won't bother us."

Soon a nose poked into our window. A black wet one. I was guessing German shepherd or rottweiller or bull mastiff by the size of its nose. A loud sniff followed.

The snow shifted when gigantic paws dug for a few seconds.

I pulled back, but kept my camera there ready for the second the damn dog moved away.

Suddenly the nose left, the digging ceased and a spray of liquid yellow showered into the window—flooding my brand-new beeper/camera.

Jagger shut his eyes. "Oh shit."

"Pauline! Pauline what is wrong with you?" my mother called out when I shot through the kitchen doorway.

I continued running through the hallway, past the wall of family photos and into the bathroom. "I'm fine." I shoved the door open, glad neither Daddy or Uncle Walt was in there, and headed toward the shelf above the toilet.

There it sat.

I grabbed the pine Renuzit and held the can away from

my face, then sprayed as if the bathroom were infested with flying creatures. When I thought of the day I'd had so far: the dog, Jagger, my camera. I inhaled. Deeply.

Ah.

Christmas.

Traditional holiday meals.

Outdoors as a kid.

And . . . family.

The scent wrapped me with comfort, working miracles much better than Prozac or Zoloft could do. I shut my eyes and inhaled again.

Bang. Bang.

"Pauline," Mother shouted. "Are you . . . Do you have the runs? Oh my Lord. Michael, get the Pepto-Bismol. Did you see how fast she came through the house? Pauline has the runs!"

My eyes flew open. Geez. "Mom, I'm fine." Suddenly I heard my father's voice shouting from the kitchen that there was no Pepto-Bismol in the refrigerator and should he run to the store?

"Darn it all. Uncle Walt must have used it up and not put it on the shopping list," my mother's voice came through the door. "Walt? Did you use the Pepto—"

I opened the door and stuck my head out. "I'm all right, Mom. I don't need any medication. I'll pick you up some Pepto-Bismol at the drugstore later. I'm fine, Daddy!"

She looked past me as if some evidence that I really was sick and just wouldn't admit it was lying on the floor of the bathroom. What kind of evidence, I had no idea. But this was my mother we were talking about here.

"Why does it smell like a forest in here?" She wiggled her nose a few times. As kids, we used to say Mom's nose was like one of those drug dogs. She could smell something burning before it actually ignited. Then she would sniff and sniff the air, asking us if something was burning. As teens, we used to purposely burn a piece of toast, throw it away, and say we knew nothing about where the smell came from as Mom sniffed until her sinuses dried.

I gave her a hug. "Your Renuzit, Mom. That's the forest scent." Then I walked past her, heading toward the front door.

"Pauline, have you gone mad? What is this? You run in here, into our bathroom and spray my Renuzit as if some skunk had passed through. That stuff is not cheap, you know."

I smiled. I would have thought she owned stock in the company or at the very least, once a year, was sent cartons of free cans as such a good, loyal customer. "I'll get you a can at the drugstore, too." Maybe I'd pick up an extra can and keep it in my purse. With this new job and Jagger, I might need some pine comfort down the road.

"I don't need any more cans of it. I have seven in the laundry cabinet. Sit down and eat something."

Although food was the last thing on my mind, the tone my mother used left little room for argument.

So, I sat at the table, eating a piece of blueberry pie she'd made from berries she and Daddy had picked the past summer and frozen. She used cream cheese below the berries on a flaky, homemade crust, in which she never spared the butter. Between the Renuzit and pie, I had almost forgotten about my injured camera.

"Delicious. This is delicious, Mom."

She gave me an odd look. "It's the same as I've made since you were born. I do, however, put a lot of work into my cooking. What is wrong with you tonight?" She cut another slice of pie. I was about to say I was full, when she set it on my father's dish. He started eating without a word. Guess nonverbal communication came with years of a happy marriage.

"I've had a bad day at my job. Just wanted to spend some time with you and Daddy and Uncle Walt."

Uncle Walt sat fast asleep in his chair. His dentures,

now stained a light purple, slipped in and out of his mouth, mid-snore.

"Did you hear that, Michael? Her *job*. See what her job is doing to her?"

Daddy nodded, took a forkful of pie and put it in his mouth. Then he winked at me.

I smiled.

Mom stood to start cleaning up before Daddy had finished his second piece. "I have a bad feeling about this job. You came here to use my Renuzit because of your job. That is silly." She leaned over toward me. "You want Renuzit, Pauline? Move back here where we can keep an eye on you, and you can spray until the room fogs up."

Again not remembering my trip back from my parents' house, I set my camera on Miles's kitchen counter and glared at it. I'd fiercely wiped it over and over with a rag Jagger had given me from his SUV. The guy had everything you could need in that Suburban. The beeper/camera sat there staring back at me.

Needless to say, I had nothing viable on Tina.

"Damn it." I had no idea if dog pee would ruin the expensive piece of equipment. I thought of calling Goldie but realized he was on his date with Miles. Nothing short of a major world disaster could get me to interrupt those two. Besides, Goldie didn't strike me as an expert on dog pee, and I didn't think a dog peeing on your camera was a usual surveillance happening.

No, I looked from the camera to Spanky, who was jumping at my leg, and decided I'd just have to try it out to see if it still worked. Thing was, I hated to touch it. I'd touched a lot worse in my nursing career, but I drew the line at dog pee. I couldn't really wash the camera either, although I was tempted to shove it into the dishwasher. I could call the company I bought it from, but couldn't take being humiliated twice—no, three times in one day—even if it was only over the phone.

I was a professional. I had to do these things on my own. So, I decided to fix myself a cup, a big one, of green tea and try the camera out. I said a few mini novenas as the microwave heated my water. I really couldn't afford a new camera. It had to be all right. And did the warranty cover dog pee?

When the tea was done, I gave Spanky a rawhide bone to occupy him and sat at the counter staring. The camera needed more time to recover, I decided. So, I sipped and watched.

Then I took out the Windex and sprayed the camera, making sure not to soak it. I washed my hands, sat down and let it sit, airing out.

My stomach knotted when I thought of having to go to work as a nurse tomorrow. Ack. Why did I let Jagger talk me into that? Because, Pauline, the guy seems to be able to get you to do what he wants. True. There was something about Jagger that a woman just couldn't say no to, and I didn't mean in a sexual way.

Although Lord knows, if he asked, "no" wouldn't be the first word on my tongue.

Midway through my tea I thought about this past week. I left a good-paying job, got a no-paying job (so far), found great friends in Goldie and Adele, met two very opposite men—Nick and Jagger—and got my camera peed on.

I finished off my tea.

Okay. Moment of truth. I picked it up and sniffed. Smelled like metal and plastic and Windex. Good sign. Truthfully, I told myself, the dog hadn't really soaked the camera completely. Most of it had landed on the snow, since the window Jagger had formed wasn't all that large.

"Okay, Spanks, guess you're my guinea pig for tonight." He looked at me with his dark black eyes, which were far too big for his head but gave him a rather cute (in a pathetic sort of way), look. "Come, Spanky."

I aimed the beeper/camera at him. He gave me a lazy look and returned to gnawing on his rawhide. "Okay. You can stay there, but keep moving. Anything. Even your little jaw. Maybe an occasional ear twitch."

I moved away, moved closer, moved to the other side of the kitchen and tried out the zoom feature. After I'd taped what I figured was enough for a test, I pressed STOP. Then I got the wire from my bag to connect it to my VCR. Jagger's rag sat on the floor near my bag. I lifted it to throw it out, had second thoughts and decided if I washed it I could keep it as a memento.

What for?

I shoved it into the kitchen garbage can and told myself to forget Jagger, for now anyway. I walked to the TV and connected the camera.

The picture came out fuzzy, but there sat darling Spanky, chewing to his heart's content. I sunk into the chair next to the TV. "Thank you, Saint T."

With that dilemma solved, I went into the pantry and looked under C for canned cream of mushroom soup. There were six cans since it was my favorite. Miles hated to see me eating the soup and always insisted it was for cooking, not to be eaten plain. I loved it on string beans topped with French-fried onions too, but, still, it had been my favorite soup since being a kid, when we couldn't eat meat on Fridays.

I took a can and opened the doggie-treat container to get a biscuit for Spanky, who was fast on my heels. The little shadow didn't miss a thing. I used the electric can opener on the counter, wiped off the excess soup, since Miles was a stickler for neatness and I was inclined to agree with him on that issue, and poured the soup into a pan. As I turned on the faucet to add the required one can of water to my soup, the phone rang.

I set the can down and lifted the receiver. Before it was even at my ear, I heard, "Pepperoni all right on your pizza?"

For a fleeting second I thought someone had a wrong number, but when the voice registered in my brain, I said, "I'm a mushroom/sausage gal."

The phone disconnected and I looked at my can of soup. I opened the cabinet, took out a container and lid and poured the soup inside to store in the refrigerator until tomorrow. No need for cream of mushroom soup, when I'd soon be eating pizza with Jagger.

I'd set the kitchen table with the china, then reset it with paper and plastic. I didn't want to give Jagger the wrong impression. Within minutes of my resetting it again with china, the doorbell chimed.

Miles had it playing a Brahms lullaby this month. He liked variety. I hurried toward the door, then decided again that I didn't want to seem overeager. I'd already stepped in it when I'd asked if it was a *date* for coffee today. I stopped to check my hair in the brass mirror that hung above the couch, then went to the door.

Spanky beat me to it and was jumping wildly as if he could smell the pizza. I opened the door.

Jagger stood with pizza box in one hand, a bag in the other. He held out the bag. "Coors."

"We have beer, but thanks."

He hesitated then walked in with Spanky jumping at his calves.

"Get down, Spanks." He did and ran to the kitchen and came out with his prize rawhide in his mouth, which he dropped at Jagger's feet.

"Thanks, buddy, but I'll stick with pizza." He followed me into the kitchen and set the box on the counter. He looked around and focused on the table. "No need to go through any trouble. Paper dishes will do."

"I . . . er . . . Spanky wants you to throw that." Thank goodness the dog was at Jagger's feet waiting patiently while the half-gnawed rawhide bone sat near his boot. Without another word, I scooped up the dishes, put them in the cabinet and got the paper ones out.

Jagger threw the bone seventeen times.

Then he took the beer out, held one out to me, which I took, while he popped the top on his.

"Glass?"

"I'm fine." He brought the pizza box to the table, sat down and opened it.

Half pepperoni. Half mushroom and sausage. "You didn't have to go through any trouble—"

"I didn't make it." He took a piece and bit off the end.

I got myself a glass and piece of pizza, then sat down. Suddenly I realized I was alone in my home with Jagger. I took a bite and tried not to stare at him.

I had noticed he had on jeans and a dark sweater of sorts under the black aviator leather jacket he always wore. A pair of black leather gloves were sticking out of his jacket pocket.

He took a long swig of beer. "We?"

I looked at him. "Excuse me?"

"You said 'we.' 'We have beer.' Who else lives here?"

I hesitated, caught off guard. I too took a long sip of beer, to buy time. "I would have thought you'd already have that information."

I think his lips formed a slight grin. He knew more than he would admit, of that I was certain.

"Miles Scarpello, one of the nurses from Saint Greg's actually owns the condo. I rent from him."

"I see. That's how you got the job."

It wasn't a question so I didn't answer, though I wanted to shout that I could have gotten it on my own. But again, I was a lousy liar. I didn't even know what an insurance-fraud investigator was until Miles sent me to the interview.

Jagger finished his slice of pizza and took another. Before he bit into it, he said, "I wanted to go over a few things about tomorrow. Then I won't bother you."

Bother? Bother? Having him sitting here, allowing my eyes to feast on his perfect bod was not a bother. "Good," I managed to say although it shocked the hell out of me that a coherent thought could come out of my mouth. "I need to know why I'm actually taking this job."

He finished his beer, got up and took another one. He popped that one open and leaned against the counter. "Doctor Macaluso is committing fraud."

"I know. That's why I'm following Tina"—I sat up straighter and set my beer down—" 'Doctor'? You mean 'Missus' Macaluso." But I doubted Jagger ever said anything he didn't mean.

"Ever hear of a medical mill?"

"I've heard of puppy mills."

He shook his head, sat back down and chuckled. "A medical mill," he said, then took a sip of beer, "is when unethical medical practitioners, in this case the doctors, work in cahoots with scheming patients to create fictitious claims. They're accident-related injuries, often the soft tissue—"

"So more difficult to prove." Wow! Where'd that come from?

Jagger stared at me. I expected him to tell me to shut up since I didn't know what I was talking about.

Instead, he said, "That's why you're working there."

"My nursing background."

He barely nodded but it was the same as if he did. "The claims are often fraudulent disability, Workers' Comp or personal-injury claims."

Fascinated, I set down my beer. "I can't believe people would do things like that."

"Then you're in the wrong business, Sherlock."

My mind got hung up on "Sherlock." Although my inner self tried to tell me Jagger was being facetious, I chose to think it endearing. "I know people commit fraud. It's just that—"

"You'd never do anything against the law."

"I . . . No. I wouldn't. That's not such a bad thing. You know?" The nerve!

He grinned. "You need to see as many patients as you can,

evaluate their injuries and see if their charts reflect their care and actual diagnosis and, most important, their treatment."

"Yikes. Anything else?"

"Yeah." He leaned over and touched my hand. "Be careful."

Twelve

With my sudden onset muteness, I could only stare at Jagger. After what seemed like hours and his possibly thinking that I, in fact, really *did* do drugs, I managed to recover. "By 'be careful' do you mean . . . don't let them see me spying on them?"

"That too."

"Too?" I swallowed. "Then you mean my life could be in danger?"

He let go of my hand, but it felt as if he was still touching me. That didn't surprise me. Being touched by Jagger was a mind-altering experience. Phantom touches were becoming old hat.

He ran his hand through his hair. "I wouldn't ask you to risk your life for a case, Pauline."

"Oh. Wow. Good." My underarms were soaked. Partly from fear of the job, partly from him being here. Forget the touching incident. With shaky hands I took my beer.

Jagger leaned over. "I said I wouldn't put you in any danger. I just need a little help."

Help? I'm helping Jagger? My hands calmed—he didn't touch me again. I waited, took a deep cleansing breath and exhaled, cleaning out the cobwebs this guy seemed to form in my brain.

He grinned.

"Okay. I'll bite. You, Jagger with no other name knows it all. Why would you need my help?"

He laughed. "If I knew everything, would I need to send you in undercover?"

"Oh. Yeah."

"Look. You, a nurse turned investigator, fell into my lap. . . ."

I knew he was talking again 'cause I saw his lips moving. But I was hung up on the "falling into his lap" part. Suddenly I saw myself falling from the ceiling into his lap. Actually saw it! Like how Ally McBeal used to have those visions on the old show with the dancing baby and all.

Suddenly I felt something.

"What?" I yelled.

I looked up to see Jagger touching my hand and staring at me. "You don't use? Do you?"

That's the second time someone had asked me that this week!

"No. I'm a nurse. I wouldn't abuse drugs."

"Sherlock, nurses have the perfect opportunity to get drugs."

"I wouldn't. My mind drifted off because . . . I'm tired. Not using."

He got up and started to collect the things from the table. "I won't keep you then."

"Wait!" Yikes. I calmed my hysterical voice. "No need to rush off. You never told me why you suspect that practice."

He held the dirty dishes for a second and looked around.

"Under the counter."

He opened it and dropped them into the trashcan. "One of the best sources for reporting fraud is a disgruntled employee."

"Who? Who is the disgruntled—"

"The less you know, the safer . . . better, it is. Disgruntled employees are our best sources. They sing like canaries."

"I see," I said, but wasn't sure if I really did. Who would squeal on their employer? Actually, I guess I would if I found out they were breaking the law. That "safer . . . better" thing was a bit disconcerting.

"You look for what seems out of the ordinary tomorrow, then we'll talk."

"Gotcha. Anything out of the ordinary. But nurses don't really do the billing—"

He bent his head and lifted his eyes toward me. Damn. I felt naked again. I lifted the napkin from my lap and stupidly held it in front of me, pretending to wipe my lips.

"Come on, Pauline. I've seen you in action. I'm guessing you can be resourceful when push comes to shove."

"Resourceful. Oh. Yeah. I'll see what I can do."

"Don't tell anyone that you are doing this. Especially anyone in that practice." He got up. Shrugged into his jacket, took his gloves out of his pocket and put them on. "Anyone, Pauline. Anywhere."

I followed him to the front door.

He stopped and turned. "No one. That means even Doctor Vance Taylor."

I wished Adele was here to push my jaw back up from my chest. "Vance? How?" I shut my mouth and watched him walk down the stairs into the cold, now dark, night. "Jagger?"

He stopped but didn't turn around.

Fine by me. I could stare at a butt like that for quite a while. But it didn't take too long before I asked, "Who the heck *are* you?" and he merely said, "Jagger."

When he drove out of the parking lot, I collapsed against the door frame. He had to be FBI. Now there was no doubt in my mind.

Well, I said to myself, he did say he would help out with my case if I helped him. And if anyone could get my money for me faster, I was all for it. I knew Goldie could, but since he was so busy himself, I decided I'd go with Jagger's offer.

Yet I wondered what the heck I was getting myself into. I wanted to ask Goldie, but Jagger had said not to tell anyone.

And he knew about Vance and me!

I decided I needed to get to bed early. If I waited until Miles came home—and I was dying to know how that date turned out—I'd more than likely be tempted to tell him in great detail about my night.

But I'd promised.

And with my Catholic-school-induced conscience—compliments of the nuns, no less—I was also true to my word.

I thought being locked in the elevator was claustrophobic. But this situation I'd gotten myself into with Jagger had me sweating, palpitating and feeling as if I was back in that elevator again—except that now it was half the size.

"Linda Stark please," I said to the receptionist as I reported for duty. It was a killer to don my nurse's clothes this morning, but I had to look the part. I'd chosen my comfortable white clogs and a blue-and-green striped top with blue scrub pants. As usual, I pulled my hair up, very nurse-like.

The receptionist, Trudy Blackwell, who apparently had never gotten out of her baby-fat stage from her youth and was wearing a paisley green smock, showed me to Linda's office.

When she knocked and opened the door, Linda got up. Trudy introduced me.

"Thanks, Trudy," Linda said, taking a stack of files from one pile on her desk and putting them in the OUT tray. Linda moved with great efficiency. Her short black cropped hair and fitted black suit gave her an air of authority. Her black Woody Allen–style glasses, however, gave me the creeps. She showed me around, ending up at the nurses' station, and introduced me to the other nurse who was working that day.

Eddy Roden, no less.

Great. Now I would have to deal with him bugging me along with trying to do my job for Jagger.

"Come on, Pauline. I'll show you where the coffee is," Eddy said. "That's the most important thing in the office."

Linda laughed as she walked away, but I got the impression that she didn't think Eddy was really funny. *Join the club*, I thought. Then again, no telling what Eddy really had in mind. After we got our coffee, he showed me what to do, and I came up with the notion that Eddy was not a happy camper.

A disgruntled employee.

And, he'd been talking to Jagger in the cafeteria the other day. I wanted to ask Eddy about it, but remembered my promise. It made sense, though, that if I talked to anyone here, the entire case could be ruined. Even Fabio's case on Tina would be, too. She'd find out who I was and put two and two together. Nope. I couldn't discuss fraud with Eddy.

We took our coffee out to the nurses' station and he showed me how the files were arranged for the patients who were in the waiting room. I set my mug down and took the first file.

Sixty-three-year-old male. Mr. Johnson Suskowski. Broken femur. I guessed no one could fake a broken bone, so I marked him off my mental list of suspects in case any patients were involved in fraud too. The main problem with Mr. Suskowski was that his doctor was Vance.

And I hadn't had a chance to call him and give him the good news that I'd be working here.

Okay, truth be told, I'd been putting that tidbit off, since I had no earthly idea of what reason I'd give him for being here. The saving grace I counted on was that Vance would be too busy seeing patients to run me through a mill of questions.

"Mr. Suskowski?" I called out to the full waiting room.

An elderly man, one of three with casts on their legs, got up and hobbled toward me. He came up to my shoulders and had the most adorable smile. He seemed to have a bit of trouble dealing with the crutches, so I stepped closer to him.

"Let me help you with those, sir. You need a wheelchair?"

"No, sweetie. I'm fine." He grunted and hobbled forward. The cast looked as if it weighed more than Mr. Suskowski, even though it was the lightweight material.

"All right," I said, thinking he wanted to retain his independence much as my Uncle Walt, who wouldn't even let me hold his elbow to walk down a set of stairs. And Uncle Walt tended toward wobbly nowadays. "Make sure you don't rest the tops of the crutches under your arms. It could damage the nerves."

He grinned. "They already told me that a long time ago. Cast is due off soon."

Once Mr. Suskowski was seated in an exam room, he told me that he'd broken his leg playing golf, when he went to fish his ball out of the brook and got his foot caught on a rock. I stuck his chart in the holder on the outside of the door and flipped the red marker over to signal the doctor that a patient was waiting inside. I told Mr. Suskowski that it would be a few minutes and turned to go get the next patient—and ran smack-dab, as they say, into Vance.

"Pauline? Again? What are you doing here?"

"Oh, well. Not much time to talk. Mr. Suskowski is waiting for you—"

He took my arm. "You are acting weird. Weirder than usual."

Coming from Vance, that wasn't a joke. If he accused me of 'using,' *he'd* end up with a broken something. "I'm filling in for Tina Macaluso."

"But what about your being burned out from nursing?"

He looked genuinely concerned, and I didn't want to make him feel any worse, so I said, "We went to school together," as if that would explain anything.

What it did do was confuse Vance enough for him to merely shake his head, reach up to get Mr. Suskowski's chart and say, "I'm too busy for this."

I smiled to myself. "Call me on Friday, and we'll make plans."

After shuffling about fifteen patients in and out over the course of the morning, my stomach was starting to growl. I'd managed to grab a fast cup of coffee but really wanted something substantial and warm. Eddy said the office closed from noon to one, so then I could go out and get lunch. Good thing he didn't ask to join me. I looked at my watch. Eleven forty-seven. I had thirteen minutes to find out whatever I could for Jagger.

Otherwise I'd be working here longer.

The annoying part was that the nursing routine had come flooding back to me without a thought. Still, I told myself, it wasn't what I wanted in my life right now. Being here was okay since there were no babies pooping, no teens shouting, no one vomiting on my shoes. And no staff for me to fire.

But as unglamorous as this job was, investigating was a hundred percent glamorous as far as I was concerned. Besides, it was a hell of a lot more exciting than ushering patients in and out of examination rooms.

Eddy passed by with a cup of coffee. The coffee area, which was right by Linda's glass-walled office, was used as a lounge. I smiled to myself over Jagger's calling me "Sherlock." He'd said I was resourceful, and even if he'd meant it sarcastically, I was going to think I was resourceful enough to find something out today.

"Eddy, any coffee left?"

He paused and took a sip, then held out his cup.

"Not from yours." *You jerk.*

He laughed. "In Linda's office. You could scrape out the bottom of the pot."

"Thanks." I hurried off before he mentioned lunch. I looked at my watch. Eleven minutes to find out what I could.

Linda sat at her desk with her Woody Allen black-framed glasses perched on her nose. When I stuck my head in the open door, she shoved a few files into the OUT tray again. I thought she really was speedy at getting done whatever it was she did. She looked up.

"No more patients until after lunch. Mind if I get some coffee?"

She didn't budge. "Help yourself."

I tried to look at her desk as I passed by the transparent partition, but she glared at me with every step. So, I took my coffee and planted myself in the chair opposite her desk. She gave me an odd look.

"It's been fun working here. I'm glad Tina mentioned it to me." Ha! I headed off any thoughts she might have of asking me to leave by reminding her that her boss's wife had told me to work here.

"Glad it's working out."

"Yeah. Bummer how those agencies don't have enough temps to help you." Comfortable that I'd cemented my relationship with her, I took a sip of coffee. Yuck! It really had come from the bottom of the pot. Jagger owed me. And I'd tell him so.

Linda looked back at her desk. "Excuse me."

"Pretend I'm not here."

She turned around, typed something on her keyboard at her computer station, then clicked the PRINT icon on her monitor and got up. When the printer spit out what she wanted, she took it, opened her desk drawer and removed her purse and walked to the door. "See you after lunch."

I looked at my watch. Three minutes, but I got up and took my cup to the sink and washed it out very slowly. I walked back to her desk and with one finger, gingerly opened the top file in the OUT tray.

Mr. Suskowski. Good. At least I knew his case.

The top of the file looked okay. It was my set of notes, followed by Vance's assessment of Mr. Suskowski's fracture. Vance had ordered an X-ray, which I'd made sure was done, although not by me, since I had no inkling of how to work the damn machine. Then I looked on the next page.

A referral sheet for an MRI.

For a second I worried there was really something wrong

with the nice man. But then I reread Vance's notes.

His notes contained no order whatsoever for an MRI.

I knew tests like that cost hundreds of dollars, if not more. And why would one be needed for a simple fracture?

Maybe someone had made a mistake in filling out the referral sheet?

Or could something really be wrong with Mr. Suskowski?

Feeling badly for a nice man who could be in ill health, I let go of the file and looked at my watch. Three minutes past twelve.

I hurried to the staff exit to find the entire suite empty. I reached for the doorknob—it didn't budge.

Shoot!

I pulled the stuck door again. Nothing.

Not being able to get out, I started to feel a bit claustrophobic. Maybe I could call maintenance, but I'd feel stupid telling them what happened. For a few seconds, I shut my eyes. "Oh, Saint T? If you're not too busy—"

"Stuck in?"

My eyes flew open, ready to see a vision of Saint Theresa holding a bouquet of roses in front of me. But it was Trudy Blackwell standing there. Phew. As much as I believe in my faith, I really wasn't ready for any saintly visions. "Hi. I was finishing my coffee and before I knew it, everyone was gone."

She laughed. "Rats running from a sunken ship. You have to know this door." She put her weight into the door. A jiggle, a shove and it opened.

Rats? Hmm. Maybe Trudy was the disgruntled employee? She might know more about billing fraud than Eddy. I thanked her and hurried out, deciding to take the stairs to the cafeteria.

The line was long today since it was after noon. I took a tray and waited my turn, reading the menu. When I had my hot dog with mustard, relish and very little onions since I didn't want to make the patients ill from my breath, I took a container of French fries and a bottle of Coke to wash down all the fat and calories.

For some reason, my new life had me eating more crap than I ever had.

I paid and scanned the room, not wanting to sit with either Eddy or Vance. Good. Neither was in sight. I walked to a table almost hidden in the back but near a window and sat down. I lifted my hot dog and put my lips over the end.

"This seat taken, ma'am?"

Startled, I bit down so hard that mustard, relish and onions shot out, landing on my scrub shirt.

Jagger's voice.

I looked up at a man about Jagger's height, wearing an expensive navy pin-striped suit with red power tie and white shirt. Had to be a doctor or some businessman. His hair was combed back and tortoise-framed glasses hid his eyes, and he had a dark black mustache over his lips.

Mentally shaking my head over hearing Jagger's voice when he wasn't even there, I said, "Er . . . no. Have a seat."

I noticed he didn't have a tray and thought it odd, so I'd eat and leave. He did, however, have a cup of coffee in his hand so he had a purpose here. Besides, I was perfectly safe in the public cafeteria.

He shoved the chair back with his foot and sat down. Man, *that* took away from his *GQ* business persona. While I pondered that move, I thought it was even more odd when he leaned in so close, and I pushed back.

"So, what'd you find out?"

I dropped my hot dog, and it landed *splat* on my tray, sending sugary Coke all over my greasy fries. They were history. Did this guy suspect *me* of snooping? I tried to think of what to say to act as if I was innocent, but before I could make up a lie, which was so hard for me to do, he touched my hand.

Jagger!

No one else's touch could make me feel as if a lit match were being held near my skin. I tried to look past the glasses and said, "Ja—"

"Are you sure you don't *use*?"

I pulled my hand away. "You ruined my lunch." I looked at my tray. "Look at my hot dog. It has Coke on the bun. And the fries are inedible."

He looked at me as if I were nuts.

And, truthfully, I sounded it.

"I'll get you another fucking hot dog, Pauline. You shouldn't eat that shit anyway, but that's your problem. Did you notice anything out of the ordinary?"

Still finding it difficult to get past the idea that this was Jagger, I clucked my tongue at him. "No. Yes. No. And *you* ate a donut yesterday."

He shook his head.

"Look, this is all new to me, this fraud stuff. Give me a break."

He took a sip of his coffee. "Right. I'm not known for my patience though." Then, he got up and walked away!

Great. Now I was stuck working here, and he wouldn't help me with Tina. Great. Great. Great. I lifted my soggy hot dog, took it out of the bun and stared at it for a good long while. Just as I put the bunless dog in my mouth, Jagger came around the corner with a tray. He set it down in front of me.

"Don't eat that thing."

On the tray sat new fries, and a fresh hot dog with mustard, relish and onions—very few onions. My mouth dropped open yet again in the company of Jagger, but this time it was because I marveled that he had noticed all that in the short time he'd sat here.

Wow. Would I ever be that perceptive? I guessed I needed that skill in this job, and told myself, while I took the new hot dog and bit into it, that I was no slouch in the perception department. Again, that came from being a nurse. Guess Fabio knew what he was doing when he hired me.

Jagger sat down. I still had to fight the urge to stare at his incredible disguise, although his voice was a dead giveaway. It was him, all right.

"You said no, then yes, then no again when I asked you if you'd seen anything. Which is it?"

I chewed faster and swallowed. "I only have five minutes left. I thought I found an MRI that was ordered, but it wasn't, but it was."

Jagger slapped himself in the head.

"Several of the docs seem suspicious to me. Tina's husband is a real jerk. Wears Armani under his lab coat. There's a Doctor Levy who is rumored to spend big bucks. A female doctor, Charlene something, looks the cleanest. Single working mom. Oh, wait. I do have something else."

He sat like a statue.

"I know, okay, I *think* I know. Well, truthfully, I'm more than likely guessing—"

He grabbed my arm. Not that it hurt, but more surprised me. "*What* do you know?"

"Either Eddy Roden or the secretary, Trudy Blackwell, is the disgruntled employee. I'm going with Trudy 'cause she just doesn't dress professionally. But, wait. Eddy has a chip on his shoulder—"

"Christ," he muttered.

"What?"

"Look, Sherlock, I *know* who the squealer is. How the hell do you think I'd know to . . . look into this practice?"

Duh. Now I slapped myself in the head. "Oh, right. So which one is it?"

He didn't move. I guessed he was contemplating whether to tell me or not. I was also guessing he'd go with not.

But he looked at me and said, "Maybe you need to know to be on the lookout." He paused, drank. "Roden."

My stomach knotted. Somehow knowing made me a bit uncomfortable. Cause if Eddy could find out that something un-kosher was going on in the office, could he then find out that I was planted there to spy too?

I took the last bite of my hot dog, forced myself to swallow, ran the napkin across my lips and polished off my

Coke. Damn, but an unhealthy meal tasted good. I got up. "I have to get back—"

"Pauline?"

I swung around to see, of all people, Nick standing next to me. He looked at Jagger and nodded.

Did he recognize him?

Seemed so, since Nick more than likely expected Jagger to be in disguise by the look he gave him. I smiled. "Hi, Nick. Well, I have to get back to work."

"You're working here?" He looked me over. "As a *nurse*?"

"Well, I—"

Jagger jumped up.

I looked at him and remembered my promise. "I'm filling in for a friend, an old schoolmate. Seems I can't get away from the nursing field." I laughed.

Jagger and Nick stared at me. Okay, so I ramble when nervous. I started to move, then paused since I couldn't get past Jagger, and he wasn't being gentlemanly enough to step aside.

"So, what are *you* doing here?" Nick asked Jagger.

Jagger took my arm. "Came here for lunch."

It seemed as if Nick wasn't buying that. Who would, with Jagger dressed up like Donald Trump?

Nick leaned against a chair. It had to be a natural move, but it seemed as if he'd set up a barricade that we couldn't get through without making a scene.

Jagger's grasp tightened.

I bit back an "ouch."

Nick looked from me to Jagger. "Lunch? Huh? This isn't exactly a five-star restaurant."

Jagger started to pull me toward Nick.

Nick did step aside, and while I let out a sigh of relief that we didn't collide and cause a scene, over his shoulder Jagger said, "Came to have lunch with Pauline."

Nick just wouldn't let up. He followed behind us. "Business?"

Jagger stopped and turned around. I had to do the same in the small space between two tables full of staff.

He lifted off his glasses in a gesture that I guessed was so Nick could see his eyes. Why? I had no idea, since no one could read Jagger's eyes. I started to turn to get back to work since I was already five minutes late and had to walk down the stairs.

Jagger pulled me to his chest and said, "Pleasure."

"You two are *dating*?"

Jagger's hold tightened. Good thing, since my legs turned to Jell-O when he said, "You've always been perceptive, Nicky."

Thirteen

I could only stare, again with that open-mouth thing, while Jagger pulled me through the cafeteria to the elevator. One thing I did manage was, "Oh, no. I'm not getting on that thing with you."

"I won't stop it this time." He talked as if nothing had happened back there, and worse yet, he actually thought I'd believe him about the elevator.

He'd told Nick we were dating!

I summoned all my mental faculties while we stood in front of the elevator. Hordes of staff passed by, some staring, some with raised eyebrows. "Dating? Dating?" Okay, so I *wasn't* using all the mental faculties I had, but it was what I could come up with right then.

He looked at his watch. "We'll talk later. You're eleven minutes late—"

"Oh shit!" I pushed past him to the stairs and ran, cursing my clogs on every one of the steps, which I nearly fell and broke my neck on. Once at the office, I stopped long enough to compose myself, less than a second, and hurried in. I went to the nurses' station and grabbed a chart.

"Your pay is going to be docked for being late," Linda said.

"Oh, I . . . no problem."

"I hope this isn't going to be a habit. We have to get patients in and out quickly. Time is money."

I hope I'm not going to be here much longer. "I know. I met a friend. . . . Well, he just wasn't himself. I had to stay a bit longer than I wanted to." Good one, Pauline! Jagger sure didn't look like himself and had to be way out of his mind to say they were dating. Not that that wasn't a good cover to fool Nick. It was, and probably the only one that would work.

But dating Jagger?

I sighed.

Linda looked at me. "You all right?"

"I'm fine, and I've never used drugs in my life." With that I walked away.

The rest of the afternoon progressed without incident. By day's end, I had seen over forty patients and didn't notice anything suspicious about them. When the clock said it was four, I grabbed my purse and headed for the door.

God, I could only hope I wouldn't have to be here any longer than this one week.

I had just dropped onto the couch with Spanky on my lap when Miles came down the stairs.

"Scrubs? What the hell are you doing dressed like that?"

Oh shit. "Once again couldn't say no to a friend."

"What about your new job?"

"Funny thing is, I can do both." Not in this state of exhaustion though. I hadn't done anything to catch Tina today. Depressed at that thought, I sighed.

"Tea?"

"Coors."

I kinda dozed off until I heard Miles shuffle out and back then set a nice cold bottle of Coors on the coffee table. He knew I didn't like a glass when the beer came in a bottle. Cans I didn't do. It tasted better from a bottle. I actually liked when it foamed at the top. I pushed forward and

Spanky jumped down and scurried off to the kitchen, where I knew Miles had left a treat in his bowl.

I looked at Miles. There was a smile on his face even through neither of us had spoken. I took a long sip of beer—then promptly swallowed. "Oh damn! I forgot. So, how was it?"

The smile turned into a grin.

"That good?"

Miles proceeded to tell me about his night with Goldie, the fabulous food, the wine, the company and how it seemed as if they'd never parted.

"I'm so glad."

"Everyone should have someone like this, Pauline. Everyone."

"By that I'm guessing you mean me."

He nodded.

Oh, no! Despite the recesses of my brain being bogged down in exhaustion, I realized I *did* have someone. I wasn't sure what Jagger had in mind about dating, or even if the subject would ever come up again, but maybe I was supposed to act as though I had a significant other. Worst of all, I didn't know whether to tell Miles and Goldie, my dear friends.

As I contemplated that problem and drained my bottle of Coors, the doorbell rang. I looked at Miles. "I'm guessing that may be your beau."

Miles always looked so adorable when he smiled like that. He got up and went to open the door.

I leaned back, shoved off my clogs and shut my eyes. I think I snored.

"I'm guessing this one is for you, Pauline."

I opened one eye . . . and jumped up. God, I hoped Jagger hadn't heard me snore!

He stood there, back to his normal attire of jeans and black aviator jacket. No glasses. No mustache.

I liked this version better.

He held his hand out to Miles. "Jagger."

Miles introduced himself, and I know he was dying to ask who the hell Jagger was and why he was there.

I came to the door. "Well, good. The introductions are out of the way." I looked at Jagger as if to ask what the heck he was doing here. He stood there as if it were perfectly normal, and clearly understood, why he had invaded my home.

"Come in," Miles finally said.

Jagger walked in, sat himself on the couch and looked at me. "Wasn't sure what you wanted to do for dinner tonight."

If I had a ruler, I'd measure Miles's and my jaw to see whose had dropped further. I think I'd win hands down 'cause I could swear I felt my bottom lip hit my breasts, and his only reached his clavicle.

Jagger ignored us and went on. "I'm in the mood for Mexican, but wouldn't mind some home-cooked tonight either."

Miles mumbled, "Pauline doesn't know how to boil water."

Jagger smiled. "Of course not. I was thinking Mrs. Sokol's cooking."

I touched Miles on the arm. "What's today?"

"Wednesday."

"Fish," I mumbled.

Jagger stood. "Fish sounds great. I'll get myself a beer while you go change. Nice to meet you, Miles." With that he headed into the kitchen.

Miles looked at me. "I'm dating him," I said, then shot up the stairs like a rocket.

Once in the safety of my room, I collapsed on my bed and wondered what I'd gotten myself into—and was it really all that bad?

My mother never refused a request for dinner. Any of us kids could pop in unexpectedly, and she'd feed us. Actually, I think she looked forward to it.

Once again I sat across from Jagger, this time in the kitchen, thank God,'cause my family had already started to eat there when we popped in uninvited. Through frequent apologies from my mother and two offers to move to the dining room, we actually got served.

To his credit, once out the door of the condo, Jagger had said he didn't intend to intrude on my parents again, and we could go eat Mexican. I wasn't sure who'd pay and with my cash flow in a drought and expecting to go Dutch treat, I insisted on my parents' house, knowing there'd be enough food to feed a medium-size third-world country—and all for free.

Besides, my mother thrived on feeding others.

"So, Mister Jagger, I'm so glad to see you again," my mother said, ladling beets onto his dish.

I think he groaned about the beets (or maybe the "Mister" part) but gave her a nice smile and said, "It's good to be here, although I hate to just drop in and eat all your wonderful food. My mouth started to water when Pauline suggested we come here."

Mental note to myself. Jagger is a smooth liar. Very smooth.

He was perceptive too. He must have noticed on the last visit that the way to my mother's heart was through culinary compliments.

Daddy nodded a few times between forkfuls of scrod, oven-baked potatoes, and beets.

"How many miles to the gallon you get on the Suburban, son?" Uncle Walt asked.

I looked over to see he had his dentures in his hand and was wiping them with a napkin. Horrified, I let my gaze wander toward Jagger without turning my head.

He smiled at toothless Uncle Walt and said, "You know, sir, I've never calculated that. But she runs smooth."

Uncle Walt popped his teeth back in. I made another mental note to put dental floss in his Christmas stocking.

Ack. Christmas in this house. Now I loved the tradition of my family all being together, but this year Jagger would be here. And all my brothers, sisters and their spouses would think Jagger and I were an item.

The thought made me drop my fork.

"Pauline, please don't chip the china," my mother said.

It wasn't really china, but dishes she'd gotten at the Stop and Buy. One place setting every week if you spent over fifty bucks. I did like them, though, since they were a Currier and Ives picture of a snow-laden farm in New England, even if it took five months to get an entire set.

The meal progressed with small talk until Mom got up to clean. Jagger jumped up too, which made me obliged to follow. My mother loved waiting on us, but I couldn't not help her. It'd make me look lazy.

In the kitchen she said, "Pauline, get out the good ice-cream dishes."

Not wanting to argue that she had a pie, an apple one, in her hand, I did as told. Jagger leaned against the wall and watched. I wondered if he even had a mother—ever. Then I wondered if, ack, the damn sexy Jagger had Stella Sokol flustered. You don't want to think of a guy affecting your mother that way. Trust me.

"Let me get that, Missus Sokol," he said as Mom tried to balance the pie and coffeepot.

To my amazement, she gave the pot up freely. My mother never let anyone help serve. If she did, she couldn't brag about the work she did. Not really brag, because it was true, but she had such pride in her housekeeping abilities and cooking.

When we had the kitchen cleaned—and the dining room too, since Mother insisted we sit in there for dessert—Jagger and I headed to the door.

He looked at Uncle Walt, who was already in the recliner with his eyes shutting and said, "Next time I'll take you for a ride around the block, sir."

Uncle Walt's eyes flew open. "I'll hold you to it, son. I'll hold you to it."

Jagger thanked my parents and soon we were in his Suburban, driving south. The condo was east. I'd eaten far too much, which was nothing new when I went to my parents' house, so I leaned back and decided I didn't have the energy to talk.

I heard a pig! My eyes flew open.

When I realized I was in Jagger's SUV and we were stopped, I knew it couldn't have been a barnyard animal that had made that godawful sound. I must have dreamt it, I thought, until I saw Jagger staring at me.

"A good ENT can yank out your adenoids."

That pig sound had been me.

Despite the air outside being a chilly thirty degrees, my face burned. Jagger didn't, however, continue to stare. Thank goodness for small miracles. I made a mental note to have my adenoids checked when my health insurance policy kicked in and looked out the window. "What are we doing here?"

"You have a job to do, don't you?"

Tina Macaluso. I'd been so exhausted from my nursing job today, I'd plumb forgot. Funny how one's mind worked once you hit thirty-four. "I forgot my beeper/camera."

Silence.

I turned to look at Jagger, who scowled back at me with a forehead more wrinkled than the skin on Uncle Walt's neck.

"Hey, things happen," I said in my own defense.

"If you want to make it in this business, Sherlock, you need to be prepared at all times. What if Tina had come into the office today and lifted a box or something else heavy?"

"I . . . you're right." I sighed. "Guess you wasted a trip out here."

He leaned over the seat.

Very close to my left shoulder.

So close, oh . . . my . . . God, that I could inhale his scent of man. Not being able to identify any commercial cologne, I named it "scent of man" 'cause he sure as hell smelled sexy and manly. Not in an Irish Spring soap-type way either.

Oh, no. More a way that made me swallow so hard I know he had to hear.

He pulled out an eyeglass case.

I cursed the pheromones.

"What? We're going to do some reading?" I chuckled.

Jagger gave me a look that said he thought I was certifiable. He opened the case. "Put these on." He held them out toward me.

I waited, not sure what to say. "Sunglasses. What? Is there a full moon or something?"

"Something, Sherlock." He pointed to one corner of the frames. I couldn't help notice him shake his head. He said, "There's a video camera in here."

"No shit!"

He shook his head yet again.

"Didn't your mother ever tell you if you keep doing that your head will roll off your shoulders?"

"I thought you were a professional."

I gingerly took the glasses he held toward me. "I'm working on it."

"Then you can learn from the best."

"Goldie?"

He curled his lip at me.

"You mean . . . Nick." I held the glasses, still marveling that a camera could fit in the frames. "Oh. Sorry."

A low growl came from Jagger's side of the car.

"What's with you two anyway?" I put the glasses to my face and looked in the mirror. "Oh my gosh, it doesn't look dark through these." I lifted them up, looked from under, then put them back on. I repeated it about seven times.

"The past is past. And, Sherlock, stop playing with those. They run about five grand."

My hands flew to my face to yank them off, but before I could touch them, Jagger grabbed me. "That's the best way to break them."

"Sorry." I relaxed my hands, but he still held on. I guess I'll always wonder, but it sure as heck seemed that he paused—while still holding me.

Within seconds, though, he'd let go and moved back to his

side of the car. I sighed as quietly as humanly possible, but he seemed to notice and sat mannequin still.

"We'll head through the woods to the back of the house."

I waited until Jagger got out, but he didn't come around to my side of the car. What was I thinking? I hurried out and made sure the door was locked since I was leaving my purse in the car. I figured he'd lock it with his key system since he more than likely had equipment in there that was worth a heck of a lot more than my purse with everything in it. Including my paltry credit-card limits.

We walked by the empty lots into the snow-covered woods. "How do you know she's at this house? And why does she have two houses? Or does she? Is this hers?" I sighed. "My feet are cold. I should have worn boots. You should have told me to wear boots. My little pinky toes are especially—"

He stopped, turned around and looked at me. "Jesus, Sherlock."

That was that. Nothing more. I guess Jagger had put me in my place for asking stupid questions tonight. Well, it seemed any question I asked him was stupid, in his opinion. So, being the inquisitive person that I am, I asked, "Whom exactly do you work for? Who—"

This time he stopped, turned, looked and turned back.

Then he merely walked away.

Left me standing in mid-word, and calf-deep in snow.

Fourteen

Right then, mid-word and calf-deep in snow, I figured I'd never really know who Jagger was and whom he worked for.

At least I was positive that he'd never tell me.

But he'd held up his end of the bargain by taking me here tonight, and lending me his . . . ack . . . expensive glasses to do my job. So, I wouldn't give FBI versus PI versus insurance-fraud investigator versus who-the-hell-knew a second thought.

I decided if I kept standing there watching him walk away, either my feet would freeze in the ground or I'd lose him in the woods. I could only see a faint light in the direction of Tina's house. With the glasses on, I was having some difficulty seeing. Not that they made it dark, but more that I plain wasn't used to wearing glasses.

And I could swear Jagger's scent clung to the glasses.

Foolish thought, Pauline, I told myself. Scents probably don't stick to plastic no matter how expensive it is. I hurried from tree to tree, once nearly falling when my right foot stepped into a hole covered by the snow. I yanked it out, hoping it wasn't some hibernating animal's hole and that I'd disturbed their sleep. And that they had teeth.

Jagger leaned against a tree near the back of Tina's house. Now I could see lights burning in most of the rooms. I was certain Tina didn't have any children, since she more than likely would have made a point to tell—no, brag—to me about the little darlings. So, why would two people need so many lights on at the same time? They couldn't be using all those rooms at once.

Maybe others didn't think of wasting electricity like my mother had drummed into my siblings' heads and mine. Of course, I voluntarily pinched my electrical pennies nowadays since leaving my nursing job.

"Do you see anyone?" I asked.

Jagger turned to me. "Keep it down. Sound travels better on these cold clear nights. And no."

He was right. I had to start thinking before acting in this job. Good thing I hadn't come out alone.

Suddenly I noticed Jagger tense. I should have been watching Tina's house, but at the moment I'd been watching him instead. I followed his sight line to the back door which started to open. Moving closer to Jagger, I caught my half-frozen left foot on a low-lying branch and landed *smack* against his side.

The man had quick reflexes.

He grabbed me before I did a belly flop in the snow and, God forbid, smashed his glasses. I pulled away and wiped the snow from my knee, which had helped save me too. "Thanks."

Again that head shaking.

I made a mental note, the list was getting quite long, to buy a bottle of Tylenol for Jagger. He had to be developing a whopper of a headache from all that shaking.

"When you need to start filming, press this." He gently took my finger, pulled off my glove and touched it to the part of the eyeglass frames that held the RECORD button. It was so tiny I wondered if I could find it on my own. Or maybe I just wanted an excuse for Jagger to touch my glove-less hand.

Stop that, Pauline, I ordered.

"Look," he whispered.

I stopped staring at him, trying with all my faculties to forget how much sexier his voice sounded in a whisper and thinking I wouldn't mind him whispering in my ear and not about Tina, and turned my attention to her backyard.

She'd come outside, with Doc Macaluso following behind. Darn. If anything needed to be lifted, he'd more than likely do it. But as they walked to the woodpile, Tina opened a canvas bag-like item that I knew was designed to hold logs. The good doc looked around a few times, then nodded toward her.

"You getting this?" Jagger asked in that low, sexy voice.

Oops. I'd forgotten to turn on the camera. I yanked my glove off with my teeth and pressed the button before Jagger turned around. "Of course I am getting it." Now, anyway.

The doc stood guard. He kept looking around like some kind of sentry. Tina was turned toward him as if waiting for a signal.

Good. Made them look guilty as hell.

Very nonchalantly she proceeded to fill the bag with wood. It had to be heavy by the number of logs in it, but Tina held it as if it were filled with feathers. As an added bonus, she bent over and picked up three logs one right after the other. "Yes," I murmured, thinking Donnie was a wimp.

Jagger didn't move, but even with the moon out, I thought maybe I saw him shake his head again.

Tina and the doc went back inside. After a few minutes, gray smoke begun to billow out of their chimney.

"Looks like they got enough to last the night." Jagger turned and started to walk back toward his SUV. After a few steps, he stopped and looked at me. "Glasses." He held out his hand.

I took them off and wondered how I was going to get the video I'd just taken with his camera.

'Cause I'd forgotten to shut it off and just filmed several seconds of Jagger's butt.

* * *

"Sounds as if you had a good time with Miles," I said to Goldie as I walked into his office with my empty mug. I decided I needed to see Goldie each morning before heading off to my nursing job and have his chicory coffee. I'd brought my own mug from home to use at the office and felt as if I really belonged when I got to leave it here. It was the one with the joke about how many Polacks does it take to screw in a lightbulb that Miles had given me for Christmas several years ago. Goldie had cleaned a part of his office out for me to use. He even gave me tips on how to apply the samples of makeup he gave me too.

Most mornings I looked pretty damn good by the time I left.

He sat at the desk, his feet, wearing black leather pumps, resting on the top. Today his slacks were more like trousers, black with a shiny silver belt buckle of a peacock. The blouse was white silk with a ruffled front similar to the other one I'd seen him in but softer-looking. His earrings were black-and-white cloth in the shape of half moons. His hair, tinted auburn today, was pulled back in a chignon held by a black-and-white bow at the nape of his neck.

Today Goldie looked more sophisticated than glitzy.

I could only guess that was Miles's effect on him.

He tapped a half black, half white, high-gloss nail to his tooth. "Suga, I only hope you find someone. Beats the hell out of being alone."

"I . . . Well, Jagger ate dinner at my parents' house with me last night." I couldn't lie to my friend. Strangers it was getting easier with.

Goldie sprung forward, his pumps tapping the floor. "You be careful, suga."

The urge to get defensive rose up but I held it back, knowing Goldie had my best interests in mind. He was more than likely right about Jagger anyway.

The guy was a mystery to me, and I was still too "green" to solve him.

"I'll be careful. So, tell me more about your date."

In the next ten minutes, Goldie filled me in on all the details right up to their dessert of cherries flambé and stopping just short of going back to his place. Those details I could do without. "I love the way your eyes light up when you talk about Miles like that."

"What about . . . his?"

I smiled. "Brighter than yours when he speaks of you." It was the truth too.

Adele stuck her head in the door. "Hey, *chéri*, how's it going?"

"Great." I wasn't sure what "it" she meant, but didn't want to elaborate and be wrong.

She held out a manila envelope. "This was just delivered for you, *chéri*."

"Me? What on earth?"

"Looks like a video," Goldie said. "Let me freshen our coffees while you pop it in the VCR." He turned and winked, taking my mug. "Unless it's X-rated."

Adele plopped onto the couch. "In that case, I'm in."

We all howled.

"I got some video of Tina last night. This has to have worked. . . . A friend lent me a camera."

Goldie whistled. "I'm impressed. You work a day job and manage to do your surveillance too. Dedication like that will get you far. Fabio eats shit like that right up."

I hated not being able to tell my friends that Jagger had helped me out, but then I would have had to tell them about my deal with Jagger. I was a truthful person if not a great investigator yet, and always kept my word.

I needn't have worried about telling them about Jagger.

The film of Tina and her husband was surprisingly short, and Goldie said it was a start but not enough to hang her with yet.

Then, clear as a movie in a theater, a picture came on the TV. Sauntering through the woods was Jagger, butt and all.

Adele whistled.

Goldie shook his head and made obscene but joking sounds.

And I sunk down into the zebra chair, wishing I could blend into the stripes, although today I wore pink flowered scrubs.

The thought never left my mind—Jagger had seen the tape too.

The orthopedic office was packed full as soon as the clock struck eight thirty. I wondered why any of the doctors would need to commit fraud, since they had to be making a bundle legitimately. Maybe they weren't involved. That was a distinct possibility, I thought, as Linda came up with a cup of coffee and handed it to me.

I'd had enough caffeine from Goldie's chicory coffee, but I took it nevertheless. "Thanks."

"I wanted to introduce you to the other doctors. Yesterday was so busy for me that I didn't have the chance."

Far as I could tell, the woman buried herself in paperwork and never left her office. What did I know about running a private practice? "That'd be nice. I already know Doctor Taylor and, although I haven't seen him here yet, Doctor Macaluso." Who I'm betting is a lying cheat.

Linda turned down the hall so I followed. In the lounge area that was connected to her office sat a young woman in a white lab coat. Linda turned to me. "Pauline Sokol, this is Doctor Charlene O'Connor."

Charlene seemed too young to be in private practice. Her black hair was curled around her ears and she wore little to no makeup that I could detect. The woman looked older than her years, and I figured she might have been on call last night and perhaps had been called into surgery. She nodded toward me. "Nice to meet you."

Linda headed to the coffeemaker and refilled her cup. "Doctor Harvey Feinstein." She nodded to a man about in his late fifties.

I guessed he was the oldest in the practice. He merely looked at me and nodded. Not a word. Okay, I pegged him as having the old surgeon "God" complex. Next was Dr. Aaron Levy, who greeted me nicely but hurried off, claiming tons of paperwork to catch up on.

I took a sip of the coffee I really didn't want and eyed the two doctors. Looking at them, so professional in white, I found it hard to believe that they or their colleagues were involved in something illegal. Then again, I guessed the prisons were full of criminals who didn't "look the type."

They both took their coffee and headed to their offices. Eddy came in and got himself a Coke from the refrigerator. "We have ten minutes till showtime," he said, then laughed.

Linda took a stack of files and went into her office and closed the door, so it was Eddy and me. I looked at him and wondered how helpful he could be. "Linda introduced me to the other two doctors."

He rolled his eyes. "I'll just bet that made your fucking day."

I shook my head. "It was nice to meet them. Doctor O'Connor looked beat though. I guess she was on call last—"

"Bitch always looks strung out."

"Drugs?" I nearly gasped.

"Kids. Single parent with two boys. Pays her ex alimony. What a crock. The guy sells cars and womanizes. Charlene got a raw deal."

Enough to make her commit fraud? Hmm. "Must be hard on her."

"Not as bad as old man Feinstein. Four kids in Ivy League colleges. He moonlights in the ER over in Hartford for extra cash. Hates it with a passion. Don't push his buttons."

Yikes! Another potential criminal. And then there was Donnie with two houses, one a mansion. Oh, great. "Guess we all have our crosses to bear."

"Give me a fucking break here. The only decent one in the bunch is Vance, as far as I can tell."

That left Aaron. "What's wrong with Doctor Levy?"

Eddy laughed. "Guy after my own heart. Likes the women. His ex has sucked him bone dry in court, but good old Aaron still finds the bucks to pay for his women."

I wasn't sure if Eddy meant pay as in dates or pay as in prostitutes. Wow, again. Goes to show how looks were so deceiving. I found it hard to believe that there were so many potential suspects in this practice.

Eddy got up. "Showtime."

I dumped the rest of my coffee in the sink and stuck the mug in the dishwasher. The lounge was quite complete as far as kitchen facilities were concerned. Linda fit into her office so well you couldn't even see her from this angle.

Eddy went to get his chart, and I picked the top one off of my pile. Thank goodness I was on Vance's side of the office, I thought, as I ushered one of his patients into an examining room.

"What brings you in today?"

Mrs. Bakersfield, an elderly woman with wrist pain said, "Well, the years are hard on someone my age. My hands just don't seem to work as they used to, dear."

I smiled in what I hoped looked sympathetic and eyed her chart. Eighty-four. I only hoped I'd see eighty-four, let alone have my body parts work correctly. "Are you in much pain?"

"Yes, dear. But that's part of the process."

I assumed she meant the circle of life, but didn't want to clarify the subject with someone who was so close to closing that circle. "Don't forget to tell the doctor about your discomfort. He can order you something to help."

"I don't take pills, dear."

I smiled while giving her credit for being so stalwart, but didn't mention that I took a pill at the drop of a hat when I had pain. Nothing too strong. Mostly Tylenol or monthly Motrin. "Doctor Taylor will be in to see you soon." I took the chart and headed toward the door.

She said, "He's a real looker. Isn't he?"

You haven't seen Jagger. I turned around. "He could be in movies."

She laughed. "He could put his shoes under my bed anytime."

I joined in her laughter.

"Who could?" Vance asked coming up behind me.

I swung around.

Mrs. Bakersfield giggled then said, "You, dear. You."

Vance gave her a nice smile and leaned toward me. "I can't make dinner this weekend. How about tonight?"

Tonight I'd hoped to be with Jagger—working. "Tonight? Gee. I'm so tired when I get done here. Guess I got out of the routine."

"We'll make it an early night."

And hit the sack? I wasn't sure if I could keep doing that to myself, or to Vance.

"Go ahead, dear. He's a looker!" Mrs. Bakersfield gave me a huge grin. Her dentures slipped in the process. While she nonchalantly and in a very ladylike way slipped them back into place, I said, "As long as I'm back by eight." I figured that gave me time to do some surveillance on Tina, even if by myself. I had come to realize that I wouldn't know when Jagger would appear or not.

I hurried out and took the next chart. Mr. Steve Marquette. Back pain. Hope he wasn't faking it like Tina. That was one ailment I'd come to realize could be faked quite well. Even if nothing showed up on an X-ray or CT scan, the patient could still be in pain. Soft tissue injuries and muscular pulls. Hard to prove.

I walked toward the waiting room. Eddy was calling out a patient's name. He turned to look at me. "Hey, Sokol, how's it going?"

"Fine, Eddy."

He waited for his patient to hobble over with her leg in a cast. "Fine? Here? Hell, maybe you should take over for Tina permanently." He laughed.

"No thank you." I held up my chart, ready to call out the patient's name.

Eddy leaned near. "You do a hell of a lot better than her fat ass."

"That's not nice."

"Hey, you haven't seen her in action. Or should I say non-action. Just 'cause her hubby is a partner here, she doesn't do shit." He held the door for his patient. "Back injury, my foot."

My eyes widened. "That's not nice either." Did Eddy know something? Could he be of help to me?

He started down the hall with his patient. "Neither is fraud."

Fraud?

Eddy and I needed to talk.

As I bent to look at my chart, I noticed Linda come out of her office. She smiled at Eddy's retreating back, then at me. I hustled to the waiting room doorway and called, "Mr. Marquette," not wanting Linda to chastise me for not working. Already she was docking my pay for yesterday.

I held the chart in one hand and waited. No one moved. I repeated, "Mr. Steve Marquette."

There were four woman on one side of the room, an elderly gentleman who didn't look like a Steve and two young boys near the door. One of them could be him. On the opposite wall sat a biker. Chains. Leather. Shades. Wow, I thought. I hope he didn't ride a Harley in this kind of weather. "Mr. Marquette."

He looked up, then stood.

"Are you Mr. Marquette?"

He nodded.

Great. The guy probably had the IQ of a *pączki* and it would be a challenge doing his history for the chart. "This way."

He followed me into the examining room.

I watched him looking at the door and holding a hand to his back. Okay, Pauline Sokol was the epitome of empathy for her patients. Maybe the guy wasn't turnip material after all. Maybe his back pain had him too preoccupied. "So, Mr. Marquette, please take a seat on the examining table."

He looked at me through the dark glasses. His hair touched his shoulders, much longer than mine. Actually, it partially covered his eyes. A deep blonde shade that was far too light for his dark eyebrows. A growth of beard covered his face and long dangly silver earrings clanged in his left ear.

There was something familiar about him, but I didn't really think I knew any bikers. Course, could have been a friend of Miles or Goldie. My life had gotten too weird lately, and that's why I thought I knew him. Overactive imagination. Had to come from spying. "What brings you here?"

He looked at me for a few seconds.

"Sir, what brings you here to the doctor's office?"

Slowly he lowered his glasses. "Thought you might want to film my butt."

Fifteen

Jagger!

I could only stare for several minutes. Maybe I should pass out and not have to deal with him—after him mentioning that I filmed his butt. But, I needed to stay conscious since I had to work and get money.

So, I summoned all my strength and said, "Oh, that video thing. I didn't know how to turn off the glasses. Camera. Don't flatter yourself."

He grinned.

Didn't buy it.

Well, I had too much to do besides get embarrassed and let him enjoy himself at my expense. "I'm guessing your back is fine, *Steve*."

"Anything so far today?"

"No." I sighed. "Seems business as usual."

He remained silent. I couldn't get over Jagger as a biker. Wow. He looked pretty . . . yummy. I reminded myself that I was having dinner with Vance, my . . . my what? I really couldn't call him my boyfriend. Didn't *want* to call him that.

What if Jagger planned for us to be together tonight?

I'd totally forgotten that we were supposed to be an *item*. Now what? I had to be truthful. My parents always taught us kids to tell the truth. Sometimes I wished I could break that habit, but, well, that was me. The little white lies I'd been telling lately that related to my case didn't count.

"Before the doctor comes in, I have to tell you . . . I have a date tonight."

He looked at me over his glasses. "And?"

"And? And aren't we . . . Well, you're the one who told Nick. I mean, I never said. You . . . I heard you tell Nick. I just wanted to tell you in case you had plans—"

He grinned. "So, you're cheating on me already?"

"I . . . no. It's just . . . Well, I've been dating Vance—"

He held up his hand. "Pauline, I *lied* to Nick."

Why on earth had I made it sound as if I owed Jagger an explanation? And, sadly, let him think that I thought we were really dating?

I pulled my shoulders straight and said, "I only wanted to tell you so that you didn't plan to help me with Tina tonight."

"That's thoughtful of you."

I turned and walked to the door. "The doctor will be right in."

A soft, deep chuckle followed me.

I had no idea what Jagger discussed with Dr. Macaluso after I'd left. Furthermore, I didn't want to know. I did my work shuffling patients from examining room, to cast room, to X-ray and out the door. Jagger had to be out the door about two hours ago, I thought, as my stomach growled, and I readied to go to lunch.

I only hoped he wasn't in the cafeteria.

I headed up there to find the lunch line wasn't as long as yesterday. I managed to get a bowl of beef barley soup, croissant with butter and hot green tea with low-fat milk. The croissant was to make me feel better after my Jagger encounter.

Eddy sat with me during lunch and made small talk. I looked around to see if anyone was close enough to eavesdrop, then said, "So, Eddy. What's your take on Tina?"

"She's fat." He took a sip of his Coke.

"Not how she looks. I mean her back problem."

"Fake. She's a fat-assed fake."

"How do you know that?"

"I've seen her bend down and pick up a penny from the fucking floor. If I had back pain, I wouldn't bother with that. Hell, I wouldn't bother to pick up a buck if my back hurt like hers is supposed to."

So Eddy had witnessed Tina's fraud. I wondered if an eyewitness account would be beneficial, and as I was making a mental note to ask Goldie, I looked at Eddy.

Eyewitnesses had to be credible.

There went that theory. I'd have to get the video on her soon.

He leaned near, his beady eyes on me. "You don't know about this place, Pauline."

"I . . . What's to know?"

Eddy's mouth opened and then shut. He stared at something or someone behind me.

I looked over my shoulder. A long line had formed now and a crowd stood waiting for the elevator. There stood Dr. Levy and Dr. Feinstein with Tina and Trudy. Everything looked normal to me. No one stood out.

But something or someone had shut Eddy's mouth.

I excused myself and decided I'd need to share this info with Jagger—if I could recognize him.

On the stairs I thought of how damn appealing he looked, no matter what he wore, and mentally patted myself on the back for not getting out of breath anymore. Obviously I was getting used to these stairs.

The rest of the afternoon went along without incident. No Jagger in disguise. No Eddy Roden acting weird. Weirder than usual. Linda was pleasant, and Trudy told me all about her children and grandchildren. I actually felt like one of the staff.

But it didn't take long for me to be reminded of how I really didn't want to practice nursing—once my feet started hurting and an elderly woman yelled at me for having to wait so long on the phone to make her appointment. I was about to tell her that nurses had nothing to do with the phones, when the door opened.

A group of six young men walked in with a guy in about his late twenties. The kids, I guessed ranging from thirteen to sixteen, all stood to the side. There were two Hispanic-looking teens, three black and a white one who was much shorter than the others. When they were in high school, my brothers would have given anything to be as tall as these kids. They all wore the gigantic pants hung low on their hips with colorful—and, hopefully, clean—underwear showing.

Trudy got up and opened the door. I didn't see any patient charts and none of the boys looked injured. They followed along with the man in his twenties to the examining room in the back of the hallway. I figured they were maybe here for basketball physicals, but then thought, that couldn't be possible. This was an orthopedic group.

Before I could figure it out, the boys came out, all carrying white plastic bags. Odd, I thought, but had no clue as to what to make of it.

Since my shift was over, I took my purse, said goodbye and went out the door. In the elevator lobby I noticed the boys taking sneakers, expensive looking Jordans, out of their bags. Maybe the ortho group donated them to promote good feet.

I went down the stairs and out to my car. When I reached to pull on my seat belt, I noticed the group of boys getting into a white van with the YMCA logo on the side. Hmm. They had to be basketball players by their height.

Too tired to care, I started my car and let myself daydream about a hot bath in the sunken tub.

I'd use honeysuckle bubble bath.

"I can't believe we're working in the same office," Vance said as he leaned across the table in Bernoulli's.

I'd been in the mood for pizza, although Vance usually insisted that wasn't dinner food. Consequently, we usually ate at some fancy restaurant. I had to put my foot down tonight, maintaining that I was too tired to get dressed up after work.

I had on my black jeans, a black-and-peach knitted sweater and black boots, since it had started to snow a few minutes before Vance had picked me up. No way was I freezing my feet for him again.

I took a bite of pizza, scooped up a mushroom that had fallen onto my dish and looked at Vance. He didn't own a pair of jeans, so tonight he wore a cashmere sweater in a deep olive that went well with his hair color, always styled to perfection. I wondered if a hair ever had the audacity to slip out of place on his head, but guessed not. His pants had to be suede and must have cost a bundle.

"More wine?" He held the bottle toward me.

"Yikes. No. I'll be asleep on my cannoli if I have any more."

"I'm guessing that's what you want for dessert."

"Um." I wrapped a stringy piece of mozzarella around my finger and popped it into my mouth. Last time I ate pizza, it was with Jagger. Ack.

Vance stared at me. "You smell nice. Honeysuckle."

"Yeah. You know, Vance, working together usually doesn't work out. I mean, maybe we should . . ." I couldn't break up with him. Not now. Not here.

And not because of Jagger.

Yet, I really wanted to.

"True. Good thing we don't have too much contact at work."

So he wasn't in the market for social freedom. Okay, I'd hold off any knee-jerk reactions, but I decided I'd put my foot down one more time tonight.

And not sleep with him.

I wasn't sure what excuse I'd use, but I'd think of something between now and eight. I had to get the subject off of our relationship so I said, "There are some awfully nice elderly patients that come to your practice." That wasn't a stretch, because Vance knew I had a fondness for my Uncle Walt and all of his elderly friends.

"I guess." He gave me an odd look.

Even though I liked the elderly, it was a strange subject to bring up, and Vance must've been thinking just that. But I decided an investigator is always on the job, and I needed to know more about that MRI. It bothered me.

What I didn't know was how I was going to bring up the subject?

And, I thought, taking a sip of wine, what if Vance didn't order that MRI? Then who did? Or, my mind started to crank, what if Vance *did* order that MRI? Why?

"Pauline?"

I looked up. Vance was standing. "I have to go."

"The men's room is to the left of the brick oven on the north end of the kitchen."

"No. Pauline. I have to leave. Didn't you hear my beeper go off?"

I hadn't. "I . . . sure. I was joking. Go ahead. I'll get a cab home."

"You sure?"

"Go. Have fun." I have no idea why that came out.

Vance looked at me. He set two twenty-dollar bills on the table.

I should have said don't worry, but I really didn't want to be stuck with the bill. Well, at least this solved my sex dilemma.

"There's been a car accident. The ER paged me."

"Oh. I hope everything is all right." I sat back and watched him leave. Once the waiter came with the bill and back with the change, I left a generous tip and walked to the door.

I forgot I needed a ride home, so I asked the hostess if I could use the phone to call a cab. She gave me a strange look.

"There aren't any cabs running after seven in Hope Valley, ma'am."

She was right. After 7 P.M. the town rolled up its streets and consequently the cabs during the winter months. Damn. I'd have to call Miles. She let me use the phone but the recorder came on. Miles was either called in to work or out with Goldie. I tried Goldie's number. Got his recorder too.

"Hi, sugars, you've reached the one and only Goldie Perlman residence. If you're a hot dude, leave a message. If you're the cops, you have the wrong number. And if you're a bill collector, Goldie Perlman is deceased."

I laughed into the phone despite the odd look from the hostess. I'd have to remind Goldie to change his message now that he and Miles were an item. I looked out the window. The snow had stopped.

A pinkish glow covered the earth as the freshly fallen snow sparkled beneath the street lamps. Well, I did have on my boots, so I decided I would walk home. Thank goodness I'd talked Vance into coming here. It was in the Italian section of Hope Valley only about six blocks from my place.

I went out into the parking lot and passed between two vans. When I got to the edge of the lot, a white car sped past, splashing slush at me and getting so close I had to jump over the curb.

Then, from behind—someone grabbed my arm!

My reflexes were amazingly keen for having had two glasses of wine, I found out. I yelled, "NO!" and slammed my fist into my attacker's abdomen. I'd seen that on TV with some feminist group.

A *whoosh* of air blew into my face. It sounded surprisingly like my name, and a curse came out with it.

Without time to think, I took my purse and swung it back, ready to slam the guy with what had to weigh about thirty pounds.

My hand was pinned behind my back before I could follow through on my swing.

"What the fuck are you doing?"

I tilted my head back and finally looked at my attacker, although I already recognized the voice.

His grip loosened.

"What am *I* doing? Is it normal for you to keep popping up all over and scaring the bejeevers out of me?"

Jagger let go. "What the fuck are bejeevers?"

"I . . . What difference does it make? I think you broke my arm." It didn't really hurt, but I rubbed at it nevertheless.

"You all right?"

I glared at him. Puffs of frozen breath came from my mouth. "I'll live."

"What are you doing walking out here?"

"There aren't any cabs after—" Out of habit, I rubbed my arm. "Wait. Why am I confessing to you? You're the one who jumped out of the shadows and accosted me."

"I didn't accost you. I saved you from that Toyota Corolla."

That much was true. My heart did a little arrhythmia at the reminder.

"I could have moved over by myself. And the car wasn't that close."

"Then why are your pants wet?"

Oh shit! I wet my pants? I looked down. Thank goodness my pants were covered in snowy slush. I hadn't realized that I was freezing until my body gave a shudder.

The next thing I knew, I was in Jagger's Suburban, wrapped in a Patriots blanket that I argued about using. Hey, I was a diehard Steelers fan and, cold or not, the Patriots were the fault of my Steelers getting knocked clear out of a chance at the Super Bowl in 2001 during the AFC championship game. The heater blasted warm air at me. Okay, that felt good.

"So, again, what were you doing out here? And what do cabs have to do with it?"

I went through the details of Vance getting paged and left

out the part that I'd decided not to sleep with him tonight—or ever again.

Jagger kept his eyes on the road as he drove out, but I had the feeling he knew what I was thinking. "So you didn't get to ask him about the MRI?"

"No. He had to leave too fast. He's only on call once every five weeks, and wouldn't you know, tonight he got called in."

"Guess that put a damper on your *date*."

The way he said "date" was odd. Was he jealous? Yeah, right! Wake up and smell the pheromones, Pauline. Jagger is not your type and you are in no way *his*.

Stick to fantasy daydreams.

"Where are we going?"

"I assumed you were walking home."

"Yes, I was. Thanks. I couldn't get a ride from anyone . . ."

He stopped at a light and looked at me as if to say, "Why should I care?"

Jagger pulled into my parking lot and turned into a space marked for visitors. "Miles home?"

I looked around. "I don't see his car."

He cut the engine and looked at me.

"Oh, you want to come in?"

"Since your boyfriend had to hurry off, I thought we could talk."

I had visions of talking and . . . never mind. "I'll make some coffee if you want."

On the way to the door, Jagger asked, "What about the rest of the day at work?"

Grass didn't grow under this guy's feet. No wonder he was good at his job. He lived it.

"I . . . Let me see." I dug my hand around in my purse and dug and dug and dug until Jagger got so frustrated he grabbed it and within seconds pulled out my keys. Then he opened the door, and we went in. Him first. "You know, there *was* something I thought was odd."

Spanky ran up to Jagger and leaped at his calves. Jagger scooped him up and held him then rubbed behind his ears.

"Why don't you let me decide."

He didn't trust my surveillance skills. And truthfully, I didn't blame him.

A beeping came from the kitchen.

"Come in here. You can let him out while I check the answering machine."

I pressed the button, figuring one of the messages was mine, looking for a ride. I found that one and deleted it. Next came Miles's coworker reminding him that tomorrow was a birthday party for one of the surgeons, and it was Miles's turn to bring in the cake. But not chocolate because Dr. Harwinton was allergic to chocolate. I wrote that message down.

Jagger came up behind me with Spanky in his arms.

"Almost done." I pressed play again. On came my mother. "Pauline, you're not home—"

I shook my head, wondered if I'd ever turn into my mother and hoped Jagger didn't think the same.

"—I really should know where you are at all times in case there is an emergency—"

My heart thudded. Did something happen to Daddy? Uncle Walt? I said a fast prayer as she continued.

"—or I need to get you for something like to remind you to tell Mister Jagger that we do grab bags on Christmas Eve."

"We do grab bags on Christmas Eve," I said.

"Don't forget to tell him that it is an item for seven dollars, and on Christmas Day the item has to be a food item. You tell him, Pauline. Don't forget, or Mister Jagger will feel badly that he is not prepared. Oh, the food item has to be seven dollars as well. Don't forget. Tell him."

"Yes, Mom." As if I didn't know the Sokols' yuletide grab-bag rules. I turned to Jagger and took Spanky from him. "We do a food—"

"I got it."

"Fine," Spunky, not one to cuddle for too long, promptly jumped out of my arms and scurried out of the kitchen.

The 3 still blinked on the answering machine. I pressed the button to hear the last message.

"Pauline," Vance's voice said. "I've just gotten out of surger—"

Ack. I hope he wasn't calling me for *that*.

And with Jagger standing right here!

I started to push the button to delete it before he finished. But for some reason didn't.

But he continued, "The accident was only one car. A bad one though. Drove off the curve on River Road. The one down past Madeline's. Right into the pilings along the boat ramp and into the water. The airbag deployed with such force—"

I shook my head at Vance's disembodied voice as if he could see me and as if to ask how any of this made any difference to me. I wondered why on earth he was giving me so much detail about his case. He never had before.

Before I could wonder any longer, his voice said, "Eddy Roden didn't make it."

Sixteen

My eyes widened and I gasped.

"God damn it," Jagger said.

We stood there silent for several seconds.

Eddy Roden was dead.

Funny how one's mind acts when they hear bad news. All I could think of right then was, It could have been me. That Corolla could have killed me. A foolish thought because despite what Jagger had said about grabbing me, I didn't think the Corolla had come that close.

"I have to make a few calls," Jagger said.

"Calls? Oh sure. You can use this phone. I'll get us something to drink. Coffee?"

He'd already dialed. "Beer."

The shocking news did warrant a beer. I walked to the fridge, took out two Coors. When I opened the drawer to get the bottle opener, I heard Jagger talking.

"Lieutenant Shatley." A few minutes of silence. "John, it's me."

I popped the top off my beer, took a sip and thought that Jagger must know this cop pretty well if he didn't have to identify himself. Maybe Jagger was a regular cop? Or an undercover cop, was more like it. It really didn't matter, I thought, when the reminder that Eddy was dead hit me.

I opened Jagger's beer and set it on the counter next to him. He nodded a thanks and took a long sip. "I need an accident report. . . . God damn it. . . . Not that. . . . Sure. . . . No. Tonight." He held his hand over the receiver. "You got a fax?"

"Fax?"

"Fax machine," he said testily.

"Sorry. No."

"I'll pick it up," he said into the phone. "Anything you got for me about the Roden accident?" He shook his head and mumbled a few curse words, a "Thanks, buddy," then hung up the phone. After that he polished off his entire beer, while I still had three fourths of mine to go.

"Another beer?" I asked, although I didn't think he needed one if he had a lot of work to do tonight.

He looked at me. "Go change your wet pants while I use the phone."

The cool material had clung to my skin, making me forget the discomfort after hearing about Eddy. I set my empty beer bottle on the counter and went to change. Jagger was already talking to someone about the make and model of the car that Eddy had been driving. I surmised it was some sort of mechanic on the line by what Jagger was asking.

Upstairs I shimmied out of the wet jeans and looked into my closet. If I changed my top Jagger might get the wrong impression. He might think that I cared what I wore for him.

And I didn't want him thinking that!

I went with reliable blue jeans and left on my sweater. Once downstairs I found Jagger, sitting at the counter writing notes on a little pad he must have carried with him because I didn't recognize it. Of course, I wouldn't put it past him to go rummaging through our drawers for whatever he needed.

He looked up. "Tell me about work today. You talk to Eddy?"

I sat opposite him. Spanky had curled up in his tiger-striped bed near the door. Exhausted and mentally drained, I paused. Did I?

"Sherlock, we have a shitload of stuff to cover tonight."

"I'm thinking. Oh, yes. I did talk to Eddy." I related the conversation of Eddy's opinion of all the doctors and Tina, and her picking up the stupid penny. I included a description of Eddy's odd expression when he'd looked past me in the cafeteria and how he had suspiciously stopped talking so abruptly.

Jagger took an occasional note, but didn't, however, look too impressed. Then again, this was Jagger. I figured he was the type to remember everything without writing things down. When I looked at his paper, I was amazed.

Doodles covered the entire page. Not only didn't he take notes, but he did sketches of Spanky, cars, planes and some things I couldn't recognize all the while he listened to me. And they were good!

I knew from the questions he asked that he didn't miss a thing. Of course, he may already have done background checks on all the staff.

"Linda's a single mom too," was all he said when I mentioned that Eddy never talked about her.

I even told him about Trudy being a grandmother. Jagger gave me a "how is that relevant" look. I couldn't help but defend myself with, "Well, she doesn't look that old."

"Anything else about today?"

"No. Yes. Wait."

He shook his head.

I curled my lip. "It hasn't been the best of nights, you know. I almost forgot. A group of boys came into the office. . . ."

I think I detected his eyebrows raise a fraction. "And?"

"And they weren't there but a few minutes." I told him how they came out with bags that I later saw were new shoes and said, "I'm guessing the doctors maybe donated them—"

Jagger gave me one of his Jagger looks.

"What?"

"Don't guess. Tell me facts."

After a short exasperated huff, I covered how they got into the YMCA van and the driver who brought them in drove them out of the parking lot.

"Capper."

"What?"

He looked a little less pissed. "Capper or runner. Has to be."

"I'm not following." I finished my beer, thinking that might either help me understand him better or make my tired brains so clouded I wouldn't care what Jagger said or thought about me.

He leaned back, his hands behind his head. He looked as beat as I felt. "He's a third-party middleman. Recruits perpetrators to commit insurance fraud. Tomorrow check to see if there are charts on those kids and billings to the insurance company."

"Oh, but they were only in the office a few minutes and didn't even see any doctor—"

"Maybe you should stick to nursing."

I didn't have a hot temper, but I did have one that got set off by insulting me. The nerve!

Before I could tell Jagger off, he continued, "I'll bet there are charts on each one of those kids, claiming soft tissue injures sustained at the Y. Most likely playing basketball, if they were all tall as you said."

"They *were* tall."

He gave me an odd look. "I got that. Sometimes these runners befriend legitimate accident victims for the medical mills."

I had a hard time believing I was working in a medical mill. All I could think of was a show I'd seen a few years ago on *60 Minutes* about puppy mills. I shuddered when I looked at my darling Spanky. But that's not what Jagger was talking about. "How can people do those things?"

"Look, Sherlock, the world is full of dishonest shits that commit crimes like fraud. Sometimes enough—"

He looked out across the room. I followed his stare, thinking something had moved or he heard a noise. Nothing seemed changed to me.

"—enough so that insurance companies go bust and criminals get rich."

"Like Tina and Donnie."

"Not many can afford two houses like that. Tomorrow check to see what kinds of cars all the staff drive."

"Cars? How am I supposed to—"

"Skip coffee with Goldie and stake out the parking lot."

I could only stare at him and wonder just how much he knew about me. Finally my mind, the spunky part, kicked in and I said, "You've been following me. Stop that. Stop following me around!"

"Look, Sherlock, if I find out that Eddy's death wasn't an accident, you can consider me your fucking shadow."

Before I could say anything else, the sound of a door slamming made me jump out of my seat and scream.

Jagger looked at me. I think he shook his head again, although he was doing that so frequently, I hardly noticed any more. "That's your front door, Sherlock. Not some .357 Magnum."

Then I think he grinned.

Embarrassed, I turned away too fast to notice if he really did. Thank goodness Miles came in, followed by Goldie.

I jumped up and gave them each a hug as if I hadn't seen them in years. They gave me a collective look of confusion. "Hey, you two. How's it going?"

Goldie raised an eyebrow and looked at me, then Jagger. "Fine, suga. What about you?"

I knew he meant What the hell is wrong with you? But he didn't ask that. Despite his flamboyance, Goldie had tact and grace.

"We're fine. I'm . . . fine. How about some coffee?"

Goldie held his abdomen. "If I drink any more, I'll burst. We ate at that new Indian Restaurant. I drank a couple gallons of water. Spicy. Yummy. What'd you two eat?"

"I had a pizza with Vance." There went my honest mouth. I never even thought to lie. It must look strange to have Jagger sitting here and me saying I'd gone out with another man, but I really couldn't explain why. Even Jagger gave me a dirty look. "We had some business to discuss," I added, very pleased with myself.

Miles busied himself playing with Spanky. Goldie gave Jagger the once-over, then looked at me. He mouthed, "Cocaine."

I shook my head. "Indian, huh? I really don't like ethnic food that much."

Miles looked up. "Hah! You're as Polish as a fucking pierogi, Sokol."

"Well, yeah. I like my mother's cooking, but not spicy food like Indian." I looked at Jagger. He stood. I'm quite certain this conversation wasn't stimulating enough for him—and I didn't blame him. I rambled on without any purpose, for no reason other than nervousness. I wanted to tell them about Jagger and I—the truth. But couldn't. Then I thought of Eddy.

Goldie sat on the stool by the counter.

"Eddy Roden was killed in a car accident tonight," I said. Jagger bent his head down but kept his gaze on me.

Miles took Spanky and held him close. "Eddy? That dude that used to work at Saint Greg's?"

I'd forgotten that they didn't know that I work with Eddy right now. Make that *worked* with him. Suddenly all my lies were colliding with each other like tiny bumper cars in my head. I didn't know who knew what or what I could say to whom about what. Or what the hell I was talking about.

"I have a headache," came out. They all glared at me.

Goldie reached into his spangled black purse and pulled out a pillbox with Mardi Gras masks on it. "Here. Tylenol."

I took one and swallowed it without water.

Miles looked rather concerned. "You sure you feel all right—"

"She has a headache," Jagger said far too briskly.

Goldie straightened in his seat. "Let's do a foursome tomorrow night for dinner."

I felt my eyes grow large. I didn't need a mirror to see how I looked. Just as I could feel Jagger's glare boring into my back. Now what?

But I didn't have to worry about that. Jagger said, "Sounds like a plan," and walked to the door. "Let's go, Pauline."

I wanted to ask where, until I turned and looked at him. That look didn't invite questioning. I placed a fast kiss on Goldie's cheek, then one on Miles's and an even faster pat on Spanky's head. Before anyone could question me, I followed Jagger out the door.

Once in Jagger's SUV, I asked, "Where are we going, and why did you agree to go out with them tomorrow?"

He drove for a few minutes without answering. "Sounded like fun."

"Fun?"

He let out a long sigh. Then he slapped himself in the head. "You need to set your private life apart from your work. We're supposed to be convincing so no one suspects that you're working for me."

Working for him! Okay, in a way I was. "I knew that."

"Then don't sound so surprised that we would agree to go out with those two jokers."

"They are my best friends!"

"Yeah, sorry."

He didn't mean it, I could tell. "No you're not, and you'd better be on your best behavior tomorrow night and not hurt either of their feelings."

He chuckled. "I'm going to have a headache myself tomorrow night, Sherlock."

"Oh no, you don't!"

He slowed, looked at me when we stopped at a light. I didn't care though. He wasn't going to insult Goldie or Miles if I could help it. So, I used my head and female intuition. "You *owe* me, Jagger."

"Owe you?" The light turned green and he sped off a bit too fast.

I didn't want to argue while he was driving, but I calmly

pointed out, "I took this nursing job to help you. You're the one who told Nick we were dating, and now we're going out with them tomorrow."

"The nursing job is a moot point. My helping you with Tina erases that debt."

Before I could argue, I looked up to see we'd pulled into the Hope Valley Police Station parking lot. For a second, I'd forgotten about Eddy. Obviously Jagger never forgot a thing. He was out and up the steps before I had my door closed.

Once inside, I became more confused about the mysterious Jagger.

Seventeen

The mysterious Jagger knew everyone.

Make that everyone—all the cops, that is—knew him. At first I wondered if he had a past criminal life, which would make sense, but Goldie wouldn't have let me even sample the "cocaine" if that were true.

Nope. I had to conclude that Jagger spent a lot of time around here for years since the oldest to the youngest cops greeted him by name. Had me leaning toward FBI again.

Jagger ushered me into an office at the end of a hallway. Files covered the gray metal desk and there was a hint of stale cigarettes. Old coffee mugs, some half full, some empty, lined the end like wounded soldiers. At first I thought this might be his office until I noticed a nameplate partially sticking out from under a piece of paper. Lieutenant S something. I couldn't see the rest. Unless "Jagger" was his first name and his last started with an S, this wasn't his office.

Of course, he more than likely wouldn't clear up the mystery of his name for me anyway.

I was about to ask what was going on when a short stocky man wearing a wrinkled brown suit came through the door. He high-fived Jagger and gave me a nod. Balding, his hair was unflatteringly combed from one side to the other as if that would hide the skin underneath. As rumpled as the man appeared, he had a friendly face. I could read this guy, and he looked genuinely glad to see Jagger. Yet he had a look of concern in his eyes. I had to guess that was for Eddy Roden.

Jagger sat with his feet resting on what little edge of the desk wasn't covered. "Pauline Sokol. John Shatley. Lieutenant Shatley."

I smiled and said, "Nice to meet you, Lieutenant," at the same time Jagger said, "Got my accident report for me?"

The lieutenant looked at me and nodded. "Same here." Then he fished around in the pile of debris on his desk. It reminded me of Fabio's desk, and the lieutenant made me think of that detective who used to be on TV. Columbo. I smiled to myself.

When I looked up, Jagger was reading something. The accident report, I assumed. After a few minutes, he got up, handed the paper back to the lieutenant and nodded. "Thanks." He walked toward the door.

I got up, held my hand out to the cop and shook when he took it. "Nice to meet you." I'd already said that but was at a loss for words. We'd breezed in and now out so quickly, I didn't have time to think.

Jagger was already halfway down the hallway. He slowed near the desk. Well at least he had some manners, I told myself, until I saw him reach over the counter and snatch a chocolate-dipped donut from a box.

So much for manners.

The desk sergeant jokingly cursed Jagger, who held the donut up and took a giant bite.

Hurrying to catch up, when I got near the desk I caught my foot on the leg of a fresh-looking teen sitting on a bench. I broke my fall by grabbing his shoulder.

"Watch it, bitch!"

Jagger spun around.

The kid looked from Jagger to me. "Sorry," he muttered.

Yikes. Now *that* look on Jagger was clearly readable.

"No. I'm the one who is . . ." Some pictures hanging above

the kid caught my eye. They weren't exactly Wanted pictures like you'd see in the post office, but a collage of newspaper clippings. The title of the bulletin board was "Have You Seen These Locals?" as if it were some sort of contest.

Jagger took another bite of his donut. "Let's go, Sherlock."

The kid grinned. One of his front teeth was missing and his hair was slicked back with enough gel to lubricate a set of automobile brakes. So many dangly silver earrings pierced his skin that I wondered he didn't get some kind of metal poisoning.

I felt sorry for someone trying to look so "cool" when he was probably hurting inside and would rather hide from the world.

The teen looked at me. "Sherlock?"

Jagger grabbed my arm. "You got a problem with that, son?"

"Er . . . nope."

"Nope, sir." Jagger started to move.

"Wait!" I hadn't meant to shout like that. The kid jumped and started to apologize profusely, calling Jagger "sir" and me "miss." Two cops at the front desk turned and stared, and Jagger asked, "What now?"

I pointed to the wall.

"Yeah?" He bit into his donut again.

"That's him."

"Him?"

"The capper."

Jagger let go and swung around. "Which one?"

I leaned near and touched a picture of the capper playing street basketball. The caption under the picture said it was a Hoop It Up game in downtown Hartford. His face was circled in yellow. I leaned nearer, "Walter 'Chewy' Barchewski. Oh my God. He's Polish!"

Jagger gave me a tug. "Come on."

"But . . . did you hear me? His name. I mean. I can't believe it."

We were now outside the police station, and I couldn't stop myself. "I mean," I repeated, "Polish!"

Jagger let go and stopped. "Jesus. Not all criminals are Wops, Sherlock. I'm sure there are a few crooked Polacks out there."

"Yes, there are. Chewy, for one."

Once at his Suburban, he unlocked the door and got in. I got in and pulled my door shut. I started to go on again about Chewy but this time was able to stop myself. Silently I thought, *I can't freaking believe it.*

"So?" I asked.

Jagger looked at me, licking the last bit of chocolate frosting from his finger. "What?" He looked down at his finger. "You wanted one too?"

"No. I didn't want a donut. What did you find out on the accident report?"

"Not much." He started the engine and backed out.

I wrapped my jacket tighter as the night temperature had more than likely dropped below zero. Good thing I hadn't had to walk home with wet pants. The heater blew air on my legs, but the engine hadn't warmed enough to make it comfortable. "That's too bad. Or maybe that's good. Maybe it really was an accident that killed Eddy, since you didn't find out much."

Jagger pulled onto Elm heading toward the river. "Yet."

"I—" Yet? Not much yet? That meant he expected to learn more eventually. "What do you expect to find?"

We turned down River Road. I felt my stomach knot. I really didn't want to see where Eddy had gotten killed.

Murder was *not* in my job description.

Jagger should have left me home. I had only agreed to follow people to film them and, if need be, snoop in office files. But when the M word came into play, I was outta here.

"Take me home."

He slowed and pulled over into the parking lot of Sam the Clam Diggers dive. "What now? You got to pee?"

"No, I don't have to go to the bathroom. I want to go

home. I didn't agree to anything that has to do with murder." There. I put my foot down.

"No one said it was murder . . . yet."

"There's that 'yet' word again. You imply that Eddy may have been killed. I don't want anything to do with—"

"I'm not driving you across town and then coming back. It's getting late and you have to go to work tomorrow."

"I may call in sick. . . ."

He leaned near.

I inhaled chocolate. Um.

"We have a deal." He remained near.

"And . . . when is the . . ." It was hard to concentrate. I swallowed, thinking that would help. Then I pulled back until my head touched the window. "When was the last time we went to spy on Tina?"

"I had planned to tonight, but Eddy inconveniently died."

Shoot. I couldn't argue with that. "But I don't want to . . . What do you think you're going to see down here anyway?"

"I don't know, Sherlock. That's why I'm here. To look. Tire marks. Broken pilings. Who the hell knows?"

He didn't let me argue anymore, but shoved the gear shift into drive and sped out of the parking lot.

"Slow down!" I ordered.

"Relax. I don't plan to visit the fishes like Eddy."

And neither did I, but feared there was a chance I might if I got caught snooping around the office tomorrow.

I was never so glad to be home as I was right then. Jagger pulled up to the doorway. Good: He wasn't getting out. I reached down to get my purse. He leaned back and pushed a few hairs from his forehead.

I guessed that made him think better. He might have a lot to think about after our little trip down River Road.

I had stayed in the SUV while Jagger got out and walked around the scene several times. The only thing I'd noticed was skid marks, which told me nothing, but I guessed Jagger could read something into them. Then there were the broken pilings near a dilapidated dock. The only thing Jagger said when he got back into the Suburban was that's where they fished out Eddy's car.

I shuddered again as I had when he'd said it. Eddy was no prize, but no one deserved to die like that. Falling into the river. How horrible. I repeated the silent prayer that I had said earlier asking Saint Theresa to have allowed Eddy to be dead or at least passed out before his car hit the water. With my phobia, I couldn't imagine being submerged in a car and not being able to get out. That's why I carried a hammer in the glove compartment.

You never knew when you'd need to smash your windows to prevent yourself from drowning. I shuddered again, wondering if a hammer would have helped Eddy.

"Good night," I said softly, since that's all the energy I had left.

Jagger touched my arm. Yikes. It wasn't a hard grab like at the police station, signaling that he was annoyed with me. No. It came more from concern.

"Look, Pauline, you really have to be extremely careful and closemouthed at the office now."

My heart beat faster. I wanted to believe it was because Jagger touched my arm, but this time I knew it came from fear.

"Actually, you can back out of the deal if you want."

"Then how are you going to investigate?"

He looked at me.

"Oh. Silly question."

He let go.

For a second, I felt disappointed.

"I can manage, although I'll admit that you're working there would speed things up," he said.

Eddy may have died because of all of this mess. Suddenly—and this is not my style—I felt a sense of responsibility to help out in Eddy's memory. I normally would run a marathon or bake a cake for any cause, but spying on alleged criminals was not me—until now.

"I'll do it for Eddy." Oh, God. I'd just committed myself.

Jagger nodded. "Since the stakes are higher now, I can't ask you to do it as a trade for Tina's case."

"What? I agree to help you longer and you renege on our deal?"

"Relax, Sherlock." He flipped a switch that unlocked my door. I opened it and started to jump out. "I'm not reneging."

That got my attention. I stopped.

"I'll cut you into the profits."

"Money!" Oh damn. I sounded pathetic. I sounded like a pathetic loser only interested in the almighty dollar.

I sounded like I saw a light at the end of my financial drought's tunnel.

"Fine. That's a deal I'll accept as long as you still help me with Tina."

"Never said I wouldn't." He stared at me for a few seconds. "Listen, Sherlock, you can't finish your case with Tina . . . yet—"

"What? You promised!"

"I know what I said. If you uncover her now, a much bigger job will be botched."

"Your case. Why does yours take precedence over my—"

"Thirty-three thousand, eight hundred ninety-two dollars and seventy-seven cents versus over three million."

Suddenly I felt as if I'd sealed my fate.

And, oh God, how I hoped my fate wasn't similar to Eddy's.

I miss Goldie's chicory coffee, I thought, as I sipped on my Dunkin Donuts hazelnut decaffeinated. Besides, it was freezing this morning and sitting in my car instead of going into the office seemed a stupid idea. Knowing what kinds of cars the doctors drove didn't seem pertinent to me. Most doctors could afford something nice, although working in a practice like the ortho one, strictly governed by insurance rules, didn't produce millionaires.

I'd turned off the engine to be less conspicuous as other

staff drove in to work. I'd wondered, if I was seen sitting in my car with the motor running, someone might think I was trying to commit suicide. A crazy thought, but somehow not that far off base when I thought of Eddy.

Maybe he knew he'd get caught, so he killed himself. I'd have to discuss that one with Jagger if he hadn't already thought of it himself.

An engine roared in the distance. I sipped my coffee and watched over the rim.

A California orange '99 Lamborghini with California plates pulled into the space marked for Dr. Levy. Levy was a common name I told myself so maybe it wasn't our Dr. Levy. Sure enough, I noticed his Italian leather shoes as he climbed out of the car and walked toward the staff entrance. Hmm. Couldn't be paying too much for call girls if he could afford alimony and that car.

Unless he was getting money from the insurance companies.

I fished around in my purse, looking for a pen and piece of paper. I knew my cars but wasn't sure if my half-frozen brain would remember who drove what. All I could find was a canceled check for Jeanine's car payment. I grabbed my Estêe Lauder All Day Starlight Pink lipstick and wrote "Levy—Lambor."

Before I could write "ghini," a black Bentley pulled into Dr. Feinstein's space. Wow. Even a 2001 Bentley Arnage had to run over two hundred grand. With four kids in Ivy League schools?

I'd liked Dr. Feinstein when I met him, but I put a lipstick star next to his name. He was my number-one suspect.

Then I saw Linda Stark get out of a silver minivan. A Dodge Caravan, older model. Jagger had said to spy on the doctors, but Linda was there and soon Trudy drove in. Now she surprised me as she got out of a candy-apple red Chevy truck! You go, girl!

Soon Vance pulled in driving his Mercedes. I sunk down in my seat. All I needed was him seeing me and asking foolish questions. Of course, "Why are you spying on the doctor's cars?" wasn't really that foolish of a question.

A noise caught my attention. Around the corner sputtered a white Toyota Corolla with a huge dent in the back fender. I assumed it was one of the staff.

But it was Charlene O'Connor. She got out and greeted Vance, and they walked into the building together. I'm not sure what shocked me more, her car or her friendliness toward Vance.

And no, I wasn't jealous!

It'd fit right into my "breaking up" plans to have him dump me. Truthfully it wasn't *that* friendly of a greeting, more my wishful thinking. Besides, I wasn't sure how old her kids were, and truthfully, I really couldn't see Vance as an instant father. Actually, I couldn't see him as a "nine months till the baby's due" father either.

In my heart I think I always knew what kept me from marrying Vance. He just wasn't Michael Sokol.

My coffee was gone and my toes were numb. Not to mention I'd fogged up the windows of my car with my breath. I knew Donnie drove a Porsche 'cause I'd seen it at his and Tina's house, and she drove a Lexus, so I didn't need to sit here any longer freezing my bejeevers off. I had the docs covered.

Made me think of Jagger.

As much as I tossed and turned last night, thinking of Eddy Roden possibly being murdered, an overwhelmingly comforting thought convinced me that Jagger wouldn't let me get hurt.

Not 'cause it was me.

He wouldn't let anyone get hurt if he could help it. I wasn't going to concentrate on the last part of that theory. Goldie said I could trust him with my life if not my heart, and I was holding that good thought for today.

I stuffed my empty cup into the Stop and Buy plastic bag that I used for a garbage bag in my car and grabbed my purse. Once in the building I had to wipe my eyes when I thought of Eddy.

Not a friend by any means, but I already missed him and felt horrible that he was dead.

When I got into the office, I nearly lost it. There on the reception desk was a bouquet of black flowers, roses, standing tall above a picture of Eddy Roden. Someone had typed the year of his birth and subsequent death on a sheet of paper and cut it out to tape it to his picture.

I'd always loved roses. They were my special flower, since Saint Theresa sent them as a sign that she heard someone's prayers, but now, looking at these black ones, which I think were actually a deep purple, I felt as if the rose scent would make me sick. Right here in the waiting room.

I opened the door to the office and heard sobbing. Trudy sat at her computer, wiping at her eyes. I walked closer.

"Morning."

She looked up and nodded.

"Can I get you something? Water?" I'm not sure why water makes someone feel better, or if it really does, when they are sad, but that's what they do in the movies, so I offered.

"He was a good boy," Trudy said, then continued sobbing.

"Yes, he was." Linda came up from behind. Her eyes were red, along with the tip of her nose.

I wondered if they really thought Eddy was a "good boy" or if their way of handling grief was to "imagine" that Eddy wasn't as bad as he seemed to me. Very similar to when a public figure dies and the press mentions all the good they did, even if half their life was spent on doing bad. Or was Linda and Trudy's display of grief meant to cover up something? Still, he shouldn't be dead.

Linda and Trudy started to tell me all the funny things Eddy used to do until Tina came walking in. She too looked as if she had been crying. What a day this was going to be. They'd all be so preoccupied over Eddy's death I wondered if anyone would get their work done.

Preoccupied.

Maybe so preoccupied that I could look at the records of the boys from the YMCA.

I looked up to heaven. Thanks Eddy.

Again, he should be here annoying me, but since he wasn't, I chose to believe that his death wasn't in vain. Now the case might take a giant leap forward if I could find some evidence to give Jagger.

After shuffling double my load of patients in and out of the examining rooms for hours, I sank down into the couch in the lounge. What had I been thinking? I didn't have time to pee, let alone go snooping in records, since now I was the only nurse on duty today. Tina came and went, but never lifted a finger to help. No great surprise.

Linda busied herself at her desk with shuffling files back and forth. I swore she moved the same ones from the IN tray to the OUT tray and back about five times. She had to be affected by Eddy's death. Finally she stopped and leaned back.

I stuck my head in her door. "How about a cup of coffee?"

She looked around. "Geez, I didn't even know anyone was here." She moved another file into the OUT tray. "That'd be great."

I thought offering to fix her coffee could soften my next question. When she took the cup and her first sip, I asked, "Are you having any luck replacing Eddy?"

She choked on the next sip.

"Oh, Linda! I'm sorry." I pulled her hands up in the air. That trick came from when I'd worked with kids and, of course, Mom always used it on her children. It would stretch out someone's rib cage enough to help them swallow better. Worked on adults too. "Keep them up a few seconds."

She coughed and let her hands down. "He just died last night!"

Taken aback by her tone, I said, "I know, and I'm so sorry. But you know, I've only hired on for this week." And nothing on God's green earth could get me to stay longer.

"And you'd leave us hanging?"

So much for coffee softening.

"Well, I do have something I need to do."

Saved by the door, I thought, as I heard it shoved open. Tina came bounding in. "I need coffee."

I need you committing fraud documented on film, thank you very much. "Hey, Tina." I went to the lounge and sat back down, deciding they could all get their own coffee. I wasn't hired as their waitress. Why the heck was Tina back anyway?

After Linda talked to Tina for a few minutes in a voice not loud enough for me to understand, Tina grabbed her purse and they left. I looked at the clock. Noon. The office would be closed for the next hour.

And I really wasn't that hungry.

I pushed myself to stand. A sudden stream of adrenaline had me in "investigative" mode. I looked down the hall. No sounds. But I couldn't take any chances, so I hurried from room to room, not sure what lie I'd use if I found someone. I didn't have to worry since I'd found no one. I stopped at the reception desk. Trudy was just going out the door.

I saw her back, today covered by a black-and-white-striped caftan, but didn't say a word, and she obviously didn't see me. A sharp click made me jump.

She'd locked the door to make sure no one could get in. I was alone and feeling a bit claustrophobic.

But this time I didn't care. I had work to do, I told myself, as I shook off the feeling of confinement. The phobia wasn't too strong since it was a set of rooms and offices and not an eight-by-eight-foot elevator with a closed door. Just the same, I knew I couldn't leave or I'd be locked out.

I went into Donnie's office on a gut instinct. Since my gut had served me so well in my nursing, I decided to trust it on this one. His office was the nicest of any of the doctors. A picture of Tina, looking quite lovely, sat on his desk. Ain't love grand. Behind his mahogany desk was a file cabinet. Had to be patients' files.

I took a Puffs Plus from my pocket, held it in my hand and tried his top desk drawer. It slid open without a groan. Inside sat several pens, papers that looked like doctor stuff and an extra pocket protector. Donnie hadn't changed. Nothing good in there.

Then, still using the tissue, I rummaged through the files in the cabinet. Not much in there for my case. Looked like real, legit patient files.

I leaned against the desk to think. The picture of Tina tumbled over. "Shit." As I went to pick it up, I noticed a key taped to the back. "Hello," I whispered and gingerly took it off so as not to rip the cardboard back of the frame.

I held the tissue, turned the key in the lock of the bottom drawer. Something said to look there, and, besides, it was the only drawer with a lock on it. I opened it and found a few charts.

They should have been filed with all the others.

Hmm. With the tissues in hand, I took out the stack. Tina Macaluso's sat on top. Why would Donnie have his wife's chart here? When I opened it and did a bit of reading, it was all clear. Donnie had treated her, or at least written up the accident report on her. After all, there was nothing to treat. It said her "injury" had occurred on a Monday morning. Lifted patient. Back injury. The hardest to prove. Interesting. Of course, by her actions I knew she was faking it, but when I thumbed through the file, a thought occurred to me.

"Monday morning" stuck in my head. From what I'd seen of her, she wasn't a morning person. I had asked Eddy about her once, and he'd said how lazy she was and that she didn't always come to work on time. Perks of being married to the boss. Then how did she get "injured" on a Monday morning?

Maybe Tina had "hurt" herself at home and was claiming it happened at work to get the money. She could have had a minor injury, and they'd gotten the idea to make some bucks—to pay for two houses. I made a mental note to run it by Jagger and check out her neighbors to see if anyone had seen her get hurt.

The other files glared at me. Had to be something important in them if the doc kept them locked in here. I picked up the stack. Eddy. Trudy. Linda. A few more names I didn't recognize, but soon found out they all were employees over the past few years. I opened poor Eddy's chart first. Two Workers' Comp claims. Hmm. One was for a sprained wrist, the other an injured leg, leading to partial disability.

Eddy didn't even limp.

The other charts all had more Workers' Comp claims on each of the employees—and I'd bet my life that they were never injured.

I looked at the clock. Damn. Armed with mucho info, I shoved the charts back, locked the desk, re-stuck the key behind Tina and hurried out.

In the hallway, I turned around—and bumped right into Dr. Levy.

"Oh, I'm so sorry." Damn! What the hell was he doing here, and did he see me in Donnie's office?

He nodded, then looked at the floor. I'd caused him to drop his medical bag. It'd opened and a disposable syringe had fallen out along with several Ace wraps.

"Sorry again." I bent to pick them up.

He tried to grab the stuff first, mumbling something about goddamn nurses and women.

Weirdo, I thought. *No wonder you have to pay for sex.* "It's still sterile since the wrapper didn't rip," I said, handing him the syringe. Obviously he was too preoccupied to have seen that I had come out of Donnie's office.

He merely looked at me, took the syringe from my hand and shoved it into his bag. "Go to lunch." With that he turned and walked through the reception area, opened the door and shut it with a click. A locked click.

I leaned against the wall and shut my eyes. "Phew."

Then my logical brain said I had less time to snoop more now, so I forced my eyes open and turned toward the reception desk.

I went to the computer Trudy worked on and pressed a key. The screen popped on with today's appointments listed. I really had no idea what I'd find on the computer since I had no idea what to look for. I didn't want to mess up any of

Trudy's files or have her find out that someone had tampered with them, so I decided to stick to investigating only hard copy. Files. Like Linda's. And Donnie's. Trudy obviously only worked on the computer.

I got up and walked down the hall headed for the area where I knew most of the active files would be found.

Linda was a neat freak, I decided. Although she looked to me like all she did was move files all day, her desk was immaculate, and not locked. I looked over the files in the IN basket. All were patients I'd seen today.

Nothing seemed odd.

So, I took the stack from the OUT tray. Half were from yesterday's patients. The bottom half from the morning, the top from the afternoon.

Bingo.

The YMCA basketball boys.

All six charts were held together with a rubber band. I opened Emanuel Louis's. Soft-tissue injury to the left leg while playing basketball. The next one was a broken wrist on Nicky Scarlucci, who I guessed was the white boy. I shut my eyes to remember if I'd seen a cast on his arm.

For several seconds I kept my eyes closed until I could picture him. Shorter than Emanuel and the others, Nicky had dark brown curly hair. He'd had on a black bubble-type jacket that teens wore nowadays and jeans, ten sizes too big, that dragged along the floor. But no cast. "Uh-huh." Nope. In my mind's eye there was no cast on Nicky. I took one last mental look before opening my eyes.

A hand grabbed my shoulder.

Eighteen

Someone grabbed my shoulder! My eyes flew open. In a split second I swung around, my hand in a tight fist—which landed smack-dab in Jagger's left eye.

"Jesus Christ!" His hands flew up to his face. "What the fuck? Why are you always attacking me? You trying to blind me or something?"

"You scared the shit out of me! Why do you insist on scaring me?" I jumped up and ran to the fridge and got out a handful of ice, which I shoved into a paper towel. "Stick this on."

"I called your name when I came in."

"You did not."

"Did too." He held the paper towel of ice to his eye. "Christ."

"I said I'm sorry, and you didn't call my name."

"Maybe you were too engrossed in the files, but I swear I did and you mumbled something that sounded like 'Uh-huh.' "

"Ack. I did." I looked at his eye. A huge red mark circled the deep brown color, and I knew that within hours he'd have a whopper of a shiner.

I wondered if he'd admit that he'd gotten it from a girl.

"Okay. I'm sorry, but you have to stop sneaking up on me. Now, what the hell are you doing here—in that?"

For the first time I took a good look at him. And Mrs. Bakersfield thought Vance looked good in white. The lab coat Jagger wore made his olive complexion a bit darker—swarthier. His hair was combed a different way so it didn't touch the nape of his neck. I wondered if he'd cut it, but thought no. He wore wire-rimmed glasses and had a gold tiny loop earring in his left ear. These disguises were too much. If I saw him in the hallway, I wouldn't have recognized him.

Yet, I would have drooled.

He ignored my question about his lab coat and asked, "What'd you find in the files that you were so preoccupied with?"

"Oh. You are going to be so proud of me." My face heated to the boiling point. Why did I say such a stupid thing?

"I'm listening."

I told him about the files in Donnie's office and my theory about Tina.

He ran a hand through his hair and nodded.

From Jagger that compliment was like getting a gold star on your kindergarten drawing.

"More than likely they misclassified their employees' injuries to make bogus Workers' Comp claims," I said.

"I guessed that."

My chest puffed out like a prize-wining turkey's. "More good news. I found the files on the YMCA boys. They have injuries listed that I didn't see any evidence of. Even if I didn't notice their injuries though, they weren't here but a few minutes, so I know they weren't seen by the doctors."

"Who handed them the bags with the shoes in them?" He leaned over my shoulder.

I inhaled "scent of man."

"Sherlock? Earth to Sherlock?" He lifted the top file I'd been looking at.

"Hmm?"

"Okay. I believe you that you don't use, but have you ever had your attention span checked out? It's shorter than a toothpick."

Suddenly I visualized him playing with that dumb toothpick in his mouth. Between his full lips. Touching. Tapping. Tasting. Oh . . . my . . . God.

I felt my chin being lifted and found myself looking directly into his eyes. And this was supposed to help me concentrate? His finger on my chin? Puleez. How could I, with fire burning my skin?

Professional, I screamed inside my head. *You are a professional, Pauline Sokol!* "What did you ask me?"

"Forget the attention-span thing. We only have thirty minutes left. The shoes?" He removed his finger.

Yikes.

I couldn't believe that we'd wasted so much time—or that my thoughts had strayed to his finger. "Oh, yeah. The shoes. I never saw who gave them to the boys. The first time I noticed the bags was when the boys walked out, and they opened them in the lobby while waiting for the elevator."

He paused a minute. Maybe he had figured out something important about the case.

He looked at me and said, "Let me get this straight. Did you get on an elevator with six giants and one short Polack, when you won't ride in an elevator with me anymore?"

Shoot. I didn't want him to know that I hadn't, so I gave him a dose of his own medicine and ignored his question. "Don't mess up the files. Linda is very anal."

He ignored me and looked through each chart.

"What I don't understand is, how do they get money out of the insurance companies?"

He kept flipping through papers as he said, "The shoes are used to get the kids to give them their insurance card info—and to keep their mouths shut. The office bills the insurance company for visits, X-rays, casts. You name it."

"Nicky's chart said that he had a broken bone, but when you snuck up on me I was trying to picture a cast on his arm, and I couldn't."

"I'll forget the sneaking-up part. Which, in fact, I didn't do. As far as the no-cast part, the fake break."

"Excuse me?"

"A con artist will take advantage of an old break, an existing injury to make a claim. I'll bet Nicky had a break not long ago."

"And they used his old X-rays."

Jagger smiled. Nice. "Atta girl, Sherlock."

"I'm learning from the best." Now I was psyched for the rest of the day.

Jagger held open the files on each kid and stared at them a few seconds, adjusting his glasses each time.

"Something wrong with your glasses?"

He stopped and looked at me. "No, Sherlock."

"Oh, it's just that you keep adjusting—" He leaned closer to one of the files whose writing was a bit smudged. "Camera!" I shouted.

"Keep it down!"

"Oh, sorry. Right," I whispered.

Damn. I hadn't taken pictures of the files in Donnie's office. I wasn't about to share that with Jagger. I'd let him assume I had and sneak back in there later.

He finally set the files back exactly in place. And here I'd warned him not to mess things up. Duh. The guy was a professional, and I'm guessing never left a trace of himself anywhere.

He was like a current of air.

First he's not here. Then he's here—without any fanfare.

And usually scaring the bejeevers out of me.

For a second I thought his disguising himself could be construed as comical, but now, looking at "Doctor" Jagger, I knew he'd found a way to get himself into places I never would be able to go. He was a master at his job.

And anything but comical.

He looked at the clock on Linda's desk. "We need to get out of here."

"Yeah. I am a bit hungry. Good thing I've got a few minutes to run to the cafeteria." I blew out a breath and went to the employee exit. "Damn, stuck again. We can't get out."

Jagger merely looked at me.

The last I saw of Jagger was him getting on the elevator and starting to tell me he was going to see Lieutenant Shatley, and that I should go back and take pictures of Donnie's files. Damn him. Then the door shut and I hurried up the stairs. Sure, he'd more than likely bring up that I was chicken to ride with him, which was 99.9 percent true, but I also had to hurry to get lunch and think about how the heck he got us out of the stuck office.

I remembered going into the waiting room where the employee door was and then Jagger opening it—from the other side! Somehow he'd gotten out of the office and let me out. I shook my head as I grabbed a ham and cheese on a croissant. Forget the calories in the buttery roll. I needed something after my brush with fear caused by Jagger.

I looked at the dessert section. Nothing interesting. I asked the woman behind the counter, "Do you have anything in chocolate?"

"Like what? Cake? Cookie?"

"Anything. Anything chocolate." When she went into the back and came out with a brownie, I wanted to leap over the counter and hug the darling. Instead, I thanked her profusely, despite her look of confusion, and hurried to pay. I didn't have time to sit and eat, so I stuck the brownie in my pocket—thank goodness it had plastic wrap on it—opened the sandwich and ate as I walked down the stairs. Then I opened the chocolate brownie and salivated.

When I hurried across the waiting room, already full of patients, Trudy looked up from her desk. "What's the matter, Pauline?"

"Watter?" I said with a mouthful of brownie.

"Matter," she clarified.

I swallowed and walked behind the desk. "I'm fine. Nothing the matter. No problems for me." Yikes. The nervous rambling was back.

The phone rang, thank goodness, and Trudy turned to answer it. I took the opportunity to get the heck out of Dodge and away from her interrogating. Okay, to be fair to Trudy, she was only asking out of concern and it was weird that I'd been eating my lunch on the run.

I rushed into the lounge to rinse out my mouth before I smiled at a patient only to discover I had a black brownie-covered tooth. When I bent over the sink, I felt someone come up from behind. I wiped my mouth with a paper towel and thought I'd kill Jagger if it was him again.

I turned around and jumped. "Oh!"

Linda stood inches away.

Oh no! Did she discover her charts had been tampered with? "Hey, how's it going?"

"It's going fine with me, Pauline, but I'm wondering about you."

"Me? I'm . . . peachy."

"Then why aren't you out there working? You're the only nurse here today. Remember? The patients aren't going to show themselves into the examining rooms."

Damn. "I know. It's just . . . sorry."

Her look, one that reminded me of my mother hollering at us kids, softened. "No. I'm the one who is sorry. I'll bet you're just flustered over Eddy."

I almost said why would I be, but quickly realized what she meant and decided to use it to my benefit. "Eddy. Poor Eddy. We went to school together. I can't get him out of my mind."

She touched my arm. I noticed a beautiful ruby ring on her finger. The doctors must pay her pretty well, I thought, since she was a single parent and sole supporter of her family. Then again, I wasn't being fair. Maybe she had a boyfriend and he'd given it to her.

Or Linda did more than just move files around.

One thing I noticed since becoming a medical-insurance-fraud investigator was that my imagination had taken on a life of its own. Problem was, I had a hard time deciding what was fact and what was my mind going out of whack.

I threw my paper towel toward the trash. It hit the floor. I bent, then looked at her. "Always bend those knees."

She glared at me.

"Bad knees are a bummer. Ever have trouble with yours?" The file in Donnie's desk was for a knee injury on Linda.

"My knees are fine."

"Have they always been?"

"Yes, Pauline. Why the sudden interest in my knees?"

"I . . . er . . . I thought Eddy had said you were out on Workers' Comp with a knee injury." *Forgive me, Eddy, but I had to use you since you are no longer around to corroborate my lies.*

She shook her head. "Must have been someone else he was talking about."

That meant Donnie and Tina filed claims on Linda—without her knowledge. I whispered, "Yes!"

"You're acting odd, Pauline."

Oops. No comeback for that, so I said, "Good. Good knees. Good for you. Always bend. Helps the back too. Excuse me, Linda."

She moved aside as if she couldn't wait until I left. As well she should with my behavior, so I bustled off to the waiting room. I peeked over my shoulder to see her standing there, arms folded over her chest—watching.

Again, reminded me of Mom.

The rest of the afternoon was a blur. Being by myself I had to concentrate on nursing and not really do a darn thing about fraud investigating. Toward the end of the day a guy came limping in dressed in a black suit, sporting a long beard and dark glasses. He had a Seeing Eye dog with him.

I stared at him for a few seconds, then mentally slapped myself upside the head.

Jagger!

I held his chart, which said Mr. Mario Pinellas, (yeah, right) in my hand and leaned over. "Gotcha this time, Jagger."

The dog growled.

The man leaned his head toward my voice and said, "*Excusa*?"

The accent was real.

The voice was higher than Jagger's.

And there was no shiner.

I swallowed, did an express novena that the dog wouldn't chew my leg off and said, "I'm sorry, sir. Please come this way, Mr. Pinellas."

I needed to get out of here.

After Mr. Pinellas was safely in the examining room, where I made sure he wouldn't fall off the table, I shoved the red clip over to signal Dr. Levy that his patient was in the room and hurried to the lounge. I promptly ran into Linda again.

"Something wrong?" she asked, standing there with a stack of charts in her hands.

I tried to see if they were the YMCA boys' ones, but couldn't. "I'm just beat."

"Oh. Good news. I hired a replacement for Eddy. She'll start Monday. You'll train her."

"Me? I've only been here a few days myself."

"Tina's coming in to help."

Yes! I hope she has to pick up a ton of stuff. "Tina? Great. She'll be a big help. I only hope that her back is all right."

Linda's eyes darkened.

Hmm. Maybe she suspected Tina was a fraud too. Interesting. "Do you have a piece of scrap paper, Linda?"

She walked to her desk and handed me a yellow Post-it on which I wrote, "beeper."

Linda looked over my shoulder, but I didn't care. She'd never know what I meant, and by her look she was getting perturbed with my weirdness and more than likely wanted this week to end faster than I did.

* * *

On the way home, I decided to check in with Goldie. I needed some friendship after the day I'd had, and I knew Miles would still be at work. I also needed to vent about how I'd forgotten to take the file pictures, and how Jagger had known.

"*Chéri*? How's it going?" Adele sat behind the reception desk, filing her nails. Not as long as Goldie's, hers were a bright pink to go with the even brighter pink silk blouse she wore with the top four buttons undone. I couldn't look at her cleavage since I knew it'd make me green with envy. Her legs, covered in sparkling black nylon, were crossed and she had on black patent-leather heels.

"Hey, Adele. Not so good today."

"Heard about Eddy. Too bad."

Did everyone know Eddy Roden? I didn't ask how she did, but figured that the tight-knit community of insurance people in Hope Valley had some underground-type communication system going. Goldie had told me about it, but I never realized the extent until now.

I nodded. "How sad."

She filed the last nail and set the emery board down. "Fabio's been looking for you. I left you a few messages on your machine at home." She motioned toward his office with her head, causing her curls to bounce. "You can beat it if you want. Adele didn't see you."

I smiled. "Thanks for that, but I'll go talk to him." What I'd say was another matter. Adele said Goldie was in his office if I needed him after talking to Fabio, and I walked down the hall.

At Fabio's door, I paused.

The thought of running out to my car became a real possibility as I heard music, I think it was Perry Como's rendition of "When the Moon Hits Your Eye Like a Big Pizza Pie" and told myself that couldn't be the name of the song while I also told myself I could do this. I could face Fabio and talk him out of firing me.

I knocked and peeked in when he said, "Yo."

"Fabio?" I hesitated at the door.

He'd been clipping his fingernails onto a piece of newspaper, and I wondered if today was manicure day at Scarpello and Tonelli Insurance Company. I only hoped he didn't do his toes.

He kept clipping. "What?"

"I . . . Adele said you wanted to see me."

"Who are you?"

If you'd look up you'd see, you dumb shit. "Pauline."

Slowly he set the clippers onto the pile of papers on the desk. He beat Lieutenant Shatley in the messiest desk department. Fabio gave a low growl and glared at me. "Well, Ms. Pauline Sokol. How nice of you to grace us with your presence here."

"Look, Fabio—"

"No, *you* look, Sokol," his voice kept getting louder until I considered it a shout. "I'm not paying you to fuck around at who knows what. No tape yet, and I need my money back soon. I have bills to fucking pay." He leaned forward for a closer look. "Why the hell are you dressed like that anyway?"

"I—" Oh no! I couldn't fabricate any lie, and found it hard to ask Saint Theresa to help with things like that.

"She's hanging out at Macaluso's office building to do her surveillance, you jerk," said Goldie coming up behind and putting his arm around my shoulder. He turned toward me. "Brilliant plan you came up with, suga." Then he winked a long, black fake eyelash at me.

I smiled and mouthed, "thanks," but worried either one would find out how close to the truth Goldie had just come.

Fabio waved at both of us. "Get your asses out of here and go do work."

We turned to go. Goldie still held onto me.

"Oh, Sokol, you got one week left on your probation. No proof on Macaluso and you can kiss your career *adios*."

Goldie's nails dug into my shoulder, but I stifled my "ouch" knowing it wasn't meant for me.

Outside the door he mumbled, "Cocksucking asshole." Then he gave me a tight squeeze and let go. "Excuse my French, suga. That guy gets under my craw."

I smiled. "Thanks for saving me in there."

"I need a drink and you look as if you could use two of 'em yourself."

We headed into his office, where he insisted I have a Hurricane in a tall, curved glass that he'd gotten at a bar called Pat O'Brien's in New Orleans. They were famous for their Hurricanes, a fruity punch-type drink with dark rum. Goldie used a pouch of the mix and his blender. He poured two drinks and handed me one.

"Thanks. You have the most well-equipped office I've ever seen."

He laughed. "You ain't shittin, suga." Goldie sunk into the zebra couch. In his banana yellow tights and long matching sweater, he looked very "jungle." Tiny orb-like lemons hung from his ears and his lipstick was a California orange much like Doc Levy's car. *I forgot to show Jagger the list of doctors' cars*, I thought, as Goldie stretched himself out like a cat. His shoes were black spike heels today.

My feet, nestled in their white clogs, hurt just looking at them. I sat across from Goldie and sipped on the Hurricane he'd handed me, and told him about the files and Jagger. Goldie was appropriately sympathetic and said that maybe Fabio would give me a bonus for the extra info I'd found. Then we both mouthed, "Yeah, sure." I smiled at him and held up my glass. "I'm going to get looped on this, you know."

He grinned. "Don't get wiped out before our double date tonight."

Ack! I'd forgotten about those plans. And here I was planning a nice hot bath, a small meal, after the croissant and brownie, and subsequent nap until it was time for bed. "I'm so beat. Maybe we could make it another day—"

"Oh no, you don't. I want to see about the Jagger thing."

By "thing" I guessed he meant our relationship. Come to

think of it, I had no way to get in touch with Jagger to cancel if I wanted to. I figured, no, I knew he'd just show up when it was time tonight.

I took a longer sip than I should have and coughed. Goldie jumped up. "Put your hands in the air, suga."

I did, having recently used that trick on Linda.

He sat back down and took a sip of his drink. "I have a bad feeling about this, suga. And I don't mind tellin' you."

What's to have feelings about? I thought. There is no *thing*. "I'm a big girl, Goldie. I can take care of myself."

"Taking care is not what I'm worried about. I told you Jagger would never hurt you." He finished his drink, ran an orange nail across his lip to catch the last droplet and said, "It's that heart of yours. I've seen you look at him, suga. I've seen you look at him, but he doesn't look back."

That hurt, although I knew Goldie didn't mean for it to. He was partly right; but what I silently disagreed with was Jagger not looking back.

No one on this earth could read Jagger's looks.

So, Goldie could be totally wrong—and it may not all be one sided.

What was I thinking!

There was no side to this conversation because Goldie was wrong on both counts. Jagger had the appeal of a sexy, out-of-reach movie star, but I wasn't delusional enough to think I'd appeal to him.

Still, I'd enjoy those daydreams.

But keep my wits about me.

And consequently my heart.

Nineteen

I told myself that Goldie was wrong. The thought wouldn't leave my brain, so I decided to do some work. Investigating, before Fabio fired me. Surely work would keep me preoccupied even though I'd spent all day at the office. I couldn't relax now anyway since soon I'd be on the "date." Not having any idea where Tina was and not wanting to fish around town for her, I went to the medical office.

Had to get pictures of Donnie's files.

After sneaking in and avoiding two janitors, I made it into the practice. One had left the front door open, which fit right into my hopes. If it had been locked, I was sunk. Never would I have the "Jagger" skills for breaking and entering. No one was in the reception area, so I slowly walked to the door leading into the hallway where the examining rooms were.

I turned the knob and held my breath.

Silence.

Thank you, Saint Theresa. I knew she was helping me, along with a few guardian angels. Had to be, or I might have suffered Eddy's fate by now. I walked into the hallway and waited. Again, no sound except the clicking of the stupid clock over the nurses' station. Some drug company had given it to the clinic. The hands were syringes and the numbers little pills. It was half-past a Percodan, so I had to hurry. There was that "date" thing tonight.

I looked down the hallway. All the doors were closed, including the ones to the docs' offices. If someone had been in here, surely their door would be open. I listened and wished I had my mother's nose for sniffing. Could come in handy sniffing around for other humans.

I gingerly walked down the hallway toward Donnie's office. At the door I waited, put my ear against the wood and listened. Good. Nothing again. I turned the knob and opened the door to darkness and flipped on the light. My beeper/camera didn't do infrared film, and I couldn't afford that right now.

I hurried to the desk, found the key on the back of the picture and whispered, "Thanks, Tina." After I opened the drawer and took out the files, which, thank goodness, had not been disturbed, I started clicking away. My heart beat faster as I accomplished my job. Felt damn good to do it—all alone.

After I had plenty of shots and everything back in order, I flipped the light switch and pulled the door, moving the handle very slowly so as not to make any squeaks. I got out the door and looked down the hallway. No one.

Then the floor creaked.

I looked down to see if I'd stepped on a loose spot in the floor. I felt frozen to the spot. I forced myself to shift my feet as if they weighed a hundred pounds each and turned. I couldn't go out the way I'd come in. The way of the creaking floor. So, I decided to head around toward the X-ray room. There was an emergency exit at the end—and I considered this an emergency.

Footsteps clicked along the hallway. Janitors probably wore sneakers or rubber-soled shoes, which wouldn't make that sound. I got near the room and saw the sign.

EMERGENCY EXIT ONLY. ALARM WILL SOUND.

I needed the exit, but not the alarm.

I turned quickly and headed back toward the lounge. Maybe I could sneak in there and get out the other way. I heard a breath—and it wasn't mine, since my breaths were stalled in my trachea. I swung into the first office I could find.

The streetlight lit the darkness enough to see I was back in—Donnie's office! Damn these hallways for being a circle.

I held onto the doorknob to make a speedy exit when the time was right.

The doorknob turned.

I gasped.

"What the fuck are you doing, Pauline?"

I froze.

The door swung open.

If I thought my heart had sped up before, it was pounding so loudly now I could hear it.

And probably *Donnie* could too.

After yanking my thoughts from fear to sanity, I said, "Oh, hey, Don. How you doing?"

"It's always been Donnie, Pauline, and the question is what the fuck are *you* doing?"

Good question.

I looked past Donnie in hopes that Jagger would be there to save me. No one. Not even a real janitor was in the office hallway right now. I needed a lie. A good one. One that would prevent Donnie from suspecting me of being an investigator.

"Geez, Donnie. You caught me." I stepped out of his office and started to go.

He grabbed my arm. "I *know* I caught you, but what the hell at?"

Suddenly a janitor (obviously sent from up above) came around the corner. I said the fastest thank-you prayer on record. "Okay. See you later, Donnie." I tried to pull away.

"You didn't answer my question, and I'm not letting go until you do."

Damn. Then, I looked at the janitor. Blonde. Built. Blue eyes. Yes! I waved to him and smiled.

Donnie looked over his shoulder.

The janitor looked at me as if I were nuts.

I leaned next to Donnie's ear. "Sh. Don't say a word to Tina or especially Linda. I think he's married, and we were going to . . . you know, Donnie. You know."

Thank goodness that he was a doctor with a brain and could figure out my message. He looked from the janitor, who was now vacuuming and making noise so he couldn't hear us, and back to me. Thank goodness the janitor couldn't hear.

"Gotcha, Pauline. You of all people." He grinned like a sex fiend. "But next time use the examining room instead." He winked at me and went into his office.

I let out a sigh and collapsed against the wall, glad that men thought of sex at the drop of the proverbial hat.

Maybe their brains really weren't their biggest . . . asset.

Then it dawned, why the heck would Donnie think, "me of all people!"

After I got home from the office, I soaked in lilac bubbles and tried to forget the day I'd had, that I had to insinuate that I was fooling around with the janitor, what Goldie had said earlier and everything about Jagger. Soon the water cooled so I rinsed, got out, toweled myself off and slipped into my white silk undies and lace bra.

I didn't choose them in any special way. They were on the top of the pile and just happened to be my sexiest. Not that I thought anyone would see them tonight! After changing outfits about seventy-five times, I settled on cream-colored wool slacks, and a cream-and-tan sweater with sparkly thingies on it that Miles had given to me last Christmas.

At first I worried the color would make my Polish, year-round pale complexion more washed out, but then I'd used the makeup tips Goldie had taught me. Came out damn good. Looked healthy and sexy.

As I slipped into black pumps, I wondered if Miles'd had Goldie in mind when he'd bought the sweater. It looked like him. But I loved it since my friend had given it to me. I swirled my hair up into a French twist-type do and looked into the mirror. Nope. Leave it down, I thought. Made me look younger and not so sophisticated. I didn't want to do sophisticated on a "date" with Jagger.

He'd probably wear jeans and leather anyway.

"You about ready?" Miles called from downstairs.

I gave myself a once-over in the mirror and looked at Spanky perched on my bed. "What ya think?"

He opened one sleepy eye and shut it.

"Men." I hurried out the door and left him to fend for himself after that. He was tiny, but quite capable of bounding off my white ruffled comforter if he chose to.

At the base of the stairs I stopped. Miles sat on the leather couch, sipping his white wine, dressed to perfection in a navy suit. Looked gorgeous. Hair neatly combed into place with his sideburns just below his ears. The room smelled of his Polo cologne yet the scent wasn't overpowering. Miles had too much class to overpower.

Goldie tapped a sparkly silver spike shoe on the carpet while he sipped on something. I guessed Scotch. He'd draped a white fur shawl of sorts over his shoulders, which went fab with his winter white pantsuit, trimmed in silver. I couldn't imagine the salary Goldie pulled in, but the clothes horse sure had taste.

But that was it. The two of them.

No Jagger.

I stepped off the last step and nonchalantly looked toward the door as if that'd make the bell ring. If he stood me up, I was quitting the ortho practice nursing job on Monday.

Miles got up. "What'll it be?" He looked at me and I started to say Jagger would be here soon, but then realized Miles was talking liquor.

"Same as you're having."

The phone rang as Miles headed into the kitchen. A few seconds later, he called out, "Jagger will meet us at Madeline's."

I blew out a breath.

Goldie took a sip and looked at me over the glass's rim.

"What?" I said. "He's meeting us there. Probably got tied up." I sat with a thud. Spanky ran down the stairs and jumped at my legs. I scooped him up and gave him an extra hug. He promptly jumped down and ran to Goldie.

"It's just that I don't want you—"

"Cocaine. I know." I didn't mean to be so testy. "Sorry about the tone."

He held up his glass. "I can be a pain in the ass sometimes."

Miles came through the door and handed me my drink. "I can vouch for that."

"Stop it, you two. Goldie, you have a heart of gold, like your name." I was dying to ask about Jagger but didn't want to seem too anxious.

He said, "He's tied up at the police station. He'll run home, change and meet us at the restaurant. Reservations aren't for another half hour so we'll be fine."

My friend knew me so well.

I took a sip of beer and let myself relax.

When we walked into the restaurant, several people stared. For a few seconds, I felt jealous that Goldie looked a hell of a lot more gorgeous than I. I don't think a customer here thought he was a man. His pantsuit covered his wrists.

I smiled at my two favorite people as the hostess ushered us to our reserved table with a view of the river. Tiny white Christmas lights glowed like fireflies outside the window. In the background faint ruffles of waves floated along with the night's breeze.

Speaking of breeze, in came Jagger.

My heart leaped to my throat. No jeans. No leather.

This time it wasn't a disguise. His hair still touched the nape of his neck but it'd been combed into a style, less fly-away. He had on a suede tan jacket with a lighter shade turtleneck and darker brown trousers that fit to perfection. My fingers shook as I took my water glass to my lips and pretended to drink. Couldn't risk choking or spewing water on my outfit. Goldie already put me to shame.

Jagger came closer, nodded and sat. "Sorry."

Miles and Goldie stared.

I know they were looking at Jagger's eye. He hadn't even tried to conceal it, although I think I would have been disappointed to see any form of makeup on him.

Goldie said, "No problem, man. Business is business. We can all relate to that." He really had class not to mention the shiner.

I was dying to find out what Jagger'd learned at the police station, but couldn't ask in front of Goldie and Miles.

The waiter came over and Jagger ordered a beer. He looked at me. "Refill?"

My wineglass was still full. Either this "date" made him so uncomfortable that he wasn't himself (which would also disappoint me) or his eyesight might have been affected. Geez, I hoped not.

I thought I'd do him a favor and get the subject out in the open and over with so I said, "Where'd you get that beauty of a shiner?"

He glared at me. Took a sip of his water and said, "Work related."

Goldie laughed. "Once I got bopped on the head by a suspect. He was lifting a huge mother load of lumber onto the back of his pickup. Back injury my derrière. I got a little too close with my camera—this was back in my 'green' years—"

"I hear you," I said and laughed.

Goldie toasted me with his Scotch. "—and the guy chased me six blocks with a hammer. Hit me with the handle. Bled like a stuck pig."

Miles gasped and touched Goldie's hand. "Head wounds always look worse than they are, sweetie."

Out of the corner of my eye, I caught Jagger. Although usually hard to read with his mysterious stone-faced expressions, that look was pure "what the hell am I doing here?" I smiled and made sure he noticed.

The dinner progressed without incident. Jagger remained

polite although I got the feeling that if he were a little kid's balloon he would be ready to pop.

By the time my tiramisu arrived, Jagger *did* look really ready to pop. Didn't take any talent to see that. But he'd been friendly enough to Miles and Goldie, so I could only assume he was in a hurry to end our "date."

I ate the dessert quickly, declined coffee and said, "Guys, I'm bushed. I think we'll head off now."

Jagger was up and out of his seat, paying the hostess, who I guessed would pass it on to the waiter, before I could sling my purse over my shoulder. I was sure Jagger had been polite enough and said proper goodbyes to Goldie and Miles, but it was such a blur I couldn't picture it in my mind. Besides, I was feeling a bit down that he wanted to end this night so fast.

Once outside, he yanked off his coat and pulled the turtleneck as if it were choking him. Damn, but the sweater clung to the muscles of his arms. Just the right size to say he worked out, yet not gigantic enough to imply that he did steroids like Popeye did spinach.

"You're going to stretch it out."

"Doesn't get much use anyway." He hit the button on his key chain and the door locks popped open.

I opened my door and got in. He'd started the engine and was already backing out before I could fasten my seat belt. "Thanks," I said.

"For what?"

"Being . . . polite to them."

He stopped at the entryway and looked over. "Hey, they're both great guys. Besides, even if they weren't, I'm not in the habit of hurting others' feelings."

I nodded but thought, What about hearts?

I sipped on the decaffeinated Hazelnut coffee Jagger handed me from the drive-thru at Dunkin Donuts. He then parked the car in the rear of the parking lot, making me wonder why we hadn't just gone inside. It would get cold out here. I knew that from my surveillance of Tina.

For several minutes he sat there sipping at his coffee. I couldn't stand it any longer. I decided to try to make conversation, and the first thing that popped into my head was, "Did Eddy commit suicide? I thought maybe that he got worried, you know, 'cause someone suspected him of ratting them out. And then I thought, if he were so worried that things might get ugly, maybe he drove into the river—"

He turned the car off, looked me square in the eye and said, "Eddy was murdered."

My hand shook, spilling droplets of Hazelnut onto my beige wool coat. Jagger didn't blink an eye, but reached down and pulled a Puffs tissue out of the container on the floor. He handed it to me while I said, "Murdered. How . . . how do you—"

"Police blame the air bag."

I wiped at my coat not even caring if it got stained. I mean, a man, a man I knew had been murdered. I'd dealt with death and dying throughout my nursing career, but I'd never even known anyone who knew a person who'd been murdered. I looked at Jagger. "So the air bag didn't deploy? Wasn't he wearing a seat belt?"

"Had on his seat belt."

I really didn't know why I was asking so many questions. Eddy was dead. Why did it matter how? But I couldn't help myself. "Then he was killed because the air bag didn't deploy?"

"It deployed all right. Crushed just about every bone in Eddy."

"That's why Vance was called out. But I don't understand. I thought the air bag would save—"

"Someone had tampered with it. Put in a much larger, more powerful one. Thus Eddy . . ."

I said a prayer for Eddy's soul. How awful to be killed like that. Of course, getting killed any way would be awful. The results would be the same.

"So, where does that leave us?" I asked.

Jagger looked out the front window, sipped his coffee and said, "Right where we were."

I quickly told him that Trudy and Linda never had the injuries the Workers' Comp claims had indicated. He looked at me as if he already knew. Then why did I need to go back there? I was hoping he'd say I could call in sick and drop that job. But then again, Eddy might have died because of this case and as I'd told myself before, I owed it to him. Well, maybe not owed, but in his memory I'd do all I could to help. I knew very little about investigating medical insurance fraud and even less about investigating murder. But I would try my damnedest—about the fraud thing! Murder was to be left to the professionals. Still, if I could help with that . . .

"But," Jagger said, "you have to be extra careful in searching around the office. You can do it though."

I wasn't sure if he meant I could do a good job investigating, or I could be extra careful. Hell, I'd try for both. "What am I supposed to be looking for to help find Eddy's murderer?"

Jagger had been taking a sip of coffee as I asked. The coffee spewed onto his dashboard. "Shit, Sherlock. *You* are not getting involved in *that*."

The emphasis on "you" and "that" made him sound like my father telling me I couldn't do something like join the air force right out of nursing school. Daddy was right back then as I would never have made it by moving away. Pauline Sokol was a stay-at-home-gal. At least a stay-in-the-same-town gal.

"I mean it, Pauline. Leave murder investigating to the pros."

"Like you?"

He looked at me. "What'd you find out about the doctors' cars?"

Touché. He wasn't going to give me a clue if he had anything to do with helping find Eddy's killer. Damn. Well, I had to remind myself it didn't matter who Jagger was or whom he worked for. The end result had to be the same. Bring criminals to justice.

"Oh, with all that about Eddy, I forgot." I set my coffee cup on the dashboard and reached for my purse.

"We don't have all night for you to rummage around in that thing if you want to go see what Tina is up to."

"Oh, yeah. Sure I do." I rummaged around without results. "I almost forgot about—"

Jagger grabbed my purse. "What the hell are you looking for?" He tipped it over onto the floorboard.

"Hey!"

There on the floor sat my cell phone, address book, tissues, used and clean, lipstick, scraps of paper with phone numbers on them—whose, I mostly had forgotten—and, gulp, a Tampax. It looked gigantic. The size of a column on an antebellum plantation house.

"Didn't your mother ever tell you not to look in a woman's purse?"

"I'm not looking *in* your purse."

"Semantics." He didn't address the mother issue, which made my inquisitive mind all the more inquisitive. "Oh, there." I reached down and picked up the paper I'd been looking for. It was pretty much a smudge of Starlight Pink.

Jagger took it from me. "Great job, Sherlock. This should be very helpful."

I grabbed it back, ripping off the top corner, which more than likely wouldn't matter. "I couldn't find a pen."

"Let me get this straight. You go to do surveillance to see what kinds of cars the docs drive without a pen. And"—he looked at the paper—"you have to use a canceled check for paper. And, the damn thing is a fucking Picasso in lipstick."

I had no recourse for that one.

"I remember what I wrote." Least I hope I did. I shut my eyes for a few seconds to picture the doctors getting out of their cars. Good thing I'd learned so much about cars from

Uncle Walt. The pictures came clear. Then I told Jagger who drove what.

"Interesting."

"What is? The fact that they all drive such expensive cars—"

"Except Doc O'Connor."

"Guess that eliminates her," I said.

Jagger took another tissue and wiped off the coffee splashed dashboard. He turned to me. "Does it?"

"I . . . I . . . Doesn't it?"

"Don't always go for the obvious, Sherlock." He shoved his empty coffee cup into the bag on the floor and turned the ignition on.

I leaned back, took my last sip of coffee and wondered if that was true. Was Charlene involved and just driving an old rattletrap to avoid suspicion? Or was one of the other doctors—all males with inflated egos—driving an expensive car that the insurance company unwittingly paid for?

Or was Jagger yanking my chain?

Damn. This wasn't easy.

Jagger turned the car in the direction of the river. Oh, no. I didn't want to go back to the scene of Eddy's death. But Jagger turned right instead of left and soon we were outside the Macalusos' smaller—but not cheap by any means—house. He pulled over a few houses away and killed his lights.

This is where I first saw Jagger.

The thought didn't have time to percolate before the garage door opened and Tina's car backed out. "How do you do that?" I asked Jagger, sounding much too much in awe of him.

He chuckled, turned on the car and started to follow Tina.

"That was just dumb luck," I argued even though he hadn't said a word.

"Not so dumb, I'd say."

"By the way, did you call the cops on me the first day I was—"

He merely turned and looked.

Shit. I knew it. Oh, well. Guess he didn't want me messing up his big case.

We turned left onto Elm and headed toward the shopping mall. A bit disappointed, I didn't think I'd get much film on Tina shopping. Unless she kept stooping to get things on lower shelves. I thought of Eddy's comment about her picking up a penny. Poor Eddy.

Tina turned into a little strip mall a few miles before the big mall. Jagger slowed, turned into the next parking lot, which was a Burger King. He faced the Suburban toward the strip mall.

There was Tina, big as life, getting out of her car. She had on a full-length brown mink coat, which made me think of a grizzly. I'm sure the mink folks wouldn't want that image of one of their obviously expensive coats in any ad though. She was just too large of a woman to make mink glamorous.

I heard a click and turned to see Jagger standing outside the door. Geez. He could give me some warning. I grabbed the contents of my purse from the floor and started to shove it back inside. It took several minutes. When I looked up, Jagger was gone. Shit.

I quickly got out of the car. When I shut it, I heard the familiar *click*, and knew he was within range to electronically lock his doors. The wind kicked up, sending my hair flying about like millions of kites on my head.

Snow covered the ground above the curb, and I noticed footprints the size of feet that I guessed were Jagger's. They headed toward the strip mall, so I followed along, my darn pumps getting soaked in the snow, not to mention my toes freezing like ten tiny ice pops.

I slipped three times but caught myself on nearby branches or cars, whichever was closest. When I got to the parking lot of the little mall, I stopped. Now what?

I looked around. There was a printing shop, which was closed at this time of night. A lawyer's office, dark too. A coffee shop whose lights burned brightly and where patrons milled in and out like bees at a hive. Maybe Tina had gone in for a cup of coffee. I walked toward it and noticed next door was a gift shop. At the end of the strip mall was Curves R You fitness center. Below the sign were silhouettes dancing what I assumed was jazzercise and ones flipping and dancing in all directions doing aerobics.

Tina had to be in the coffee shop, I thought, so I walked closer. A crowd of people drinking and talking formed outside. Watching them had me freezing. They all looked as if they weren't in any hurry. Wishing I lived in Florida, I peered past a man sipping a latte, but couldn't see much inside. The windows were decorated with cups of steaming coffee, donuts and various posters, leaving little clear glass to view through.

So, I opened the door and looked in. A line formed near the cash register, several couples sat at tables but none looked like Tina in her mink coat. She might be in the ladies' room, I told myself, but I had no intention of spying on her in there.

This place didn't look promising, so I moved away from the door when a rude man said, "In or out, lady."

I was so cold now, my feet were numb, and I knew the tip of my nose made Rudolph's pale in comparison. Bundling up, I moved closer to the door of the exercise place. With a shiver, I opened the door and stepped into the foyer. I intended to warm up and leave in a few minutes before someone came to see if I wanted to join.

Thank you very much, but Pauline Sokol was an ardent jogger and fit, in my opinion, for her age. I pushed back my hair since the wind had done a number on it. A woman came through the door to go inside. "Excuse me," I said and moved to the side. When I watched her go in, something caught my eye.

The door to a large room opened. A group jumped and bobbled to The Village People's "YMCA" song—and there in the back of the class was Tina!

Yes!

I moved inside the place and started to fiddle around in my purse. I hadn't wanted to wear my beeper/camera at dinner in case it got bumped off. I sure couldn't afford another, and wouldn't take a loan from Uncle Walt again. My fingers weren't having any luck so I stuck my head in the purse.

"Looking for this?"

My head flew out of my bag. There Jagger stood with my beeper/camera.

I grabbed it from his hand. "What the hell are you doing with—"

"You left it on the floor. I didn't want to lose Tina, so I hurried out. When I knew where she was, I came back to get you. What the hell have you been doing?"

"Me?" My voice came out rather hysterically.

A young woman in neon green spandex came near. "Can I help you two with something?"

I said, "No—"

Jagger said, "Yes, ma'am."

"Suzy," she corrected with a smile aimed only at him.

What was I? Chopped sauerkraut?

"Suz, my wife is interested in your programs. Mind if we look around, hon?"

Hon?

Where'd he get off calling a twenty-something *hon*? Was that legal?

Before I could get unwarrantedly jealous, the word *wife* hit me. Ack!

She batted her eyelashes, not nearly as long and full as Goldie's, at my "husband" and the next thing I knew, we had a ringside seat in a room that looked over the pool, racquetball court and gym, where Tina danced like a marionette sans any back pain.

"Suzy Exercise Queen" went on and on about the facilities. When she excused herself, he leaned over and said, "Get filming."

I'd shoved the camera into my pocket earlier. Now I took it out and held it in front of my eye.

Jagger reached over, turned it around.

Shoot. I'd wondered why I couldn't see anything. But now it was correct and Tina was bending, spinning and jumping so that *my* back hurt watching. Soon the class was cooling down.

"Hurry before little Suzy comes back or we run into Tina on the way out," Jagger ordered.

"I can't make the camera go any faster." My voice came out as if I were pissed. Not because he was rushing me—I knew we had to get out, or get caught—but because I was still hung up on that "hon." I told myself repeatedly that Jagger had slipped into one of his disguises with the term of endearment. But shoot, I was still pissed.

Me, he called Sherlock.

But truthfully, Pauline, I told myself, *you get a tingly feeling inside when he says that.* I'd come to learn that when he called me Pauline he was dead serious.

Suddenly my arm was yanked down, my camera slipping from my hand. Jagger's hand was on mine, his other hand snatching my camera out of the air—and in back of him was a startled Suzy—no doubt wondering what kind of nut holds a beeper to her eye.

"Nope," I said, "Doesn't need new batteries." A bimbo like Suz should buy that or at least be so confused that she could care less.

"Well, we've seen enough, hon. You have a brochure for my wife?" He looked at Suzy.

I yanked my arm away and grabbed my camera, not giving a damn if Suzy was weirded out by us. She started to say something that either had "brochure" in it or "security."

We didn't stay around long enough to find out.

I'd never hustled as fast across a slippery parking lot as I did tonight. Once in Jagger's car, I insisted he crank up the heater even though he said the air would be too cold until the engine warmed.

Cold air blew on my legs.

"You're doing that on purpose," I accused, but he only switched the fan on higher and didn't say a word.

Soon we'd pulled into the big mall near Sears. I looked around. Christmas shoppers. Damn! In my new lifestyle change, I'd forgotten it was only about ten days until Christmas.

And only half of my shopping was done.

Usually I was done by Halloween.

Certainly Jagger didn't bring me here, knowing that. Or—I looked over at him—maybe he did. A tiny thread of paranoia involving him reading my mind had been forming since day one. *Don't be dumb*, I said to myself. "What brings us here?"

He was getting out again without me. "Since we're in the neighborhood, what the hell is a seven-dollar grab bag anyway?"

I laughed. "With inflation it should be about a fifteen-dollar grab bag nowadays, but my folks are traditionalists, and thrifty."

"You have to help me find something." This time he waited outside the door.

How cute. Jagger needed my help and what was even cuter was his concern that he get the grab-bag issue straight.

What an interesting, albeit confusing, man.

"How about this?" Jagger asked, holding up a gaudy red, green and white candle.

I curled my lips at him. "Let me answer that with Would you want to get that in *your* grab bag?"

He plunked it down. I thought he'd break it and have to buy a broken gaudy candle, but it didn't even crack.

"What the hell. I can't do this."

Yes! Christmas would be saved! "That's fine. I'll make up a doozie of an excuse to my mother as to why you couldn't make Christmas—"

"I'll be there. Besides, you suck at lying."

He did have a point, I thought.

He grabbed my arm. "What'd *you* get?"

"I . . . a shovel that folds and you can keep in the trunk of your car."

"Fine. I want that."

"But—" He had me heading into Sears before I knew it.

"Show me where you got it."

I took him over to the shovel department and he purchased a shovel like the one I'd bought. They were still on sale for $7.00. When he went to pay, I nonchalantly leaned over to see the name or names on his credit card, only to have Jagger's face appear in my view. "I want to get something for your mother."

I pulled back. At least he hadn't accused me of snooping, although I had no doubt he suspected as much. "You don't have to do that."

"I do what I want."

"Oh, right. I noticed that. What did you have in mind?"

He took the bag from the clerk, who gave us a strange look. "If I knew, I wouldn't have asked you."

No kidding. "Mother has very few needs. Maybe some new potholders—"

"I want something for her, not the house. Don't you women get pissed over gifts like that? Blenders. Irons."

"Did your wife?" My hand flew to my mouth I think even a few seconds before the words came out. "I . . ."

He stopped and looked at me. Jagger did that a lot and those looks meant things. Things I had no idea about. He was certainly a poor example to use for reading body language, I thought again.

Instead of chastising me, he said, "Good job, Sherlock."

Wow! He thought it was great that I did some investigating about his past! "Thanks. Nice to have you be proud of me for finding out—"

"Proud of you?" He chuckled. It was a low sound, coming from the depths of his throat—more a growl actually. "Proud of you, Pauline? Proud that you snooped into my life? Yeah,

I'm tickled purple." He turned and walked out of the store.

"Pink," I corrected, fast on his heals and feeling embarrassed that I didn't "get" his sarcasm to begin with. When we were out in the mall, I caught up to his side. I'm not sure, but I think he may have slowed a bit. I decided to let the "wife" thing go. "My mother likes candies, and there's a Lindt chocolate store near Macy's upstairs—" I grabbed his arm. "There's Mr. Suskowski!" I yelled into Jagger's ear.

Jagger stopped. "Don't yell in the mall. You'll draw attention to us."

"We're not spying on anyone here." But suddenly I realized he didn't want anyone thinking we were a couple. Damn.

"Who's Mister—"

Before Jagger could finish, I hurried over to Foot Locker, where Mr. S was trying on a pair of shoes. I slowed when I walked in, deciding it wasn't smart to startle an elderly gentleman. Besides, I didn't want him to know that I'd seen him.

Jagger stood near the doorway.

I grabbed a running shoe from the shelf and pretended to look at it. A teen with spiked red hair came up. "Help you, lady?"

I looked at him. "Oh. Yes, I take a seven. Do you have this in a seven?" Mr. S was getting up to pay.

The kid grumbled something. "That's a man's shoe, lady."

I gave him a dirty look and said, "I *am* a man," then shoved the shoe at him and walked to the cash register. From the corner of my eye I could see the kid staring, running a hand through the spikes on his head, and Jagger, grinning.

The hell with both of them.

"Oh, hi," I said, coming up to Mr. Suskowski. He gave me a confused look. Maybe it wasn't him. But, yes, I really thought it was. "Don't you remember me? From the orthopedic doctors' office?"

He smiled. "Oh, the nurse."

"Yes. Right. How are you doing?"

"Got myself a new pair of Nikes. That's how I'm doing.

Cost a good chunk of my Social Security check, but the podiatrist said they'd be good for my feet. Even with the cast they fit all right." He shook his head.

I wondered if the podiatrist had stock in Nike. "These kinds of shoes are very comfortable and supportive, although, you're right, they are expensive."

The clerk running Mr. Suskowski's credit card through the little black machine gave me a dirty look, as if I was trying to talk him out of the purchase.

I smiled at him and said, "So, are you feeling better?"

"Best as can be expected at my age. Well, nice to see you, although I don't remember your name. Not that I have dementia like my brother, Dick, but we'd only met that short time. I guess I didn't feel it necessary to remember."

Wow. Put in my place. Of course, to Mr. S's credit, I was acting a bit nosy. "Yes, well, have a nice Christmas. I hope your MRI isn't scheduled too near the holiday."

Now he looked at me as if *I* had dementia. "Maybe you got me mixed up with another patient, little lady."

"I . . . Didn't Doctor Taylor tell you that he was ordering an MRI for you?"

He shook his head no. "My wife is going to worry about me. She's meeting me down by JC Penney's. Well, good holiday to you too."

"Wait!"

The clerk looked ready to call Security and Mr. S looked frightened. I softened my voice and smiled. "Silly me. I guess I did get you mixed up. You're not going to have an MRI?"

He hurried off, nearly running into a chuckling Jagger on the way out. But Mr. Suskowski did call out over his shoulder, "No MRI, and don't follow me!"

Twenty

I'd sunk to accosting elderly gentlemen.

They'd more than likely put that on my tombstone, I thought as I hurried up the stairs to my room. Jagger had dropped me off at home and left after a brief thanks—followed by several snickers—for helping him with his Christmas shopping.

He had listened to my entire conversation with Mr. Suskowski.

On the ride home we did get into a serious mode and talk about that MRI. The man never had one, nor was he scheduled to. I'd have to check out who ordered it. But damn, that was Vance's signature on the chart.

Although the good part of my night—getting more video of Tina—had been sandwiched between my "double date" and the senior citizen accosting, I was thrilled to have succeeded at something in my new career. I had all the confidence in the world where nursing was concerned, but investigating? Yikes. I set my alarm clock an hour early to head over to Scarpello and Tonelli Insurance Company to present the video to Fabio.

Even though Jagger had asked me not to finish my case, I had to give Fabio something or I'd be looking for a new job soon. What to do? I'd go to Fabio and see—

By this time Monday, I might even be paid!

Having no idea how that worked or if I had to wait until Fabio got his money back from Tina, I decided I wouldn't worry about it. I would soon be accepting a new case and feeding my anorexic bank account.

I cursed and hoped Jeanine got four flat tires, wherever the hell she was.

Part of the money would go to Saint Stanislaus Church for Uncle Walt's loan and, admittedly, I overspent on shopping (in the past!), but now I would be able to pay my credit card bills and soon be out of debt. One would think a single thirty-something woman would be sitting pretty with her finances, but I wasn't alone in the overspending department. After working so hard lately, though, I would be cutting up more than one store's credit card very soon.

When I stripped off my outfit and slipped into my flannel pj's with Mickey Mouse dancing about on them, I thought of Tina. She'd worn black leggings, black shorts, Spandex no less, and a black tank top. Tina gave new meaning to the term that black was slenderizing. I had to admit, for her size she did keep up pretty well with the instructor. Tina was light on her feet, as they say—and shit out of luck, as I say, when it came to bilking the insurance company out of money.

Spanky snuggled halfway under my pillow. I wondered if he was burrowing to get away as I told him the details of my night, including my assessment of Jagger, who bought presents for my mother, father and even Uncle Walt.

Jagger had gone with the Lindt chocolates for Mom and a Meerschaum tobacco pipe for my father, who only played with sticking pipe cleaners in them and never lit the darn things, I told Spanky. All Meerschaums were hand carved, I clarified, continuing on to say that my father would be impressed, although I *had* tried to talk Jagger out of such an expensive pipe.

He bought it anyway, and also seven car magazines for Uncle Walt.

"What a guy," I told Spanky's tail since that was the only

part sticking out. "And, Spanks, I think I'm done with my tailing, excuse the pun, of one Tina Macaluso, fraudulent claimant."

Done.

Spanky stuck his head out, glared at me.

I stood still for several seconds. "Oh . . . my . . . God. You're right, Spanks. Now I won't have any reason to have Jagger help me."

I flopped onto the bed, nearly catapulting Spanky's five-pound body off onto my dresser. I caught him in time and thought, now I *have* to keep helping Jagger out with the ortho case.

Or face never seeing him again.

I needn't have worried about when I'd get paid, I thought the following Monday, as Fabio went on and on about there still not being enough video surveillance for his taste. He liked his "clients" to be proven frauds without a shadow of a doubt. Even though I'd discovered additional fraud, the pictures hadn't been developed yet, and he wasn't a happy camper.

Consequently, I hadn't seen the last of Tina.

And I needn't have worried about breaking a promise to Jagger either—or not having him help me anymore.

"You have to get her lifting something she wouldn't even do with a good back, Sokol. And why the hell is all your surveillance at night?"

Ack. I couldn't explain that one.

"What? You spend all your day getting beauty sleep?" he asked, leering at my chest.

I instinctively placed my hands over my green-and-red paisley—for the Christmas season—scrubs.

"You know, doll," he said in a condescending voice, I thought you'd have the smarts to know too, that we need pictures, hard-copy photographs, doll, to put in the file. If we go to the DA with any info, they don't have fucking VCRs on their desks. They need to see pictures, doll. Fucking pictures."

Yikes. I hadn't thought about that, and as annoying as Fabio was, he was right. If, however, he called me "doll" one more time, I'd haul off and let him have my best uppercut as evidenced by Jagger's black eye. I should have had the smarts to think about the picture thing though.

The other day Goldie had been stapling photographs into a file, and I knew what they were for. It was just that so much had happened lately, that tidbit of investigative information had slipped my mind. Well, I *was* a green newbie, for crying out loud.

But—the thought surged into my brain—*Jagger wasn't.*

He should have told me!

Why didn't he?

Why would he keep . . .

He didn't want me to end this case, but he still could have told me about pictures.

I was going to make him pay for that one.

"I'll get more video and some pictures soon," was all I could come up with. Jeanine's car payment was due on Wednesday and here it was Monday and I hadn't gotten paid yet.

I walked out of Fabio's office in a financial funk.

And pissed beyond belief at the mysterious, out-for-himself Jagger.

"Hey, *chéri*, what's wrong?"

The lie came out way too easy: "Nothing. I'm fine." I didn't like fibbing to Adele. With Fabio, I could spin the truth around and around until his balding head was dizzy, but lying to people I liked didn't come easy—and wasn't fun.

After a quick cup of coffee with Adele, since Goldie (Damn! I could have used his friendship right then) was out on a case, I said goodbye and drove to my other job.

Linda'd managed to convince me to stay on a bit, to train the new nurse.

Well, at least there was a bright side to my day: Tina would be helping out too.

And, after learning what Jagger had done to me, I would be quitting today even if it wasn't supposed to be my last day, I thought, as I pulled into the parking lot of the professional building.

An old Toyota soared past me. "Jerk!" I yelled. It was similar to Dr. O'Connor's car and I hoped a physician much like herself would have the brains not to be so reckless, but this person sure didn't. The only thing the driver had going for him was that he was wearing a Steelers's cap. Go Steelers!

Suddenly I got angry that I'd missed two of their Monday-night football games since taking on these two jobs.

I'd have to get Uncle Walt to give me the blow-by-blow account. His mind was a steel trap when it came to watching our favorite team.

In the lounge I ran into Tina sitting on the couch with another woman dressed in scrubs next to her. I figured she was the replacement. I had to stifle my urge to ask Tina how jazzercise went. She looked at me oddly and suddenly I worried that she'd seen Jagger and me Friday night.

At least I didn't have to worry about any "motherly" chastising glares from Linda. In the alcove where her office blended with the lounge sat her desk. Uncluttered. Unoccupied.

Maybe I could plan to sneak a peek at some more files during lunchtime if the bitch, excuse my French, was gone.

"Hey, Tina." I nodded at the other nurse.

Tina took a sip of coffee and a giant bite of a honey-dipped donut. I mentally shook my head at that. "Pauline Sokol, this is Annie Hatfield. Annie's taking Eddy's place."

No emotion on her part when she mentioned Eddy. I would have at least expected a tear in her eye. I felt a bit choked up, and I didn't know him half as well.

Maybe Tina really was involved, although murder seemed out of the question. She *was* a nurse, for crying out loud. Then again, she was involved in *beaucoup* fraud. I had the tendency to think the best of everyone until proven otherwise. Even then, I tried to think of some good things about them.

Geez. He'd only been dead forty-eight hours and she'd acted so cool when she'd mentioned his name.

With the introductory formalities over, I went to bring in my first patient.

Mrs. Bakersfield's chart was on top. Too bad. The poor woman was only just here. It must be a bitch growing old and having parts not work. I smiled at her. "I know why you're back."

She got up and hobbled over. "My knees?"

"No, ma'am. You just can't keep away from that handsome Doctor Taylor."

She slapped my arm and laughed. "You know it."

Once I had her settled on the examining table, I found out her knee, the right one, really had been bothering her. I put the chart on the door and said the doctor would be in soon. Soon. *Yeah, right*, I thought. This practice overbooked way too often, in my opinion.

Today only three of the five doctors had office hours, with Doc O'Connor and Doc Levy off, yet the waiting room was packed. I snuck a peek at the appointment sheet over Trudy's shoulder. Not one empty slot. No wonder the poor patients complained of having to wait so long for the phone to be answered and having to wait even longer to see a doctor once they got here.

Something made me go back to the exam room and pick up Mrs. B's chart. Maybe intuition. Maybe some outside force. Or maybe my overactive imagination since turning investigator had me open it and look at Vance's notes from the other day.

Nothing out of the ordinary. I turned it over and read that Mrs. B had had X-rays. Right here in the office. I leaned against the wall. I didn't remember taking her to X-ray.

On Friday, Doctor O'Connor had had to do the honors, since before going to medical school, she'd told me, she was an X-ray technician.

She remembered Vance being an intern that year.

I'd said I couldn't picture Vance as a "newbie" and we'd laughed about it. She told me what he was like and how his wealthy father kept checking up on him, even arguing with the professors if Vance got less than straight As.

That was my Vance.

I stuck my head in the door and asked, "Doing all right, Mrs. B?"

She nodded. "Fine, dearie."

"Oh, by the way. Did you have an X-ray the last time you were here?"

"No, dearie. I haven't had any since two years ago when I had pneumonia. I'd remember if they did, since they always put you on that hard, torturous table."

Yet there was a note that X-rays *were* done—and the charge more than likely sent to the Global Carriers Insurance Company, which was right here in Hope Valley.

When I went out to put her file in the stack, Trudy was alone. I looked around. No other staff there. I leaned near.

Trudy jumped.

"Oh, sorry. Hope I didn't cause your back any pain." Donnie's Workers' Comp claim on Trudy was also for back pain. The guy had no imagination.

She gave me an odd look. "Never had a back problem."

Damn, I wished I could call Jagger. Two helpful tidbits of info today! I had to remember to ask him for a phone number although I guessed the guy was never anywhere where there was a phone and wasn't sure if he'd give me his cell phone number. Maybe he thought I'd try to trace it and find out his real name and where he lived, or—more likely—think I'd keep calling him.

I smiled about the fact that he'd thought I'd done some investigating on him, when in fact Goldie had told me about Jagger's having been married.

Shoot. I wished I hadn't thought about that, 'cause now my mind drifted off, wondering what kind of woman Jagger would marry.

Or, more important, what kind of woman would want to marry him.

I looked at the clock. Five minutes to noon. The waiting room was empty. The morning had flown by with no one having X-rays taken (that I observed). They hadn't because Tina told me if anyone needed them we'd have to call a radiology technician from downstairs.

I wondered why she wasn't trained but then remembered Eddy saying how lazy she was. Poor guy. Dead and more than likely overworked prior to that.

Tina had already rushed the last patient out of one of the examining rooms, telling Annie, who had spent part of the morning at the desk with Trudy while Tina did God knows what (probably slept) that the cafeteria got real crowded and they needed to hurry or have to wait in line.

Thank goodness I ate only what was needed to survive and didn't make food a priority. I held back in the lounge, but she spotted me.

"You coming?"

"I . . . I'll be there in a few minutes." Quick, Pauline, think of an out. I waited a few seconds, cranked my brain into spinning the truth mode and said, "I think I lost an earring. I'll take a look, then meet you in the cafeteria."

She looked at me. "You have two on."

I reached up to touch my ear. "Of course I have two on. . . ." Oh shit! "But I had an extra pair in the pocket of my scrubs and now I only have one."

And no way was I going to show her my empty pocket.

"Make sure the door locks behind you on the way out." She started toward the door with Annie in tow.

I smiled and waited. Soon I'd get to my real work. I started to turn and smacked into Donnie yet again. "Oh, sorry."

He gave me an odd look. "Go to lunch."

"Earring lost. Thanks for the concern."

I think he growled as he turned and left.

I heard footsteps heading toward the waiting room and focused on my search of the office to once again make sure I'd be alone. Each examining-room door was open, so it only took a hot second to see no one was in them. Dr. Macaluso's office door was closed, as were the offices of the two docs who were off today. Still, I knocked and tried to open them.

All three were locked.

The other two were empty.

Fine by me. I knew no one was in them. I hurried down the hall to the X-ray room. That door was always closed, as if carcinogenic rays would sneak out and zap us all. It would only take a second to see that room was empty, since no X-rays had been done today.

I grabbed the handle, gave it a quick turn. At the same time I heard voices down the hallway behind me.

Tina called, "Pauline? I forgot my purse. You in the can?"

Shit. I opened the door anyway before she could see me since it'd complete my snooping and give me more time with the files once Tina actually left.

There, lying faceup on the X-ray table, was Linda Stark.

It didn't take my medical background to see the pasty, cyanotic color of *death* on her face.

Twenty-one

Linda Stark was *dead.*

D. E. A. D.

It didn't take my newfound investigative skills to see that she didn't climb up onto the hard, cold X-ray table to die all by herself.

Someone had killed her and put her here.

Or killed her right here. Eeew.

Either way, she was dead. Murdered! Had to be.

Oh, I looked around the room and saw no sign of a struggle, although I had no idea what I was looking for.

Okay, the logical side of my brain had taken over, indicating my years as a professional registered nurse had paid off. I was cool under pressure. Kept a clear head in the face of an emergency.

But, still. *Dead.*

Linda lay so still. Eyes closed. Right hand hanging down with that giant ruby ring glaring at me. Immediately I erased her off the list of suspects. Maybe she knew something and squealed about it like Eddy—and now had paid the ultimate price.

I couldn't help but stare at her body until the illogical, impulsive side of my brain kicked in—and I screamed my lungs out loud enough to wake the dead.

Linda, however, remained completely still.

I hurried to the doorway, but couldn't just leave.

Tina bounded down the hall followed by Annie. "What the hell is wrong with you—" Tina looked in the door.

We all stood screaming in the hallway like clichéd hysterical females until a janitor ran in from the waiting-room area. He dropped his mop before he got to the doorway. Dressed in a Yankees baseball cap, blue-tinted glasses and dark gray jumpsuit, the guy nearly knocked me over.

I grabbed his arm for support as he leaned against me. Tina and Annie continued screaming.

"What the fuck is wrong now, Sherlock?"

I'd thought having janitor Jagger here would be a comfort. But watching the police investigate Linda's death and having them question me relentlessly, or so it seemed, I faced the reality that even Jagger's presence didn't help. Trudy, who arrived back from lunch early, had fixed a cup of Chamomile tea for all three of us. I sipped mine and watched Jagger as he sat by the reception desk talking to Lieutenant Shatley.

Nope. I didn't feel all that much better.

Because, I had to confess to myself, *two* people now were murdered, and I highly suspected it was all related to medical insurance fraud.

I wondered if the lieutenant knew how much I was involved with Jagger. Well, not involved as he'd suggested we were to Nick, but in helping with the case. I wanted the lieutenant to think I was a real insurance-fraud investigator.

Not a suspect, as cops sometimes make one feel.

The cops milled around, and Tina and Annie had to help Trudy cancel the afternoon appointments. The cops would have the place to themselves.

I looked at the clock. If they said I could leave, I'd be

outta here in seconds. And I didn't plan to look back, since I was about to quit this job anyway. I only hoped the cops wouldn't tell me not to leave town.

Funny how my active imagination kicked in. I knew I had nothing to do with Linda's murder, or alleged murder, but the men in blue, and the lieutenant in wrinkled brown had asked me—and, I assumed, the others—questions that made me second-guess myself.

I sat there waiting, sipping my tea and remembered a time I'd gotten a letter saying I was being sued for a car accident. It was a hit and run in New Haven several months earlier. I wracked my brain to remember if I'd been in New Haven, and had I really hit a car and left?

Logically I knew I hadn't, but just looking at the letter from some attorney named Grossman, I was second-guessing myself.

After coming to my senses, I called the New Haven police, only to find out that on the accident report someone had written an L that looked like a C. My license plate was CZG196 and the criminal's car was LZG196.

So, I had to keep my wits about me not to have Hope Valley's finest make me second-guess myself again.

I never even killed flies in the condo. I'd open the window and set them free, which annoyed Miles to no end since often times another flying creature would sneak in while I was liberating the flies.

"Pauline?"

I looked up to see Jagger standing over me. I never even saw him come over. "Yeah."

"Let's get out of here." He turned to go.

I pushed up to stand. "I'm free to go?"

Jagger shook his head and didn't turn around. "You watch a lot of TV?"

I shoved my cup into the sink without stopping to rinse it out. "No, I don't. I only wanted to know if the lieutenant needed me anymore."

"He's got your number."

"Speaking of numbers," I said as I got my purse out of the cabinet, "how about yours? If you didn't show up, I would have had to call you."

"I'll be around."

He'll be around! Well, I had to admit, he did show up at all the right times, but what if he didn't? "What if you aren't, and I need you? I mean, what if I'd stumbled into the X-ray room and—" A chill chased up my spine at the thought.

Even Jagger paused.

"That could have been me."

He looked a few seconds, lifted the Yankees cap, and ran a hand through his hair. "No, it couldn't." He opened the door and started to walk out into the empty waiting room.

I grabbed his arm to slow him down. For a second he looked as if he might slug me, but he didn't. He kept walking with me hanging on him. "You know something? What . . . You know what happened to Linda? Tell me. Who did this? The same person who killed—"

He shoved his hand over mine. "Calm down."

It was like a verbal slap in the face.

He let go as we got out in the elevator lobby. "Get in," he commanded when the door opened.

I started to protest, but Vance came out of the office at that moment. I didn't want to go into any details about my fear of riding the elevator, so I very reluctantly got in.

Vance looked from janitor Jagger to me and got in. "What a bummer finding Linda, Pauline."

I nodded.

Jagger stood distressingly yet—I was certain, purposely—close on my left.

Vance kept staring at me. "Maybe you want to stop somewhere and get a drink?"

Jagger nudged me with his knee.

My first reaction was to elbow him, but I ignored him and said, "It's only around noon, Vance. If I drank now, I'd be done for the day."

"Maybe you need that." He shut his eyes a second and rubbed a finger along his temple.

Poor Vance, I thought, *so uptight he can't even allow himself the luxury of running his fingers through his hair.* "No. I don't need liquor. I'm going home for a nice hot floral bubble bath."

I heard a low growl from my left.

The doors opened on the ground floor, and I realized my pulse hadn't quickened and my breathing was normal. Being preoccupied, I'd survived the elevator ride.

Vance stepped out and turned around. He gave Jagger, who still stood near, a dirty look. "Don't you have work to do? Floors to polish?"

Yikes!

I readied for Jagger to haul off and land a good one on Vance's perfectly chiseled chin, but he merely tipped his hat and turned down the hall.

Damn. I needed to talk to him some more and the jerk wouldn't give me his number. I didn't want to sit home alone (Miles was at work now), thinking of murder and having no one to talk to.

Two murders.

Vance was rambling about a drink again. "Please, Pauline. A nice Sherry or Cognac."

Jagger was hovering in the lobby. By the time I turned to Vance, said "I really can't" and looked back, the lobby was empty.

"Sorry to be so pushy. This hasn't been the best of weeks."

"I hear you."

He leaned, gave me a kiss on my forehead and turned toward the entrance doors.

"Wait!"

Vance swung around. "You changed your mind?"

I shook my head. "Did you order an MRI on Mr. Suskowski?"

I wasn't sure if the confused look was from my question or my peculiar behavior. "Did you?"

"No. He doesn't need an MRI for any reason."

I felt that stupid chill along my back again. "Oh. Bye." I thought better than to ask about Mrs. Bakersfield and the X-ray. Too much asking could ruin Jagger's case.

"I guess I'll go to the hospital for early rounds. If you need me, page me." He hesitated, I'm sure out of concern for me, then turned and left.

I stood in the foyer, watching people come and go for several minutes until I felt something behind me. This time it wasn't that chill.

More like heat.

Without turning I said, "He never ordered the MRI, Jagger."

Feeling quite proud of myself, I drove out of the parking lot after Jagger had gotten into his SUV and headed out first. For a change, I'd actually guessed that he was behind me, and consequently he didn't scare the pants off me this time.

Of course, that's what I chose to think. He more than likely *let* me know he was there in some Jagger-like way, since he, hopefully, had figured I'd had enough of a shock for one day, thank you very much.

Before he'd left he asked me if Tina was in the office all morning. I told him that I honestly didn't know, since I was busy and didn't keep tabs on her. Did he suspect Tina had killed Linda? Oh my. He wouldn't have told me if I asked, so I didn't.

My tummy growled. I hadn't had any lunch and it'd been several hours since finding poor Linda. I added her name to my mental list of prayers for the dead. I wondered if she'd run into Eddy in heaven, or if Eddy actually had arrived there, or if Eddy ever would. I put my money on purgatory for him, which was a heck of a lot better than hell. Then again, Linda didn't seem as if she'd be on Saint Peter's invitation list either.

Unnerved by Linda's death but having dealt with it so many times in my nursing career, I decided I needed to do a little more work to take my mind off today. So, I headed to Tina's smaller house, not certain why. When I pulled into the subdivision, I noticed a neighbor walking a dog near Tina's. I pulled to the curb, shut my engine off and got out and walked toward her.

She turned at the corner. Damn. I hurried along, not certain what I was going to do or say. A man came out of a brown saltbox house across the street and looked at me. Oddly. Okay, he had reason to. This small, exclusive neighborhood was not a place strangers frequented for walks. I paused, but before I could smile at him, he rushed back into his house. I turned and looked down the street.

I'd lost the dog lady.

I stood there awhile, then turned around. A man dressed in a hooded green parka and winter facemask jumped behind a parked car. Shit. I turned back around, hoping he was merely out for a walk. Why would he hide like that? He didn't look like the man from the house I'd just seen. Much taller. Jagger?

Why would Jagger hide? Not his style. Besides, he always wore black. My racing heart said I should get the heck out of there, evidence or not. I quickened my pace, careful not to slip on the snowy sidewalks. As I broke into a jog, I could hear snow crunching behind me.

It got louder. I ran faster.

Before I knew it, my feet were up in the air, my clogs directly in front of my face. I landed with a painful thud. The crunching behind me stopped.

Then I saw a police cruiser pull around the corner.

I swung my snow-covered head around to see who was behind me.

No one. Not even a flash of brown. I was never so glad to see a police car.

Before the cops got closer to me, the dog lady came around the corner, and ran up to me.

"Are you all right?"

With a groan, I pulled myself up, thankful that these classy people didn't shovel snow very well and I'd had a nice cushion to fall on. "Thanks. I'm fine." I wanted to ask if she saw anyone behind me, but thought that would scare her off. The police cruiser slowed. She waved to him, and he passed by. Phew. Looked like the same cop Jagger talked to here, the first time I spied on Tina. Brown saltbox probably called him on me.

"Well, if you are all right, I need to get Kirby inside. Snow sticks in his pads."

"I'm a friend of Tina Macaluso," I quickly said. "Do you know which house is hers?"

"You're in front of it. Some friend." The dog looked as if it might pee on my clogs so I stepped into the snow. Also the woman's tone didn't seem too friendly now—maybe she wasn't a Macaluso fan. That'd be my bet.

"Thanks. A shame how she hurt her back."

The lady started to walk forward. "My husband is always telling Tina she shouldn't shovel. Never learn. Some people never learn."

Shoveling!

I looked at the snow as if it could tell me the truth, but instead asked, "Is that what happened? I'm so embarrassed. On her get-well card I put that I was sorry she was injured at work."

The woman looked at me. "Her injury lasted all of five minutes, then she was out skiing that evening. You look more hurt with your little tumble than she did."

I stared at her as if she might tell me more, but then again, I had pretty much what I needed. Tina wasn't hurt at work, and although barely hurt at home, she had filed a Workers' Comp claim for the dough.

That helped ground me after the day I'd had.

A Subway shop was on my way home so I decided I'd get a sandwich, eat it, and take that much-needed bubble bath now that my muscles were moaning. I drove up to the drive-thru, told the disembodied voice in the speaker that I didn't have any coupons when it asked and ordered a roast chicken breast with real mayonnaise, (hey, I deserved it today), lettuce and extra onions.

I got the grinder and decided that after my bath I'd run over to Fabio's office. I needed a Goldie fix. He could cheer me up, even if I couldn't tell him all the details of my day.

At my stoop, I fiddled in my purse, cursing that I wasn't thinking clearly and now I couldn't find my keys. To make my day perfect, icy pellets danced against the windowpanes and my head. "Shit. Shit. Shit."

"When will you ever learn?"

This time Jagger stood near his Suburban, which he'd parked in Miles's space in front of our door. Since he paid most of the bills, for now anyway, Miles earned the closest space. I had no problem with that unless it was raining ice, like right now. Days like this I wished I could pay all the bills.

Jagger came up the walkway. I searched frantically, determined he wasn't going to spill the contents of my bag, on the sidewalk this time. There! I pulled out my keys and stuck the right one in the door.

"It's open," he said, opening the door and walking past me.

"How? What?" I hurried in and shut the door before Spanky made the great escape. "How the hell did you know? Miles never forgets to lock the door."

I set my purse and sandwich down, picked up Spanky. "I need a hug. I need a hug." He licked my cheek as I stared at Jagger. "Well?"

My tone was perfect. Demanding. No outlet for him. Perfect bitch.

"Do you think I'd let you come in here without checking it out first?" He rubbed Spanky's head, turned and walked into the kitchen. "What kind of sub we sharing?"

Spanky jumped down, no doubt expecting a treat in his bowl from Jagger, and my jaw hit my chest yet again.

I wanted to shout he had no right, no business breaking

into my home, but in all fairness, I said "thank you" and followed Spanky into the kitchen.

Jagger already had two Coors out, no glasses, and was sitting at the table, doodling, sipping his beer. As I let Spanky out the back door for a few seconds, I wondered if anything in that notebook was useful to this case. It didn't take the dog long before he was right back in, shaking ice off his fur.

I sat at the table, set my sub down and started to open the bag. "Roast chicken with mayo, lettuce and extra onions." I took half and set it on a napkin next to his pad.

He nodded his thanks.

"Found out today that Tina did, in fact, hurt her back at home, but not enough for a sustained injury." I wasn't about to share that I'd been followed, fell in the snow, and a neighbor had probably called the cops on me.

He looked at me.

"I spoke to her neighbor," I said.

His face froze.

"Relax. I didn't give my name, and I said I was a friend."

He toasted me with his Coors, then took a sip.

I smiled inside.

I took a bite of my sub. I have no idea why Fabio popped into my head—other than fear had me all muddled up—and the fact that he'd mentioned the G word the day he'd hired me. I said, "Where can I get . . . a gun?"

Of course, two murders had something to do with my asking.

Jagger took his time, no great surprise. Actually, I thought he was once again going to ignore my question. But he picked up his beer, finished it off and looked my way. "Why?"

"Why? Why? Oh, I don't know. Maybe two murders might have something to do with it." I felt something at my leg and looked down to see Spanky begging. After ripping a tiny piece of chicken off my sub, I told him to sit and he gently took it from my fingers.

"Ever *use* a gun?"

"I've never seen a real gun."

Jagger shook his head in an "I thought so" kind of mode.

"I can learn." Yikes. I really was talking nonsense. I really didn't want to be in the same building, much less the same room with a gun. I knew Jagger must carry one by that bulge I'd seen, which, by the way, I hadn't noticed lately. Great. My protector—unarmed.

Then again, he might have it hidden.

Then again, I had to stop the first thought that came into my head, which was that I wouldn't mind frisking him to find out.

So much for the gun argument. I'd let it go—for now. "By the way," I said, still thinking of Fabio. I took another bite. "How come you never told me that I should be taking still photos of Tina committing fraud?"

He grinned.

"Stop that! You should have told me. I could have finished this case and . . . and been done with her, gotten paid and started working on something else."

"I told you, it would mess up my case. Besides, I said I'd pay you."

That's right. I had forgotten that. But now I wasn't sure if, even for Eddy and now Linda's memory, I could keep helping Jag . . . Wait! "You son of a bitch!"

He got up. I thought he was going to run out but then again, this was Jagger.

He didn't run.

From anything. Of that I was certain.

Instead, he walked to the refrigerator, opened the door, and took out another Coors. "Such language. Very uncharacteristic for you, Sherlock."

About ready to apologize, I paused. No, wait. I was pissed! "I'm not talking recently. You didn't tell me about taking pictures of Tina . . . I could have gotten several with the opportunities I'd had . . . but you didn't want my case closed long before Eddy was killed."

"So I could keep you helping me. I told you that."

I could only look at him.

The staring lasted for several moments, until I blinked. "Now you did, but earlier on—"

He shrugged.

"It's true? You were using me from the start."

He sat back down, twisted the cap off his beer. "Partly."

Mentally I counted to five. Too eager to hear this, I didn't want to waste time going up to ten. "You're going to have to explain that one."

"Look, you know I needed your help. Earlier on I didn't want you to finish so that you would stay on that nursing job. Lately, I couldn't have you finish and have Tina picked up. That would blow my case, as I said. And Sherlock, you've been doing a fine job."

"Fine?"

He shook his head and blew out a long breath. "Okay. A great job."

"That's better." My roast chicken sub with real mayo held no appeal now that I'd gotten so riled. I normally didn't give Spanky people food, but it seemed a shame to waste it. I broke it up into tiny pieces, got up and put it in his dish.

The dog went insane.

But his insanity couldn't beat mine. Jagger drove me nuts. Would he really have lied to me or at least kept the truth from me in order to *use* me like that?

Yeah, he'd just said so.

"I find it hard to believe that you couldn't have gotten the info I've helped you with on your own. After all, you *are* Jagger."

He raised his beer to me again, then chuckled. "True enough. I could have, but it would have taken longer." He leaned back, took a sip of beer.

"What's the big hurry with you? You don't exactly look as if you need the money—"

"I don't do it for the money, Pauline."

Wow. I was seeing a very serious side of Jagger. If not for the money, then what? Could he really be that interested in solving crime because he felt obligated to or, more likely, because he was that dedicated?

I looked at him, wishing he'd show some emotion, some facial expression other than pure sexiness, so I could read him. No such luck. I demanded, "Who the hell do you work for?"

Twenty-two

"No gun," Jagger said, got up and walked to the door.

I hadn't noticed, but Spanky was standing there wiggling as if he needed to go out. Jagger opened the door and Spanky bounded out. Jagger waited a few minutes and let Spanky back in, then picked the dog up as if to warm him.

Wow. A human, an actual touching side to such a complex man. I cleared my thoughts and didn't allow him to ignore me this time. "I demand to know who you work for."

He ran a finger across Spanky's head. Very gently. I could see the control—well, maybe a hint of a struggle to maintain it. I thought of the kid's balloon again, and sure didn't want Jagger to explode.

To use a cliché, fear was not my cup of tea. But in that instant, I realized there was a bit of fear in me when I looked at Jagger. Interesting. I trusted him with my life, yet I was a bit afraid of him at the same time.

He set Spanky down, took a toothpick out of his pocket (that's where they materialized from!), peeled off the cellophane and tapped it against his tooth. Then he chewed on it a bit. He looked me in the eyes. "You don't need to know."

"Hmm?" I'd been momentarily mesmerized by the toothpick thing. I yanked my glare from him and his stupid toothpick, looked past him to see the ice coming down harder and said, "I *want* to know."

"If I tell you FBI, then what? Hmm? Then what will be different?"

"I . . . well . . ."

Before I could answer he said, "If I tell you some fucking insurance company . . . that I'm an investigator for some fucking insurance company, then what will that matter? Or undercover cop. Maybe you'd like to hear that I'm a cop? Or PI? Huh? What the hell difference would any of that make?"

I got up, kept my chin held high and walked out.

Damn him.

Jagger didn't follow me. At first I expected it, then I sat on the leather couch and waited. It really didn't matter, I guessed, but the less I knew about him, the more I wanted to know. If I asked myself why, I wouldn't have a clue.

And I'd bet my darling Spanky that Jagger knew this was killing me and that made it all the more fun for him—and gave him all the more reason *not* to tell me.

Silence filled the air. Not even Spanky's little barks could be heard. I wondered if Jagger'd gone out the back door, or a window, or some mysterious exit that only Jagger was capable of knowing about. Then the phone rang.

I got up to get it and this time heard Spanky in the kitchen. He was making the little doggie sounds that he made when someone tickled his tummy.

So much for Jagger's Houdini routine.

I held the receiver to my ear. "Hello."

Miles's voice came on. "Hey. I'm stuck at work. Didn't want you to worry. I'll bunk down here tonight—"

"No!" I hadn't meant to shout, but if Miles didn't come home, I'd be alone with Jagger until he took it upon himself to leave. "I mean, why not? Why are you staying at the hospital? Those beds with plastic mattress covers are the pits. You won't sleep a wink. They'll make you sweat."

"No kidding. But have you looked outside?"

"I . . . it's raining."

"No, it's icing. There are weather advisories out and a major accident on Interstate 91. We've already had two OR cases out of it. I can't drive in this stuff. Even four-wheel drive doesn't do shit on ice."

I couldn't insist that he risk his life just so I wouldn't be alone with Jagger.

And—the horrible thought struck me—I couldn't insist Jagger leave in an ice storm either.

Of course, if he chose to on his own . . .

"Don't you leave the condo, Pauline. The cops are warning everyone to stay inside until tomorrow when the weather warms. Promise?"

I said goodbye and started to set the receiver down, when he added, "And tell Jagger to stay there too."

Damn!

Jagger came in as I hung up. "Miles is staying at the hospital." Maybe I shouldn't have told Jagger that. Now he knew we were alone.

And, Pauline, I asked myself, *What the hell difference would that make to him?*

"Good. Now we can discuss business."

At first I thought he might be ready to tell me whom he worked for, but then I looked at his serious face and decided I would not bring that subject up again. Not anytime soon anyway.

Make that for now.

"Fine. That sub wasn't much. Are you hungry?"

"I'll get a bite on my way home." He sat on the leather stuffed chair opposite me.

"You can't go."

One eyebrow raised. "Excuse me?"

"Miles . . . Miles said there's a weather advisory for the ice storm. He said no one is supposed to be out in it. It does make it harder on the emergency crews if people don't pay attention to the police."

He looked at me.

"Okay, so maybe you *are* the police, but I don't care."

He crossed his legs and leaned back. "Good. Then you won't be bothering me about who I work for."

"No, I meant I don't care if you are the police or FBI or a con artist yourself. You can't drive on ice unless you have spiked tires or chains. Do you have chains in that Suburban of yours? Well, you do have just about everything else, so I wouldn't be surprised—"

He blew out a breath in my direction. "I don't have chains or spiked tires. I'm hungry. Let's fix something and talk." He got up and walked to the kitchen. "That make you happy, Pauline?"

Ack. There was that tone and my real name. I followed him in and said, "Tickled purple. Let's see what we have to eat."

He already had the refrigerator door open. I should be upset that he made himself at home, as usual, but I wasn't. Actually it was nice that he didn't expect me to wait on him.

We heated up some leftover macaroni and cheese Miles had made. It was always wonderful 'cause he used extra Monterey Jack cheese, canned milk, and two whipped eggs in it to give it consistency. Jagger ate as if he was starving.

We'd switched to Coke for Jagger and water for me. No drink with the equivalent of ten teaspoonfuls of sugar was passing my lips tonight. All I needed was to add five pounds to my frame right in front of Jagger. I took a sip of water and watched him take a bite of macaroni. "So, what do you want to discuss?"

He swallowed and looked my way. "We need to wrap up this case."

"We?"

"I need you to stay at the office at least another week."

I choked on a noodle. My hands flew up in the air and Jagger sat watching. "Aren't you going to do something to help me?"

"If you needed me to, I would. You're still talking, so you're not choking."

If I needed him to, he would. I sat back and thought of that. I know Jagger meant right here and now, but I also got the impression he meant more. He meant he'd be there if I needed him in the case, too.

"I really can't go back there."

"They've bilked the insurance companies, mostly Global Carriers, out of an excess of three million dollars. Remember?"

"Oh my!" With two dead bodies and all, I'd actually forgotten that. "By just lying on patients' records? Seems hard to believe."

He finished his Coke, held up his glass. I nodded toward the refrigerator and said, "Help yourself."

He did and as he sat back down, said, "They've been at it for some time. Years."

I gasped.

"Stop being so surprised, Sherlock. If you want to make it in this business you've got to detach yourself. No emotions—"

"What about fear? Fear for my life."

"Nothing is going to happen to you."

Because he wouldn't let it.

I should be peeing in my pants at the thought of two murders, but a calm had settled inside me, and it hadn't come from the macaroni. "Wow. Years?"

He nodded. "If Eddy hadn't sung, they'd be at it until they got caught. Some disgruntled employee, often on the take too, gets pissed. Maybe thinks they deserve more. I got that impression from Eddy. He wasn't squealing out of the goodness of his heart. So, Eddy, in the mind of his cohorts, died because of a lack of loyalty."

That made me feel a bit better, although I still felt sorry for Eddy and Linda. "What about Linda?"

Jagger finished his meal, got up and rinsed off his dish, which he set in the sink. I'd have to put them in the dishwasher before Miles came home tomorrow. Jagger turned, leaned against the sink and produced another toothpick, which he chewed down on.

"Did you ever smoke?"

He gave me an odd look. Quite a habit he'd picked up. "It's not a substitute for smoking. Toothpicks help me think."

No arguing against that kind of logic. "So, what about Linda? Why was she killed?"

He stayed put, chewing. "She did billing. Had to be involved in some way. Whether she was one of the ringleaders, your guess is as good as mine."

Not the way my mind worked lately. I'd more than likely guess that Linda killed herself. I looked up. "Do you think Linda committed suicide? I mean, maybe she knew they'd find out and end up in prison. She didn't strike me as someone who liked to follow orders."

Jagger chewed and stared. "Gee, I hadn't thought of that."

"Really?" I was so excited. But when I saw a tiny twitch of his lip, I wondered if he were being honest with me. He wanted me to go back there, so maybe he was lying. Trying to get me psyched to do more investigating by thinking I knew something he didn't.

Shit. My adrenaline surged. I really did want to help solve this case. "I don't believe you for a minute, but . . . oh God, I can't believe I'm about to say this—"

"You'll be safe. You have my word." With that, he walked out of the room.

I remained still, thinking how he was able to finish my sentences. I heard him talking and knew he was using his cell phone in the other room.

I'd agreed to go back to the ortho group.

I put my dishes in the sink with Jagger's and thought I'd clean it up tomorrow. Physically and now emotionally drained, I needed some sleep.

But the thought of whether I would be able to sleep, with Jagger here, did cross my mind.

In the living room, I took out an extra blanket and pillow Miles kept in the closet for when he fell asleep watching TV. I fixed up the couch for Jagger, who was still talking on the phone. Trying not to eavesdrop, yet dying to hear what he said, I concluded he was talking to the police.

My suspicions were confirmed when he hung up, came into the living room and sat on the soft chair to take off his boots. "The cops will be around, under cover. No need to worry."

"Easy for you to say." I started up the stairs with Spanky fast on my heels. At the top I turned and looked over the railing. "I said I'd do it, but there is one stipulation. . . ."

"I'm not tellin you who I—"

"I'm past that." *No, I'm not, but I'll drop it for now*. "I want . . . need at least your cell phone number."

"I said I'd be around when you need me." He started to undo the buttons on his shirt.

Despite my exhaustion, I knew if I watched him strip off his shirt, sleep would elude me. "I know what you said, and I believe you'll be around. But I want the added cushion of knowing I can call—"

"Five-five-five, six-eight-nine-one."

The last thing I saw was the muscles, smooth, obviously firm, of his back before the light switched off, and I swung around so fast I tripped over Spanky, landing smack on the carpeted hallway.

In the darkness below, I swear I heard him shake his head.

"I'm fine," I grumbled and went into my room.

Like my mother, I wasn't the world's best sleeper. Tossing and turning through sleepless nights was not a stranger to me. I lay in bed, thinking about how Jagger was on my couch.

I remembered seeing one fifteen on my digital clock, then two forty-five, then three and something close to three thirty, but by then my vision blurred, and I must have fallen asleep.

The sun heated my room. I could tell by the comforting

feeling when I snuggled deeper into the recesses of my gigantic overstuffed down comforter. I reached out to pet Spanky's little body as I always do. I ran my hand around where he usually nestled.

No dog. Slowly one eye opened, then the other. "Spanks?" Nothing. I sat bolt upright and almost flew out of the bed. Spanky might have had to go out and couldn't hold it. One thing Miles didn't care for was dog piddle on the white carpet, even though our little guy only went about five drops. Spanky had been housetrained for years, but maybe, I thought, the people food had upset his little tummy.

Then I smelled something and relaxed.

Thank goodness it was a pleasant, appetizing smell, making me rethink Spanky's disappearance. I shut my eyes, bundled up more and inhaled.

Bacon.

I smelled bacon. Then I did in fact get up. Jagger was downstairs! And unless Miles had come home early, which I didn't suspect since I thought he had another shift to do, Jagger was cooking.

A man after my own mother's heart.

If she found out about that, I feared she'd start her matchmaking nonsense. As I was the only single child in our family, mother took to fixing me up every so often, until I put my foot down and started canceling the dates she made for me. That embarrassed her, so she stopped.

I stood up and looked out the window. The parking lot was a veritable sheet of ice, sparkling like some fairyland in the morning sun. I touched the windowpane. Cool to the touch yet not real cold. The temperature must be above freezing. The ice would melt soon.

Then Jagger could leave.

I reached to grab my yellow-and-white-striped robe, then paused. What was I thinking? I couldn't go downstairs in that. I had to shower and get dressed.

In the shower I kept, foolishly I might add, looking at the locked door as if I expected Jagger to come rushing in.

I didn't take the time to wash my hair, so I quickly used the green apple shower wash on the sponge and rinsed away the soap and my stupid thoughts. Why did I keep thinking he was after my bod? He'd never even made a pass at me—yet.

It had to be about my attraction, albeit out-of-whack attraction, to him. I laughed out loud. My attraction to him was as much a fantasy as the sparkling parking lot.

Once out of the shower and dressed in jeans and a long royal blue turtleneck sweater that made my gray eyes appear bluish, I went downstairs to the kitchen.

The table was set with Miles's good china. Coffee percolated. Bacon hissed. Spanky lay in the sunlight near the French doors, and I guessed his tummy was full, since he didn't jump up. Jagger sat at the table, doodling. I noticed the shiner around his eye had dulled to a yellowish purple today. I felt a twinge of guilt for slugging him.

"Something smells good." I went to the table, took my cup from the saucer and walked to the counter.

"I'd think an investigator like yourself, Sherlock, could identify the aroma." He didn't budge. Kept doodling.

I laughed—alone. "Bacon. There. I've learned from the best. Besides, it was just a figure of speech." I walked back to the table, stopping to pet Spanky on the head.

He opened a sleepy eye at me as if to say, "Leave me alone," and promptly shut it.

I sat opposite Jagger and put Equal and milk into my coffee. I preferred tea in the morning, having taken to drinking green tea since I'd heard it had health benefits, but today the coffee tasted wonderful. Maybe because I got to sleep late after the rotten night I'd had. Maybe because I was actually starved and it wasn't my usual breakfast choice.

Or maybe it tasted so wonderful because Jagger had made it.

I really couldn't let my mother know about this. We ate in relative silence, then I told him I would clean up since he cooked. Jagger gave Spanky a pat on the head. The little traitor actually opened both eyes, licked Jagger's hand, and then I think the damn Benedict Arnold dog smiled.

"I'm off now," was all Jagger said before heading out.

I followed him to the living room. "That was nice, the breakfast. Thanks."

He nodded and opened the door.

A little stuffed black-and-white dog tumbled into the entryway near Jagger's feet. He bent, picked it up.

A note was tied to the red ribbon of the dog's neck.

"What the heck is that? Looks like my Spanky. I wonder if some kids left it—"

Jagger looked at me.

"This didn't come from any kids."

Twenty-three

I could only stare.

Jagger kept his head down, looking at the note. The stuffed Spanky tucked under his arm now looked rather grotesque. Its button eyes had been pulled off. I swallowed hard and sucked in a deep breath. Spanky curled up near the fireplace without a care. I let my breath out very slowly. "What . . . is it? What does it say?"

Jagger folded it up. "You don't need to know."

"I . . . *What*? What do you mean, I don't need to know?"

He stuffed it into his pocket. "Just that. If I let you read it, you'll go off on a tangent, misinterpreting—"

"And not continue to work for you."

"Let me ask you something, Pauline."

Serious. He was dead serious. "What?"

"Do you trust me?"

I looked at him a few seconds. Not being able to read his dark eyes, yet feeling that calm still deep inside when he looked at me, I said, "You're not being fair."

"I didn't ask you if I was fair. I'm the first to admit I'm not. Hell, sometimes I'm downright selfish. I can be a taker if the need suits me. Jagger does what Jagger wants."

He shoved the stupid dog under his other arm. I guessed it

was so I couldn't keep staring at it the way I'd been doing. "Then why should I trust you?"

"That's up to you to decide." With that, he turned and gingerly walked across the grass instead of the icy sidewalk.

Patches had melted but there were still slick spots. The roads, however, seemed much better since the traffic was traveling at a decent speed.

Over his shoulder he said, "Get inside and lock the door. Don't answer it without finding out who it is. Don't open it unless it's someone you know. I'll take this to Lieutenant Shatley." At the door of his car, he stopped and looked at me. "You never answered my question."

I touched the handle of my door and held my chin up high. Not an easy feat to do when your heart is doing a jig in your chest.

He waited, watching.

"Yes."

Jagger had nodded and gotten into his SUV before I could shut and lock my door. I really did trust him, but being here alone had me a bit concerned. Who knew where I lived? How did they find that out? And why didn't Jagger stay with me?

I hurried inside, slammed the door, locked it, rechecked the locks and collapsed against the door as if my one hundred fifteen pounds could keep someone from opening it. I stayed there, thinking.

Maybe the note wasn't for me. Maybe it was a mistake. Or maybe it was meant for Jagger. Someone knew he was here. Someone was following him.

Maybe that's why he left. Silly, he had work to do and even if someone was following him, he wouldn't hide out. I rechecked the locks again, hurried over to Spanky and picked him up despite his low growl. "Too bad, buddy, I need a hug right now."

The phone rang.

Spanky jumped, or maybe it only appeared as if he jumped because I did.

For a few seconds I could only stare. Was my life going to be run by fear? Did I really *have* anything to fear? No one should suspect me. I'd been very discreet at work and had never gotten caught.

Ring. Ring.

I sucked in a breath and walked to the phone. When I lifted the receiver, I heard, "Five-five-five three, six-eight-nine-one. Write it down this time."

Then a dial tone.

I opened the drawer and took out the notepad Miles kept there for phone messages. At least Miles was prepared, I thought, as I jotted down Jagger's cell phone number.

I tucked it into my pants pocket but not before memorizing it. I ran the numbers through my head one more time.

The doorbell rang.

I shouted something foul, and Spanky jumped up and ran toward the door, barking.

Keep calm, Pauline. You are a professional. This became my mantra until I forced my feet to move toward the door. Miles wouldn't ring the bell unless he forgot his key.

Maybe Jagger had come back?

Spanky kept barking. I could only hope that whoever it was didn't know the dog weighed only five pounds and could be frightened away by any loud sound.

The bell rang again.

I grabbed a pillow from the couch and walked closer. What the hell? Did I think I could smother an attacker? I threw it down and stood there.

"Suga? Open up! You all right?"

Bang. Bang.

Tears sprang to my eyes. Goldie! I hurried to open the door. "Goldie!" Spanky jumped and ran toward the kitchen, and Goldie took my hands into his.

"You're not all right. You look like shit. Scared shit. Or is it shitless?" He had a large gym bag with him. A large black bag with purple and green and yellow Mardi Gras masks on it. He would make a perfect ambassador for tourism in the city of New Orleans. "You gonna let me in all the way, suga?"

"I'm so sorry. I—" I took a step back. "Oh my God! You're not dressed!"

He closed the door and laughed. "I'm not exactly naked, suga. I'm taking a day off, and on my days off I like to go casual."

Casual was an understatement.

I'd been so scared before when I opened the door that I hadn't noticed Goldie wasn't in drag. His hair was cropped short, blond with tiny spikes in the front. Dark sunglasses with tortoiseshell frames covered his eyes. His complexion was smooth and tanned. I reached out and touched his face. "No makeup."

He laughed and set the bag on a chair. "Casual Tuesday. No muss. No fuss."

I couldn't help stare at his chest. It was so much flatter.

He looked at me. "Water bra."

I smiled and nodded as if I knew what a water bra was. I did, however, assume the cups were filled with water. Wow. Soft and full and round without any surgery or hormones. "You look good. Real good. Not that you don't look good in . . . you always look gorgeous."

He slung off his brown leather jacket with a dyed brown lambswool collar on it, and put it on a chair and shoved his sunglasses to the top of his head. "Sun's a bitch today with all that melting ice. Too much glare hurts my eyes." If anyone had told me Goldie would be wearing jeans—although tighter than the casing on a kielbasa—I'd have said they were crazy.

Masculine wasn't a term I'd use to describe Goldie when not wearing drag. He still had some feminine features, like his little pert nose, soft skin, and big round eyes. But he was cute.

I couldn't help but go over and hug him again. I've never been known as a touchy-feely type, but lately—that is, since taking on this new job—I had urges to be held by someone or to hug someone or something. Spanky took the brunt of my hugging, even if he didn't welcome it. "Sorry. I needed that."

Goldie laughed. "Hey, we all need somebody sometime. Isn't that a song?"

"I don't know," I said, feeling downright giddy to have his company. "What's in the bag?"

"Gym clothes." He turned toward the kitchen. "Don't you offer your guests a drink?"

"It's only ten thirty and gym clothes?"

He laughed again. "Hey, you think I was born with this bod? No siree, suga. I'm on my way home from Gold's Gym."

I joined in his laughter. "What'll it be?"

Spanky stood near the door, wiggling. The poor thing. I wished he'd learn to bark when he needed to go out. One day I knew I'd find him standing there with his little paws crossed, trying not to wet the floor.

"Coffee." Goldie said, following me into the kitchen. "Oh, boy!"

"What? Oh boy what?"

I swung around. Had somebody climbed the brick wall and taken Spanky? "What!"

He nodded at the sink. "Wait till my Miles sees that."

"I'm going to finish cleaning up. As a matter of fact, I was going to go for a run, then clean up. Have you heard from him today? Is he working the day shift?"

Goldie nodded. He took a piece of bacon from a plate and nibbled on it.

"Yuck. Why don't you nuke that?"

"It's fine. A run sounds fine too. I'll join you."

Taken aback, yet not wanting to be insulting since Goldie didn't strike me as the running type, I nodded. "Okay. If you really want to."

After he helped me clean up, since the dirty dishes bothered him as much as they'd bother Miles, I went upstairs to change, and Goldie changed into his running clothes in the downstairs bathroom.

We did our stretches in the living room and went out, but not before I checked about a hundred times to see if I had my key, and about two hundred times to see if the door was locked.

Goldie followed me out the front entrance, through the parking lot and over to the jogging run that had been made for the condo association members. I was impressed that he kept up without labored breathing.

When we turned the corner to the only area that was surrounded on both sides by woods, I slowed. Goldie came up from behind.

"What's . . . wrong?" He kept jogging in place as I did.

Don't be foolish, I told myself. *No one is following us.* "I thought I heard something in the woods. Must have been a squirrel."

"Varmints are everywhere." He took a deep breath. "Race you back!"

"You're on!"

He was off before I could answer. I gave a quick look around behind me and ran my little size sevens off.

I'd never run so fast in my life. I tried to tell myself it was my competitive nature driving me forward onto Goldie's heels, but if I were true to myself, I'd admit it was dumb fear that someone was following me.

Maybe it was Jagger.

Yes, I liked that thought.

We made it to the parking lot in record time. Goldie first, with me on his heels. Damn it. He raised his hands and danced around like Rocky.

"Don't get . . . carried away. You had a head start."

"By . . . about . . . a second."

Amid laughter, Goldie kept blowing out loud breaths and bending at the waist. "I'm . . . beat."

We cooled down by walking slower around the parking lot, which had now thawed completely. Puddles covered the cement, and we jumped over them to get back to my door.

Once I'd opened it and we walked in, Goldie collapsed on the sofa. I chose the stuffed chair cause it was closer to the door. "Thanks."

"For what, suga? Beating the pants off of you?"

"No." I smiled at him. "For . . . being you."

He nodded.

"Only a friend like you would show up on a day off and jog with me. You're a doll to think of coming over here since you knew Miles wasn't here. You have no idea how much I needed that." Then I told him about Linda.

Goldie bit at his lip and ran a long red nail over it. I guessed it was too much work to take off the nails when he didn't dress in drag. He looked up at me. I'd never seen him so serious.

It scared me.

Of course, I was way too touchy lately. To be a professional in my field, I had to toughen up. "What is it?"

"I . . . I like you too much to lie."

My heart started to speed up. "Lie?"

"I didn't just come to visit you."

Suddenly I felt disappointed and, truthfully, a bit hurt. "Oh?"

"Look, suga." He got up and came over. Without an argument, I let him take my hand and lift me from the chair. Now I wasn't liking this one bit.

"What is going on? Why did you really come here?"

He gave me a hug, which had my stomach in knots.

"Jagger told me to."

After I'd gotten over the shock that Jagger felt it necessary to send a "bodyguard" over, Goldie and I shared a beer even though it wasn't noon yet. We didn't talk about how much he knew about the case I was helping Jagger with and it really didn't matter.

I reminded myself that Jagger was no slouch for thinking about my safety—until my internal devil's advocate said that maybe the reason Jagger didn't want anything to happen to me was that he was still *using* me for the case.

Just how dedicated *was* Jagger?

Twenty-four

I tried to contemplate Jagger sending Goldie over to act as my protector. Partly I was pissed that Jagger thought I couldn't take care of myself. Then I realized I couldn't—in the face of murder. Partly I was pissed that I couldn't. Maybe I really did need a gun.

That thought scared the bejeevers out of me.

Goldie kept looking at his watch. I figured he had someplace he'd rather be than babysitting me, so I said, "You don't have to stay, you know."

He looked from his watch to me. "I'm lots of things, suga, but stupid isn't one of them."

"Hmm? I don't get you."

"Jagger *told* me to—"

"Ah. Now I see. But he doesn't have to know—"

Goldie chuckled. "He always knows."

Yikes. Had no comeback for that.

A chill flew up my spine. Just as I felt this unbelievable sense of calm and safety when around Jagger, I also felt he really did know far more than he should. I tapped my nail to my tooth. "How do you think he does that?"

Goldie shook his head. "If I knew, suga, I'd be chasing the big bucks that he does."

I leaned back on the couch. Spanky jumped at my leg so I lifted him up, and he promptly snuggled under one of the black-and-white-striped pillows that Miles had gotten when he did the living room monochromatically. He didn't count the white as a color. "You think he does it all for the money?"

With a shrug, Goldie said, "I have no fucking idea. Excuse my French."

"Actually I asked him something similar, and he said it wasn't for the money."

Goldie all-out laughed. "I'm not sure you, or anyone for that matter, can believe what Jagger says. The guy gets us all believing what he wants. That's been my take on him since meeting him about five years ago."

"I guess you're right. But you still don't have to stay. Are you meeting Miles for lunch?"

The usual sparkle in Goldie's eyes brightened.

"I see you are. Please don't stay—"

The doorbell rang. We both jumped. I figured Goldie might not be the best babysitter for me, being preoccupied with Miles. We sat, silent, for a few seconds.

"I'll get it." He stood and walked to the door.

I really wanted to remain on the couch, hidden behind the pillows like Spanky, but I repeated my mantra that I was a professional and had to act accordingly. So, I sat up straighter and decided in a few seconds I'd stand.

Goldie peeked out the beveled-glass side panel. I could see his shoulders relax. "Some hot-looking babe with dark hair. Not a one out of place either."

Ack. My shoulders tensed. Vance. If any other guy had said a hot-looking babe, I would have thought it a female, but this was Goldie's take.

I got up and looked out the window. The bell rang again. "Vance. Never known for his patience."

Goldie unlocked the door and said, "Hey." He stepped aside, but Vance stood there like a fool, staring.

I mentally shook my head so as not to appear rude. "Hey, Vance. Come on in." Goldie and I moved farther to the side.

"Hello," Vance said, still staring at poor Goldie.

For a few seconds, I thought Vance might be wondering about Goldie's feminine appearance, but then I realized he was scrutinizing him. The damn fool was jealous. Then I also realized I couldn't tell Goldie that Vance and I had dated, and I use that term lightly, for many—far too many—years.

So, I went with, "Goldie Perlman, this is Doctor Vance Taylor. He is one of the orthopedists who works at the group where I've been filling in."

Vance looked pissed at the introduction.

Goldie looked mildly amused that Vance looked pissed, and being the astute investigator I knew him to be, also looked as if he knew my explanation was very incomplete. But I couldn't go into any detail.

Vance finally came in and stood in the middle of the room. Spanky slithered farther into the pillows. I'd always been convinced the dog didn't much care for Vance, although he'd never been mean to him. Actually, he didn't pay any attention to the little guy. Not like Jagger.

Don't start! I told myself.

"What brings you here?" I asked Vance and noticed he was carrying a white paper bag.

He held the bag closely and looked from Goldie to me. "I . . . brought lunch. Thought since yesterday was such a horrible day with you finding—" He sucked in a breath.

One would think a doctor would deal better with death. Although, to be fair to Vance, orthopedic surgeons don't often face death with their patients, and the murder of an employee, make that two employees, wasn't exactly a usual occurrence.

Let's hope not, I thought.

"I'm fine about yesterday. Not that Linda died, but I can handle my being there. It's sad though."

Goldie nodded as if he'd known Linda, but Vance, with

his usual stiff upper lip, merely stood there, holding the stupid bag. But I was hungry so I said, "What'd you bring?"

"Two Rubens. Two."

Goldie grinned. "Sounds delicious."

I think Vance tightened his hold on the bag.

Then Goldie, being the kind individual I'd come to love as a friend, said, "Too bad I can't stay."

I could actually see Vance's body relax. Goldie knew if Vance was here, Jagger wouldn't get pissed, so this was his golden opportunity to escape. I smiled and said, "That was great fun running together, Gold. We need to do it more often. Enjoy your lunch with Miles."

He politely said goodbye to Vance and scurried out. I followed Vance into the kitchen and got out some china dishes. Vance never would go for the paper plates. Spanky, who would normally be fast on our heels at the scent of food, remained sequestered on the couch, pillows camouflaging his five pounds.

"Yummy," I said with a mouthful. "Where'd you get these?"

Vance looked at me as if to say Don't talk with your mouth full, but said, "That coffee shop over by the mall. In the little strip mall by the printers."

I knew the place well after stalking Tina there. Which reminded me: Today would be a perfect day to get her on film. I had to finish the case soon, even if I didn't turn it all in to Fabio, since Jagger had me going back to the office. "I've seen the place. Good food."

Vance hadn't touched his. Wow. He usually ate everything on his plate when we went to dinner. I always assumed it was because he didn't want to waste food that he was paying for. I wondered if his parents made him "clean his plate" as a kid and if they were as rigid as Vance. My best guess from the few times I ate dinner there was they weren't. Vance wasn't much like his father, a prominent wealthy neurosurgeon; but Vance himself wasn't poor by any means. Frugal, no doubt.

Not poor, like I would be if I didn't get rid of Vance and

go find Tina. Where the heck was Jagger? I wondered. He should be here to help me finish my case and meet his deal.

Several strings of sauerkraut had fallen from my sandwich onto my dish. I finished my sandwich and busied myself picking each one up and eating it. With the last one held to my open lips, I looked across the table.

Vance sat staring. Today must be his staring day, I thought.

"Sorry," I said and popped the sauerkraut into my mouth.

He shook his head. "Your eating habits aren't on my mind right now, Pauline."

Oh God. I hope he didn't come here for *that*.

"Oh?"

"I mean, Pauline, someone killed Linda and Eddy. Why do I have such bad luck?"

"I'm not following." I got up and took a glass from the cabinet. "Water?"

"Beer if you have one."

Wow. Beer for Vance? He *was* upset. Poor guy. Guess it was a bummer to switch jobs and find out the practice wasn't exactly what you had in mind. I got him a Budweiser, saving the last Coors Light for myself. I figured I'd need it after Vance left. Hopefully soon. But I couldn't chase him out in the rotten mood he was in. I handed him the bottle.

He looked at me. "Pauline, you're not yourself today either. A glass?"

"Oops." I got him one of the good ones with the gold rim that I hated since they couldn't be put in the microwave. Actually, there wasn't anything I'd nuke in such a fancy glass, but I still didn't like them. They were Vance. The beer bottle was me—and Jagger.

Vance poured his beer into the glass and took a sip. "I don't know what to do, Pauline. I came here to see what your thoughts were."

"On?"

"On my leaving the practice." He took a long sip. A mustache of foam settled above his lip. It took several seconds for him to pick up a napkin and wipe it off.

Vance really wasn't himself. I actually felt sorry for him. "Geez. You just started there." Knowing what I did about the investigation, I couldn't be too objective. "Then again, there have been two murders associated with the practice. I—"

His eyes widened. "You think my life is in danger?"

Damn. With the sense of security I felt with Jagger, I hadn't thought about that. I wanted to say no since he'd only started there, and according to Jagger, the perpetrators had been involved in fraud for a long time. "I don't think so."

"Did you see anything, Pauline?"

"Nope. Just a dead Linda. Now back to your job dilemma. I've found out that if you don't like your job, or something about it, you need to do something about that."

He looked at me and raised an eyebrow. "Yes, but you quit nursing since you were burned out and what do you do? Take a nursing job."

Yikes. It did look stupid, but I couldn't say it was because I was investigating there. I snorted. Not very ladylike, but enough to get any ideas of *that* out of Vance's mind. "It does seem odd, but truthfully, I only did it to help out Tina. You know we went to school together."

"Yeah, I know. Donnie and I were residents together, too. But that doesn't answer my question."

"It's not an easy one, Vance. I think if you're not happy or you're concerned, then you need to move on to something else."

"It's not easy to just up and leave a practice, Pauline."

"I know that, but you asked my opinion." Geez. He was annoying me and not only 'cause I wanted him to leave so I could follow Tina.

"I'm sorry. You're right. Maybe I should take that staff position at Saint Greg's."

"They offered you one?"

He nodded. "Several months ago, when I mentioned to Doctor Greenstern, the head of Ortho, that I wasn't happy in a two-man practice."

"But, Vance, would you be happy on staff? You'd have to

deal with interns and residents, and the pay can't be the same."

He stiffened. Money always did that to Vance. "That's the main drawback."

"The pay?"

"No, the interns and residents. They could mess up my patients. I really don't like someone interfering in my treatments."

I knew that to be true. Plus Vance had little patience and wouldn't do well teaching. But, I still think the money issue wasn't far from the truth either. "Well, then it's back to staying put. I'm sure the police will get everything straightened out and find out who is responsible."

He nodded. "I guess I shouldn't be too hasty. I spoke with Donald and Charlene. They're not thinking of leaving."

Why would they? I thought. They might be making millions on fraud. "Then it's settled." I got up and cleaned off the table, hoping he'd get the hint. "Look, the sandwich was great and I hope I helped you, but I need to . . ." Damn. Need to what? I really wished I could be a faster-thinking liar. "I . . . Did I tell you my parents and Uncle Walt went to visit my aunt Florence in Pennsylvania for two days?"

He looked at me as if I were nuts. "Why would you?"

True. "Oh, I thought I'd mentioned it. Anyway, I have to go over and feed Uncle Walt's bird, Perry. He's a canary so Uncle Walt named him after Perry Como. You know the singer—"

Vance got up, most likely annoyed with my rambling with all that was on his mind. "I know who Perry Como is. How about dinner tonight?"

"I . . . I promised my mother I'd eat what she left so it won't spoil. You know how she worries that I don't eat enough." No, he probably didn't, but what the heck. "You could join me." Perfect out. Vance wouldn't be caught dead at my parents' house. I'd taken him there once back in 1998, and I think he suffered some kind of culture shock. We never discussed it, nor did I ever invite him to the split-level that smelled like kielbasa and kraut again. Hey, I told myself, I was getting better at these lies.

We said our goodbyes and after a quick peck on my cheek, Vance was out the door. The sun was brilliant now. The roads dry. And I was heading off to find Tina Macaluso.

Good thing I'd started that lie to Vance, because my parents really were away. I didn't have to feed Perry since Uncle Walt, in fact, didn't have a bird, but I could "hide out" at their house and not have to worry or have a babysitter over the weekend. And that meant Goldie and Miles could be alone.

I drove back and forth between the Macalusos' two houses three times, cursing Jagger all the way. How did he know where to find her? And where was he? I kept looking for him to pop out from behind a tree while I sat waiting for Tina, who could not even fit behind a tree. I couldn't even use the same ruse Miles had, when he'd dialed her up from his cell phone. If I called her, she'd see my name on caller ID.

Then, my luck changed. The front door of the mansion opened up and out she walked. Today she was in her bright yellow parka. I thought of fake canary Perry—only on a larger scale. Donnie was close on her heels. Damn. I really wanted to get Tina alone, but had no choice in the matter. When they pulled out of the driveway I started my car, and soon was nearly sucking on their tailpipe.

First they stopped at the coffee shop in the strip mall. Oh shit. I hoped Tina wasn't going in for Jazzercise again. I really couldn't think of a way to sneak in if Suzy was on duty. Thank goodness, the Macalusos went into the coffee shop and came out a few minutes later with a white bag. It made me wonder if they had bought Rubens, like Vance.

It's funny, the dumb things one's mind comes up with while on surveillance. It was much more fun working with Jagger along. Not because it was him, but because he was someone to talk to and pass the time with. Goldie would do as well, I told myself, then realized the Macalusos were on the road headed toward the professional building.

Were they going to the office?

Sure enough, a few minutes later they pulled into the back of the office building. That's where the staff parked, although what with the police clearing out the building to go over it, the lot was empty except for a few cars.

Shoot, I hoped they didn't belong to the police. I figured they might have finished their work here by now, and I didn't figure they'd park so far away from the building like the cleaning people had to. They had to use their assigned spaces even on weekends, since some of the staff, especially the doctors, might go to their offices. And heaven forbid they'd have to walk from farther away.

I wondered, as I watched the Macalusos' car, if janitor Jagger would show up.

Tina got out, and Donnie drove off.

Yes! It would be much easier to follow her without having him along to hide from too. Besides, I pretty well had my evidence on him for Workers' Comp fraud. She went into the building through the back door. Thank goodness I still had a key. In the fury of finding Linda's body yesterday, I hadn't remembered to return the key. And now Jagger had me coming back anyway. I hadn't asked Trudy, who I guessed would be in charge until Linda was officially replaced, if I should come back. I doubted she'd throw me out since they were now short-staffed even worse.

I waited until Donnie's Porsche was out of sight, then pulled into the parking lot next to a car I'd guessed belonged to one of the cleaning people. Then I took my camera out of my purse, which I locked in the trunk. It wasn't a good idea to lug it around when sneaking up on Tina. I put the camera and my keys into my jacket pocket.

Within a few minutes I was walking up the stairs very slowly, stopping at every landing to listen.

Nothing.

No footsteps coming from below. Thank goodness. If the forensic guys were still working, they must have gone on a lunch break. I really would have peed my pants if someone, Donnie perhaps, came up from downstairs. At the next landing, I opened the door to the elevator lobby where the office was. No one was around. A janitor's bucket and cart, like the ones in hotels that the maids leave out in the hallway, sat nearby. Apparently the cops were letting them clean some areas that they were done investigating.

Now what?

The door to the office was closed. Tina had to have gone in by now since, I assumed, she took the elevator. I looked back and forth and walked toward the cart. A set of keys hung on the side. Hmm. Maybe there was a janitor's closet on this floor. I took the keys, not sure why, and walked past the door to the office. Sure enough, a door was open at the end of the hallway. I needn't have pilfered the keys.

Mops, chemicals, buckets. A janitor's closet is not a pretty sight to someone with a cleaning phobia. I left that up to Miles and Hilly, the woman who came in weekly, since he insisted on paying for her to clean his condo, which he inevitably recleaned. I leaned against the door and wondered what to do.

When I looked up, it was like a heavenly vision. Janitor's overalls. Similar to the ones Jagger had worn that day. A bit big for me, but, hey, this wasn't a fashion show. I slipped the overalls over my jacket to take up some of the slack and stuck my camera in the overalls.

I'd die of heat, but determined to get paid by Fabio soon, I told myself, I could pretend it was like Alaska in this building, if that's what it took. I grabbed a Dodgers baseball cap and shoved my hair under it. I groaned at the thought of wearing someone else's hat, but when I thought of getting paid, I ignored the grossness factor.

I confiscated the mop and bucket and rolled it into the waiting room of the ortho office. No one was in that area, thank goodness. I heard radio music coming from the lounge area. No sign of any cops. Good. The music would help me sneak around. Tina had to be in there. I only hoped she was lifting something heavy.

With mop in hand, I walked toward the lounge.

I don't know who screamed louder, Tina or myself. Then I realized my screaming was in my head—a reaction to her—although I amazingly had the wherewithal not to make a sound out loud.

I tipped my hat to her and prayed she didn't recognize me. "Ma'am," I said, trying to disguise my voice.

"You fool. You scared me."

That was it? Good. She didn't call me "fool Pauline," so I figured I could mop while she . . . What *was* she doing?

Linda's desk was covered in papers.

She never left it like that. Tina had to have spread them out. On the floor sat several file boxes. Heavy ones, I hoped.

Within seconds, Tina had gone back to ignoring me, and through the open doorway I could see her looking at the papers. I mopped the floor in the lounge and looked down to realize I'd moved onto the carpet. Dumb idea to mop a carpet, so I moved closer to the refrigerator.

She turned to look at me through the glass partition. She looked nervous. And why wouldn't someone who was bilking the insurance company out of millions? I touched my pocket to feel the camera.

"I have work to do. The hallway needs mopping," she called out.

Shit. I couldn't say no. I nodded and carried my mop toward the hall. I hoped the door was open enough for me to peek through and take a few pictures.

After that, Tina never paid me a second thought or got up to close the door. Instead, she lifted a stack of papers and started to *shred* them over a file box.

Twenty-five

Shredding documents, even if by hand, didn't seem like logical office work to me. Stunk to high heaven, in fact.

Now I knew why she did the dirty work, though. Donnie couldn't risk injuring his precious surgeon's hands. I got that from Vance all the time. Besides, it made sense. By the looks of things, Tina could win one of those competitions where contestants tried to tear a New York City phone book in half in one fell swoop.

Watching her fury, I thought she was getting into this shredding business like gangbusters. Then she got up.

I got out my camera.

She grabbed a rather large stack of papers and, to my horror and delight, became a madwoman. She twisted and turned like a hula dancer.

I snapped in sync.

When papers would fall, she bent—not using her knees, I might add—and picked them up at record speed. And the papers did fly.

I caught her looking at the clock and figured Donnie had given her a time frame to work in. The thing I still wondered was, What were those papers?

Maybe fake bills? Tina and Donnie must have made some extra bucks on the Workers' Comp fraud, and that's how they could own two houses.

My original mission had been to get pictures of her committing Workers' Compensation fraud—and today was my lucky day, so it didn't matter right now what the papers were.

After several minutes, my camera wouldn't click anymore. I looked down to see I'd taken twenty-eight pictures on a twenty-seven-picture roll. I knew it was pushing it to go past the allotted number, but I'd lost track in my frantic effort to keep up with Tina.

At least the last two shots were of her picking up the file boxes with angst on her face, which I was going to promote as showing how heavy the boxes were, and moving them to the other side of the room by the door.

I should have just left, since I had what I'd come for, but I couldn't move.

I needed to know what she was doing.

I needed to know what files she was destroying.

And I needed to find out before I got caught.

Jagger would, after all, need this info.

The files had to have something to do with the unorthodox running of this practice. Linda was killed yesterday. I guessed it was because of something she knew or was a party to. And Tina was making confetti out of files from Linda's desk. I remembered how Linda would move files from the IN tray to the OUT tray and back and forth when I came into the room. Maybe there was something to that. Maybe she did that to distract me or whoever else came in. Or maybe it was to mix up the files.

A funny feeling stuck in my gut.

I think I'd stumbled upon the answer to Jagger's case.

The question was, how the hell was I going to help, when the papers were smaller than the nail on my pinky finger?

A pain pierced my back.

I spun around, thinking I'd been shot. No one in the hallway. I ran my hand along the back of the overalls and looked at it. Clean. No blood. Then it dawned on me that my imagination had gone haywire for a second. I'd been hunched over for so long, my back muscles were rebelling. I moved to the side to stretch. Stretching always helped.

In my haste to ease the pain, I bumped into the wall.

"Who's out there?" Tina shouted. "That you, janitor?"

My eyes widened. My mouth went so dry that I thought no words would ever come out again. And my heart beat so loudly I knew, just knew, Tina would be at the door any second.

She stuck her head out the open door.

I stumbled against the wall while grabbing for my mop.

"I'm going to report you, you drunk. Get the hell back to mopping that floor and then leave." She turned and shoved the door.

I stuck my foot out in time to stop it from slamming shut. Ouch. Not a good move, although necessary. I peeked in, thinking. What the heck. She was going to report a short, fat janitor in a Dodger's baseball cap for working while drunk.

I was in the clear.

I looked inside.

She wasn't there!

I leaned closer. The bill of the hat prevented me from sticking my face too far inside. I shoved it to the back. Several strands of hair fell into my face. Damn! I tried to stick them up, but didn't have much luck. I let them go and opened the door in time to see Tina near Linda's desk, picking up the last box.

I waited until I heard a door close.

Then I hurried in.

If I followed her out the back entrance that Jagger had used to sneak up on me, what then? What should I do? I couldn't get any info out of the tiny pieces of files. Damn it all. Still, wait until the police found out she was shredding and stealing files. Even if her husband was part owner of this place, I didn't think they'd like it.

I dropped my camera on the desk and slumped into Linda's chair in a huff.

Three papers flew, like Uncle Walt's fake canary, out from under the desk. Well, they really didn't fly of their own accord but merely jumped into the air from the breeze I created when I collapsed into the chair.

For some reason, I thought of Jagger.

Damn. I should call him and tell him about this, but I'd left my cell phone in the car, and I knew he wouldn't want me using the office phone in case they could trace his number.

I bent to pick up the papers.

Mr. Suskowski had had two MRIs, according to this insurance form. And Mrs. Bakersfield had had one too. It was of her skull, when she'd come in for her knee. I know the backbone is connected to the shoulder bone and the shoulder bone connected to the . . . the damn song started in my head but I couldn't remember any more of it.

But what I did remember was that these two patients didn't have any of these tests done, and Mrs. Bakersfield's skull wasn't connected to her knee.

And again, Vance's signature was on the form.

I leaned back in the chair. Was Vance in on the fraud? How could he be? He'd only been here a short time, and Jagger had said the illegal filing of fake insurance claims had been going on for years.

Something stunk.

I took a Kleenex tissue from the cute cat holder on Linda's desk, although I figured maybe I shouldn't touch it. But since the crime-scene tape was gone, the cops had to have gone over this place since yesterday. I used the tissue on the handle of the desk drawer anyway.

I listened for Tina to return although I figured she had left, since the boxes were gone. Damn. That would have been a great shot, to get her carrying two file boxes out the door. But I had perfect evidence already.

I smiled, even though alone in the room, and whispered,

"Pauline Sokol, you devil of a medical-insurance-fraud investigator." My next thought was that I'd have to get business cards made. I opened the last drawer on the bottom. Nothing. Nothing out of the ordinary.

I leaned back and looked at the desk. "Big help you've been."

Saint Teresa had to be thinking of me.

I leaned closer. There on the front of the desk was a lovely piece of oak molding. Linda's desk was the prettiest in the office. At least I thought so, since I was partial to oak. The doctors mostly had mahogany, except for Charlene, who had an old metal one. The woman must be in as bad a financial situation as I was. She had kids to feed.

Was she bad off enough to commit fraud?

I touched the molding, then pushed it very gently. Nothing. Damn it.

And here I thought I was so clever.

"Someone in there? That you, Bobby?" a man's voice called out.

My hand shot forward. The tips of my fingers jammed into the molding. The man shouted once more, sounding closer.

I looked down to see that the molding had moved. I stuck my finger near the top: Bingo!

I pressed the button, the hidden drawer popped out, and I mentally shouted, "Yes, Uncle Walt!"

There sat a book. Not just any book I noticed, when I heard someone shove open the door between the waiting room and hallway.

I grabbed the book and hightailed it out the back door before the real janitor could finish his cursing when he nearly broke his neck on the mop I'd left in the hallway.

Once out the back door, I charged down the stairs to the ground floor, where I peered through the wire-glass window in the exit door. Good. No Porsche. Phew. I ran to my car, unlocked the door and jumped in.

I was out past the mall before I realized that I still had on the janitor overalls.

Feeling like a criminal, although I knew I wasn't, even if I had stolen the overalls, I pulled into the mall parking lot. After looking around several times, I shimmied out of the outfit, balled it up, and got out. Nonchalantly I walked toward the brown metal Dumpster and promptly, up on tiptoe, flung it inside.

I looked around again, saw no one was paying attention and went to my car. I took my purse out of the trunk, got inside the car, and looked at the book on the seat. It sat there so innocently in its bright yellow cover with black writing. A big pencil was silhouetted against the title.

Forgery for Idiots.

My first thought was, Linda was no moron. My second was that *she* ordered the MRIs and forged Vance's signature.

Vance needed to know. He was fearing for his life, and now I had evidence that said he need not worry.

I had to convince Jagger to let Vance in on it once the case was handed over to the DA's office and indictments handed down. Of course Linda was dead.

But the Macalusos knew to shred Linda's files.

I looked in the mirror and grinned. Pauline Sokol was an official investigator. I could get the pictures in my camera developed at the one-hour photo booth in the mall.

I looked around.

No camera.

I must have left it in the overalls. Damn! How would I . . . No, wait. I had dropped it on Linda's desk. It had to still be there. Thank goodness, again, for the key to the professional building and the office. The real janitor wouldn't pay me any mind now.

I reached into my purse and grabbed my cell phone. I shut my eyes to recall Jagger's number. I was so excited to tell him what I'd found. Okay, calm down. I couldn't think of the number. Foolishly, yet out of past experience, I looked around for a black Suburban. None.

I leaned back in my seat and forced my brain to remember. Okay, I had it. I punched out a set of numbers.

"Charlie's Eatery," a young man said.

Shoot. "Sorry, wrong number." The cell phone beeped at me. "Okay, so I got a wrong—" It beeped again. I looked at the screen.

Low battery.

Shoot again. I transposed the last two numbers and held the receiver to my ear.

"Yeah."

My heart thudded. Jagger's voice.

"It's me. I have some—"

Beep. Beep.

"What?"

I think I heard him call my name, but I interrupted with, "I have some information. I'm going to the off—"

Beep.

I'm pretty sure the final *beep* came before my words.

"Jagger? Jagger?" I looked at the phone as if it were its fault that I hadn't thought to charge its battery in several days. "Damn you."

I threw the phone onto the seat. Oh well, I'd get the camera, come back here and call Jagger from a pay phone. Too anxious to get my camera back, I didn't want to take the time now.

I would think walking into a mostly empty office building would feel eerie, but I'd started to get used to it by the time I made it up the third flight of stairs. If the janitor caught me, I could say I had business here and my proof would be my key.

I walked into the office door without seeing anyone. Come to think of it, there weren't any cars in the parking lot. This time I'd used the front door instead of going to the back as I had when following Tina.

I unlocked the outer door and walked through the waiting

room, down the hall and into the lounge. There it was in Linda's office, on the desk. My camera. Yes!

I went over and took it. This time I made sure to stuff it into my purse. Then I walked out into the hallway.

Just to double-check, I leaned over and looked deep inside my bag. There it sat. "Good," I said, then straightened up.

And screamed.

Twenty-six

I think I broke something in my throat from screaming so loudly.

Vance stood there, glaring at me.

"Wha . . . wha . . ." That was it. Either I'd been so traumatized that I couldn't speak, or I really had broken something important. "Oh, thank goodness it's you," I finally squeaked out in pain.

"What the hell are you doing here, Pauline?" He took my arm and led me into his office.

Charts were scattered across his desk. Vance was more anal than Miles and never left a mess, so I knew he'd been working. I assumed he had come to review patient records to help in his decision of whether to stay or leave here.

"Sit down." He walked to the sideboard and poured me a glass of water.

I took it, nodded a thanks, and drank some. Maybe it would lubricate my larynx and it'd work again.

Vance sat across from me in his fine black leather chair. "So? What are you doing here?"

I shut my eyes and opened them. My heart rate was still about three times the speed it should be. My hands shook so that droplets of water danced out of the glass, landing on my Steelers parka.

"Pauline? Answer me!"

My father's voice came out of Vance's mouth. At least the stern tone did like when my brothers and sisters and I had done something wrong. Then, as if animated, I started to talk. No, I started to ramble. "I came to follow Tina, I had to get more pictures. She . . . shredded. The papers on the floor, jumped from under the desk. I left my camera. Well, I didn't know I had."

Vance stared at me. The familiar eyes that I'd known for so many years had me feeling as if I could ramble on without being interrupted.

"At the mall, I didn't have my camera. I shoved the janitor overalls in the Dumpster. Then I came back here to get . . . Oh, Vance. Linda's book!"

He leaned near. "What book?"

"She . . . your signature. Forgery. Morons. She forged . . . for MRIs, X-rays . . . Lord only knows what else. No wonder someone . . . someone found out, Vance. That's why they killed her." I sucked in a huge breath and shouted, "She forged your signature. I found the insurance forms that said you ordered the tests when you didn't. . . ."

Vance's eyes grew dark.

Now I'd admitted repeatedly that I could never read Jagger's facial expression. But Vance had always been an open book.

Anger.

Disgust.

No . . . Wait. What was it now?

Coldness.

His expression grew cold. It hadn't felt eerie being in the empty building before, but now, sitting across from a man I'd known and dated for years—and had slept with—an ominous feeling crossed over the mahogany desk to stab at my heart.

I swallowed. "Linda . . . didn't forge your name."

Vance stood. "She did forge all the other doctors' names though." He came around the desk.

I started to stand. He shoved me down with a force that I would never expect from someone wanting to protect his hands. He lifted a few strands of my hair, let them run through his fingers.

I shuddered.

Vance had never been repulsive to me, or I wouldn't have slept with him. I wasn't that desperate.

But now he was. Repulsive, that is.

He leaned close to my ear. I heard him say, "You should have stayed at Saint Greg's."

Speaking of staying somewhere, I damn sure couldn't stay here. I pushed at his arm. He yanked me close to him, bending my arm behind my back.

This wasn't the Vance I knew.

"Let me go. You're hurting my arm."

"Soon . . . you won't feel any pain."

Now *that* was something a girl could go her entire life without hearing and she'd be fine. "What do you mean?" Although I had a pretty good idea.

Linda didn't feel any pain now.

Neither did Eddy.

Before I knew it, Vance was dragging me around his desk. I tried to elbow him, but he knew his bones all right and snapped my arm with such force, even his eyes lit up. That's when the pain shot up to my shoulder. I screamed. I looked down to see the bend in my arm. "You . . . broke . . . it," was all I could wail.

Vance opened his desk and pulled out a gun. Yikes. I didn't know a .357 Magnum from a Glock 33 other than from the movies, but I did know that his having broken my arm and now brandishing a gun at me, no matter what kind, was not a good sign.

I ignored the pain and begged Saint Theresa to have Jagger be outside the door.

Vance pointed toward the hallway. "Go." He released his hold on me and pushed me ahead of him.

I stumbled but regained my balance. "My arm. It hurts. Can't you cast it . . ."

Vance hesitated. Good sign. I appealed to his mercy or his Hippocratic oath. Then to my dismay, he said, "You won't need it. Go."

I walked to the door. "You don't have to shove the barrel in my back. I know you're armed." I held my arm to immobilize it as much as I could. Nausea had bile seeping up my throat. "I'm going to—" Before I could finish, vomit splattered the hallway carpet.

"Christ, Pauline."

"You're the one who broke my arm!" Tears trickled out of my eyes. Partly from fear. Partly from pain. But no matter the cause, I refused to let them flow—and give Vance any satisfaction.

He took my other arm and led me out into the hallway. No janitor. No Jagger. If I lived, I vowed to charge the battery on my phone daily.

"I didn't mean to hurt you, Pauline."

"Only kill me?"

"I . . . Some things can't be helped."

"Oh, right. How foolish of me to cast any blame on you."

He dragged me to the elevator.

If I thought my heart was pounding before, now it was doing double-time.

Vance pressed the button.

"So, tell me, Vance. Why did you kill Linda if she wasn't forging your name?"

He looked at me. I could see an old familiarity in his eyes. We'd known each other a long time. I guess he, too, remembered that, and opened up to me. "I didn't kill her. Charlene . . ."

I slumped against the wall. "Charlene killed Linda?"

"She had to. After Linda found out Eddy had ratted on us.

He actually bragged about it to Tina when he was drunk. Charlene had his—"

"Air bag tampered with," I whispered.

"How did you—"

I waved my good hand. The pain had dulled since I had supported the break as best I could. Then again, maybe impending death had trivialized a little thing like a broken arm. But I was feeling a bit shocky. "It doesn't matter."

Or did it?

With nothing left up my sleeve, I said, "The practice is under investigation for medical insurance fraud."

Vance's eyes widened. "You never were a good liar."

"That's true. Only this time, I'm not lying. Eddy squealed to the right people."

"I've always known you were smart, Pauline, but now you've gone too far. Now you have to—I should have put an end to this when you were jogging this morning."

Goldie being there had saved my life.

"You've been following me."

"Then fucking Tina and Donnie show up here and interfere yet again."

"They're in on it with you?"

He merely looked at me.

The elevator door opened.

"Shoot me here. I won't go in."

Vance touched my cheek. In his defense, it was quite tenderly. "I told you two years ago to seek some professional help for your claustrophobia. Maybe now you'd be more cooperative if you had."

I shook my head, now more pissed than scared. "Just what I want to do. Make it easier on you, you prick."

"Don't get vulgar, Pauline."

He caught me off guard and before I knew it, we were in the elevator. "No!" I reached out to grab the door.

Vance shoved my hand away just before the door hit it.

The sweat that had beaded on my forehead was now trickling down my face in telling drops. "Thanks for nothing."

He pushed the button to go up. I could barely think. "Vance, I . . . can't . . . breathe."

"Don't get hysterical on me, Pauline. That was Linda's downfall. Just like her greed. She wore that stupid ruby ring that reminded me of her greed every day. She'd claimed it was a token to remind all of us of what we could have if we worked together, but that's not how I saw it. She freaked when we found out Eddy had squealed. I had told her to be calm, cause once Eddy was out of the picture everything would be fine. We would take our money and—"

"You were having an affair with Linda?"

He looked at me as if I were insane. Me? Yeah, right. Look who's calling the kettle black.

"Linda wanted to have an affair with Charlene. Charlene didn't swing both ways. Pissed Linda off."

Suddenly I ignored my claustrophobia as best I could. I had to hear it all. "I'm confused," I said.

I played my ace, knowing Vance couldn't stand stupidity and had very little patience for someone not understanding something he thought was perfectly clear. That's why he could never work with interns and residents.

"Pauline, I thought you were smarter than that."

"Apparently I'm not."

He looked at me with a hint of his old affection. "I guess I owe it to you to explain."

Just as I nodded, he hit the emergency stop button on the elevator.

Oh Lord, not again.

This time, though, my life really was at stake. I ordered my brain not to believe that just because the elevator was stopped and the door was closed that I would panic and die.

The gun in Vance's hand, however, was good reason to believe I might.

So, I sucked in the already stale air of the elevator, ignoring the familiar scent of Vance's expensive cologne and said, "After all we've been through, all you've meant to me, I think you do too."

He looked at me and laughed.

Uh-oh. I think the guy just cracked.

He stopped long enough to say, "I never meant anything to you other than a good fuck."

No sense telling lies on my deathbed. "It never was *that* good. I'm surprised you never said anything before."

"We fulfilled a need for each other. And I . . . I love . . ."

I shouldn't feel sorry for someone who broke my arm, ouch, made me puke on the floor, and forced me at gunpoint into an elevator, but I did. I actually felt sorry for Vance. I really had to toughen up. "You love me?"

He curled his lips. "No, Pauline. I love Charlene."

"What?" I didn't mean to sound like a jealous woman, but shoot, he loved *Charlene*? "Now you *really* owe me an explanation."

The walls closed in.

How I wished it wasn't so late, and that the building hadn't been shut down for the investigation. Normally, it would be crawling with people. Doctors and nurses who could cast my arm and maybe stop the bleeding after Vance . . . shot me.

"I met Charlene when I was an intern—"

"Then why date me?"

"Well, if you'd let me explain." He dropped the gun to his side.

I couldn't take my eyes off it, until I ordered myself to. He couldn't see me staring at it or he'd tighten his hold and be more cautious.

"She was married. I wouldn't come between someone and their spouse."

But you'd commit fraud and murder. I thought better than to say that. Vance was on a roll. I let him go on as I kept glancing at the gun and wiping the sweat from my forehead.

"Then her marriage became rocky. I only meant to comfort her, but . . . things happened. You know how that is. I needed you to take any suspicion off of Charlene and I being together."

"Glad to have helped."

"Thank you," he said, then continued in a monotone. "She had two kids, and her ex left town. Bastard of an ex. Left her high and dry. So, I couldn't get openly mixed up with her."

"Daddy wouldn't approve."

He nodded.

I cursed his father for messing with Vance's mind.

'Cause look where it got him.

"But I still wanted to be with her even if secretly. That's why you and I didn't go out that often."

No great loss there, buddy. I looked at him and nodded.

"But with her kids, and paying off huge debts her husband had left her, Charlene wasn't financially well off. Even for a doctor."

"That's why you didn't marry her." It wasn't a question. I knew Vance. Even though he loved her, and I didn't doubt that, he would be a failure in the eyes of his father if he didn't become wealthy. A woman and two kids needing that much money would be a drain on that plan.

"So you decided to commit fraud to get more money?"

He gave me a "What? Are you stupid?" look. "No, Pauline. Don't interrupt. Charlene and Donnie came up with the idea. They attended a medical seminar back in '98 over in England, where some consultants, who were subsequently caught and charged, discussed medical fraud, the fools. They actually would *teach* doctors how to commit fraud, under the pretense of teaching you how to watch out for it. Charlene and Donnie started out small. One claim here. A false claim there. One night when Charlene and I had finished making love . . ." He looked at me.

I yanked my eyes from the gun.

"Sorry. I don't mean to rub our sex life in your face."

"No problem. I understand how you felt about her."

"Feel."

Yeah, right. And he'd proposed to me a time or two. I'd never really been in love and now I was dying to tell my mother that she was wrong about me marrying Vance after all the numerous times she'd tried to talk me into it.

I only hoped I would get the chance to tell her.

I'd started to feel a bit dizzy either from shock or claustrophobia or Vance. But I bit my lip a few times, figuring the pain would keep my mind clear.

"Anyway, after sex she'd told me about the money she and Donnie were making. I couldn't believe how easy it was."

"So that's why you came to this practice."

"You *are* smart. But it did take me a long time. I do have a conscience, you know, Pauline."

Had one. "I know, Vance. But, really, you broke the law and two people are dead."

"It was their own fault. Eddy squealed and Linda had a fight with Charlene. Linda secretly loved Charlene, and when Charlene wouldn't . . . go for her . . . Linda threatened to report all of us. Charlene had to inject her to end the threats."

"By inject I'm guessing you mean with a deadly drug."

"Pavulon."

I gasped. "A neuromuscular blocker? Without a respirator, a person dies."

He sighed. "That was the idea."

Linda had suffocated when her muscles relaxed so much that her lungs didn't function and her diaphragm didn't work. How awful. Yet clever, since it wouldn't be easily traced. Paralyzed to death with a simple injection.

"What about Tina and Donnie? Weren't you afraid they'd tell someone?"

"Ha! They're up to their eyeballs in debt. They need the money a hell of a lot more than Charlene and I."

"So Tina was shredding evidence so you all wouldn't get caught?"

He looked confused.

"Oh, hell. I was following Tina. My new job is as a medical insurance fraud investigator."

He laughed. "How ironic."

"I'm glad you see humor in that." I rubbed my arm.

"If I had my bag, I'd give you a shot of morphine for the

pain. I figured you were snooping around for something. I thought you suspected me of something. Actually, I thought Eddy had told you about all of it. I'd seen you talking to him and that other man, whoever he is, far too often."

He was softening. Maybe I could catch him off guard. I didn't allow myself to think of the "other man." Jagger. "So you tried to scare me with the stuffed Spanky."

"Spanky never liked me."

Good taste.

"So I thought it was appropriate to put a note of warning on his little collar, telling you to give up this job. I thought it would scare you enough never to come back here."

"Good thinking."

"Why didn't it?"

Oh, hell. "Because I never got to see it. The police have it. They'll get you eventually, Vance."

"With you out of the way, they'll have no proof. I used surgical gloves. They'll never trace the note to me. And . . . whatever I tell you will go no further than these walls."

He might be right if Jagger wasn't on the case.

"Why couldn't you have gotten scared off when I followed you near Tina's house that day? Would have been to your benefit, Pauline."

"You own a green parka." I'd never suspected Vance to be a stalker. Not his style. Guess greed changed people.

He smiled—no, he grinned, a very clichéd sinister grin.

"I don't understand why Tina faked an injury—"

"Fat greedy bitch. If they had let me control things, and had listened, we'd all be millionaires and no one would ever have known."

Again, not with the likes of Jagger around.

Jagger.

"They never listened to me. Even Charlene has her faults. I told her running you over would be a mistake—"

"That *was* her at the restaurant! And that guy in the Steelers hat zooming out of here was her too."

"She had to get away after injecting Linda. No one was

going to use the X-ray room that morning, so it was a perfect setup."

I shivered. Linda had lain there paralyzed until she could no longer breathe and died.

"So, Vance, how did you get away with giving those basketball players new shoes to lie for you?"

He curled his lip. I could tell that "fake break" stuff wasn't his style. He really hadn't wanted to involve others in the deception. "A man from the YMCA told all of us doctors that the kids needed new shoes. We used it as a tax write-off."

The capper who gave us Polish people a bad name. So that's how they allayed suspicion about the shoes. I wasn't far off in my thinking on that one.

"So all along it was you doctors and nurses that were committing the fraud. And here I thought the Mafia was involved." Okay, that wasn't really true, but in this situation, I lied. There never had been any truth to the old rumors of Tina's family being involved with the Mafia from our nursing-school days. But Vance didn't have to know that.

I thought I heard a noise in the distance, but then Vance started to speak. "I don't know what the hell you're talking about. I'd never had anything to do with the Mafia. My family is pristine in their reputation."

Until their son became a murderer.

I wondered if I'd ever see my family. Mom, or Dad, or Uncle Walt. Tears welled up in my eyes. "I want to see my family." Sobs followed.

Vance looked more confused than before. But he knew how I felt about my family, so he bought it. He reached over and wiped a tear from my cheek. "It'll be all right. It'll be fine, Pauline."

How could death be fine? I realized that Vance *was* cracking, but not in a violent sort of way. No, his style was more mellow, more emotional.

So, I had to use that.

I cried louder.

"Pauline. Please. You know I don't like tears."

"I . . . can't . . . help . . . it."

He reached into his suit pocket and pulled out a linen handkerchief. Wow. He really had suffered a meltdown to let me use his linen on my nose.

I blew loudly.

He shut his eyes.

A loud banging came from above, outside the elevator.

Vance looked up.

I lunged, ignored the pain in my arm, and managed to grab his gun.

Boom!

Twenty-seven

December 24

I looked at the Christmas tree in my mother's living room and smiled. Daddy always waited until Christmas Eve to get a good buy. Thing was, he inevitably got one that was about two feet too tall, and then he cut off the top, making it out of shape.

It warmed my heart to see the familiar hacked-up, out-of-shape tree.

It also warmed my heart to see my family milling about dressed in festive holiday attire—and I was alive to see it. That felt pretty damn good too.

I ran my hand across my neon pink cast and shut my eyes. How clearly I could picture Vance lying on the elevator floor, me with his gun pointed at him as if I'd known how to shoot, and my other hand slamming the elevator button to make it go.

When the door had opened, Jagger yanked me out in a nanosecond. Vance's gun went off a second time and hit the same spot on the ceiling that I'd shot earlier. All I could say as Jagger held me was, "I couldn't do that again if I tried."

It'd been over a week since I'd seen or heard from Jagger.

I opened my eyes. The six-o'clock news was on the television. No matter what the occasion, Daddy had to watch the news. If he saw it at lunchtime, he wouldn't watch it at six. I always wanted to point out that a lot could happen in the world between noon and six, but, well, that was Daddy.

I loved him as he was, as I loved all the rest of my family too. Each had their own quirks, but hey, they were *my* quirky family. It'd been tough the first few days after the incident with Vance since the news covered the case over and over. My poor parents had just about made me move in with them.

I inhaled.

Pine Renuzit.

Suddenly that thought wasn't so bad.

Yikes! It had to be the fact of nearly being killed that had my mind discombobulated. Sure, I loved the folks, but moving back . . . ack. Still, it was great to see that the six-o'clock news now covered sightings of Santa. My nieces and nephews were ecstatic each time a reporter mentioned spotting the old man at the North Pole.

I looked into the kitchen to see Goldie, wearing the lovely mauve striped silk scarf I'd just given him as a Christmas Eve gift, dancing about to "Jingle Bells" while he bounced my niece Hanna around.

Miles was quoting from the cookbook I'd given him, and my mother and he stood arguing about how much vinegar went into the dried mushroom soup. Oh, she'd given Miles and Goldie condoms as stocking stuffers. Gotta love her.

Uncle Walt sat at the table with his fork in his hand even though dinner wouldn't be ready for about an hour. I'd learned earlier that Jagger had come over a few days ago and given Uncle Walt a ride around the block in his Suburban.

I sighed.

Ring. Ring.

"Pauline, don't just stand there in a fog. Get the door," Mom called from the kitchen.

"Sure." I hadn't taken a head count, but thought we were all here. Come to think of it, I hadn't seen ex-nun Mary and her husband. "Merry"—I opened the door—"Christmas!"

"Yeah."

"Jagger."

He walked in and stood in the foyer, where he shrugged off the freshly fallen snow. It cascaded to the floor like frozen diamonds. "You were expecting Santa?"

No, this is way better, I thought, then looked outside to see it would be a white Christmas after all.

"Well? Aren't you going to take these?" He held out a gigantic Christmas bag.

"Aren't you going to use *that*?" my mother said coming up from behind.

We looked at her.

She pointed to the ceiling.

Mistletoe. I actually think it'd been hanging there since 1969, but it never got much use from me.

"Mother. No—"

Jagger pulled me closer and planted a kiss on my *cheek*.

Close up I could see that his shiner, faded to a dull yellow, was nearly gone. Good thing, or I'd have to explain it to my folks. I had enough on my mind, like if he let me go right now, I'd collapse against my mother and probably crush her. Then who would clean up?

I summoned my mental faculties and said, "Come in. We haven't started to eat yet."

"I need to talk to you first," he said. "Merry Christmas, Missus Sokol."

She nodded.

"Talk to me? Sure."

My mother raised her hands. "I'll leave you two alone."

Mom!

Jagger followed me into the study and shut the door. "I had to wrap up a few things about the case, but here." He took an envelope out of his pocket.

I stared at it. "I didn't get you a Christmas present 'cause—"

"I said I'd pay you for the job."

At least my crimson complexion was festive with my green wool pants and green sweater.

He held out the bag. "Where do grab bags go?"

"I'll take them."

He handed me the gift. "Look, I tried to get to you as soon as I had figured out Vance was involved. Your god damn cell phone conked out. It took me forever to find you. Then . . . then the elevator . . ."

I shut my eyes. I couldn't go through that scene again. I opened my eyes. "I know. In my excitement of the new job, I forgot to charge the phone."

He shook his head.

"Fabio ever pay you?"

"That's how I finished my Christmas shopping. He was pleased, well, as pleased as Fabio would admit to, about the extra fraud I'd discovered. He also said he'd give me a new case—"

Jagger groaned.

"I'm learning."

"Then you need to learn not to go into empty buildings alone, unarmed—"

"Hey, I shot that elevator—twice."

"Let's just say you've grown as an investigator, since you didn't get yourself killed."

I smiled. He'd just about admitted that I had done all right. Knowing him, though, that was the best I'd get as far as compliments went.

He shook his head. "The DA has the case now. Seems your buddy Vance, the Macalusos and Charlene will all be spending Christmas in jail, courtesy of the state."

"Vance is not my buddy," was all I could say.

Jagger once again shook his head, then turned to my father's old rolltop desk. He picked up a pen and took my arm. Then, he wrote a doodle of Spanky on my cast and his cell phone number.

"I memorized it."

He covered my cast. "Go ahead."

Shoot. "Um . . . five . . . two . . . two . . . I know there's a two in it somewhere." I pulled free. "Senior moment."

"Auntie Pauline," my nephew Charlie stuck his head in the door. "Babci said to come into the living room for grab bags."

Jagger pushed past me and followed Charlie.

I stood there and smiled. He was actually excited about something. How cute. He'd never done grab bags in his life, I assumed. But from what I knew about Jagger now, he'd never admit it.

I'd come to see a gentle side of a man who would hate to hear that—and would deny it vehemently. A man who would make a point to give an eighty-year-old man a ride. Who would throw a bone seventeen times for a five-pound dog. Or a man who would make me feel safe, even when I couldn't see him.

Suddenly it really didn't matter whom he worked for, why he was so driven or what went on in his and Nick's past. Right now, I could care less.

After the presents were exchanged—and I stopped complaining that I'd gotten a folding shovel, because that's what I'd put in—Jagger motioned for me. I followed him to the fireplace, where he reached into his bag. One box was left in it. He took it out and handed it to me.

I began to say something, but he touched his finger to my lips. Then he leaned forward and kissed me—on the lips!

A warmth headed down to my insides, stopping just short of my panties when I reminded myself that I was in my parents' house.

"Merry Christmas," he whispered into my ear.

I'll never wash that ear again.

I started to drop the box, but caught it before making more of a fool of myself.

"Open it," he said.

My fingers shook. I kept trying, but they wouldn't work. He reached over and touched my hand. Then he pulled one end of the paper to start it for me. My heart did a Christmas jig of its own. Soon I had the paper torn and read on the box, "Motorola wireless? But I have a cell phone."

"Comes with *two* chargers, Sherlock. One for your house. One for your car."

I looked at him and laughed.

"And if you don't use it, I'm going to have a microchip put on your tooth. As a matter of fact . . . say ah."

USA TODAY BESTSELLING AUTHOR

MARY DAHEIM

THE BED-AND-BREAKFAST MYSTERIES

HOCUS CROAKUS

0-380-81564-8/$6.99 US/$9.99 Can

The discovery of the Great Mandolini's attractive assistant (and ex-wife) skewered on one of his props has put a crimp in the magician's act.

SILVER SCREAM

0-380-81563-X/$6.99 US/$9.99 Can

Soon after a less-than-lauded screening of his new film, genius super-producer Bruno Zepf is discovered drowned in the kitchen sink.

SUTURE SELF

0-380-81561-3/$6.99 US/$9.99 Can

Although cousins Judith and Renie survive their hospital stays for minor surgeries, the ex-pro quarterback next door is permanently sacked after his knee surgery.

And new in hardcover

THIS OLD SOUSE

0-380-97869-5/$23.95 US/$36.95 Can

Available wherever books are sold
or please call 1-800-331-3761 to order.

www.AuthorTracker.com

DAH 0504